To Jean & Peter —

I HOPE YOU ENJOY THIS
STORY OF CHICDHOOD AND
LOSS SET IN WESTERN
COLORADO ——

Harry C Brown

SUNDAYS
IN
AUGUST

SUNDAYS IN AUGUST

A Novel by Harry Clifford Brown

SUNSTONE PRESS

SANTA FE

Sunstone books may be purchased for educational, business, or sales promotional use. For information please write: Special Markets Department, Sunstone Press, P.O. Box 2321, Santa Fe, New Mexico 87504-2321.

10 9 8 7 6 5 4 3 2

Library of Congress Cataloging in Publication Data:
Brown, Harry Clifford, 1953–
    Sundays in August / by Harry Clifford Brown. — 1st ed.
        p. cm.
    ISBN: 0-86534-261-X
    I. Title.
PS3552. R68554S86   1997
813′ .54—dc21   97-25073
                                        CIP

Published by   SUNSTONE PRESS
                Post Office Box 2321
                Santa Fe, NM 87504-2321 / USA
                (505) 988-4418 / *orders only* (800) 243-5644
                FAX (505) 988-1025

To my mom and dad—Lou and Ernie,
to my sister and brother—Donna and Bill,
and in memory of my teacher and friend—Mai Robinson

I knew that that word was like the others:
just a shape to fill a lack . . .

—William Faulkner, *As I Lay Dying*

1

"How can he hear an earthworm?"

Franklin and I are crouched behind the evergreens alongside the red brick house our pa built. Franklin holds his index finger to his lips and we begin crawling, Indian-style, toward the robin. It bounces away on wiry feet.

"If he hears worms, he can probably hear us. Huh, Franklin?"

"Shhhh."

The robin stops and jerks his head from side to side as if there are notches in his neck like the wheels of a clock: click click to the left, click click right. I feel the wet soaking through the knees of my pants and see the green stains smudged against Franklin's in front of me and can smell the grass; Mom says I was born with the nose of a beagle.

Franklin slowly comes up off his hands, kneeling on the grass with the rubber dagger cocked behind his head. The robin bounces toward us a few feet and then its head dips low as though it's going to take off. But it doesn't. Franklin throws the dagger and the handle strikes the robin's neck and it flattens in the grass with its wings spread.

"You got it, Franklin."

We're standing now, staring across the lawn at the robin. I look at Franklin and he's running his front teeth over his bottom lip. We walk over together and look down.

"Is he dead?"

Franklin squats and cups his hands under the bird and scoops it up. Its small head rolls limply over Franklin's fingers, feathers parting along the bird's throat.

"Is he dead, Franklin?"

I follow Franklin along the back fence to the alley. He carries the bird's body out in front of him as if it's a bowl of Mom's homemade vegetable soup and he doesn't want to spill any of it. But it isn't soup. It's a handful of feathers and Franklin lays it down on the soft dirt next to the fence. Franklin walks over and takes a shovel from the shed. He digs a hole big enough for a football and places the bird in it, folding its wings up underneath. He fills the dirt back in and tamps it all around with the flat of the shovel. We stare down at the small mound of dirt, and then I follow Franklin up the sidewalk and on into our house.

* * *

Our house doesn't stand in Grand River anymore. I knew before coming it wouldn't be here, but after thirty-five years—thirty-five years to the day of knowing what we did was right—I've come back to see for myself.

From the interstate, the orchards lie below. Picking ladders poke up here and there among the peach trees, and a tractor pulls a flat-bed trailer of bushel baskets and wooden crates along the canal road. A trail of dust lifts into the dry air behind it, flattens out and lingers white in the sun over the canal. It's harvest time in the valley and the ditch water flashes like strips of tin between the straight rows of trees.

The main street coming into Grand River is wider now, four lanes instead of two, and shopping areas with supermarkets and speciality shops take up entire blocks where only fields once stood. The parking lots are empty, except for a few stray shopping carts, and the avenues quieter than I ever thought possible, even for a Sunday. Maybe, I think, the entire town has locked up and gone to church.

Heat collects here along the empty pavement, quivers on the air in low distorting waves. And illusions of water, like puddles of liquid glass, stand in front of me across these streets, only to break apart and disappear as I drive toward them. Maybe the Grand River I knew is now like this, a mirage existing only in my memory and then, with my return, dissipating into the heat.

The first place I see, but didn't come to see, is the church. It's bigger now with a new addition built on the back and a newly paved parking lot across the street. There's a tall white cross on the grass near the walk and a screened-in marquee announcing the times for sermons, Sunday school, and choral practices. The same stained-glass windows are there, though, set into the side of the building and in the front, the same big wooden double doors. The doors are swung wide and as I drive by, organ music surges out of them, trailing off after me down the street like an old enemy coming to meet me from my past.

I drive on past the glare of cars spilling out of the parking lot along the curb, past Smitty's Hardware Store and Crown Appliance and the F.W.

Woolworths, past City Park: the baseball stadium where we watched the Grand River Eagles play under the lights, the football field where the high school played its games, the public swimming pool where we spent summers trying to swim with what seemed like every other kid in Grand River, and the playground next to where the zoo once stood and the lions once roared. I drive down Gateway Avenue to the corner—Mr. Dugan's filling station used to be here but now there's a bank—and then left along the Indian Wash to Willow Avenue and Orchard View Grade School.

I pull over here in front of the school, get out of the car, and begin walking. The neighborhood is still and because of the quiet, changed. Where are the kids?

The chit-chit-chit of sprinkler water stuttering across freshly mown grass and the distant bark of a dog come to me now and then, but even these are lost in the emptiness of the streets. The vacant lots where we climbed trees, built forts, and captured enemy soldiers are no longer vacant, only more homes with the same neatly clipped lawns and swept walks and flower beds. The Livers' stucco house has been torn down and replaced with a rough-cedar structure, the kind in decorating magazines. And the Phillip's house has a new garage built onto it with split-cedar shakes on the roof that don't match the vinyl siding. Even the pavement under my feet feels different, its texture softer and smoother than when I was a kid here forever running through these streets.

Maybe that's it; maybe the difference is I'm not running. Maybe the neighborhood would come back to me in one exhilarating sprint down an alleyway or through somebody's yard the way we used to cut across blocks to save time. Maybe all would reappear, blurred in the speed of my own legs. But the neighborhood can never be the same, just as I can never be. The neighborhood has grown up.

I come to the corner of our street; in front of me stands Mrs. Henderson's house. At first I think it has been torn down and replaced but then realize only the porch has been removed. It's still painted white and the yard is as tidy as ever with tall iris and gladiola growing in back. I can almost see Mrs. Henderson in there among them, rooting around in her straw hat and loudly printed summer dress, nylons rolled down around her ankles, muttering earthy threats to the weeds she's yanking up. Good old Mrs. Henderson. As much as I dread doing it, I check the name on the mailbox and, sure enough, her house becomes as different as everything else I've seen.

I walk slowly down my old street like I think anyone would on a Sunday afternoon, but I find myself glancing about as a kid might in the dark, specters moving in around him. But instead of darkness there's the sun straight up at its most intense. Taking a handkerchief from my back pocket, I wipe sweat off my face and from around my neck. It's no wonder there's no one on these streets. The heat. Who can stand this heat? And then, suddenly, I'm there.

Old man Hillar's house next door is empty with a realtor's sign stuck in the lawn near the sidewalk. I stare at the large red letters and the black numerals of the realtor's telephone number underneath, and I feel the sun hot on my hair and the cotton of my shirt wet against my skin. And then I take a deep breath and turn to the spot where I spent the first ten-and-a-half years of my life.

The house stands squarely facing me. An ordinary house. I see nothing unusual about it and as I should have expected, nothing familiar. I knew before coming it wouldn't be our house standing here. Just a house like any other house on any other street in Grand River; with grass, a hedge, a driveway, a carport with a car parked in it, a fence in back. And what had I expected? Nothing, I decide, is ever what you wish it to be.

And then I see the elm. It's standing behind a house across the street. I've never laid eyes on this house before because there was a vacant lot here when we lived on this street. But the tree I've seen. I've thought of this tree often over the years and perhaps to protect myself from disappointment, expected it to look smaller and more withered. But it doesn't. Gazing up, I sense its growth has been in perfect harmony with my own. I feel, standing here, as though I'm greeting a childhood friend whom I naturally expected to become different across the last thirty-five years, but who has only grown different in all the ways I have and, happily to me, has remained the same.

I walk over and run my hand over its cool rough bark. I look up along its trunk, thick limbs twisting into thinner branches, leaves a mass of freckles against the sun. The elm has been standing in this heat for more than thirty-five years, I think. And today I'm standing with it and in my mind, always have been.

I walk away, back down the streets, along the quiet walks toward the grade school and my car. Now I'm ready for the last place I've come to see.

* * *

A gray jay, summer-fat from campground refuse, hops along a branch turning its head at me as I get out of my car and start down the bank to Johnson Reservoir. High above me the trees creak and the breeze lifts the jay's feathers atop its head and across its chest. Spruce Mesa must have had a lot of snow this year because the water is high on the dam and at places, almost reaches up into the trees. A path is worn smooth around the reservoir, and people sit below against rocks or on camp stools watching their poles move with the wind coming off the water.

A man with a friendly face and a young boy sitting at his side greets me and tells me he and his grandson haven't had any luck and wants to know if it's any better where I've come from. I tell him I just got here, but I keep moving along the path and say nothing else. I wish I could say more, tell him the fish down below are biting like crazy or that salmon eggs are a good bet at this time of the afternoon or at least explain to him why I don't want to talk, why the sight of him and his grandson fishing together is so disturbing.

As I turn away from the lake and start off into the trees, I notice the path up ahead abruptly forks left. My father and I had never needed a path to show us the way into Lambert Lake; there wasn't one. But now there is, so I follow it a ways through the brush and skunk cabbage, through the shadows of white fir and Engleman spruce before breaking out into the upper end of a clearing.

I know this place; it's the summer bog. And at the edge where it meets the forest, six stumps jut up bone-white and erect as marble gravestones. What were once six trees are now part of the path and lie before me across the bog, split end-to-end. As a boy, this bog had always sung to me with a chorus of frogs and if Pa let me, I would slop off into it with my pant legs rolled up and my feet bare just for the joy of hearing the frogs close to me, of feeling their throats bump against my fingers. But now this path cuts through the bog and the frogs are gone, and all I can hear is the sucking sound of the tree trunks rolling and squashing down in the mud and then lifting up behind me as I pass over them.

Pa and I usually walked around this clearing. But in late spring or, some years, early summer we were able to cross it because it would still be thawing. At that time of year, when the clearing had not yet become a bog, our footsteps sloshed and were loud the way every noise is in a forest blanketed with snow. After we had reached the other side and gone back into the trees where the ground begins to fall quickly away toward the lake, our footsteps would crunch and I could hear Pa breathing and the tree boughs brush against the wicker of his creel. The snow stood deep there on that embankment and sometimes Pa would break through to his waist and have to struggle back out, holding his pole above his head and elbowing himself up and out with one arm. My father was used to struggle, though, and he would stand there for a moment until he caught his breath, his face red and the hair under his straw fishing hat as wet as the snow. We would continue then, a little more deliberately, Pa testing the snow's weight with his own before taking another step. I felt secure following my father's footsteps, hearing him breathing, knowing I wouldn't break through or go sliding down into the rocks below.

But now I'm alone and it's at summer's end and there is no snow. Light, no longer sifting down through the branches, lies muted at my feet, the shadows deepening as I work my way farther and farther down the embankment. I don't remember it taking this long.

Just as I feel the first swells of panic wash over me, I see it: a silver sliver flashing through the trees. I stop and gulp the mountain air and then tramp down through the underbrush and trees over the lava rock to the water's edge. I sling off my pack and stand in the sun reflecting off the lake, strips of tinsel undulating in the breeze. I stand for a long time and then the darkening comes and dusk settles around like strewn sand across the sky.

I shake my head, half-chilled, and wonder what I'm doing here. But I know what I'm doing—just as I knew thirty-five years before—so I turn away from the lake and walk up the bank underneath the spruce trees and begin gathering wood. Using a flat rock, I dig out dandelions and grass, clearing an area on the ground, and then pile larger rocks around the edge. I break dried twigs off the branches and pile them in the middle. From a pocket of my pack I take out a box of matches; I strike one, cupping my hand over its head, and bring it to the twigs. They catch, making sharp snapping noises, so I place a couple of sticks across them and then blow gently until the sticks catch, too. I take a couple of heavy branches and place them on top. Soon the flames leap and the sap pops loudly and the fire burns green and blue.

I put on my jean jacket, spread my sleeping bag near the fire, and stretch out on my side along the fire's warmth. With my head propped in one hand, I stare into the fire burning hot against the night, stare through the flames jumping and the wood crackling until he finally appears, until he's there just as I knew he would be, standing on the other side of the fire near the water's edge: a ten-and-a-half year old boy with a fishing pole in his hand.

* * *

"Pa! Any luck!?!"

He shook his head. My father stood on the other side of the inlet and flicked lures into the eddy from the stream that fell down through the rocks and into the deep water. The spear-like tops of spruce trees swayed against the sky above him, and I could hear the wind kick up and sough through the branches and over the forest floor. Whitecaps began to break out in the middle as I traced the foamy outline of the lake with my eyes. Then the wind died as suddenly as it had begun and the mosquitoes came out.

My red and white bobber rolled with the lake water. The fishing line remained slack; there hadn't been a bite for almost two hours. I tightened the line with a couple of turns of my reel as I heard the whine of an engine off in the distance. On the far side of the lake, a pale-blue and white 4-wheel-drive truck appeared from a break in the trees, bouncing from side to side over rocks and ruts before bucking to a stop. Its aluminum camper shone silver in the afternoon sun. Two doors slammed, one and then the other, and I heard two men talking, their voices thin but clear in the crisp mountain air. I didn't know there was a back trail leading into Lambert Lake. We had always parked our jeep down below at the small reservoir and spent an hour and a half hiking in.

My father changed gear now and cast a homespun muskrat fly with his long willowy fly rod. The leader at the end of his line made an S above him before the smooth snap of his wrist sent it singing down on the water's surface. Usually he snapped it two, three, four times before he was satisfied. Then he would wait for a fat rainbow trout to nose up and lip the fly before running with it.

Suddenly, my own pole bounced and bowed. I grabbed the cork end with my right hand and fingered the line in my left in order to feel the trout's life. As I gave the pole a jerk to set the hook I saw something fall; I saw it off the edge of my cheek and then I heard the thud. The trout was fighting, breaking water. When I turned, my father was stretched out along the water's edge.

His hands lay straight down on either side, half closed with the palms facing upward, his fingers waving like legs of an insect upturned. His face sat sideways in mud, eyes staring away from the lake into the cold bank. Icy water lapped at the sleeve of his flannel shirt. I straddled him and grabbed him under the arms. But I couldn't move him. My hands cupped around my mouth as I gave a shrill whistle, a whistle Pa had taught me when I was only six, but the slight breeze blowing across the lake toward me caught my sound like the webbing of a baseball mitt and threw it back.

I cradled my father's large head, lifted it in my hands and turned it toward the water. He was warm and I felt the sticky sweat that had accumulated around his neck and under his jaw. I grabbed his right shoulder with both hands and managed to pull him a half turn out of the water. Another tug and he lay on his back, purple deepening in his chapped lips. Again I whistled and then shouted but the two men on the other side didn't hear me.

I sat down and looked at him. His mouth hung open as though he had just fallen asleep in his easy chair. Often, after a few beers he would doze in front of the Motorola and snore. But now my father wasn't snoring. The deep lines across his forehead and between his bushy eyebrows were relaxed and he looked younger than his fifty-two years.

A large fly, black with a phosphorescent glaze of green, began playing about his mouth. I took off my baseball cap and fanned but it continued, buzzing around and lighting when it could. Finally, I placed the cap over my father's draining face.

"Petey, I got a new cap for you today. Just like the kind Maris and Mantle wear."

"Thanks, Pa."

"Don't go an' let that ornery brother of yours gyp you out of it. Ya hear? It's not everybody that has a New York Yankees' baseball cap."

"I know, Pa. I won't."

"Now go get me a beer, Petey. Your dad's tired. That loading dock can kill a man."

"Okay, Pa."

I jumped to my feet and headed around Lambert Lake toward the glint of sun reflecting off the distant shoreline.

* * *

The two men were broad-shouldered and tall and looked like brothers. They wore identical olive-green waders and unlit cigars were tucked in their mouths. The shorter one had a droopy mustache and he started chewing the end of his cigar when I suddenly appeared from a tangle of brush, wet and out of breath.

"My pa!"

"Hey, what's wrong, fella?"

"My pa."

"What happened?"

"I don't know."

I carried my father's tackle box and I could hear the lures and sinkers jounce as I scrambled over logs and across streams. In my other hand I held his casting and fly rods. The two men spoke to each other in low solemn voices when they would stop, stooping to one knee to catch their breaths. They glanced at me then but wouldn't look me in the eye. Sometimes they traded places, the one in front who carried my father by his legs would go to the back and my father's arms. My father's head dangled from side to side between the tall men's legs as they walked. His brown gray-flecked hair hung wet and his mouth yawned wide. The whites of his eyes rolled back. I tried to look at the lake but it was only a reflection of the clouds gathering overhead and I couldn't focus. Only my father's upside down face between the triangle of the men's working thighs remained distinct.

They loaded my father into the camper shell. One of them squeezed my shoulder and took Pa's fishing poles and broke them down for me. He placed them across a gun rack in the back window of the cab and began loading the gear they had left out. I wondered about my own pole, wondered if the fish unhooked itself or if it would die on the end of the line, my hook forever lodged in its mouth. The other man, the one with the mustache, lay under the truck draping chains over the two back tires.

"You can sit up front with us, Pete."

"I want to stay back here with Pa."

"It's a long way into town. Why don't you sit up front?"

"I'm okay."

I sat on the makeshift bed, a piece of foam rubber glued to a sheet of plywood spanning the width of the camper. My father lay before me on the floor, his legs underneath the plywood with the camping gear. Through the rectangular window I saw the men talking as the truck lurched over the rutty jeep trail. The engine groaned and wheezed and the haze of blue fumes it belched filled the camper and clashed with the stench of my father's excrement. Pine branches scraped the length of the aluminum shell like fingernails across a chalkboard and sent shivers up my back and neck. A mountain of gray lava rock outside seemed to press down on me from out of the sky as we made our way over streambeds and potholes. Once, the truck hunkered down in a deep rut and the men had to jack up the front end and wedge flat rocks and sticks under the tires before we could continue. My father's limp body absorbed each jolt as if it were somehow connected with the truck's progress. He lay on his stomach, large shoulders and back rolling in rhythm to the truck's labour and when we would pass over a particularily rough spot, the back of his hands slapped the metal floor.

Finally, we came to a clearing of skunk cabbage and range grass where the men got out and removed the chains. The clean-shaven one tapped on the side window and asked if I wanted to get out for a minute. I didn't so they got back in and turned off the trail onto a smooth dirt road. The steady hum of the engine was comforting and my father now lay still.

As we came down off the mountain and headed toward Grand River it grew dark and a loud tumble of thunder broke overhead. I closed my eyes and listened to raindrops pelt the aluminum camper shell with a hollow plink and gradually, methodically fuze into a single drumming above me. The rain fell and the wet earth washed in through the camper windows and brought with it the smell of wet horses.

A man wearing a straw hat and carrying a green hose comes and sprays off the horses and their hides steam like hot wash hanging out to dry.

"Get on this one with your sis, Petey. Up ya go."

"Horsey big, Petey."

Mary wears a white ribbon in her hair. It tickles my nose as I clutch to her. I feel my father next to me, walking alongside the plodding horse, and the roar of lions from City Park Zoo swallow up the din of voices from the public swimming pool nearby. Through Mary's wispy down of sun-bleached hair, I see Franklin on the horse in front of us kicking at it with the heels of his cowboy boots to make it go faster. Mom, in her summer dress and sun hat, walks beside him. She carries Erwin on her hip with one hand and holds a cigarette with the other.

"Don't let go of Mary, Petey. That's a big boy."

The horses are tethered to metal bars which fan out from the center of a ring like spokes from a giant wheel. I can see many things from here: the green fence of the baseball park, the scattered pink dots of cotton candy, the small concrete zoo with the monkeys and aged lions behind its bars. Around and around we go and I can feel the horse's muscles methodically work the damp ground far below. The park jiggles and I'm hot and dizzy and the stench of fresh manure hangs about me. I don't want to ride the horse anymore; I want to go home. I turn to my father, to tell him I want down from the horse, but he is no longer there. My father has left, gone away somewhere and I reach for Mary as I slip from the horse toward the muddy earth.

"Pa!"

The men cut the truck over to the shoulder and let me out of the camper and take me to the side of the road and hold my head in the driving rain.

2

By the time we reached St. Matthew's Hospital, the rain had stopped. The gutters were still full, though, and there was water standing in puddles around the parking lot. Three orderlies in white shirts and pants with black shoes pushed a roller bed out through the emergency room doorway and over to the truck. A nurse began talking to the two men. I stayed in the cab and watched through the window as the orderlies slid Pa out and onto the bed. They covered him with a sheet and then rolled my pa away. The two men and the nurse walked over and opened the door.

"Pete, this is Nurse Hays. She wants you to go with her now. Okay?"

I got out and the two men handed me our fishing gear and patted me on the back as I went with the nurse into the hospital. I turned and looked back through the glass doors as the taillights of the truck that had carried my father moved away into the half-light outside.

After answering a lot of questions—my name, address, telephone number, birth date, father's name, mother's name, number of brothers and sisters—I sat down in a wheelchair the nurse brought, cradling the fishing poles and tackle box across my lap. The nurse's shoes squeaked against the waxed tile as she wheeled me down a long antiseptic hallway and into an elevator. I asked if I could call home but she said my family had already been notified and were on their way.

I was placed in a room with another kid who had his arm in a sling. He looked about Franklin's age, fourteen, and he eyed me curiously. The nurse took the fishing gear and made me take my clothes off and change into a gown that was slit up the back. I had to lie down as the nurse gave me a shot in my bottom and then left the room. The other kid was grinning.

"What's wrong with you?"

"Nothin'."

"Nothin'? Then why you in here?"

"I don't know."

"You don't know why you're in here?"

"No."

"You're not sick?"

"I don't know."

"You don't know nothin', do you? Maybe you're crazy."

"No, I'm not."

"Then why you in here? Something has to be wrong with you or they wouldn't put you in here."

"My pa . . . my pa sent me here 'cause I don't feel good."

"Oh. Where's your pa?"

I felt dizzy and a cold skim of sweat rose up over my face. My pa was downstairs waiting. Pretty soon I would feel better and we would get our fishing poles and go back home and everything would be like it was. We'd play catch in the back yard or go downstairs where I'd watch him build a table or chair and then help him clean up, sweeping the sawdust and wood shavings into neat piles. Or maybe we'd just go home and watch TV, my pa and I; maybe that's what we'd do.

The kid next to me was moving his mouth but there was no sound. All I could hear was a faint humming in my ears. I stared at the shiny tile floor thinking about home and Mary. Mary would know what to say. She always knew.

My sister was only two-and-a-half years older than I but had the ability to say the right thing at the right time. I remember one time Franklin hit a baseball through old man Hillar's garage window next door. It was an accident but old man Hillar didn't see it that way. He came storming out his back door cussing and snorting and demanding to know who the culprit was. The whole neighborhood gang was standing there and it could have been any of us. But Franklin admitted it right away and said he would pay for the window out of money he had saved from mowing lawns all summer. Old man Hillar looked surprised and a little disappointed, as though Franklin had ruined his chance of scaring a confession out of us. He took off the dirty yellow John Deere cap and rubbed his burred scalp with the palm of his hand before pulling the cap back tightly over his head. He wouldn't hear of it, by god. Franklin would pay all right. He was going to call the police.

That's when Mary arrived. She called him "Mr. Hillar, sir," stopping him about halfway to his door, and then remarked how old and ugly the garage was anyway. Franklin gawked at her like she was crazy, as though she had insulted the judge just before sentencing. But before old man Hillar could react, Mary suggested in a calm even voice that perhaps a couple of coats of paint was just what that garage needed. He chewed on this for a moment and then a toothless grin broke across the old man's face and he nodded in agreement.

We weren't sure if Franklin was relieved or not. Maybe that was because Franklin wasn't sure either. He spent a long time painting that garage.

Franklin didn't come to the hospital, though, because Mom was home in bed. Erwin was only six so Franklin had to stay home and watch him. But Mary came and she brought a grocery sack with her.

"Pete?" Mary shook my shoulder and I opened my eyes. She sat on the edge of the bed, her hair falling to the side of her face. "Pete, are you okay?"

"Hi, Mare."

With one finger she traced the loose strands of hair around behind her right ear and the shadow fell away. I could see her nose was red and her eyes swollen like a couple of mosquito bites.

"I brought some things for you." Mary peered into the paper sack on her lap. "There's a toothbrush and toothpaste and a comb and a change of clothes. Mom said you should have clean clothes for when they let you out." She set the sack on the night stand and neatly folded the top closed, creasing the paper over with her thumb.

"Mom also said you should give me your dirty clothes so we can wash them." She looked around the bed at the drawn curtains. "Where are your clothes, Petey?"

I shrugged. "I dunno."

"Well, that's okay. I'll ask the nurse. Hope they didn't have to burn them." She glanced down at me and tried to smile.

"Mary, he just fell."

Mary stood, turned away, and clutched her arms as though suddenly chilled.

"You know how stinky Franklin's clothes can get when he works over at Mr. Dugan's gas station." She looked up at the ceiling, holding onto herself and shaking her head.

"Mom says Franklin smells like a refinery every time he comes home. She says his room smells like one, too. I don't know why Franklin doesn't like his work clothes to be clean. I guess he figures they'll just get to smelling the same way so why bother."

Mary smiled at the ceiling, still shaking her head. "What a brother, that Franklin. Isn't he something, Petey? Pretty soon he won't want any of his clothes washed." She gave out a short laugh.

"And then he'll quit bathing and brushing his teeth and combing his hair and he'll get himself a pair of those old overalls like Mr. Hillar wears, the kind that snaps over the shoulder with all those little pockets in front where you can keep pencils and things. He'll start wearing those overalls and nothing else. Wouldn't that be funny? Then he'd probably quit school and go to work at the gas station full time."

Mary's eyes dropped and she looked at me, still smiling. "But I can't imagine him doing that, can you? Everybody knows how much Franklin hates school but I don't think he'd just quit."

Mary sat back down on the edge of the bed and placed her hand on my head. "Are you sure you're okay, Petey?" She brushed my hair back, smiling hard.

"Yeah, I'm okay. Where's Mom?"

"She's home in bed, resting."

"Oh."

"Is there anything else I can bring you?"

I shook my head, looking up at my big sister smiling down on me. "How'd you get here, Mare?"

"On my bicycle." She stroked my hair.

"Mary?"

"Yes, Petey."

I swallowed, looking at the white curtains and the tile floor and the white sheets and bedspread. I looked back up at her. "He just fell."

Mary's smile froze.

"Me and Pa was fishin' and he just fell."

And then Mary's smile cracked and broke and she buried what was left of it in the pillow above my head.

* * *

The next day I was driven home in an official hospital car by a Catholic nun wearing a light gray and white habit. The gown hung in folds and only her round face poked out, like someone sniffing the early morning air before emerging from a tent. Her face was hot-red, not cold-red, as if the garment were suffocating her. A heavy silver cross hung from a chain around her neck and another cross, white with a bearded man against it, dangled from the rearview mirror.

Peering at me through thick bifocal glasses that made her eyes look as big as silver dollars, she explained that my mother was too upset to pick me up herself. She then offered me a lemon sucker she retrieved from the front pocket of her gown and as she drove, tried to talk to me about sports. Her intentions were good so I played along for a while, watching the man on the cross sway and turn with the sway and turn of the car, until she asked me if I thought the New York Giants were going to win the World Series.

I got out of the car near the front gate of our picket fence, and the nun said good-bye and asked God to go with me. Franklin and Erwin were playing splits with Franklin's pocketknife. They looked up at me, legs spread, and wondered who the funny-looking woman with the cloth around her head might be.

"Who was that?"

"Sister Irene."

"Sister Irene?"

"Yeah, she's a nun."

"Why'd she bring you home?"

"Beats me."

Franklin threw the pocketknife and buried the blade into the ground next to Erwin. Erwin stepped over with one foot and pulled it out.

"Where's Mom?"

"Inside with Mary."

"Is she okay?"

"I don't know. She's sleepin'."

Now it was Erwin's turn and he grabbed the knife handle with his gritty little hands and threw it next to Franklin. The point caught momentarily in a tuft of crabgrass and then the knife tipped over from the weight of its handle. Franklin bent over and studied it.

"No good, Win."

"Uh-huh."

"Nope, it has to stick in the dirt. This is a leaner." Franklin picked it up and wiped the blade on his pant leg. Erwin didn't move, his legs still spread.

"Why'd they put you in the hospital?"

"I guess 'cause I ralphed."

"Where'd you ralph?"

"Coming down from the lake."

Franklin pinched the flat of the blade between his thumb and index finger and flicked it into the ground on the other side of Erwin. Erwin stretched as far as he could, his left hand on the ground balancing himself, and pulled out the knife with his fingertips.

"How'd it happen?"

"What?"

"You know. Pa."

Franklin was watching Erwin trying to throw the knife while keeping his balance.

"We was fishin' and he just fell."

Erwin raised the knife above his head and threw it but it landed flat against the grass.

"I don't like splits. I wanna play chicken."

Erwin was unbeatable at chicken because he was so close to the ground, only one reason Franklin didn't like to play it. The other being that the summer before Erwin had decided to end the game in a flourish and stuck the two-inch blade one inch into Franklin's left foot.

"We can't play chicken, Win. You know what Pa said."

"Pa ain't here."

Erwin didn't know what he had said. Franklin and I just looked at him. Then Franklin folded up his pocketknife and put it in his pocket and the two of them walked up the steps and into the house, leaving me standing alone in the front yard not knowing what to do.

It had always been that way: Franklin and Erwin. Despite their eight-year difference in age, they were rarely apart. Ever since Erwin could walk Franklin had made him his own personal project. He took pride in Erwin because Erwin was so tough for his age.

One of Franklin's favorite pastimes was taking Erwin to the semi-pro baseball games at City Park. Kids from all over the valley would flock there to watch the Grand River Eagles play under the lights. Franklin and Erwin couldn't have cared less about the Eagles—if they weren't the Yankees, they weren't a baseball team—and the only baseball they saw on those balmy summer nights was through the slats out from behind half-empty bleachers. After sneaking in over the left-field fence, Franklin and Erwin stood back there and shagged foul balls. For every ball retrieved, they received ten cents and ten cents bought a comic book at the corner grocery store or a pop or two candy bars. But they weren't the only kids tracing the trajectory of those little leather dimes, arcing up above the lights and out of City Park Stadium. There were many others, and to make any money not only meant being able to run fast or, lacking that, knowing where the ball landed by the sound it made coming off the bat, but also being able to hold onto it once it was in your possession. That often meant a fistfight. And that's what Erwin did best, thanks to Franklin's training.

Between doubleheaders or when the action slowed, Franklin got Erwin into fights. Most of the kids were older than Erwin but that didn't matter much. For Erwin it was just another face to punch and Erwin punched exceedingly well. He never questioned why someone walked up to him and shoved him or called him a name. Like running after foul balls, fighting was just something he did and something he liked to do. Erwin had no idea

Franklin was behind it, that Franklin was telling this endless stream of opponents that he had overheard some little twerp call them a name or say something about their mothers. All Erwin knew was that he could hardly trust anyone. And the only person he trusted, other than Mary, was Franklin—the one person he should have trusted least. But even if Erwin knew what Franklin was up to, it probably wouldn't have mattered much because unlike most big-brother-little-brother relationships, Franklin and Erwin were a team.

And so they sat, like players on a bench when I finally worked up the courage to walk into the house. They were pinched together in the stuffed rocker with elbows resting on their knees, staring across the living room at our mother who lay on the couch before them.

As my eyes adjusted to the darkness I could see her blue terry-cloth bathrobe and fuzzy pink slippers lying at the end of the couch where she had kicked them off. Mary sat next to her and wiped her face and neck with a damp cloth. The curtains had been drawn against the heat and when Mary heard the door and saw the light from outside crease the room, she turned around and looked at me.

"Hi, Mare."

"Pete." Mary stood up and hugged me.

"Are you okay?"

"Yeah, Mare. How's Mom?"

Mary bit her lip and wiped Mom's face again. A fan whirred from the bedroom down the hallway, but the living room sweltered and Mom's skin shone with sweat. Her face looked swollen, her hair wet around it and matted flat to her head. Mom was naturally thin which made her face and head appear larger than normal.

"I think she's asleep, again. The doctor gave her some pills to calm her down and I guess they made her groggy."

Mary took the cloth off Mom's forehead and walked into the bathroom to rinse it out.

"She didn't just take pills."

"What, Franklin?"

"She drank something."

"She what?"

"Drank some booze."

"Mom?"

"Go look in the trash and see for yourself."

Our mom had never drunk as much as a sip of anything in her whole life. And even if she wanted to she couldn't because of her illness. But she never heckled Pa about drinking beer after work or on weekends after he had mowed the lawn or at square-dancing parties. Even when old man Hillar would go on an occasional binge hollering and swearing late into the night, Mom wouldn't complain except to say she wished he would choose a more civil hour for his ravings. It wasn't religion, either, that kept her from it. She wasn't a churchgoer although she had definite beliefs about things. No, drinking was just something she had never done without making a big fuss about it and looking down at her, I couldn't believe she had drunk anything now.

Mary returned and placed the cloth back on Mom's forehead. "Here, Pete. Take this."

"What is it?"

"For your stomach."

"I'm all right."

"Please? You'll feel better. The nurse told me you threw up."

I took the two tablets from Mary and popped them into my mouth.

"Sorry I couldn't come to the hospital this morning, Petey."

"That's okay."

"With Mom like this I just couldn't leave."

"I know. Is she all right?'

Mary nodded quickly. "She's just sleepy, that's all."

Franklin and Erwin got up and walked over to the couch and the four of us looked down at our mother. She had been sick as long as we could remember. Doctor Fritz, a short round man with round glinty glasses, had delivered all of us and with each one, Mom's health had gotten worse. It was as if giving life took a little bit away from her own. After Erwin was born, the doctor told Pa that examining our mother was like looking into a beautifully crafted home only to find the furniture within turned upside down with some of the upholstery torn. Knowing our father's love of carpentry, he always spoke in terms of building or remodeling or tearing something down and Pa liked him for it.

"Maybe it's time to call Doctor Fritz back, Mare."

Franklin put his arm around Erwin's shoulder and looked at Mary.

"Maybe so." Mary went into the hall closet, took out a white sheet, and began unfolding it.

"Mary, what are you doing?"

She looked up at me. "We need to keep her covered."

Mary walked over to our mother, shaking the sheet out. I turned quickly away and went into the kitchen and leaned against the sink where, underneath, the trash was kept. I turned on the faucet and stuck my face under the white hissing water, letting it run over my eyes, nose, and mouth. I opened my mouth and let it fill before turning the faucet off. Opening the cupboard under the sink, I reached in and grabbed the trash basket and began to tip it forward—Mom wouldn't drink, she had never drunk anything in her whole life—but I set the wastebasket back down, instead, and shut the cupboard and walked downstairs into Pa's workshop.

Pa's table saw stood in the middle of the concrete floor with sawdust swept up underneath. It was the new Black and Decker Mom had given him for Christmas. In front of it on the workbench lay his skillsaw tilted to one side against the blade guard and a plane with wood shavings still curled around it. From a peg on the side of the bench hung Pa's leather nail belt, the inside dark and shiny from sweat and from rubbing against his belly. Across the room along the basement wall lay two-by-fours and one-by-eights and scraps of plywood, sheetrock, and particle board and strips of baseboard and trim. The smell of the lumber—the pine and oak and cedar—and the sawdust and shavings were everywhere, and when my father was down here working I watched and could see the flecks of wood in his hair and smell the wood on him even when he went outside for more lumber.

I had watched him for hours working with this wood and I never quite believed what he could do with it, as if by magic. Curves and angles and swirls and knobs came from it as though the shapes were there all along just waiting to be found like the fossils Franklin and I discovered across the canal in the shale of the nearby hills. But it was my father doing all this with his hands, giving it its lines and texture and finish. But the most amazing part wasn't that our father had built practically everything we owned in our house—desks, the bookcase, our mother's china closet, chairs, dressers, and even fancy coat racks with designs all over them—but that he had actually built the house itself. The entire house. It was magic.

And now a coffee table lay upside down across two sawhorses. He had just glued the legs in place and was going to finish sanding it before he put the varnish on. I ran my hand along the table's length and then up the curve of one leg and out to where it flared at the end. The wood felt cool and hard against my fingertips and solid like everything Pa made. And then I remembered why he was making it: Mom's birthday.

I turned away and walked across the workshop to my bedroom. I shut the door and watched sawdust lift into the air where the sun slanted down through the small basement window. The specks gave off color as they sifted down like snowflakes in Mom's crystal winter scene. I walked through the light to the built-in drawers and took out the bottom one and set it on the floor. Feet-first I crawled into the wall and using a handle I had screwed into the back of the drawer, pulled it in after me.

Usually, I turned on the flashlight or lit a candle in here to look at my football and baseball magazines or at the rain-crinkled PLAYBOY I had found up by the brickyard. Or I'd shine the light on my heroes I had plastered around me on the bare studs and on the underside of the stairwell—Paul Hornung, Roger Maris, Jim Brown, Wilt "the Stilt" Chamberlain, Whitey Ford. But this time I only lay down in the perfect black darkness against the old stained mattress with the smell of gasoline all around.

When Franklin first got the job at Mr. Dugan's gas station a couple of summers before, I used to like to go there and watch him work the pumps. After a car pulled in, he would grab the nozzle and start the gas flowing and then hustle around checking the tires and oil and squeegeeing off the windshield before the numbers quit dinging. Because Franklin was only twelve then and not allowed to handle money, he had to service one car and then go straight to the next one to do the same thing. It was like one continuous race that didn't finish until Mr. Dugan closed the station at half past nine.

After Franklin got home, the smell of gasoline was everywhere and he reeked of it even after taking a shower. It was in his hair and on his clothes and even seemed to seep out his pores when he sweat. Mom had made the mistake of washing his dirty work clothes with everyone else's that first time and our whole family smelled for a while. After that, she washed his work clothes separately and then only every other week.

Franklin took to dousing himself with Pa's Old Spice and stuffing his dirty clothes behind his drawers under the stairway to hide the smell. And because my bedroom was on the other side of the stairwell, it began to stink almost as much as Franklin's. But the worst part was that my secret hiding place was filled with it.

I didn't say anything to Franklin or throw his clothes out because then he would have known where I was hiding and nobody knew that. But I did stop going to the station so much to watch him. After a while I got used to the smell like any smell you're around all the time and I didn't even notice it much. But now as I lay in the cool black dark, I noticed the smell because I was concentrating on it, breathing it, trying not to hear the circular screams of the siren outside.

I hadn't heard it until it was right in our driveway and had stopped. Some things aren't noticed until they've quit. By the time I had crawled out and run upstairs they had her on a stretcher and halfway out the door. Mary clutched a throw pillow to her mouth, a scream building in her eyes. Erwin lay curled up in the rocker, sucking his thumb. Franklin held the screen door, and he kept holding it long after they slid our mother into the ambulance and drove away.

"Petey, what did you do?"

"Huh-uh." I shake my head.

"Give me that you naughty boy." Momma takes the paintbrush from me. I start crying. She rubs at the dripping paint on the screen with a cloth but I can see she's smiling. I feel some better. She turns and lifts me into the air.

"Petey, what am I going to do with you, buster."

I giggle as she holds me aloft and jiggles me.

"Frank? Petey's helping us. He painted the screen."

Papa is here and he isn't laughing and I don't feel so good again. He squats at the screen and scrubs at it with a wire brush. He looks up at me and Momma. "I told you to watch him, Marge."

Papa seems angry and I begin crying. Momma bounces me against her left breast, my chin resting over the slant of her neck where it meets her shoulder.

"Shhhh. He didn't mean to. It's just a screen."

Papa straightens up, his hands resting on his hips. He looks down at the screen and then back at me and Momma.

"It's not coming off. And it's not just a screen, Marge. It's our house."

3

Uncle Herbert, Mom's only brother, arrived from Wichita, Kansas, the next morning for the funeral. It was his Christian duty. The four of us, pressed at the front window sill with our pajamas still on, peered out at him through our breath rolling out against the cool pane.

The last time we had seen Uncle Herbert was Christmas two years before. That was the Christmas he lost our presents changing buses in Denver. They were stolen, he said. The time before that his basement apartment was burglarized. Most years our mother invited Uncle Herbert to stay with us through New Years but, invitation or not, he usually stuck around long after we took the lights and bulbs off the tree and picked the carpet clean of tinsel and pine needles. All the cold turkey sandwiches were eaten and the two big hams Mom baked for New Year's day gone—yet Uncle Herbert remained. But I never heard Pa say anything bad about Uncle Herbert or ask him to leave; our mother wouldn't put up with that because Uncle Herbert was the only living relative we had.

That last Christmas, though, Pa's gold watch the teamsters gave him for twenty-five years of service turned up missing. And Uncle Herbert hadn't been back since.

But there he was on our front porch, impatiently waiting for someone to answer his knock. Taking a dark brown fedora off his head and setting down his vinyl suitcase, he knocked again, louder. His black pasted-down hair shone like a bowling ball in the morning light, and he wore a tan suit with padded shoulders and baggy trousers that draped over his shoes. A wide red tie with a green pheasant painted on it hung loosely around his skinny neck. He knocked once more, turning the hat in his hands.

Finally, Mrs. Henderson, the neighbor lady who stayed with us that night, huffed her way upstairs from doing the laundry and opened the door.

"Pardon me, madam. Isn't this the Caviness residence?"

"It sure is."

"And there are the children. Hello, children. It's your Uncle Herbert come to visit from Wichita."

"You best come in and sit down, Uncle Herbert."

"The name's Herbert T. Merriweather from Wichita, Kansas, madam. And who, may I ask, might you be?"

"The name's Hazel Mildred Henderson from down the street. Now get on in here, I've got somethin' to tell you."

"Well, of course! The famous Mrs. Henderson I've heard so much about. I'm Margaret's brother. Where is Marge, my dear?"

"You better have a seat, Mr. Merriweather."

"My dear Mrs. Henderson, I have already been informed of my beloved brother-in-law, whom I loved as only a brother can. It grieves me to think he departed this world so prematurely but the Lord, Mrs. Henderson, does work in mysterious ways and it is not my place to question the divine plan the Almighty has for each and every one of us. Now, where is that darlin' little sister of mine?" Hair oil burned from Uncle Herbert's head and filled the living room with a heavy presence as he waited for Mrs. Henderson's reply. He didn't have to wait long.

"Mr. Merriweather, I don't know how to tell you this but your darlin' little sister done got up and died just one day after her mister."

Uncle Herbert crumpled to the hardwood floor. It took all of us to heft him up lengthwise onto the couch where he stayed all morning. But we were used to seeing Uncle Herbert lie on the couch because that's where he usually parked himself when he visited us. Around noon he asked Mary to turn on the Motorola, so we didn't much worry about him after that.

Turning on the television was the first thing Uncle Herbert did in the morning and turning it off was the last thing he did at night. We got only one station in Grand River and Uncle Herbert complained about that. In Wichita, he said, they had three or four channels. Pa always said it didn't much matter because a person only has one set of eyes, anyway. "Variety," Uncle Herbert would then say, "is the spice of life, my dear man." And Pa's lips would turn white as winter icicles.

"Mrs. Henderson, dear, please do bring me a nice cup of tea. I have the most dreadful thirst."

She stood at the stove, spatula in hand, frying hamburgers for supper. The beef hissed and crackled against the cast-iron skillet and the grease spit up against the side of the refrigerator. Mrs. Henderson pressed the patties with the flat of the spatula and set it down on the stove-top. She took a Lipton tea bag from the cupboard, plopped it into a cup of hot tap water, and took it into the living room.

"Here you go."

"You're a dear. Thank you."

She returned to the kitchen and scooped up the hamburgers with the spatula and slid them, one by one, onto a platter covered with butcher's paper to absorb the grease. We were used to Mrs. Henderson cooking for us. When Mom was sick or away, she always stayed with us. Sometimes we even called her "Gram," but that was more because of the chocolate Graham-cracker cookies she made than anything else.

"Mrs. Henderson? Isn't this tea just a wee bit on the tepid side?"

Mom used to wait on Uncle Herbert hand and foot even when she didn't feel up to it. Uncle Herbert always told her she shouldn't do so much because of her condition, as he referred to it, as though any other words for what she had might dirty his mouth. Her condition should be respected and treated as a "formidable foe whose temper best not be aroused." Uncle Herbert only said things like that after dessert. Dessert seemed to lubricate Uncle Herbert's tongue.

Franklin, Erwin, and I smeared ketchup and mustard on our hamburger buns and piled on dill pickle and onion slices. The plump patties were now on a platter in the middle of the table and we forked them onto our plates and dug in.

Mary was in her room where she had spent most of the day. She usually ate less than any of us but she was still a little chubby. Mom used to tell her it was because she had such a big heart.

"What is that wonderful aroma, Mrs. Henderson? Something surely does smell good in there." Uncle Herbert stuck his long thin nose into the kitchen and dramatically sniffed the air. He could have been laid and set in concrete but the smell of cooking food would have brought him bolt upright.

"How absolutely quaint—hamburgers for supper. Marge, that poor dear, would have never thought of it." Uncle Herbert took a hankie from his pocket and dabbed at his eyes.

Mrs. Henderson sat at the table with us, working the hamburger in her mouth and studying Uncle Herbert. "If eatin' burgers for supper is such a upsettin' idea for you, I'll just save you one for breakfast. How's that?"

Uncle Herbert put his hankie away and sat down. "No, it's not that . . . it's just my baby sister . . . succumbing as she did." Uncle Herbert reached for a bun and began applying mustard.

"Now you shush and quit being weepy around the children. I just get 'em settled down and you start up. It ain't easy for nobody. Now have some chips and a burger and you'll feel better."

Uncle Herbert ate two hamburgers and then returned to the living room and lay down to watch more television. Franklin and I had to dry the dishes because Mary never did come out. But after Mrs. Henderson put Erwin to bed—he and Mary shared the same room—she told us not to worry because Mary was already asleep.

* * *

The day before the funeral was dreary. Billowy thunderheads rolled up out of the Utah desert in the west and wet the fruit orchards and the sunflowers and asparagus that grew wild along the ditch banks. The rain came hard and clean, swelled the gutters, and turned the ditch water iron-red. And with it came wind that blew the rain up under the eaves and hard against the front window pane.

The red sandstone of Rimrock National Park shone wet in the distance and in late afternoon caught the first break of sunlight in glassy streaks along its rim. The rain let up then, clouds breaking like great loaves of bread being torn apart. The front window was still streaked where the water had run as I stood gazing out at Erwin sloshing his way up and down the gutters. He hugged a Folger's coffee can in his left arm and with the right sleeve of his slicker rolled up, studied the water and curb for earthworms.

Erwin loved earthworms and anything else that crawled or jumped. In the summertime he caught grasshoppers, crickets, ants, caterpillars, butterflies, moths, and even spiders. Frogs, toads, snakes, and lizards weren't safe around Erwin, either. Once he discovered a baby rabbit in a freshly cut hayfield. He carried it home and Mom helped him place it in a big grocery box with a dish of water and some lettuce and carrots. But it was a wild rabbit, a cottontail, and it died after only a couple of days. Erwin carried the box and the dead rabbit back to the field and dumped it out onto the stubbled ground without saying a word. Erwin never caught anything that didn't die.

By the time he came back into the house with his can full of earthworms, Uncle Herbert was taking one of his regular afternoon naps. It was his third day with us and the side of his face had sprouted a rash. Lying on the couch, he would slowly run his long white fingers back and forth over the sharp edge of his cheek and jaw like he was reading Braille, as though the puffy contours of his skin held the answer to some profound question. His eyes stared at the television then but didn't blink. As his rash spread, so too did his silence until he didn't say much of anything to anybody unless it had to do with what we were going to have for the next meal.

I don't know whose idea it was or why we even did it. It wasn't because

Uncle Herbert was any worse than he usually was. In fact, his not talking much should have made his stay easier. When he wasn't lying down watching television, he was eating and when he wasn't eating, he was sleeping. Mrs. Henderson was still doing most of the cooking, and washing one more plate wasn't such a big deal although Franklin and I hated washing dishes anytime. He wasn't taking advantage of Mary's big heart because Mary still spent most of her time in the bedroom. No, I don't know why we did it. Maybe it was just because he was there. And maybe that was enough of a reason.

Erwin clunked the coffee can down on the step just inside the back door. He shucked off his wet slicker and sat on the floor to pull off his rubber boots. Franklin stood over him just inside the kitchen doorway.

"How many'd you get, Win?"

"Bunches."

Franklin squatted and looked down at the clump of shifting and stretching earthworms. "Way to go, Win. There must be a thousand in there."

Erwin's boots were off now so he picked up the can as a hunter might pick up his game and went into the kitchen, his drenched hair plastered to his head.

"Where ya want 'em?"

"Up there on the counter."

Erwin reached up with both hands and set the coffee can on the counter next to a glass casserole dish. Franklin began pouring the worms into the dish.

"I wanna do it. I caught 'em."

Franklin put the can in Erwin's outstretched hands and helped guide the worms into the dish. They slipped and slid over the glass like a crowd of sprawling skaters over ice before plopping out in one swarming heap. Franklin turned on the cold water and began rinsing and untangling them.

"How'd you find all these, Win?"

"I dunno. Just did."

I opened the refrigerator for the cheese. Mom and Pa liked all kinds—Cheddar, Swiss, Velveeta, Pimento, Parmesan—and we usually ate some at every meal, whether melted over macaroni or pressed between saltine crackers.

"What kind, Franklin?"

"Don't matter. Any kind, just so it tastes good."

I put a block of Longhorn Cheddar, a package of Swiss, and for texture, a few clumps of Velveeta into a sauce pan, struck a match, and turned on the gas burner. The gas caught with a whoosh, like the sound of your breath when the wind is knocked out of you. The cheeses spread out, melting together and forming little heat pockets that bubbled up into a sauce.

"Ready, Franklin?"

"Ready."

The mess of earthworms were now spread out over the bottom of the casserole dish in a deep layer that sloped up toward the middle. Franklin was holding the sauce pan with a potholder as we bunched together to watch.

"I wanna do it. I caught 'em."

"Come on, Win, this is the most important part."

Erwin stood on his tiptoes and peered into the dish as though it were an aquarium full of exotic fish. Franklin then positioned the sauce pan over the earthworms and aimed a steady stream onto the middle of the cluster. The sauce cascaded outward from there, blanketing the squirming worms and glazing them into a whole.

"They're still movin'."

Erwin pointed at the side of the casserole dish which was about eye-level to him. Franklin and I bent down and looked.

"Yep. They're still moving around all right."

Franklin took a butter knife from the silverware drawer and circled the inside of the dish so cheese could seep between the worms and the glass. The blanket of cheese was now quiet and there was no more movement.

"Go wake Uncle Herbert, Pete."

"I don't want to. You wake him."

"Hurry, Pete, it's going to get cold and Mrs. Henderson'll be back. I'll get the plates out."

"What do I say?"

"Tell him supper's ready."

"But he's going to ask what we're having. He always does."

"Tell him anything. Tell him Mary cooked some Chinese noodles just for him."

I walked down the hallway to Mom and Pa's bedroom. Light seeped underneath the door. I raised my hand, hesitated, and then lightly knocked.

"Uncle Herbert?"

A rustling sound came from inside and then stopped. Thinking maybe the sound was Uncle Herbert stirring under the sheets, I started to leave but then heard the closet door roll shut. I stepped back, turned the knob, and eased the door open.

"Uncle Herbert?"

There, across our parents' bed, lay not Uncle Herbert but envelopes and sheets of paper, some loose and some clipped or stapled together. The drawers of Mom and Pa's twin dressers hung open with some of their things draped over the edge. I stepped over a shoe box of business envelopes and looked up at Uncle Herbert standing—frozen—across the room, clutching papers to his chest. His eyes were closed and in front of him sat the cedar chest, its top open and pictures and more loose paper strewn around it on the floor. The big wedding picture of Mom and Pa, which usually sat atop the chest on a fancy white doily Mom had crocheted for their fifteenth wedding anniversary, leaned crookedly in the corner.

"Uncle Herbert . . . supper's ready."

Uncle Herbert opened his eyes and glanced quickly around.

"Uh . . . yes . . . well . . . I . . . uh . . ."

He stooped to put the papers on the bed, thought better of it, turned, looked around again, and then just let them flutter from his arms down into the cedar chest.

"Yes, Peter, dinner . . . thank you, thank you very much . . . I'll be, uh . . . I'll be right there."

A smile so thin it barely masked a grimace creased his narrow face as I turned to leave.

"Peter?"

I stopped and looked back at Uncle Herbert who had now turned, holding the lid of the cedar chest behind him.

"I was just . . . uh . . . kind of, uh, straightening up a bit."

I nodded as he closed the lid and sat down on the chest. He brought a glass of brown liquid from the floor.

"Peter, would you please sit down for a moment?"

Taking a swallow, he reached out with his free hand, cleared a spot on the bed in front of him and patted it, indicating for me to sit.

"Uncle Herbert, it's going to get cold. Franklin and Win are waitin' for us."

"Please, Peter. As your only kin, your mother's only brother . . ."

I glanced around the bedroom at the strewn papers and boxes and clothing and then carefully stepped around and over them to the far side of the bed.

"I must take occasion to, uh, tell you some things . . . things of the utmost importance. There you go. Sit down."

Sitting on the edge of the bed, I could clearly see red veins in the whites of his eyes and smell the pungent odor of stale aftershave and whatever it was he drank.

"Peter, your mother . . . my darlin' little sister . . ."

Tiny sweat bubbles beaded above his thin upper lip as he stared into the glass, swirling the liquid within.

"Margaret and Frank, they . . . they were . . ."

He took another drink, the sharp slice of Adam's apple disappearing then descending into place under the thin rubbery skin of his throat.

"What's your age?"

"What?"

"Your age. How old are you now?"

"Ten, goin' on eleven."

He nodded, glancing around at the bedroom and then tilting his head back as he drained the rest of the drink. He set the glass down on the cedar chest.

"For my headache."

"Huh?"

"My headache, medicine for my headache."

"Oh."

Uncle Herbert suddenly slapped his knees and tried another smile. "Eleven. Now there's an age for you."

"Goin' on eleven."

"Well, yes, uh . . . eleven, going on eleven, what the hell's the . . ." He grabbed the glass, looked into it, and then clunked it back down.

"We all have certain responsibilities, Peter. Things we must do." He looked past me over my left shoulder. "I have things I have to do, you have things you have to do, Mary, Franklin, Derwin . . ."

"Erwin."

"Erwin. We all have things we must do. And as the only next of kin, I've got the most things, the most responsibility. Marge and Frank would have wanted it that way."

Looking down, his head suddenly jerked to the side, the lower jaw yanked over as though he were palsied or loosening the knot of a very tight tie. "Well?"

I looked at Uncle Herbert and blinked. "What?"

He brought his gaze up and met mine. "Let's go eat supper."

I jumped up and started around the bed, but Uncle Herbert caught me by the elbow. "And, Peter . . . this mess . . ." He swung his other hand around the room. ". . . and this conversation, we will, as of now, forever forget. Understand?"

I nodded and then followed Uncle Herbert out of our parent's bedroom and into the kitchen for a supper we would, most certainly, forever not forget.

* * *

Franklin had set the table with special dishes Mom kept in the china closet. They were rimmed in gold with two wisps of golden wheat painted on either side. But they looked awkward next to the plastic glasses we always used. I guess Franklin thought the crystal wine goblets Mom had collected would be going too far. Uncle Herbert didn't notice, anyway.

"That's what I love about Oriental food, such subtle smells." Uncle Herbert raised his nose and closed his eyes. "So wonderfully faint, yet so exquisite. How did Mary ever learn to cook Chinese?"

"Mom teached her."

"Taught her, Peter."

"Taught her."

"I didn't know Margaret could cook Chinese food. Her own brother and there are still things I never knew about that wonderful woman. Where is Mary?"

Franklin set the Chinese casserole dish in the middle of the table as Uncle Herbert settled into Pa's place.

Erwin sat on his hands directly across from him, his tongue out and moving back and forth across his bottom lip like the pendulum in a grandfather clock. He fixed on Uncle Herbert as though watching the final out of the World Series.

"Mary went back to bed. She's still not feelin' too good."

Nothing Franklin could have said would have pleased Uncle Herbert more and he complimented her the same way he applied hair oil, excessively: when God created Mary, He created perfection; a carbon copy of her mother; a more loving girl did not exist; to think that this grieving child had so devoutedly wrenched herself away from her own troubles just long enough to prepare her faithful uncle a banquet fit for heaven; there was much to be learned from this simple act of kindness.

"Let us pray. Dear God Almighty, thank you, Lord, for providing this nourishment this day and, Jesus, bless the head of one Mary Caviness who so lovingly prepared Your food for her most thankful kin. And please, God, continue to provide for these poor homeless children who, by Your divine will, were dispossessed of their beloved parents and please help them find two new parents who will love them as their own. In Jesus' name we pray, Amen."

Steam from the casserole dish rose between us as Franklin and I turned to look at Erwin. Earlier, Erwin said he wanted to be the one to serve Uncle Herbert. But now, except for his tongue, Erwin wasn't moving.

"Well, let's dig in, young men."

Franklin looked at me and I stared back. Uncle Herbert picked up the long cutting knife.

"I'll do it." I took the knife from Uncle Herbert.

"Thank you, Peter. I was beginning to wonder if we weren't just going to look at it instead of eat it. It's certainly a work of art." Uncle Herbert shook his head, pleased.

I placed the tip of the cutting knife in the middle at the thickest point and cut toward me as though cutting a pie. I cut clean, sawing the knife in two long strokes. Uncle Herbert slipped the spatula underneath and brought it up and over and onto his plate.

Erwin's tongue stopped moving. We stared at our plates.

"Aren't you boys hungry?"

Uncle Herbert stuffed a napkin between the collar of his open shirt and picked up his knife and fork. He slipped the tines into the cheese and on through and cut a small section.

Erwin abruptly stood and walked quickly toward the bathroom. "Gotta go."

Uncle Herbert lifted the fork to his lips and put it into his mouth as he watched Erwin leave.

"What's wrong with your little brother?"

The fork came out clean and the tines went back into the cheese. Uncle Herbert chewed.

Franklin cleared his throat. "I don't know."

Uncle Herbert swallowed and then cut a larger piece. The fork slid under it, moved to his mouth, and again disappeared. "This is, as Mrs. Henderson said, an extremely difficult time for all of us, but the Lord will provide."

Before fully chewing and swallowing this second bite, Uncle Herbert already had another piece up and into his mouth. "Yes, the Lord knows what we need and He giveth."

Uncle Herbert looked down at his plate and wiped around his mouth with the starched napkin. "And the Lord taketh away."

He stared at his plate and stopped chewing. His head bent forward and he squinted as though he were a coin collector trying to make out the date on an Indian nickel or, better, a biologist inspecting a new species. With the end of his fork, he turned back the cooled outer layer of cheese. Underneath, a severed noodle lay in two long pieces and then, with a curious prod from Uncle Herbert's fork, wiggled against the grain of our mother's best china.

Franklin and I reached the back door just as Erwin did from the bathroom. With a loud whoop, we rushed outside to the screech of Uncle Herbert's chair against the linoleum floor and then the cough and splatter of the Lord taking Uncle Herbert's meal away.

* * *

The rain was gone and only its scent remained, filtering up from the soaked earth through the grass standing sharp in the August night, up from the shale and alkali and clay hills, and across from the dusted sagebrush of the desert floor. Broken pieces of glass, washed clean by the rain, lay below the elm in muted light from the corner street lamp, glinting like jewels in the weeds and charcoal shadows of the vacant lot. Across the street, through the leaves, a single light glowed against the curtain of our living-room window.

From the tree house high in the elm, our house looked small and empty. Its gabled roof which, like the rest of the house, had appeared so huge when our father was nailing the new wooden shingles in place the summer before, was now diminished, as though our father's presence was what gave it its immensity. Now that he was gone, it had somehow shrunk.

"I wonder if Mary's okay? I shouldn't have told him she made it."

I pulled the army blanket we used for the tree-house roof up around my shoulders. Franklin shifted back between the fork of two branches.

"You had to else he wouldn't of swallowed it. He knows who did it now, anyhow. Mary's all right."

"I'm cold." Erwin pulled the end of the army blanket over his lap. A piece of innertube we used as a slingshot flapped above us between two limbs and one of the lions in City Park Zoo roared from across town, a distant baritone moan swelling the night air.

"Lions do that 'cause they're mad. Huh, Franklin?"

Franklin and I glanced down at our little brother and then continued staring out through the leaves and branches at our house. Franklin shrugged. "Beats me, Win. Maybe because they're bored."

I helped Erwin pull the corner of the blanket up under his chin. "Where do you think Uncle Herbert went, Franklin?"

"I don't know. Maybe he went to get a jar of salmon eggs for dessert."

I didn't laugh as Erwin huddled in closer and a louder roar echoed across the valley, followed by a second more subdued one.

"Lions get mad, huh? That's why they like to eat people."

Franklin waved a mosquito from his ear and shook his head. "Lions don't like to eat people, Win. They just do that if they have to. Maybe when they're starvin' or being shot at or something."

"But they can't eat nobody now 'cause they're in them cages. Huh, Franklin?"

"Nope. Not unless they get out."

Erwin looked up at his big brother. "They can't get out, though. Can they, Franklin?"

Franklin shook his head just as another one let out a roar. "Not unless they can get a hold of the zoo keeper or his keys, I guess."

Erwin nodded, wide-eyed, and fell silent as the roars continued.

"Maybe Uncle Herbert went back to Wichita, Franklin."

"He didn't have his bag when he came out."

"Maybe he just forgot it."

Franklin didn't say anything.

"I'm going down. We can't stay up here all night."

"You do, Pete, and you're crazy. He might come back anytime."

"I don't care."

"You better care. You're the one that gave it to him."

"Yeah, but you made it, Franklin."

"That don't matter to Uncle Herbert, stupid. He just knows you gave it to him."

I sat back and we waited. The lions gradually quieted as darkness gathered like smoke around the corner streetlight.

"What about Mrs. Henderson?"

"I called her before and told her we already ate."

"I'm hungry."

"You're always hungry, Win."

"I didn't eat nothin'."

"Don't worry. We'll have a bunch of stuff to eat tomorrow."

Leaning back against a branch, I gazed up through the limbs and leaves at the stars across the black canopy of the world. "You ever been to a funeral, Franklin?"

"Nope."

"What do they do at them?"

"Beats me. Guess we'll find out."

"Is it in a church?"

"At a funeral place. Don't you know nothin'?"

I brought my gaze down to Franklin. "Isn't it like a church?"

"I don't know. I said I never been to one."

Two headlights turned through the darkness at the far end of the street, straightened, grew larger, and stopped in front of our house. A man got out of a long white car and we could hear voices.

"It's Uncle Herbert!"

"Shhhh."

He opened the door as he talked to the driver leaning across the seat. We couldn't see the driver's face or hear what they were saying but the ceiling light inside the car shone off his bare head. They shook hands and Uncle Herbert got out. The bald man straightened back up behind the steering wheel and eased the automobile away from the curb. Uncle Herbert opened the fence gate, watching the taillights move off down our street and disappear around the corner. He turned and then trudged up the sidewalk and into the house.

We waited until all the house lights blinked out and we were sure Uncle Herbert was in bed. We slipped down the thick trunk and around to the back door. Franklin opened it with the key Pa had given him when he started his job at Dugan's gas station. Easing the door shut behind us, we tiptoed down the stairway into the basement.

"What do we do now, Franklin?"

"Sleep."

"What about Uncle Herbert?"

"He won't do nothin'."

"What if he does?"

"Come on, Win."

"Win going to sleep with you?"

"Yep."

Franklin and Erwin stepped into Franklin's bedroom and shut the door. I went quickly through Pa's workshop to my bedroom. I kicked off my shoes and pants and slid into bed. Through the wall from the other side of the staircase I could hear Franklin's muffled voice talking to Erwin. I lay listening to the house settle above me, the copper pipes contract and the flooring give and the hum of the refrigerator. And finally convinced Uncle Herbert wasn't going to come creeping downstairs for revenge, I pulled the sheets up over my head and fell asleep.

4

On the day of the funeral I heard footsteps—as though the footsteps I fearfully expected before falling asleep had stalked me across my world of dreams and now caught up with me as I awoke.

"Pete? Uncle Herbert wants you to get up. We're supposed to be there pretty soon."

Mary stood at the foot of the bed, wrapped in threads of light coming through the small basement window. Her features were lost in the brilliance behind her and I could only make out wisps of blond hair that shone like a halo.

"I thought it was this afternoon."

"It is, Pete. It's already afternoon."

I rubbed sleep from my eyes and sat up, but the light behind Mary's head stabbed at me like shards of splintered glass.

"Sit down, I can't see you."

"Pete, we're going to be late."

I scooted over and she sat on the edge. Her large green eyes were still swollen and her cheeks, which were losing their little-girl roundness, were blotchy and red.

"You okay, Mare?"

"I'm all right."

"Is Uncle Herbert mad?"

"He's quiet but I don't think he's mad. Why should he be mad?"

"Nothin'. I just thought . . . never mind."

Mary stared down at a pink hair ribbon she twisted around her fingers. She wore her white Easter dress and it pulled and bunched under her arms. Mom had made the dress for her that spring but it was already too small in front. Mary had a closet-full of dresses Mom sewed for her but she preferred wearing jeans and T-shirts like Franklin, Erwin, and me.

Mary had been like one of the guys in the neighborhood. She pitched a baseball like any of us and although she couldn't run very fast, she usually hit well enough to reach first base. Playing football, she was impossible to block and tackled almost as well as Buddy Phillips, the best tackler on our block. In fact, it was after one of those tackles that Pa told Mary she couldn't play football anymore. Mary didn't understand. She sat on the front steps and watched after that. That was the year before, the year she began wearing the dresses.

"Pete, are you afraid?"

"'Bout what?"

"What's going to happen to us."

"Mrs. Henderson'll take care of us."

Mary smiled. "Mrs. Henderson is getting old, Pete. It's not fair she should have to take care of us now."

"She likes us, Mare."

Mary's eyes filled as she gazed back down at the ribbon now wound tightly around her fingers, reddening the ends. I shifted onto my side waiting for Mary to say something like she always did, something that would make me feel better.

"We're going to be late, Pete." Mary stood up and walked to the door.

"Hey, Mare. Remember last year when you tackled Jimmy Reece and Pa said you couldn't play football anymore?"

"Yes."

"Why did Pa say that?"

Mary looked at me and smiled. "Because young ladies don't play football, Pete."

"What do they do then?"

The smile slowly faded as she looked back down at the ribbon in her hands and bit her lip. "I'm not sure. Daddy never told me that."

And then she was gone and that was the last time I talked to Mary about our father, the last time before the Lord found her another one.

* * *

Uncle Herbert pulled our parents' '57 Pontiac up alongside a black limousine glaring white under the sun. As we got out, a slight man no bigger than Franklin walked out from underneath the brick canopy of Shade's Funeral Home toward us. He adjusted his tie as he walked and using the palm of his small hand, smoothed a handkerchief folded in the breast pocket of his dark blue suit.

"Hi there, Lawrence."

"Well, hello, Mrs. Henderson. How nice to see you, again."

"Nice to see you too, Lawrence, and just so it stays that way and ain't one-sided."

Mr. Shade laughed shrilly and clasped his hands under his chin, shaking his head.

"This here's Herbert T. Merriweather, Marge Caviness' brother."

"Lawrence Shade. My pleasure."

Uncle Herbert nodded and the two shook hands.

"And these here are the children: Frank Junior, Peter, Mary Lynnette, and Erwin."

"Nice to meet you young people and my deepest condolences to you."

Mr. Shade pressed each one of our hands in turn and peered into our eyes as though trying to locate a cinder. His face was smooth as varnish except for twin creases between his sparse eyebrows, which deepened with seriousness as he studied us and then relaxed when he straightened and motioned us inside. We followed him out of the heat into a wood-paneled hallway full of somber organ music and the chilly hum of swamp-cooler air. Our footsteps fell muffled onto a thick red carpet before stopping in front of a door.

"You can wait in here."

"Lawrence, is Frank and Marge . . ."

"No, we've just moved them up front. I'll let you know, Mrs. Henderson. Shouldn't be more than twenty minutes. Make yourselves comfortable."

We stepped inside and Mr. Shade quietly shut the door with one hand pressed against the crack as though there might be a baby asleep somewhere.

"My, my, look at them flowers, children!"

Mrs. Henderson stooped as she would in her garden and began removing sympathy cards tucked into floral arrangements with little plastic tridents. The flowers—propped up with wire and metal staples, adorned with ribbon and bunting, and sprayed fresh with floral perfume—stretched the length of the entire wall. Instead of her usual straw gardening hat, Mrs. Henderson wore a black felt pillbox covered with black mesh and a plastic yellow rose plunked to the side. The smell of too much perfume was on her as though in her old age she needed at least half a bottle of Wild Gardenia to catch even the slightest whiff herself.

"Looky here. These gladiolas are from Gladys Cramer. Why, they're beautiful! She oughtn't done that. And these chrysanthemums! My, my, who sent these? Let's see—it's a Hallmark—says: 'In life there's love from Heaven above / And in death below our body does go / But our spirit within goes up to Him / For He is the Lord from whom we're restored. Our deepest sympathy, the Clymers.' Who's the Clymers?"

Franklin and Erwin moved over and sat on a velvet sofa under a cut-glass window. Franklin propped his elbows on his knees, cupped his chin in his hands, and gazed out across the acres of manicured lawn outside. Erwin busied his fingers with races up the pant legs of his trousers, whispering conversations between the imagined runners. Mrs. Henderson collected the rest of the envelopes and handed them to Mary who stood speechlessly next to her, staring at the clipped flowers.

I waited by the door and watched Uncle Herbert. He stood alone in the middle of the room fingering the red blotches that stood out on his cheek and along his jaw line and staring down at the carpet. Uncle Herbert seemed always to be alone, even when there were other people around. And now, maybe in my own guilt for what we had done to him, he seemed more alone than ever before. He finally looked up, caught me watching him, and managed a wan smile. I smiled weakly back and at the time thought this was a truce or a sign of shared sorrow between us, but I was soon to find out that Uncle Herbert's smile meant something else, something entirely different.

* * *

His name was Reverend Calloway and as he introduced himself, I was reminded of a clown I saw the summer before at a rodeo that had come to town. The clown was to keep the bulls away from the cowboys so none of the contestants would be trampled or gored. The clown mocked and teased the bull, mimicking it by pawing at the ground with his feet and pointing his index fingers up from his head. Then when the bull charged, he jumped into the safety of a barrel where he was protected from the bull's fury. Reverend Calloway had the same ruddy complexion and perspiring bare head as that clown.

The family seating area was off to the side and faced the podium at a right angle. Through a filmy curtain drawn before us, I watched the dim shapes of Mr. Shade's attendants carrying floral arrangements to the front and I could hear the rustle of ribbon and bunting as they walked. Soon, coughs and the squeak of sweaty pant legs against varnished pews and the rub of ladies' nylons filled the chapel. Reverend Calloway shuffled his papers against the podium and for a brief moment, silence fell all around like the peaceful weight of an autumn snowstorm.

"'The Lord is my shepherd; I shall not want. He maketh me to lie down in green pastures: He leadeth me beside the still waters. He restoreth my soul: He leadeth me in the paths of righteousness for His name's sake. Yea, though I walk through the valley of the shadow of death, I will fear no evil: for thou art with me; thy rod and thy staff they comfort me. Thou preparest a table before me in the presence of mine enemies: thou anointest my head with oil; my cup runneth over. Surely goodness and mercy shall follow me all the days of my life: And I will dwell in the house of the Lord forever.' Amen."

The curtains slowly part and I see two boxes, black and shiny as beetles' backs, and the top of two heads and hear Mary catch her breath and hold it like she used to do when we had breath-holding contests in the bathtub.

"Welcome fellow servants of the Lord, Jesus Christ, to a glorious occasion for through His divine will God has summoned two of his servants to reside with Him in eternal and everlasting life."

Top of two heads and it's hot and I begin sweating.

"Jesus said, 'Let not your heart be troubled: ye believe in God, believe also in me. In my Father's house are many mansions; if it were not so, I would have told you. I go to prepare a place for you . . .'"

Franklin holds me under the covers and I'm sweating. I yell but Mom and Pa are upstairs and can't hear me because the blankets smother my screaming and Franklin's laughing and I want to kill him but he's got me pinned all around with his hands and knees.

"Mom! Pa!"

"'Thomas saith unto Him, Lord, we know not whither thou goest; and how can we know the way? Jesus saith unto him, I am the way, the truth, and the life: no man cometh unto the Father but by me.'"

It's no use, no one can hear me so I lie quietly but I can't breathe and I'm panting and feel my pajamas sticking to my moist skin.

"This, friends, is a celebration of life renewing itself for death is just a transitional stage from one life to another. Life as we know it on this world is the inferior life . . ."

It's no fun for Franklin when I lie quietly so he finally lets me up and I jump off the bed and run out of the room, sobbing. "Baby, baby—look at the baby run." I go upstairs and there's hardly any light on so I stand in the kitchen and catch my breath in double hitches.

"Before you lie the bodies of Margaret and Franklin Caviness as you and I and their families knew them. But Jesus, ladies and gentlemen, knows their souls . . ."

I walk toward my parents' room and there's a faint glow under the door so I push it open and there's a big naked bird on the bed. Its featherless wings are splayed wide, flapping to either side, and it's making a funny wheezing and grunting sound. It's trying to heave its body up but it's stuck and only rocks back and forth.

"Oh, friends, I've seen this before. Praise God! Two loving people dedicated to the Lord's will, dying together because of their unselfish love for Jesus Christ and, through Him, for one another. 'O the depth of the riches both of the wisdom and knowledge of God! How unsearchable are His judgments . . .'"

The bird shudders and collapses with a gasp and lies strangely still and I want to scream. But I don't scream. I clamp my arm over my mouth and run back through the kitchen and downstairs to tell Franklin.

"Almighty God, those who die with You shall live with You in joy and blessedness. We give You heartfelt thanks for the great gift You bestow upon Your servants now. In Jesus' name we pray. Amen."

But I don't tell Franklin because I know he won't believe me and I know I don't want to believe it either. And if I do say it, it means maybe it's true so I shut up and don't say anything.

"Franklin and Margaret Caviness were joined in holy wedlock on August 16th, 1946. They conceived and bore four healthy children: Franklin Junior, Mary Lynnette, Peter Henry, and Erwin Nathaniel. May we at this time offer these lovely children our sincerest condolences."

Mary's there but I don't tell her either. I don't say anything to anybody. I tell Mary lots of things but I don't tell her this. Mary's crying anyway and I don't want to upset her more. Then I think: maybe she already knows.

"Oh, Lord, give these young servants strength and the knowledge of Your love in this time of grief and sorrow. Let them know, Jesus, that You are the way and the will and the life. At this time and all others we say blessed be the God and the Father of our Lord, Jesus Christ. Amen."

I look at Mary—her hands clasped tightly to her mouth, tears seeping out of tightly closed eyes.

"'Blessed are the poor in spirit, for theirs is the kingdom of Heaven. Blessed are those who mourn, for they shall be comforted.' Friends, let not your hearts be troubled. Heaven awaits you who follow our Father, Jesus Christ, and in His divine wisdom He shall teach you the way."

Mary slumps to the floor on her knees just as the first chiff of organ music catches and thickens the hot air.

"Now is the time, ladies and gentlemen. Do not linger! Do not dally about for today is the day of reckoning! 'Seek and ye shall find.' Ask God for His forgiveness and make a commitment to Jesus Christ right now, friends, and you, too, shall find eternal happiness."

A young man in a dark suit appears and helps Mary to her feet and leads her away toward the podium.

"Praise God! One of His children has chosen to follow Him. Kneel right down there, child, and ask the Lord Jesus Christ forgiveness for your sins. Ask Him to enter your life and to walk with you all the days of your life. Glory be to God in Heaven!"

Mary kneels near the shiny boxes and people I've never seen before gather around her like erect ants over prey. Reverend Calloway leaves the podium and waves one hand in the air as the other grips Mary's head. With face heavenward and eyes closed tightly, he begins speaking but I can't make out his words over the crying and wailing.

The same young man comes back down the aisle looking straight at me. I turn away but can still feel his eyes on me and then he takes my arm and I look back at Franklin and Erwin and Mrs. Henderson. I feel as though I'm floating as I'm led to the front.

Mary is praying on the side where our mother lies. But it really isn't Mom, her face smoothed back and powdered white like bread dough, her hair set out against red satin as neatly as pictures she used to embroider on throw pillows. Mary is crying and saying things I've never heard her say before and then I realize she's repeating what the preacher is saying above her. The young man has me kneel beside her and I can just see the profile of our mother's face over the side of the box and it looks like a halloween mask, the rubber kind that stretches over your face and has holes for your eyes, nose, and mouth.

The young man tells me to ask our father for forgiveness and I wonder if he knows about the fishing trip. I wonder if he knows I tried to get help. I tried to help Pa. There was nothing else I could do. And he keeps telling me to ask forgiveness but really there was nothing I could do. Pa fell. It just happened. It wasn't my fault, he just fell. I hear a voice outside myself. I hear it faintly and it keeps repeating, turning over and over louder each time like a returning echo until it rings crazily inside me and I recognize it as my own: "Forgive me, Father. Forgive me. Forgive me. Forgive me."

* * *

Erwin wet his pants. He tried to conceal it with his crumpled funeral program but the dark stain reached all the way down the inside of one pants leg, causing him to cross and uncross his legs. Next to him stood Franklin rolling his program into a tight cylinder as though, being the eldest, it was our future he held in his hands and he was steeling himself. Mary was on the other side of Erwin with her arm around his shoulders, patting him and looking strangely happy. I stood next to Mary, and Uncle Herbert stood behind, sweat pouring off his forehead.

We were waiting in the chapel lobby for Mrs. Henderson, but a passerby—if there had been one—might have thought we were posing for a family picture. Instead, we were looking at one. On the wall hung a painting of Jesus Christ and a group of men. They were sitting and standing around a long wooden table with food spread out over it. Jesus wore a loose white robe and gaunt passive expression. Mrs. Anderson, my fourth-grade teacher, had taken our class to a museum where I saw pictures of World War II—faces framed in barbed wire with bones protruding from under loose skin. Jesus' eyes stared at me just as the people's eyes in those pictures had, making me feel as though we were the ones inside the picture being looked at instead of the other way around.

"Okay, everybody, let's go outside."

Mrs. Henderson dabbed her eyes with a shredded yellow tissue and led us out a side door where we piled into the back of the limousine. One of Mr. Shade's attendants drove us down a narrow blacktop to a far corner of the cemetery. A stiff hot wind had kicked up and people stood waiting for us in scattered knots as a way of protecting each other. We got out and walked over to folding chairs set up next to the two freshly dug holes. Cut sod lay in rolls to the side, exposed roots already caked dry in the wind and heat. Two flags—a Colorado state flag and an American flag—stood on opposite ends of the chairs and flapped sharply in the wind like the snap of Franklin's towel after he'd dried off from a shower.

As we sat down, the people moved into a semi-circle behind us. I noticed some of Pa's co-workers from the loading dock—Joe Ferguson, Wally Booth, Dick Garcia, and big old Trunk Willis—edge through the crowd over to the rear end of a hearse that had just pulled up. They slid the two caskets out as easily as they unloaded freight at the loading dock. The people parted and then fell in behind as the men carried the boxes over to the side of the holes and set them on metal frames. A wreath of flowers embraced each casket, petals and leaves turning violently in the wind. Led by Trunk Willis, the men stepped quietly to the side, folded their hands, and bowed their heads.

Trunk Willis used to sometimes come over to our house to play horse-shoes and drink beer with Pa after work. Trunk had a very large nose on a small head and with his equally large body, looked a little like an elephant. Pa said Trunk had repeatedly broken his nose playing junior college foot-ball because they couldn't find a helmet small enough to stay on his head and not slide crashing down over his face. Pa also said Trunk was one of the nicest, most decent men he'd ever met and, looking over at him, I knew Pa was right—Trunk was wiping that battered old nose of his with a large hand-kerchief as though it had just been crushed for the hundredth and final time.

Reverend Calloway, black robe whipped smooth against his wide hips by the gusts behind him, stood before us with a Bible in his hand. To his side and at the head of the two graves, set a glossy-faced marble grave-stone with words newly etched across its surface:

MARGARET LOUISE CAVINESS, SEPTEMBER 11, 1922–AUGUST 20, 1962
FRANKLIN RAYMOND CAVINESS, FEBRUARY 18, 1910–AUGUST 19, 1962
MAY THEY REST IN PEACE

Reverend Calloway opened the Bible and began to read, his words like snatches of paper flying by us in the wind. "In Genesis 3, verse 19, the Lord God saith to Adam: 'In the sweat of thy face shalt thou eat bread, for dust thou art, and unto dust shalt thou return.' Let us pray. Dear God, our Fa-ther, thank You for having mercy upon our souls so that we may live in Your Kingdom in eternal happiness. We ask of You today to give us strength so we might be better Christians and better able to fight the inimical foe of evil that stands between each and every one of us and eternal blissfulness. You have moved before us today, Lord, and we give you heartfelt thanks for Your presence and message of salvation. Your will shall be carried out, Your message of salvation voiced. In Jesus' name we pray. Amen."

A white sun hat somersaulted across the lawn as the preacher closed his Bible and, eyes cast skyward, rolled back on his heels. A thin string of people, mostly old and mostly Mrs. Henderson's friends, came by in front and pressed our hands and said in one way or another they were sorry. Gladys Cramer was there and mean Rickie Livers' mom and even old man Hillar, toeing the grass and hemming and hawing as though he were caught between trying to forget all the havoc we had caused in his life and feeling sorry for us.

"Yous kids be good now, damn it. Do your ma and pa proud, ya hear?"

He made a good stab at it anyway; it was the closest thing to a pleas-antry old man Hillar had ever muttered at us.

The crowd slowly disbanded. Reverend Calloway shook hands with a few last guests he seemed to know—I recognized them as some of the people who had earlier circled around Mary and me, praying. We sat on the folding chairs, staring at the two caskets and two holes. And then Trunk Willis was standing there, his head lowered and his massive shoulders slumped forward.

"Sorry about your ma and pa. If there's anything I can do . . ."

He hesitated, uneasily rotating his straw hat in his hands, and then walked away. Watching him lumber slowly up to the blacktop, I decided he didn't look like an elephant at all; he looked a lot like my pa.

Reverend Calloway finally came over and Uncle Herbert stood and they shook hands as though they were completing a business deal. Next, the preacher stepped over and hugged Mary's head to his full stomach. She stood up and hugged back, her face lost in his billowing black robe. They said a few things before he moved over to where Franklin had just gotten up.

"How are you doing, Frank Junior? You're the man of the family now, son, so you best ask the Lord for strength like your sister did here."

Reverend Calloway motioned to Mary as Franklin stared at the grass.

"Ask and He shall answer. Believe in the Lord Jesus and He'll give you everything you'll need. Isn't that right, son?"

After a second's hesitation, Reverend Calloway grasped Franklin's hand, shook it, and then let it drop limply to his side.

"Well, here's Peter. Now there's a handshake for you."

Reverend Calloway glanced triumphantly at Franklin to see if he was watching us shake hands. The preacher's hand felt soft and fleshy like a well-oiled catcher's mitt. When he let loose, I slipped my hand into my pocket and swished it around.

"The Lord spoke and comforted you and Mary today, Peter. Don't take that lightly, son. Ask Jesus Christ for guidance and He will show you the way to eternal happiness. Praise God."

Reverend Calloway smiled his clown's smile and turned his attention to Erwin who was sitting on Mrs. Henderson's lap. The wind had died some, the flags flapping softly above us, and cars moved in a long line up the blacktop toward the chapel as I watched two teenagers in a far corner of the cemetery remove shovels and a rake from the back of an old pickup truck.

"There's a big one. Hi there, big guy."

The preacher bent down, hands on knees, to get a better look at Erwin. "Do you love Jesus, son?"

Erwin didn't move and Mrs. Henderson behind him said nothing, her mouth as tight-lipped as a ventriloquist's.

"Well, Jesus loves you and to prove it He's going to be your new daddy. Now how would you like that?"

I thought Mrs. Henderson was just about to burst out with something when Reverend Calloway, still smiling, reached toward Erwin's stern downcast face to playfully tweak his cheek. And as if the preacher pushed the exact button to trigger a response, Erwin straightened one of his knotty little knees and with the hollow sound of a walnut being cracked, kicked Reverend Calloway just below the kneecap with the pointed toe of his black leather oxford.

5

The wind died and the passing cottonwoods, their long shadows mottled gray across the country road, fluttered against the light sifting through them. And all that happened momentarily hid under the drone of the Pontiac, under the stored chatter of Mrs. Henderson, and under our innocence about what was going to happen next.

"Now, I'm right down the street if you and the kids need anything. Just holler."

Uncle Herbert bent sideways, his arm across the top of the seat to get a better view of Mrs. Henderson as she got out of the passenger's side.

"Please, Mrs. Henderson, I beg of you. Won't you spend the night? You're such a comfort to the children. I would be indebted to you. Just this one night?"

"Mr. Merriweather, I do declare. For the umpteenth time, no. The sooner you get used to this business the better off you'll be. Marge and Frank would've agreed with me and that's that. Come here, Winnie. Give me a kiss, child. You dear girl, Mary. Don't you worry, honey. Everything'll be just fine. Peter, take care of your sister. You're getting to be a big boy now. And Franklin, you heard what the preacher said, you're the man of the family. Make your momma and poppa proud, boy. 'Night, everybody. And don't forget what I said about that rash if you don't want anything to happen like it did to my nephew, Earl, I was telling you about. Mark my words, if it festers up on you they'll have to cut you open from ear to ear."

Mrs. Henderson slammed the door shut, causing Uncle Herbert to close his eyes and massage his temples with the tips of his fingers.

"Thank you for the comforting words, Mrs. Henderson. We shall no doubt hear from you tomorrow."

She waddled to the front step. Her ankles had swollen from what she said was a combination of the drive back from Shade's Funeral Home and "gettin' all worked up" at the ceremony. Mrs. Henderson said that every Tuesday night during the commercial breaks of another wrenching episode of *Ben Casey* she would have to walk around her coffee table and take deep breaths in relief of those poor swollen ankles; it had something to do with circulation and the bend of her knees when sitting and the fact that her feet never sweat. And maybe, I guessed, that she felt things clear to her toes and all her fluids got bound up down there—it was the only connection I could make between swollen ankles, nonsweating feet, and high emotion.

The porch door banged behind her and we could hear her muttering above the rustle of her massive handbag as she dived into its contents. With a jingle of keys, which she gaily displayed waving above her head, we backed out of her driveway and covered the short distance down the street to our dark empty house. It was just dusk as we pulled into the driveway, the horizon at the edge of the desert a grayish-orange glow.

Uncle Herbert opened the back door and we were greeted by a smell so familiar as to usually go unnoticed; it wasn't the smell of anything in particular, just a blend of things: foods we had eaten, cigarettes smoked, newspapers read, cleansers used, aerosols sprayed, and even conversations we had spoken. The smell hung as clearly and solidly in front of us as the door that opened to it.

On the kitchen table was a large ham with potato salad, fruit salads, pies, and home-baked breads spread around it. A bowl of peaches sat on the counter nearby with a tall bottle of cola. Uncle Herbert walked over and inspected each dish by carefully lifting the tin foil with his long fingers and peering inside. Satsified, he plucked a peach from the bowl and went into the bathroom and locked the door.

"Where'd we get all the food?"

"Neighbors, I guess, and Mrs. Henderson. And, of course, the Lord Jesus."

These last words Mary spoke softly, as if testing the feel of them in her mouth. Franklin looked uncomfortably to the side and then grabbed Erwin around the neck and rubbed his knuckles back and forth across Erwin's head.

"Let's shoot marbles."

"We can't, Win. We gotta eat."

"I ain't hungry."

"Sure you are. Or did you just want to go outside and find your supper in the gutter?"

"Yeah, let's eat worms for supper!"

Erwin laughed loudly but then abruptly stopped—Uncle Herbert stood watching from the hallway.

"Set the table, people."

We pulled the table out and Mary finished slicing the ham. Uncle Herbert sat at Mom's place between Erwin and Mary and without saying a word ate three slices of ham, half the bowl of potato salad, and enough rolls to start his own bakery. Taking a hefty slice of Mrs. Henderson's cherry pie, he got up and went into Mom and Pa's bedroom, closing the door behind him.

It was dark outside and Erwin's head nodded in front of him, finally coming to rest on his small expanding chest. Mary gathered him up and carried him into their bedroom, and Franklin quickly followed and went downstairs. Soon all the lights were out except the kitchen's and the house closed silently around me.

The grease under the ham began to turn white. The fruit-salad jello ran a little so I wrote my name in it with the end of my fork and watched the letters run into each other and disappear. I got out of my chair and crawled over to Pa's place to see how things looked from there. The white ham bone glared under the kitchen light and for the most part everything looked the same—though I knew it wasn't.

I eased up from the table and walked into the living room. The sofa was dimpled as though Mom were still lying there resting. On the coffee table sat the pink ceramic ashtray Franklin made for her in shop class. A cigarette, its ash burning long, balanced on the lip of the tray and a couple of butts stuck crumpled into it. The Motorola was on and its picture bathed Mom's face and forehead. Pa sat across the room in his stuffed rocker, feet propped up on the hassock. He wore his wire-rimmed spectacles as he perused *The Grand River Sentinel.* His bifocal lenses gleamed in the light from the reading lamp behind him and I could see newspaper print reflected in them. Soon he would get up and go downstairs where he'd spend the rest of the evening in the roar and sawdust of the table saw or electric sander. For now, though, it was quiet and I could hear the night air stirring Mom's wind chime I had given her for her birthday.

"Hear your wind chime, Mom?"

But a high tinkling was all that answered. I backed out of the room into the light of the kitchen. It was dark down the hall toward Mary and Erwin's room. If I went down there I might disturb Uncle Herbert, the last thing I wanted to do. Quickly, I walked through the kitchen to the top of the stairs. I turned the stairwell light on and the kitchen light off. The stairs creaked as

I tiptoed down into the basement. Franklin's bedroom light was off but I knocked on his door anyway. He didn't answer so I took a deep breath and rushed through Pa's darkened workshop to my bedroom. I fumbled with the light switch on my cowboy lamp next to my bed and finally turned it on. The basement was cool but I could feel a sudden sweat popping out. I hurried back to the stairwell and flicked off that switch. Turning to run back to my bedroom, I sensed someone's presence. I held my breath. A shadow moved toward me from the far corner. I closed my eyes: Uncle Herbert was holding a large butcher knife in his hands, an ugly grin across his face. I could feel his warm breath fall on my face as he raised the knife.

"What the heck are you doing, Pete?"

As my eyes flew open so did my arms and I threw myself around Franklin.

"Get away from me, you queer-bait! What the heck are you doing sneaking around turning lights off and on? Maybe I ought to get Uncle Herbert and have him take you back to the hospital the way you're acting. Quit crying, ya baby."

Franklin turned the hallway light on.

"I'm not cryin'!"

"Well, your eyeballs are sweating, then. Look at you, your nose is running and everything."

"So, I can cry if I want to."

"Yeah, like you and Mary did at the funeral? Pa would of wupped you if he'd saw you up there in front of everybody."

"Pa's not here."

He glared and then brushed by me toward his room.

"He isn't here, is he, Franklin?"

Franklin stopped and without looking back, shook his head.

"What were you doing in Pa's workshop?"

"Sittin'."

"In the dark?"

Franklin turned around. "Yeah, in the dark. I'm not scared of it like you."

"Why were you sitting in the dark?"

"I don't know, I just was. I was thinking."

"'Bout what?"

"Things."

"What do you think's going to happen to us, Franklin?"

"If Uncle Herbert leaves, I don't know."

"Who said Uncle Herbert's going to leave?"

"After what we did to him, you think he's going to stay?"

"Maybe Mrs. Henderson'll stay with us."

"That old rattle-trap? You heard what she said, 'Gotta start gettin' used to it.'"

"Yeah, and 'you're the man of the family.'"

Franklin looked dejectedly down as though I had hit on the exact thing he had been mulling over. Until then, most of his worries had to do with a blossoming acne problem and what to do with those strange creatures of the opposite sex. Not only had his head been spun dizzy with his first year in junior high but with co-educational gym classes, he found his anatomy doing strange things too. In fact, Mr. Gunter, the vice-principal, had caught him behind the gymnasium with his hand tangled up in the front of Della Mae Nagel's 35-D-cup brassiere. Franklin had won a wager with Lee Hooker over whether or not Della Mae wore falsies, but the only things he collected on were ten swats from the end of Mr. Gunter's bottom-polished paddle, a hand full of foam rubber, and a good chewing out from Pa. Pa was angrier about Franklin's association with Lee Hooker than he was about Della Mae Nagel's D-cup.

Lee Hooker was shady. He was famous in our neighborhood for his vaselined ducktail which glistened as brilliantly as the leather multi-zippered motorcycle jacket he sported. Lee Hooker was at least a head shorter than Franklin but powerfully built for his age, rumored to be anywhere from four-teen to seventeen and a half. He had introduced Franklin to the best way he knew of handling the pressures of seventh grade: smoking cigarettes. And Lee Hooker was an expert on seventh grade. He had spent the last three years in it.

I saw them strutting home from school one day, shirttails out and a couple of Lucky Strikes dangling. Franklin looked awkward next to stocky Lee Hooker, probably due to his lack of practice in this new promenade and the spurt of growth that had suddenly raised his pant legs to mid-shin. But Franklin had quit the company of Lee Hooker—and smoking—because Lee Hooker was sent up to reform school in Buena Vista for hot wiring a '55 Buick.

As I watched Franklin bravely set his jaw, all the problems with school and Lee Hooker and Della Mae Nagel's underthings seemed ages ago. He took a deep breath and as he had done all day, successfully fought back tears. I wondered if I could ever be as strong as Franklin.

"Hey, Franklin, it's still pretty early. Want to go climb the elm or something?"

"Huh-uh. Going to go to sleep."

"Franklin, uh, mind if I sleep with you?"

"What's wrong with your bed? Still afraid?"

"No, I just . . . never mind."

Franklin turned off the stairwell light and went into his bedroom, shutting the door. I hurried back through the workshop and into my room. I lay on the bed with the lamp on and stared at the Green Bay Packers' pennant on my wall. Finally, I went to my bottom drawer, pulled it out, and crawled under the stairs into my secret hiding place. It was cool and the walls and cement floor felt good. I lay quietly and could smell Franklin's work clothes. He hadn't been at the station for a couple of days now but the smell of gasoline was still there. It now seemed as much a part of the walls as the nails Pa had driven into them.

I closed my eyes and imagined Franklin and me doing things together, going fishing like the two brothers up at the lake and maybe even chewing cigars or netting each other's big fat rainbow trout. I wondered what I could do to make myself tougher, to be more like my big brother. If I'd ever quit crying and not be such a baby, maybe Franklin would take me to the Eagles' baseball games to shag fly balls.

I felt myself drifting away with the crack of the bat and the roar of the crowd when suddenly I jerked awake. I heard a faint noise, high and broken. I sat up and tried to make it out. It was from somewhere just outside the stairwell wall. Then it came to me.

I lay slowly down in the dark of my hiding place and listened for a long time—listened, wide-eyed, until my big brother on the other side of the stairwell finally hushed and fell asleep.

6

Uncle Herbert's rash needed attention from the best skin man in the country who, it seems, practiced medicine in Wichita, Kansas. That fact, Uncle Herbert hated to say, meant he had to be going—immediately. In the meantime, he said, Mrs. Henderson had agreed to stay with us. After his condition improved, he would return and "take care of us as any God-fearing man would." At the time, none of us knew what that meant.

So, firmly placing his hat on his head and grabbing the handle of his vinyl suitcase, Uncle Herbert said good-bye as though he were just going down to the corner store for milk. Instead, a taxi pulled up. And as he hurried out to it, Mrs. Henderson appeared.

"Herbert Merriweather! Herbert Merriweather, just a darn minute! I gotta talk to you!"

Seeing Mrs. Henderson bustling up the street waving her hand in the air, he ducked into the taxi, which bolted away like a horse prodded with an electric shock.

"Why, you . . . Children, where did that uncle of yours go off to?"

"Wichita."

"Wichita!?! Why, that no good for nothin' scalawag! I should've known it. I got to thinking last night after you dropped me off and I dang near come back over. What'd he say?"

"Said he'd be back after he got his rash cleared up and you'd take care of us until then."

"My, my, my. He's a slippery one all right. Turn your head for half a second and he's pointing his in a new direction. Come on, let's get in the house. You'll catch pneumonia out here. Gettin' nippy already. It's gonna be a cold one come winter. Winnie still in bed?"

"Uh-huh."

"Well, better get him up. Ain't gonna fix breakfast twice, not even for that little scamp. Franklin, what's wrong with you, boy? Looks like you seen a ghost."

"Nothin'. I just don't think Uncle Herbert's comin' back."

"With any luck, he ain't. Not if he knows what's good for him. You like your uncle, boy?"

"Naw. I just don't know what to do with Mom and Pa gone. Don't know if Mr. Dugan'll hire me full-time at the station and I'm supposed to be in eighth grade and I kind of hate quitting and suppose they won't let me anyway and . . ."

"Just hold on there, Franklin. You're not quittin' school and that's that. Let me worry about that other stuff. You just watch out for your sister and brothers and let me take care of the rest."

"Mrs. Henderson, you don't think Uncle Herbert's coming back?"

"Mary Lynnette, honey, your momma told me a long time ago about Herbert T. Merriweather. He's never done a honest day's work in his life and if he does come back I'll have him tarred and feathered and hangin' from the nearest tree branch. Your momma was a wonderful woman and, I swear, I'll never know how she ended up with a brother like that one. Now you kids run along and get dressed. You're gonna be late for school."

"Mrs. Henderson, it's Saturday and we don't start school for another week."

"Don't you sass back at me, Peter Caviness. Just 'cause your Uncle Herbert's gone don't mean you can get all smart-alecky. I'm gettin' along in years but don't think I can't use a paddle if I have to."

As we filed back into our house, I heard Mrs. Henderson mutter under her breath: "My Lord, why does goin' to funerals always feel like Sundays in August?"

* * *

After breakfast, I headed out back. The lawn lay damp in the morning cool and uncut grass stretched down the middle of it and grew high along the fence and around Mom's rose bed by the alley. Pa had mowed the front yard the Saturday before and was mowing the back when the rain stopped him. He was going to finish when we came home from fishing. Now the mower sat over a grease spot up against the fence, its catcher half-full of grass gone fetid in the sun.

Another pile sat out behind the concrete incinerator where Pa burned leaves in the fall. Its sour-sweet odor drew flies like filings to a magnet so I rolled up a *Grand River Sentinel* I found in old man Hillar's garbage can and swatted a few. Tiring of that, I pulled out a broken yardstick and dragged it rat-a-tat-tat along the picket fences that lined the alleyways toward the playground.

Rickie Livers and three kids I had never seen were already shooting hoops. The bouncing basketball echoed off the brick walls of Orchard View Grade School and when it dropped through the chain netting, made a sound like crushed ice scooped into a tall glass. The three new kids wore clean white T-shirts, black hightops, and the same flat-top haircuts. Rickie Livers wore what he usually wore: a dirty pair of gym shorts, no shoes, and a salad-bowl haircut too far gone to be noticed.

"Hey, Caviness. Wanna play a little B-ball? Me an' Tony here'll stand you three."

"No, thanks. I got better things to do."

"Like what? Suckin' your old lady's hind teat?"

"Wait 'til I tell Franklin what you said."

"You puss, Caviness. Go ahead and tell him. Franklin'll just laugh. He don't care what I say to you. Even Erwin can pound you, puss."

I reached down and picked up a handful of pea gravel which spread out thinly across the dirt playground. "Take it back, Rickie."

"Take it back, Rickie. Screw you, Peter-head."

Rickie Livers turned around to the backboard with the basketball and took a shot. The rocks felt moist in my hand as I gripped them and watched the ball arc, hesitate through the net, then drop to the ground. He grabbed it again and took another shot just as I let loose with the gravel. As he went up for the rebound, rocks came down onto his head.

"You son-of-a . . ."

I was used to being chased by Rickie Livers; he had done so ever since his family moved to Grand River three years before. He was the oldest of five brothers and two sisters, all of whom had the same orange hair and freckles. The freckles on the younger Livers, though, were usually hidden under what they had eaten for breakfast or had collected in the weeds and dirt of their back yard. They had an amazing ability to blend in with their surroundings but if you couldn't see through to the color of their skin and hair, you could always recognize a Livers by how few clothes they wore.

There was no Mr. Livers, only these dusty reminders of him, and Mrs. Livers usually stayed inside their stucco house with her pets—about fifteen yapping chihuahuas. For these, Mrs. Livers knitted brightly colored sweaters and in winter it was said that the Livers' residence could easily win the annual Christmas-decoration contest if Mrs. Livers would only leave her shivering dogs out longer than it took them to pee a hole in the snow. As it was, only her children stayed outside until all hours and now I could once again hear her near-naked eldest huffing behind me as I raced down the alleyways toward home and the vacant lot.

I was the best tree climber in our neighborhood and when I jumped up at full tilt and caught a branch and scissored my legs up and over another one, I knew I was safe. And so did Rickie Livers.

"You chicken-shit, Caviness! Wait 'til I get my hands on you! You're ass is grass, Peter-head!"

Rickie Livers stalked away then, jutting his middle finger up at me as he went. I shinnied to the top of the elm and settled between two branches just thick enough to hold my weight. Below me, asphalt-shingled roofs shone like the patchwork on quilt bedspreads Mom stitched. I could see everything from here: the Morrison's peach orchard running from the north side of Willow Avenue all the way to the canal road, the elephant-gray hills where we sledded in the winter and jumped our bikes in the summer, the pink face of the Ute Range stretching out along the valley into Utah, the red sandstone of Rimrock National Park lifting up out of the desert on the other side of the river, and in the distant haze to the east, Spruce Mesa, its rim dark blue beneath the pale of morning light.

I turned my face to the sun filtering through the leaves and branches and closed my eyes. A sheet of orange and yellow light leapt before me and I could feel the heat against my eyelids.

"Guess we better throw in a couple more, Petey."

I reach over and take a handfull of dry twigs and a thick split of spruce and put the twigs on the glowing coals and lay the wood over them. The twigs smolder and then the wood catches. A flame jumps with the breeze and flickers orange against the black night.

"Thanks, Petey."

Bullfrogs croak from the shallow grassy water around the edge of the lake and the fire pops. Pa hands me an aspen limb he has whittled to a sharp point with his pocketknife. I take a hotdog from the package in the ice chest and cradle it snug in my hand and drive the point through from the end and hold it over the fire. It sweats and blisters brown on the underside and I hear the juice drip and sizzle in the ashes. The aspen limb turns in my fingers.

"Think I'll go try some flies. With this moonlight, just might be the ticket."

"Okay, Pa."

He sits on a camp stool and pulls his waders up and fastens them to the belt loops on his jeans. The fire lights up the side of his face as he kneels down on one knee to look into his tackle box.

"Maybe a wooly-worm'll do it."

Pa takes it out and ties it to the fishing line leader. My hotdog is cooked all around now so I take a bun from the ice chest and tuck the dog into it and slide it off the stick.

"Keep her goin', Petey. I'll probably want some coffee when I get back."

"Good luck, Pa."

I squeeze yellow mustard along the inside of my bun and take a bite and can hear Pa's rubber waders squeak against the wet grass as his footsteps fall away from the crack of the fire toward the lake. A white flake of ash curls out of the flame and I watch it rise through the tall gray funnel of heat and disappear into the night.

* * *

The sun was high as I climbed down. The only shade lay in splotches around the base of the elm. Here in the fine dirt, wind-swept between shoulders of roots shrugging out of the ground, sat pockets of ant lion dens. Searching the trunk, I found a red and black ant zigzagging over the bark. I knocked it into the palm of my hand and pinched it lightly between my thumb and index finger, squatted down, and dropped it into one of the pockets. It landed in the center and began struggling along the side of the den as loose dirt fell back behind.

"Hey, you know where the playgroun' is?"

A dark-skinned boy stood looking down at me.

"Yeah, just go down that street a couple of blocks an' take a left. You can't miss it. It's on the right."

"Thanks, man. Hey, what you doing?"

"Ant lions." I pointed down at the dirt and he squatted next to me.

"What's a ant lion?"

"They eat ants."

"He really a lion, man?"

"I guess to a ant he is."

Puffs of dirt flicked up from the center of the pocket.

"That him?"

"Yeah."

The ant fell back to the center but scrambled up along the other side.

"What's you name?"

"Pete."

"Hey, Pete. I'm Luis Manzanares but my frien's call me Fudgie."

"Fudgie? Why do they call you that?"

"I don' know, man, but don' laugh at my name or I mess you up. No one don' laugh at Fudgie Manzanares."

"Sorry, I just never heard a name like that before."

"That's okay, man. Where you live?"

"'Cross the street over there."

"Eee, nice house."

"Thanks."

I looked back down at the ant running as if on a treadmill.

"You live around here?"

"No, in Mexico."

"Mexico?"

"Sí. Me an' my family come here to pick fruit."

"Pickin' season's already started. Why aren't you in the orchards?"

"My Papa's sick."

The ant again fell back to the center where the ant lion snapped onto it and held it still between its pinchers.

"Eee, carajo! He got it!"

Fudgie and I leaned closer as the ant lion wrestled the ant underneath the dirt.

"Where he taking it now, man?"

"Down to eat it. What's wrong with your pa?"

"I don' know but he's real sick."

"Is he in the hospital?"

"No, José an' Helen's house."

"Who's that?"

"Papa's cousin. They real smart, too, man. José is a lawyer an' Helen is a nurse. Helen an' my sister is taking care of him."

The ant disappeared but there was still movement.

"Where's your mom."

"She wen' back to Mexico with my brothers. Those ant lions, too?"

"Yeah, all of 'em are."

Fudgie searched the ground.

"When you going back to Mexico?"

"I don' know, man."

"What about school? We start in a couple of weeks."

"I don' go to school. School's for sissies. I work in the fields with my family. What you family do?"

Fudgie was on his hands and knees now, his hand parting back a tall stand of kochia weed. His free hand made a quick grab.

"How you catch these, man?"

"It's easier to find one on the tree."

I put my hand flat against the trunk and soon another ant crawled up my wrist where I plucked it off.

"Here."

Fudgie took the ant and closed his fingers around it. With a quick flick he threw it down at the dens but the ant landed between two pockets and scurried into the weeds.

"I guess I don' do so good, huh?"

We got up and looked at each other. A wide grin stretched across his face and two friendly brown eyes studied me from under a shock of black hair that fell at an angle across his forehead. He was shorter than I but stockier with a deep chest and thick shoulders and arms. He stuck out his hand.

"*Adiós*, Pete."

I shook it.

"You going to the playground now?"

"*Sí*, man."

"What you going to do there?"

"I don' know. I never been there. You wan' to go with me, man?"

"Yeah, I guess so. I can show you where it's at."

We walked through the weeds across the vacant lot and started down the street toward Orchard View Grade School.

"What you say you family do?"

"Lots of stuff."

"Like what?"

"Well, you see our house?"

Fudgie nodded.

"My pa built it."

"He did?"

"Yeah."

"Eee, I wan' to meet you papa, man."

By the time we reached the playground, Rickie Livers' basketball game had bloomed into a full-court battle and I could see Franklin bobbing around about half a head above everyone else but at about half their speed.

"Well, this is it. Was nice talkin' to you."

"Hey, man, you can' leave now. We jus' got here. We'll show these guys how to play, man."

"I don't play much, Fudgie. Besides, I got to go home and do something."

"Come on, man, these guys don' stan' a chance. You an' me, we'll kick their . . ."

"Hey, Caviness! Pretty brave of you to show up here, again."

"Fudgie, I gotta go."

"What's he mean, man?"

"Caviness, I told Franklin what I said and he could care less. Huh, Franklin? Fact, he said I could pound you into the ground and he don't care."

Rickie Livers walked slowly toward us, talking every step as if trying to collar a stray dog. Franklin stayed on the court and bounced the basketball.

"Shouldn't have throwed rocks at us, Caviness. You knew I'd get even with you sooner or later. I'm too close for you to run now and you know it so go ahead and try. Gettin' real brave, Caviness."

I sensed Fudgie stiffen beside me as Rickie Livers stopped in front of me, a smirk distorting his face.

"What, did you finally find a friend, Caviness? Hey, greaseball, I think you better run on home to your momma 'cause your friend here's gonna get hooked a couple of times and there's gonna be some blood."

I could still hear the bounce of the basketball as the other kids streamed over from the court. Rickie Livers' glared at me and his face grew even redder than normal.

"Nobody's gonna help you, Caviness. Not even little greaseball, here. I'm gonna stomp you, puss."

"Hook 'im, Rickie!"

"Come on, Livers, hook 'im!"

I had never stood up to Rickie Livers before and now I had no choice. Although I didn't look at him, I could still feel Fudgie's body tense beside me as the knot drew tighter and noisier. And then there was no noise at all. Rickie Livers' bony knuckles sprang from nowhere and exploded against the side of my nose.

A sharp pain pierced my head and through blurred vision I could see

Rickie Livers' other arm rear back. I quickly moved my head to the side and his fist grazed my ear but his arm continued around my neck. He had me in a headlock, bulldogging me to the ground. Dirt flew into my face and the playground jiggled and tilted as I struggled to my knees. And then there was the light blue sky framed with distorted screaming faces swirling in a circle above me with Rickie Livers' red freckled face in the center. Another fist came down and turned everything black for a moment but suddenly I could feel Rickie Livers' kicking, punching body lifted off me. When I looked up again, my arms held to my sides, it was Franklin looking down at me, but then he too was yanked off. I sat up, dazed, and watched Luis Manzanares punch my big brother.

"Fudgie! Fudgie, he's my brother!"

With fist cocked and his other hand pinning Franklin's head against the ground, he froze.

"Oh, man, I didn' know. I'm sorry. I thought you was helping this other guy, man."

"It's okay, Fudgie. You didn't know."

Franklin stood, holding his right eye, focusing down at Fudgie with his other.

"Who's this?"

The rest of the gang was quiet now, staring at Fudgie, and the only sound came from Rickie Livers walking away from the circle, sniffling. I got up and tasted the warm sticky drain of blood in my throat and felt a steady drip at the tip of my nose. I looked first at Fudgie and then at Franklin.

"His name's Luis Manzanares, but his friends call him Fudgie."

* * *

"That spic cold-cocked me. I didn't even see it comin'."

As we arrived on our block, Franklin's eyelid looked like a marble, a bluish-purple shooter.

"Why'd he do it?"

"'Cause he's my friend. And he's not a spic."

"Come on, I was only trying to save you. Rickie Livers liked to killed you. Least you didn't run this time."

"Yeah, and did you hear him cryin'?"

"Not from anything you did. That Mexican kid creamed him."

"He did?"

Franklin didn't reply, just cradled his eye in his hand.

"Did Rickie Livers really tell you what he said to me?"

"Yeah, that he called you a puss."

"That's not all he said, Franklin."

It was suppertime in Grand River and neighbors were watering their yards, the spray hissing from sprinkler heads and casting miniature rainbows in the low light slanting through the mist. Old man Hillar was home from Smitty's Hardware Store, bent over an oily cardboard box of what looked like washing machine parts.

What old man Hillar lacked socially he made up for mechanically and almost everyone on our street at one time or another had taken something to him to be repaired—toasters that shorted out, vacuum cleaners that no longer picked up, cuckoo clocks that didn't cuckoo, television sets that didn't turn on. In exchange, his neighbors not only made him the best-fed bachelor around but also did their best to ignore the junkyard state of his back yard. When, in his endless tinkering, old man Hillar found the broken part he was after, he simply let it fly over his shoulder where it landed willy-nilly among its broken brethren rusting there in the dirt.

Hearing our back gate, he squinted out at us from under the bill of his dirty yellow John Deere cap.

"Goin' to hell."

"What?"

"You two, damn it. Hadn't even been a week and look at yous."

Franklin shook his head as we trudged up the walk and into the house.

"And look at yous, you old goat."

I laughed at my brother and followed him downstairs into the bathroom. Franklin stared in the mirror, gently fingering his swollen eye.

"What a shiner."

He wet a washcloth and instead of pressing it to himself, held it out to me.

"Here."

"Don't you need it?"

"Nothing's going to help this. And look at you. You look like, well, like you're goin' to hell."

I took the washcloth and peered into the mirror: dried blood and dirt crusted around my nose and mouth and smeared across my cheek where I had tried to wipe it off using the back of my hand. Franklin went into his bedroom while I washed. Wringing out the washcloth, I took it in to him. He lay on his bed, staring at the ceiling.

"Here, Franklin. I'm done."

"Don't need it."

"Your eye looks pretty bad."

"I said I don't need it. Now leave me alone."

I carried the washcloth back into the bathroom and hung it over the shower curtain rod. I then pulled off my shirt, threw it into the dirty-clothes hamper in the utility room, and went back outside.

Old man Hillar was still standing behind his garage, rummaging through the box. His cap was now pulled low over his forehead in concentration and he held a long-necked screwdriver which he plied to one of the innermost parts of the machine he worked on. As I made my first attempt, yanking the cord up as hard as I could, the cough and sputter brought his eyes from under the cap and over to me.

"Choke it! You gots to choke the son-of-a-bitch!"

I steadied myself and pulled up again, this time with both hands. The engine caught, shuttered, and belched gray smoke. I could see him still jawing at me—the stubble on his chin moving as if he were working a piece of gristle between his teeth—but I didn't hear a word and giving the mower more juice, felt too good to care what old man Hillar ever said again and went roaring down the middle of the yard through the tall hot grass.

7

Luis Rodrigo Manzanares was the seventh of eight children born to Manuel Ernesto Manzanares and Rosita Maria Gonzales de Manzanares. He was the youngest son in a male-dominated family whose eldest and youngest were female, sandwiching six robust boys which occasioned Manny Manzanares to observe, "a *hita* in the fron' an' a *hita* in the back, both en's covered with brains, like a tortilla, so the meat no fall out."

Manny Manzanares owned a small curio shop in San Felipe where he eked out a living by selling anything from authentic handmade Mexican sandals, which he bought by the gross from an American black-market manufacturer in Tijuana, to silver jewelry that mysteriously turned tourists' skin green.

Fudgie told me the shaky business transactions his father conducted with rich Californians vacationing in Baja were a constant irritant between Fudgie's father and his devout Catholic mother. So upset would Mrs. Manzanares become, that she would sometimes catch a ride out of San Felipe on her second cousin's bottled-water truck and stay as long as a week in San Isadora on the Pacific side of Baja at her sister's house. One such departure was the week of September 16th, Mexican Independence Day, when tourists swelled the dusty streets of San Felipe and Manny had his biannual drinking binge, swilling tequila with his uncle Tony Manzanares. As Fudgie's mother packed her suitcase, his father would try to explain that his drinking was out of respect for Uncle Tony, a family tradition. But she wouldn't listen and Manny's drinking out of respect for Uncle Tony would soon become drinking out of loneliness for his absent wife.

When it was a full moon and the grunion were running, drawing Mexicans and Americans alike to the small coastal village, a black-shawled Rosita Maria Gonzales de Manzanares could be seen inside the sun-bleached Virgin of Guadalupe Catholic Church kneeling in prayer and asking forgiveness for her heathenish materialistic husband. On those days, Manny Manzanares was to be stepped lightly around. He loved his wife completely and the thought of her praying over his soul gave Manny mournful eyes that could instantly turn to red coals if one of his children acted up. During these times, Fudgie and his older brothers would sneak out of the small adobe house early and not come back until suppertime when their mother had usually returned.

But finally, after six difficult years in the curio business, Manny Manzanares and his wife compromised. Manny would run the business half the year and then seek honest labor the remaining six months. Uncle Tony managed the shop in his absence.

Originally it was thought that Manny and his two eldest sons, Felipe Leon and Rudolfo Fidel, could easily find employment on one of the many boats that fished the Bay of California. But fishermen were not rich and any deck hands were recruited from the ranks of their greatly populated families.

So, after many frustrating days of traipsing up and down the coast with his two sons in tow, Manny left San Felipe alone. About one week later, Fudgie's family received a letter that he had found a job on a fishing boat out of La Bomba at the mouth of the Río Colorado. He urged Felipe and Rudy to join him immediately because he had gotten them jobs on the same vessel and they were due to leave port in three days.

Fudgie was only six then but he could still remember his mother and two elder brothers keeping him awake late into the night, heatedly arguing about his brothers' departure. But the next morning they were gone and Mrs. Manzanares' tear-swollen eyes stared vacantly at her rosary the rest of the day.

Soon, Mrs. Manzanares received another letter stating that Felipe and Rudy had arrived safely and not to worry. She didn't hear from them again for more than two months but then, as abruptly as they had left, Manny Manzanares and his two sons reappeared. Manny's wife crossed herself many times that day and scolded them like a relieved owner scolds a lost dog.

The three had been on a very successful boat, it turned out, and they had made more money than ever before. But that is all Manny Manzanares would say, shrugging off questions or answering them with questions of his own.

At the time, no one noticed Manny's reluctance to talk. He and his boys were home and that was all that was important. It was better than a holiday as Mrs. Manzanares and Fudgie's elder sister, Felicia, took the chili peppers

70

hanging in red clumps on the back porch and ground and mixed them into a salsa to pour over freshly rolled flour tortillas filled with shredded chicken. Manny and his two proud sons even drank some wine Uncle Tony had fermented while Mrs. Manzanares pretended not to notice. Everyone was happy in the Manzanares household that night.

The next morning, however, Fudgie was jarred awake by his mother's yelling and his father's loud defensive voice. Fudgie had never heard them argue like that and he wondered if they had drunk too much wine, making them loco. But Fudgie knew his mother would never drink except at communion and that his father could hold his liquor, having seen him drink half a bottle of tequila with Uncle Tony at the local cantina the Christmas before and then sling Uncle Tony over his shoulder and carry him home without so much as a swagger. The wine, though, had nothing to do with it. His father had lied. He hadn't been on a fishing boat at all. They had slipped across the border into the United States and had been picking fruit in California.

Mrs. Manzanares couldn't be calmed. Not only had her husband taken their sons to the country she most hated, he had done it illegally. Manny's excuse that the family had to eat and with a couple of seasons' wages they could buy another shop and never have to sweat for another man again, didn't pacify Fudgie's mother. She spent the rest of the day and half of the next in church praying to the Virgin of Guadalupe for repentance.

However, as water evaporates from its vessel over time, so too did Rosita Maria Gonzales de Manzanares' wrath. Such was the dissipation, in fact, that she struck an agreement with her husband and occasionally watched the curio shop in exchange for stocking the shelves with religious paraphernalia instead of rock neckties and T-shirts and rubber scorpions. Life in San Felipe returned to normal and, curiously, Fudgie's mother complained much less about her husband's shop.

Nevertheless, the following spring loud voices rang out again as the two argued into the night about the virtues and vices of seeking employment in the United States.

Fudgie didn't know what finally caused his mother to relent. He discounted the fact that the next Christmas was the best they had ever had, with enough money left over to buy a new rooster and two more laying hens. Fudgie's guess was that his mother knew her husband would go regardless of what she might say and rather than have him leave on a sour note, she would simply rationalize. After all, wasn't the annual Mexican exodus a means of bringing prosperity to Mexico? Mexico was poor, the United States rich. Let the United States share their wealth with their poor southern neighbor. Hadn't they forcibly taken what originally belonged to Mexico anyway? In fact, the United States had taken a lot more than land. They had taken the life of Rosita Gonzales' great grandfather in the Mexican War.

She had never voiced these things but Fudgie had often heard her mumble disparaging remarks under her breath when a particularly unsavory American would swagger into the shop and try on this hat or that belt, or laugh condescendingly at the army of plastic Jesuses Manny had lined in rows next to the box of clay crosses. So maybe one too many Americans had laughed—or she thought they had laughed—and that is why she not only agreed but finally joined Manny in the annual trek to the United States. Eventually, Rosita and Manny took the entire family.

After too many years and too many grueling experiences, especially her husband's illness, Fudgie's mother had enough. Leaving him in the hands of her friend, Helen Lucero, and her two youngest to keep him company (knowing Carmalita would be much help to Helen and Luis less likely to get into trouble), Mrs. Manzanares had returned to Mexico with her two middle sons, Gabriel Fernando, age fifteen, and Noah Manuel, seventeen.

She was reluctant to go, Fudgie told me, but Manny had argued convincingly that it was too troublesome for all of them to remain in the United States with him sick. The Luceros should be burdened as little as possible. Besides, as soon as his health improved, he and the two youngest would easily find rides back to Mexico because soon the peach harvest would be finished and their countrymen returning home. After a tearful farewell, Mrs. Manzanares, Gabriel, and Noah boarded a Greyhound bus bound for Calexico, California, where they again crossed over into their homeland.

"When'd your mom leave?"

"Las' month."

It was Sunday, the morning after the Rickie Livers' battle and we were swinging from the elm tree, our legs entwined in an old faded truck tire.

"When you goin' back?"

"When my papa is better."

"What'll you do 'til then?"

"I don' know. We usually picking fruit now."

"Can't you pick?"

"Papa won' let me without him. How 'bout you, man. Don' you work?"

"Sure, I mowed the lawn."

"You make money?"

"No, but Franklin does. He works at Dugan's gas station."

"He make a lot of money, man?"

"Dollar an hour."

"Eee, *carajo*. I wan' to work at a gas station."

Our street was quiet, Sunday papers lying in driveways and curtains still pulled against the morning light. Mrs. Henderson had spent the night with us and when she saw Franklin's black eye and my red nose, slowly shook her head and said she didn't know there was a civil war going on; Walter Cronkite hadn't said a thing about it. But, surprisingly, that's all she had said.

Mary still spent most of the time in her room and I could tell Mrs. Henderson was beginning to worry because she was always going in to check on her. Erwin was acting differently, too, spending more and more time with Mary and less time outside with Franklin. Usually, Erwin hated to be inside.

"What's your sister's name, Fudgie?"

"Carmalita."

"Carmalita Manzanares. That's a mouthful."

"*Sí*, man. But not for Carmalita. She is beautiful, my sister."

"She is?"

"You wan' to meet her, man? I will introduce you."

"How old is she?"

"She is twelve but everyone think she is my older sister." He laughed.

"So how old are you?"

"Thirteen. A teenager, no?"

"Same as Mary. I'm goin' on eleven."

"I thought you was twelve, but I won' tell Carmalita."

He winked and we grinned at each other.

"Peter Caviness! Come down out of that tree. Time to get ready for church."

Mrs. Henderson paused on the front porch before picking up *The Grand River Sentinel* and stepping back into the house.

"Is that you momma?"

"Fudgie, I gotta go."

"Okay, man."

"But I'll see you when I get back, okay?"

"Okay. *Adiós, amigo*."

He lifted his chin good-bye as I jumped down and ran across the street and into the house. Franklin was at the kitchen table in the clothes he wore to the funeral. Mary, in her white Easter dress, stood at the sink with Mrs. Henderson.

"Get on in there, Pete. Tub's waiting for you. That preacher's going to be here any minute."

"Isn't Win goin'?"

"I don't think that preacher wants to see Winnie for a while. Least not until his leg feels better." She started to laugh but glanced at Mary instead, who was drying dishes, and then back at me.

"Now hurry it up. Your suit's hanging up in there, too."

I went into the bathroom, pulled my T-shirt off, and stepped out of my cut-offs. Steam rose from the tub, fogging the mirror. I stuck one foot in to test the water and jerked it back. Mrs. Henderson must have thought she could boil off a summer's worth of dirt and steam the wrinkles out of my suit all in one sitting.

Starting the cold water, I rubbed a small hole of steam from the glass and looked at my nose. It was still red from Rickie Livers' knuckles and a little swollen. Uncle Herbert had always said Mary and I had the straight slightly upturned Merriweather nose like our mother's; the Cadillac of noses he called it. Franklin and Erwin, he said, had the more flat working-class Caviness nose. Pa said a Caviness nose was flat from the grindstone but Uncle Herbert pretended not to hear, like he always did when Pa said something he didn't like, and then continued studying Franklin and Erwin's profiles as he might look over the dented grillwork of a well-used Edsel (that is, if Uncle Herbert ever had the means to be in the market for a well-used Edsel—much less a Cadillac). Now my nose looked a little flat, too, and I wished more than anything Uncle Herbert was still around just so I could show it to him.

I toweled off the rest of the mirror. My hair stood sunbleached white against the tan of my face. My arms and legs were sleeved brown with summer, too, and the rest of my body looked as white as the bean sprouts Mrs. Henderson kept trying to get us to eat. The outline of my shorts and T-shirt appeared, at a glance, like I was still wearing clothes but as my fingertips traced down along the hollow between protruding ribs to my rigid white center, the tingle of nakedness spread over me.

"I'll show you if you show me."

Beanie Livers, Rickie's little sister, wads the skirt of her dress using a dirty little fist. Her eyes are serious and they look at mine.

"Ain't nothin'. I see my brothers all the time."

Beanie Livers doesn't smile and I've never seen her face so dirty. But I've never seen her up this close, either. The frayed sheet that is our tent has unhooked itself from one folding chair and flaps softly in the breeze.

"You first."

Beanie Livers moves her eyes and stares out through the tent door, her tongue working the inside of her cheek, and slowly lifts her skirt. She hooks a thumb behind the elastic waistband of her panties and looks back at me.

"Ready?"

I nod and, not taking her eyes from mine, she bends slowly down, hesitates, and then straightens up still clutching the front of her dress. I look down at yellow panties hanging around her ankles over bare feet.

"Now you."

Pulling at the top button of my jean cutoffs, I'm still looking down at Beanie's feet and underwear. Then I'm unbuttoned and my fingers wrestle with the zipper and I hear a screen door slam somewhere in the distance. But I don't hear it the way you do something you're listening for and, bending over a little, I get the zipper down and part the fly of my underwear and there I am—and there's Beanie—and butterflies lift in my stomach and settle down as moths against the corner street lamps and beat their wings and the steam rises up against the glass and I begin to lose myself in it.

"Pete! Preacher's here! Come on out, boy."

8

Reverend Calloway was fat in a soft overstuffed sort of way. The kind of fat that comes from spending too much time in comfortable places, when the body begins to spread out like the furniture it's resting on. Reverend Calloway was easy-chair fat and as he hurried up the marble steps of the First Pentecostal Church, his wide hips jiggled under the parted white linen of his summer suit coat.

Before entering, he paused and wiped sweat from his flushed face using a cloth which appeared from an inside breast pocket as a magician's might from a top hat or coat sleeve. The pink carnation on his lapel matched the color of his tie and as he cinched the knot, pink flesh melted over his starched collar.

Placing Mary's arm firmly through his own, Reverend Calloway smiled into the wooden door in front of him and ran the heel of his hand across his scalp, slicking moist strands into place. He pulled the door open and with Franklin and me following, led our sister across the empty lobby to a set of swinging doors.

"See you after the service, boys. Have a good class."

The doors opened, waiting heads turned, and the preacher waddled up the middle aisle like a duck taking its duckling for a first swim. But it was our sister he took with him and Mary looked back as the doors slowly closed between us.

One morning a couple of summers before, Mary had been picked up at our house by an army-green school bus with RIVER VALLEY 4-H stenciled across it in big white lettering and camping gear and suitcases tied to the top. She had the same look on her face then, gazing out the back window as it drove away. We didn't see her for two weeks after that and Erwin, not used to sleeping without her, cried himself to sleep almost every night until she came back. Franklin ribbed Erwin about being such a baby—if word got out in the neighborhood, Erwin's tough reputation might be finished—but I could tell Franklin wasn't feeling so hot about Mary's being gone either. When we played baseball, we couldn't find anyone else to ump and when we had a dispute, there was no one around to settle the argument.

And now, as the preacher sat Mary right there with him behind his pulpit, things seemed confused, as though we should have been arguing about all this, all that was happening to us, but didn't know who to argue with. And for the first time, we couldn't look to Mary because Mary was suddenly a player—a player drafted to the other side.

"Where did he say for us to go, Franklin?"

"Sunday school, wherever that is."

Tall stained-glass windows stood in the walls around us, coloring the light streaming through. One was a mother holding a baby to her breast. The baby's head glowed yellow in the sun under its mother's gaze. At the opposite end of the lobby, two men wearing the same pink carnations as Reverend Calloway's suddenly appeared at the top of a staircase.

"Come on, Pete. Over here."

I followed Franklin across the lobby in the other direction from the men and through what looked like a closet door. It was cement-cool in there, like our basement at home, and dark. A dim light illuminated the corner of a narrow flight of stairs that turned downward at a right angle.

"I don't think it'd be there, Franklin."

"Course not. You really want to go to Sunday school?"

Franklin stepped down and peeked around the corner and waved. "Come on."

We walked down the stairs to a long hallway lit with fixtureless light bulbs. To one side stretched the cement foundation of the church and to the other, an unpainted plasterboard wall with puttied nail heads and four doors strewn the length of it.

"Let's go, Franklin. We shouldn't be down here."

"Scared, again?"

"Naw, I just don't . . ."

Abruptly, the first door cracked open and a tall man in overalls stood looking at us.

"We didn't do nothin'. Just trying to find our Sunday school class, that's all."

The man's bushy eyebrows raised. "Hold on there, young fella. Didn't say you did do anything, did I? I just heard you two blowing smoke at each other and thought I'd see who it was. Rarely get anyone down here, you know, especially on Sundays." He looked from Franklin to me and then back to Franklin as though he had asked a question that he was waiting for one of us to answer. "Well, come on in here and have a seat."

We poked our heads into a cramped room and looked around. Lining the walls were shelves cluttered with paint cans and cleaning fluids. Against the wall on a wooden table sat a stack of books with the top one open and lying face down. A toolbox was flung open on the floor and half its contents were scattered around. In the corner a green garden hose looped over and around a wash pail.

"Pull up a box there and take a load off your feet, men. Go ahead. There you go. Now, what's your names."

"Franklin, and this here's Pete."

"Are you brothers?"

"Yeah."

"Well, nice to meet you, Franklin and Pete. I'm William but everybody around here calls me Willie so you can, too. Your whole family go to church here?"

"Naw, today's our first day."

"Well, good, good. Might as well get acquainted from the ground floor up. Huh, boys?"

"Yeah, I guess."

"This here's my office where I make all my important decisions. You guys like it? Did all the decorating myself, kind of post-Civil War pre-Reconstruction decor."

"What do you do down here?"

"Oh, all kinds of things. Mostly think. Like just now I was thinking how thirsty I am and how I could go for some Welch's. Would you men like some grape juice? I'll be back in a second."

Willie got up from his paint-speckled chair and left the room. We looked at each other and shrugged. This was better than going to some stuffy Sunday school class. Willie returned with three large cups, two in one hand. His hands looked like Pa's, brown and broad with veins snaking over the backs and disappearing into craggy knuckles and long powerful fingers. He could have carried a dozen cups. He held his drink up to us.

"'For the mind's blind eye, the heart's ease, and the liver's craw. Down the hatch all.'"

Willie drank deeply and when he lowered his cup, half-empty, his eyes shone.

"Ah, fine nectar. How's the grape juice, boys?"

"Good."

"Nothing like a little communion to get the day started, right?"

Willie took another drink and set his cup down. With a flickering smile, he reached into the front pocket of his bib overalls and brought out a pipe the shape of a saxophone. He packed it full with tobacco from a leather pouch he retrieved from atop a can of paint.

"So, how did you lucky lads stumble onto the First Pentecostal Church?"

Willie raised his leg and strummed a wooden match along the pant seam of his overalls. The match crackled and fired with a hiss. He brought it to the tobacco and drew. A pleasantly sweet smoke billowed up, mingling with the smell of turpentine and fresh paint.

"Well, our sister got invited so we came, too."

"I see. Where's your sis?"

"Up there."

"Ah, at the regular service."

"Yeah."

"Well, you boys aren't missing much. That is, unless you like being screamed and shouted at for a couple of hours. Of course, not that you don't get to yell back once in a while, it's just that your selection is a little limited. A 'hallelujah' here and a 'praise the Lord' there is just about the size of it."

Willie reached for his cup and finished with a gulp. I noticed for the first time the puff of white hair that crowned his head. His skin was like oiled leather, creased and pliable.

"Be gone with it, men. There's more grape to be squeezed and gulleted. Don't want to get Bacchus mad at us."

"Who's that?"

"The bartender, and a fine one he is, Pete. The bartender of bartenders—the original." Willie smiled. "How old are you two?"

"Fourteen and Pete's ten."

"Goin' on eleven."

"Why, I would have guessed Pete's thirteen and you're about sixteen, Franklin. Two good lookin' young bucks like you, I'll bet you've got girls strung from one end of this town to the other. Right?"

"No, not really." Franklin and I laughed.

"And modest to boot! Oh, they're a lucky lot that've found your two's favor. Now let's refill those cups."

"Can we come?"

"Hmmm. Bacchus is a tempermental one, Pete. You never quite know what he's going to pull. Maybe I'll just go see if I can't wrangle a few bottles out of him while he's still in good humor. That way we won't have to keep interrupting this fine conversation. Be right back."

Willie set his cup down and left.

"Good juice, huh, Franklin?"

"Yeah. I wonder where he gets it."

"Bacchus. Didn't you hear him? He's the bartender."

"There's no bartender in church, stupid. He was just joking. Willie likes to joke. If Willie was our Sunday school teacher, I wouldn't mind comin'."

"Me neither."

He returned with two bottles, one in each hand, and set them on a shelf. Wrapping his hand around the middle of the shorter bottle and gripping its white lid with his other, he twisted it off with a turn of his thick wrist. He took our cups and poured, then replaced the lid and grasped the other bottle which was long and slender through the neck.

"Pardon me, gentlemen, this is my own private stock. I don't think you'd like this much, anyway. It's kind of sour." He popped the cork and filled his cup.

"Here's to my new friends, Franklin and Pete. *Salute.*" Willie brought the cup to his mouth and then looked into it before setting it on the floor. He lit another match, this time using the edge of his thumbnail, and restoked his pipe with short sucks that dented his cheeks.

"You guys live nearby?"

"No, clear on the other side of town."

"Oh, your folks brought you over, huh?"

Franklin looked down and then over at me as I took another drink of grape juice. "The preacher brang us."

"Reverend Calloway?"

"Yeah."

Willie leaned back in his chair, puffing his pipe, and studied the white wisps of smoke that rose and disappeared.

"How'd you two hook up with the preacher?"

Franklin shrugged. I kept my mouth against the lip of the cup, taking little sips.

"Just did, I guess. He likes Mary."

"Your sister?"

"Yeah."

"How old's Mary?"

"Thirteen."

"So you guys just kind of came along for the ride, huh?"

"Yeah, kinda."

"What's your folks think about Reverend Calloway? They like him?"

Franklin stared into the empty cup, which he rotated between his legs using his fingers.

"They never met him. Can I have some more juice?"

"Why sure you can, Franklin. You can have all the juice you can drink. If there's one thing The First Pentecostal Church isn't short of, it's juice. I know because I help Bacchus order it." Willie winked. "Here you go."

We held out our cups. He topped his off from the longer bottle, wedged the cork back, and set the bottle down. Using the end of a match he took from the front pocket of his overalls, Willie stirred the bowl of his pipe and relit it.

"Sorry to ask you so many questions, men. It's just that I usually don't get anyone down here I can talk to. 'Willie, mow the lawn' or 'Willie, wax the floor' is about the only conversation I get out of these lint-heads." He took another drink.

"What's a lint-head, Willie?"

Willie's face reddened and he coughed. From his back pocket, he pulled out a blue and white checkered handkerchief and wiped his eyes.

"You okay, Willie?"

"Yeah, I'm fine, boys. I just didn't expect such an astute question so early in the morning. Well, let's see, Pete, what is a lint-head, anyway?" Willie tapped ash from his pipe against the heel of his boot and smoothed it across the cement floor with his foot, leaving black streaks. "A lint-head is somebody who collects lint up here, kind of like an attic." He thumped his middle finger against his temple.

"Now take this room for example. It's a sight cluttered but it isn't empty and it isn't dirty. Your noggin is okay if it's a little cluttered. That means you're just moving things around trying to get them straightened out. But if you never do that, all those things you have stored will just sit and collect lint. A lot of those people upstairs have done just that, Pete. They let someone else do their thinking for them, so all their heads are good for is collecting lint or maybe putting on one of those fancy Sunday hats. Follow me?"

"Yeah, our Uncle Herbert wears a hat, too."

"He does? Well, that doesn't necessarily mean he's a lint-head, Pete, just because he wears a hat."

"Yeah, it does."

Willie looked at Franklin and chuckled. "Well, I don't know your Uncle Herbert so I can't say one way or the other. Sometimes it's hard to tell who's a lint-head and who isn't."

"Is the preacher a lint-head, Willie?"

He took a sip, stuffed his handkerchief back into his hip pocket, and gazed over into his toolbox as though he saw something in it he didn't like.

"With a capital L."

Franklin and I started laughing and Willie, realizing what he had said, laughed with us.

"Now don't you two go calling anyone lint-head, especially the preacher. It'll be our own secret little word, okay?"

"Winnie kicked the preacher in the knee."

"Pete!"

"Well, he did, Franklin."

"Who kicked the preacher?"

"Our little brother, Erwin. The preacher told us that Jesus is going to be our new pa so Win kicked him."

"Where was this?"

Willie had a big grin on his face but Franklin was scowling. I looked down into my grape juice which was as purple as the petunias Mom used to grow in the brick planter under our front picture window.

"At Mom and Pa's funeral."

Willie looked at me, his smile melting as sure as a dropped popsicle on a Grand River sidewalk. I could see Franklin drop his gaze into his drink. No one said anything.

Sometimes when Pa came home from the loading dock he was so tired he didn't talk. He'd sit at the kitchen table with a tall glass of beer Mom poured, shake some salt into it, and then unlace his work boots. I could smell the leather wet with sweat and when he yanked those boots off, his white cotton socks were orangish-yellow around the edges and his feet would smell that same color. Mom and the rest of us wouldn't say anything either. It was as if Pa's tiredness filled the whole house—didn't exactly make us tired but made us feel his tiredness and by being silent, we helped ease it for him. Willie's silence was like that. He just sat there for a long time and let us drink grape juice.

Soon organ music sifted down through the floor above us and people sang and I wondered if Mary was singing, too, and then it fell quiet.

"I lost my folks when I was young. Was taken in by a buddy's parents who treated me just like they treated him, not very good." He smiled. "We moved from Wisconsin to Ohio and then Uncle Sam adopted me and took me traveling in Europe—Italy, Germany, France. After the war I moved to New York for a while and then came out here. I guess I've lived in a lot of places in my life but, you know, whenever I think of home I think about that house in Wisconsin before my parents died. Even now." Willie puffed on his pipe.

"Is it true, Willie?"

"What's that, Pete?"

"Is Jesus really our new pa?"

Willie stood up and walked to the table. He picked up the open book. "I'm afraid I can't answer that for you, Pete. For me Jesus is just another name in a history book." Willie thumbed over a couple pages. "But I'm afraid there's an awful lot of people who disagree with me on that. You've got to make that decision on your own."

"Who is he?"

"The better question is who was he, and to answer that isn't easy. Like all history, there are so many opinions that it's difficult to know exactly what was and what wasn't. The only way we can recapture the past is through words and words are imperfect little creatures. They're also powerful and can change history into something it wasn't, into a mythology or, uh, a kind of fantasy world. But words are all we've got for such things." Willie put the book back, face-down, on the stack of other books. "So to answer your question, I don't know who he was." He took a drink and set his cup down.

"But for what it's worth, gentlemen, here's my two cents. Jesus Christ was a man who lived a couple thousand years ago and by most accounts, a darn good man. He had a lot of opinions about life and because of those opinions, he was both loved and hated. The people who hated him killed him and the people who loved him wrote about him. These writings were put into a book, the Bible. But like many books, the Bible is part history, part hearsay, and part myth and Jesus Christ became, in the minds of those people who loved him, what I don't think any man can become—a god. Today these people are called Christians and they call Jesus Christ their savior. If you get enough people to believe something, it can almost become truth. But only almost—nothing can change what's already gone on, not even a beautifully written book." Willie sat down and let out a sigh.

"So when Reverend Calloway said Jesus Christ is going to be your new pa, he meant that you're going to become Christians and follow the words of Jesus—or, I should say, the words people say are Jesus'. But remember, a fella can only make his own noise and nobody else's."

"But how can he be our new pa if he's dead?"

"Christians believe Jesus didn't die, Pete."

"You afraid to die, Willie?"

"Nope. Nothing to be afraid of. Just think of dying as going to sleep. It doesn't hurt to sleep, does it?"

"No, but sometimes I get bad nightmares."

"Well, Pete, so do I. But when you go to sleep that last time I don't think there'll be any of that. I can almost promise you. Your mom and dad are just sleeping up a storm right now. So you can feel darn good about that. It took a lot of hard work to bring up a couple of fine young men like you two. They deserve a good rest."

"Where do those people think Jesus is, Willie, if he didn't die?"

"Well, Franklin, Christians believe that Jesus didn't die and that he lives in Heaven with God, and anyone who becomes a Christian and follows the word of God won't die either."

"Never?"

"Never."

Franklin looked up from his cup.

"No wonder they want to be Christians."

"Out of the mouths of babes. Franklin, you just hit the nail on the old head."

"Hey, Willie . . . oh, sorry. Hope I'm not interrupting anything." A young man with a dark suit and pink carnation stared at Franklin and me from the doorway. It was the guy at the funeral who led Mary and me to the front.

"No, Dave. Just having a little fellowship with a couple of old buddies. What can I do for you?"

"Pastor Calloway wants you to dim the last two rows of lights for the final segment of the sermon."

"Have to get the right effect, that's for sure, huh, Dave? If he wants to maybe I could rig up some thunder and lightning, too. You know, fire and brimstone and all that good stuff. Excuse me, gentlemen. I will be back shortly, just make yourselves comfortable."

Willie winked and wavered slightly as he stood. The young man glanced at us as they left. Franklin and I returned to our grape juice and thought about Willie.

"I wonder why Willie works here if he don't like lintheads?"

"Pete, I don't think that's grape juice Willie's drinking."

"Sure it is. His own stock."

"Yeah, you can say that again. Look at that bottle. It's just like those bottles old man Hillar keeps in the window of his shed. It's wine."

Franklin took the bottle, pulled the cork, and sniffed.

"Yep, that's wine all right."

"How do you know? You never had none."

"Did, too. Me and Lee Hooker drank a whole bottle once."

Franklin put the bottle to his lips.

"Is it good, Franklin?"

When he brought the bottle down, Franklin's face puckered like the skin on a fallen grape. He wiped his mouth on the back of his hand.

"Course it is."

"Let me try some."

"I don't know, Pete."

"Come on, Franklin, you did."

"Okay, but if you tell anybody I'll pound you."

"I won't."

Franklin handed the bottle over and I pressed my lips to its mouth and leaned my head back, letting the wine gurgle down my throat. It was sour and watered my eyes. I smacked my lips like Willie.

"Shoot, Pete! You almost drank the whole thing! Now Willie's going to know we took some!"

"You had just as much!"

"Don't get all excited, you baby. We'll just have to drink the rest and get him another bottle."

Franklin took two more eye-clenching swigs and gave the bottle over.

"Drink the rest, there's just a little left, and hide it over there under that shelf."

I drained the bottle, wedged the cork in place, and slid it on its side under the bottom shelf between two plastic jugs.

"Come on. Let's go get him another before he comes back."

"Where'd he get it?"

"I don't know but he went this way."

We ran down the narrow hallway, checking the doors, and found the far one unlocked. Franklin eased it open and a sheet of light unfolded into the darkness. We could just make out the side of a case.

"Go get one, Pete. Hurry."

"You get it."

"Come on, Pete. Grab one before he gets back."

Franklin shoved me into the room. Glancing around, I shuffled over and felt the smooth round chill on my hands. I worked my fingers around a bottle, pulled it out, and hurried back to the light and Franklin.

"Here. Let's get."

"Wait. This isn't wine: WELCH'S GRAPE JUICE. This is grape juice, you dummy. Take it back."

"You do it."

"Come on, Pete. I have to watch for Willie. Hurry!"

Hugging the bottle thrust back to me, I moved toward the stack of bottles again, found the empty slot, and slid the bottle back.

"Hurry up!"

"I can't see nothin'!"

Flourescent lights suddenly flickered on and I stood in a large storeroom full of boxes.

"There, I found the switch. Look over there, Pete. In the corner."

A row of grape juice lined the side wall and square cardboard boxes of cups and napkins were stacked to the ceiling, covering the entire back wall.

"Where?"

"There, next to that gold thing. In the green box."

I ran over to a gold stand with three candles stuck in the end of it like the tines of a pitchfork. Beads of wax hung frozen down the sides of the candles and the wicks were burnt black. Below, on the floor, a tall green and brown box sat half-opened.

"Found it!"

"Good. Bring two, just in case."

I grabbed the necks, one in each hand, and walked hunched over in quick short steps toward Franklin.

"Grab one."

"Got it. Let's get out of here."

Franklin flicked the light switch off and we hurried back down the hallway. We set the wine on the table and Franklin rummaged though the toolbox and took out a screwdriver.

"What are you going to do with that?"

"Open the bottle, what do you think. Have to get the cork out."

Franklin sliced through the plastic with the end of the screwdriver and peeled it quickly from the bottle's head. He poked at the cork and flicked pieces out. Putting down the screwdriver, he reached into his pants and brought out a pocketknife. He opened it and using the small blade, carved out more cork but it began slipping downward. Franklin stumbled forward and bumped his leg on the table's edge.

"This is going to take forever."

He cut into what was left of the cork, pushing it in pieces into the wine.

"How you going to get the cork out now, Franklin?"

Jamming his middle finger into the bottle, Franklin tipped the bottle sideways and fished for the cork. Wine sloshed out onto his hand and down the sleeve of his white shirt.

"Shoot!" Franklin straightened up and steadied himself by holding onto the back of Willie's chair. "Here she goes." He gripped the bottle as though it were a Louisville Slugger and he was stepping to home plate with it. He threw back his head and drank.

"You get some?"

Franklin coughed and picked a piece of cork from the tip of his tongue. "You try."

I took the bottle. The floor tilted and I leaned into it. When I brought the bottle down, wine came up through my nose, feeling like the blood after Rickie Livers' punch. I wiped it away with the cuff of my shirt. "Nothin', Franklin. I didn't get nothin'."

Franklin leaned against the wall. "The empty bottle. Get the empty bottle. What'd you do with it?"

I walked sideways to the shelf and grabbed hold. I moved my hands down to the next shelf, the one beneath that, and then the last one before balancing myself on the floor on all fours. Flattening to my belly, I fumbled between the two plastic containers and pulled out the empty bottle. Franklin swayed above me. I lifted the bottle over my head and he took it. I climbed back up the shelf, hand-over-hand as if it were a ladder, and stood upright. Franklin tried to pour wine into the empty bottle but it dripped over his hands onto the floor. "That'll do 'er."

"The floor, Franklin. Look what you did to the floor."

Franklin pushed himself off the wall and staggered back to Willie's chair and plopped down. "I kinda like the floor, Peter-head."

Franklin grinned and set the bottle on its edge, but it teetered and fell from his fingers. He lunged but it hit and rolled away off the table, crashing to the cement.

"Oh, no! Ya broke it!"

Franklin's head slumped against his forearm now resting on the table as he looked down at the wine and pieces of glass. "No shit, Shirley-locks."

Down the corner of the shelf I slid and sat on the floor. Wine seeped along the wall behind the table. I closed my eyes and felt the turn of the earth like a skate key twisted at the end of a shoestring and then let go. Erwin and I used to get dizzy like this in the front yard, looking up at the sky and clouds while going around and around in circles. Then we would fall and lie on the grass and feel the earth turn under us. We would lie and watch the clouds, lions and dragons and old witches with hooked noses and wild hair staring down at us and we would see them and call them by name and sometimes argue about what they were or what we thought they were. But the earth would slowly come to a stop like the rides at the carnival that came through Grand River every summer, and the clouds slowed, too, until they were barely moving at all. And then we would stand and do it again.

But now nothing stopped or even slowed down and I knew I couldn't stand even if I wanted to. I opened my eyes and there was Franklin's head still slumped on the table and even though his head didn't move independent of his body, and his body and the table and chair and the entire room and everything in it didn't move independent of anything else, it all swam around me together. Then the door opened and there was Willie, his eyes gray as the cement around him and there was the preacher, too, fat and his face stained red as the spilled wine against the white of my dress shirt. The preacher's voice came loud into the room but I couldn't understand the words and he stood over Franklin yet Franklin didn't move, except with everything else. And then the preacher was looking down at me and at the same time the weight of my head rolled to the side and there was our sister standing next to him with someone who looked exactly like her and I didn't know which one was her and which one wasn't.

As my head found the cool hard cement floor, the preacher looked fatter than ever. The preacher, in fact, was rolling in fat.

9

The light flicks off. Momma comes and sits down and pulls the sheet up, smooths it around my shoulders and under my chin. Her head is black against the square of light from the doorway. I can't see her face but her smell is there, powdery and clean but mediciney, too. Momma always takes medicine, little pills that look like M&M candies. She tilts her head back and washes them down with a cup of water. By the look on her face, I know they don't taste like M&Ms. Sometimes Momma calls me her little pill.

"Night, Petey."

"Momma."

"Now I lay me down . . ."

". . . down to sleep. I pray the Lord . . ."

". . . my soul . . ."

". . . my soul to keep. And if I die before I wake, I pray the Lord my soul to take."

"God bless . . ."

"God bless Momma and Papa and Mary and Frankie."

"And the house . . ."

"And the house we live in."

"Amen."

"Amen."

"Good night, Buster."

Momma's lips press wet against my nose and forehead, her hair falling along my cheek and ear. I smell the wetness on my nose, sweet and sour, a little like the vinegar she pickles cucumbers in every summer.

"Sleep, Petey. Sandman's comin. Close your eyes."

Her hand strokes my hair back a couple of times. She stands. Her slim outline moves to the doorway and stops. She looks back and I can see the basketball there—Franklin said Momma swallowed a basketball and I believed him for a while. Now I don't but we still call it Momma's basketball, even Papa. Sometimes she takes my hand and places it on her. Then I'm sure it's not a basketball—basketballs don't do that. Momma says I did the same thing but not as hard. I don't understand what she means and she smiles and gives me a big hug and I don't even know what I did.

"Good night, Petey."

The door shuts quietly without a click. The crack of light at the bottom goes out and I hear her climb the stairs and walk across the kitchen floor above me. Everything is dark now. My eyes are open and I look up into the blackness. Momma's gone. My nose is still damp, though, and I can still smell her.

"And if I die before I wake . . ."

I blink and see little dots of different colors, green and yellow and orange against the black. I follow them around the room until I can finally see the ceiling. Then I stare, stare at it long and hard until I can't stare anymore.

But I still have one more thing to do so I squinch my eyes up tightly and think as hard as I can and say what I always say, softly into my blankets so no one can hear. "Please, God, don't let Momma die before I wake."

And then it's done and it's quiet and there's nothing left but night.

* * *

"That's right, Sergeant, ten and fourteen. No, a sister, also. Mary, thirteen. Oh, yes, a younger brother named, uh, Ervin, I think. Six or seven. An ill-behaved little . . ."

I opened my eyes. A ribbon of sunlight fell between curtains over the bed I lay on, across a desk where the preacher stood, and up the wall to the ceiling. It lit up a black telephone and a stack of papers in a metal holder, like the basket our mom loaded empty milk bottles into every Monday morning.

"Right now they're staying with a neighbor lady, a Mrs. Hazel Henderson. No, there's only an uncle. Herbert Merriweather. A fine, God-fearing man."

Mary came into the room still wearing the white Easter dress. She walked over through the light—her hair catching there like the quick bright glow of a match head struck in the wind—and moved behind the preacher to the other side of the desk.

"Frank and, uh, Marjorie. Or maybe it was Margaret. One of the two."

Mary stood looking down at her fingers she traced along the edge of the desk. She didn't see me and I lay quietly and watched her.

"I can't quite remember, Sergeant. In their forties, I think. He passed on from a heart attack, I believe, and apparently she had been sick for some time."

Mary looked up at the preacher and I thought she might say something. Though usually quiet, Mary sometimes talked when no one expected it. But she didn't say anything and I realized now maybe that's why she didn't, because I thought she would.

One time the year before when everyone sat quietly around the supper table after report cards had come, waiting for Pa to say something, Mary began talking. Not to anyone in particular and not even for the sake of breaking through the quiet, just talking because she had something to say. And even in those nervous moments we listened—even Pa—and felt better knowing there was something else in the world, something more than the D+ I got in Science or the F Franklin got for skipping study hall too many times with Lee Hooker.

It really didn't matter what she said, just so she talked and we could listen to her voice. But soon, when Franklin and I were feeling too comfortable and thought we might be able to finish the last bite of supper and slip quietly out of the kitchen, Pa let out a big sigh and, pushing away from the table and rubbing his belly through his T-shirt, looked directly at us—not sternly, just at us.

Then everyone knew it was Pa's turn to speak. Mary fell silent and followed Mom up from the table and helped her clear the dishes. With the tinkle of silverware and glasses and plates being washed, dried and put away, Pa said all the things we knew he was going to. But now, thanks to Mary, Pa's voice had lost its edge—as though she had taken some of Pa's sandpaper to it and had smoothed the roughness away.

"Well, at least we can rest now, knowing you have him locked up. What charges have you filed?"

Mary gazed up at the wall behind the desk. Plaques hung there with the words ACHIEVEMENT and REAL ESTATE and CERTIFICATE in heavy black lettering. Underneath these words was the name Gus Calloway.

"Nothing formal? What do you mean nothing formal, Sergeant? Don't you realize what a threat this man is?"

Above all the plaques with the preacher's name hung another one, larger with a thick gold frame and fancy-written words that read:

BLESSED ARE THE MEEK;
FOR THEY SHALL INHERIT THE EARTH.

"What about theft? That wine he drank was property of my church, sir! It's sacramental! The blood of our savior! The theft of it is a crime against the Almighty, Himself!"

Mary turned from the desk and seeing me lying on the bed, hurried over and clasped my hand in hers. The preacher had the telephone in one hand and suddenly pounded the desk with his other.

"No, I can't wait until tomorrow! I'm coming down there tonight! And I'm bringing the boys!"

Reverend Calloway slammed down the telephone. He leaned heavily on his hands over the desk, shaking his head and gulping deep breaths. Then, as though just remembering we were there, he turned around and smiled, smoothing long strands across his bald head. He came over to us and sat on the bed. I felt my body slip toward the depression he made in the mattress.

"Peter?"

The preacher stroked my head. I rolled away to the side and felt an ache crawl up my neck and settle behind my eyes. My tongue lay swollen and dry in my mouth as though someone had sprinkled sawdust across it.

"Peter, are you going to be sick?"

I shook my head.

"Would you like some water?"

Reverend Calloway pushed himself up and left the room. Mary squeezed my hand. I opened my eyes and turned toward her.

"Pete, are you okay?"

"Yeah."

"You look so pale." Tears welled in her eyes and she didn't blink to keep them from falling. "Isn't it awful? When is it going to stop?"

"Don't worry, Mare. I'm okay. We just got a little sick, that's all."

"How could he do that to you?"

"Do what? Who?"

Mary took a deep breath and wiped under one eye with the back of her hand. "That terrible man, that janitor."

The preacher came back and sat down again. He handed me a glass of water, and propping myself on my elbows, I drank.

"Not so fast, son. You'll get sick, again."

Reverend Calloway took the glass and set it on a nightstand. He turned on the lamp. The light reflected in half-moons off the walls and in the glow I could see his watery eyes study me from behind his pink round nose.

"Mary, go see how Frank Junior is doing. I want to talk to Peter alone for a moment."

Mary let loose of my hand and her slips rustled underneath the Easter dress as she walked out of the bedroom.

"Peter, tell me what happened this morning."

"Where's Franklin?"

"He's in the other room asleep. Now, how did you two meet up with William Truman?"

"Willie?"

"Yes, Willie. The janitor. What happened? What did he do?"

"Nothin'."

"Peter, this is a very serious matter. Very serious. A crime has been committed in my church. Do you understand? A crime against God right in His own house. Now tell me what William Truman did. God will forgive you, son, if you just tell me the truth."

"Willie didn't do nothin'."

The preacher stood. Pulling at his nose, he studied the thickly carpeted floor and walked slowly over to the desk. Wrinkles lined the back of his white linen suit coat and when he turned around and started back, I could see the carnation on his lapel was beginning to turn brown around the edges. He no longer wore a tie and at the open throat of his shirt was the white cotton of an undershirt, barely visible against pale skin. He looked down at me, his nose redder than before.

"Peter, do you remember what happened to you and Mary the other day at the funeral?" He sat back down on the bed. "God spoke to you. He chose you. He asked you to follow Him, Peter. And do you know what you said? You said yes. You accepted Jesus Christ. It should be the most wonderful day of your life. You're a Christian now, son. And today the Lord is asking you to help Him. He's asking you to be brave and to be strong and to help Him. You don't want to disappoint God, do you, Peter?"

I shook my head.

"Good boy. I didn't think so." The preacher smiled. "Now, Peter, tell me—tell God—what happened this morning. How did you and Frank Junior meet up with William Truman?"

Sunlight angled low through the curtain and lit higher up on the wall behind the desk.

"We was trying to find the Sunday school class."

"Sunday school class? In the basement?"

"Yeah, you didn't tell us where it was at."

"Well, I must have. Of course I did. If you two would have paid attention instead of . . ." Reverend Calloway closed his eyes for a moment as though he were concentrating on something and then a slight smile parted his lips as he reopened his eyes. "So you went down into the basement. Then what, Peter?"

"Nothin'. We just talked."

"With Truman? About what? Give me an example, Peter. What did you talk about?"

"Well, Willie told us about the lintheads."

"Lintheads?"

"Yeah, you know, how they got lint in their heads 'cause they don't move stuff around and it's like a attic and you can't tell which ones are lintheads and which ones aren't."

The preacher suddenly got up. His nose was brilliant red now and his eyes icy and black peering over it.

"What else did he say about the lintheads?"

Willie had said it was our own secret word so I just looked at the ceiling.

"He said I'm a linthead, didn't he, Peter?"

I shrugged my shoulders.

"So you and Frank Junior just talked to him? You didn't do anything else?"

"Not much."

"What else, Peter? Don't let God down now, son. Tell me what happened."

"Well, Willie smoked his pipe and he give me and Franklin some juice."

Reverend Calloway's steely eyes widened and he sat back down on the edge of the bed.

"Juice? What kind of juice, son?"

"Some grape juice."

A smile played about the preacher's lips and he ran his tongue over them as though trying to lick the smile away as he might a chocolate-malt mustache.

"Peter, Willie gave you grape juice?"

"Yeah."

"And he told you it was grape juice?"

"Well, yeah."

"And did Willie drink some of this grape juice, too?"

"Yeah, but . . ."

"Hallelujah! You've just made the Lord very happy, Peter. Praise God. That's enough for now, son. We've got to get going. Come."

* * *

The shadows grew long with evening and were finally lost in the gathering twilight. And then dusk came to Grand River and behind it, night with its spray of stars spreading east to west, from the rim of Spruce Mesa over the valley to the red sandstone of Rimrock National Park. In the darkness the air was cooled and in the stars the geese, honking along the banks of the Colorado River, fell silently across the water.

Franklin sat slumped against the door beside me. He had only been awake long enough to move from Reverend Calloway's house to the preacher's new car. Normally, Franklin didn't get to sleep until late—with pumping gas and doing his schoolwork and messing around with his friends on weekends and all—but this wasn't normally and now his mouth hung open and his face flashed white from the pairs of passing car lights outside.

The car radio was tuned to a religious program. The voice that blared out seemed to rise and fall with the billboards and telephone poles looming up out of the darkness at the side of the road. Mary sat in the front seat with Reverend Calloway and quietly listened as the preacher explained what she was hearing on the radio sermon. Finally, the noise clicked off and the preacher quit talking, leaving only the steady hum of his Lincoln Continental.

The corner streetlight flickered dimly as we turned onto our street and I could hear moths bumping at it and the thrum of June bugs as we got out of the car and went up the walk into our house. Mrs. Henderson was watching television with Erwin while busying her hands with a wicker basket full of yellow yarn. Her knitting needles clicked rhythmically as she stared into the Motorola.

"That Ed Sullivan! I swear! If he don't get the dangedest darn acts on his show. Look at that big old thing standin' up there! Don't need to go to no circus when you got him around."

Erwin, sitting cross-legged in front of the television, wearing his light blue pajamas with sewn-in feet and a picture of the Lone Ranger and Tonto painted across his chest, laughed and pointed at the elephant but when he turned and saw the preacher, he stopped laughing and scooted back against the television screen.

Mary went quickly to him, knelt down, and hugged him. "Hi, Winnie."

"Where'd ya go for so long?"

"Church. You can go next time if you want, okay?"

"I don't wanna."

"Why?"

Erwin pointed at Reverend Calloway who now stood to the side of Mrs. Henderson, waiting for her to take her eyes off the television.

"Move over, children . . . why, look at that, Winnie! That big old thing's going to squeeze the stuffin' out of that fella!" Mrs. Henderson rocked forward on her feet toward the television, hugging the wicker basket to her lap until her backside lifted up off the stuffed rocker as if squatting in an outhouse on a cold morning. "My, my—look at that, child!"

She rolled back on her heels and plopped back onto the rocker, shaking her head. She unglued herself from the television then and panned across the living room like a searchlight, fixing her gaze onto Franklin and me.

"What an' the devil happened to you two?"

"Excuse me for interrupting, Mrs. Henderson, but I have to talk to you. I can explain everything."

"'Bout time you got back with these kids. Didn't know you was going to keep them all day and half the night, too."

Setting her basket of yarn on the floor, she hoisted herself upright and walked stiffly over to where Franklin was just settling groggily onto the couch. The side of Franklin's face was red and wrinkled into the pattern of the preacher's car upholstery and his brown hair stuck up in different directions like fur on the guinea pig Erwin used to keep in a wire cage.

"Franklin Caviness, what an' Sam Hill did you spill all over that shirt?"

She looked over at me, grabbed my arm, and held it up underneath the living-room lamp. With her head tilted back and her eyes cast downward, she inspected the purple splotches on my sleeve.

"Excuse me, Mrs. Henderson. That's just what I was about to explain. Could we please speak in privacy?"

"You kids go on and get ready for bed. Me an' the preacher here have some talkin' to do."

"Pardon me once again, Mrs. Henderson, but Frank Junior and Peter have to go with me for a short while."

"They what? It's dang near nine o'clock. You're sure givin' 'em a bellyfull of church for their first day."

Franklin blanched as if Mrs. Henderson had kicked him where it counts. She studied him as he took in a deep breath and let out a low moan.

"Please, Mrs. Henderson. I can explain everything."

"Okay, you kids, go to your rooms for a while. Winnie, it's about time you went to bed anyway, child."

Mary gazed at Franklin and me as she took Erwin by the hand and led him down the hallway.

Franklin pushed himself up off the couch and I followed him downstairs. His bed was strewn with Topps baseball trading cards and when he flopped down on his back, some fell to the floor.

Franklin's room was crammed with stuff. Model airplanes hung from the ceiling by thumbtacks and fishing line. The top of the desk Pa built him was a parking lot of model cars and dragsters, with a Soap Box Derby trophy he had won two years before sitting in the middle. Two dresser drawers were flung half open with socks and underwear spilling over them. In the corner, Louisville Sluggers leaned like teepee poles and his Mickey Mantle autographed fielder's mitt that he had traded for a rusty boyscout's knife was balanced on top of them. The walls were covered with Yankee pennants, a poster of Chubby Checker doing the twist, a larger one of Roger Maris hitting his 61st home run, pictures of more race cars and more sports heroes, and right at the foot of his bed where he could lie gazing at it, a new picture of Marilyn Monroe that he had ripped from that month's issue of *Life Magazine*.

Franklin was in love with Marilyn Monroe—he had watched "The Misfits" three times in a row, seeing both matinees and the late feature all in the same day—and when she died two Sundays before our father did, Franklin refused to believe it.

"Franklin, what are we going to do?"

"Sleep."

"Didn't you hear the preacher? He's taking us with him."

"So?"

"He's going to take us to the police station."

Franklin's eyes snapped open. "The police station?" He sat up, grabbed his head, and then sank slowly back to his pillow. "You're crazy."

"No, honest, Franklin. I heard him talking on the telephone."

Franklin looked at me through his fingers from one open eye. "You sure?"

"Yeah, I heard him. Mary was there, too."

"Cross your heart and hope to die?"

"Cross my heart and hope to die."

Franklin rubbed his face with the palms of his hands. "What else did the preacher say?"

"He asked me some stuff about Willie."

"Willie? What did he ask?"

"He wanted to know what happened."

"Did you tell him?"

"Yeah, kind of."

Franklin sat up and glared at me. "You told him about the wine?"

"No. I said Willie give us some grape juice."

"That's all you said?"

"Yeah."

"You sure?"

"Yeah, I'm sure."

"Then why's the preacher taking us to the police station?"

"I don't know."

"Frank Junior? Peter? Are you down there, boys? It's time to go."

Our eyes locked to one another's at the sound of the preacher's voice and then we trudged upstairs and into the living room. Mrs. Henderson was parked on the edge of the hassock with her legs pressed together, her head bent down. On her lap she twisted a yellow tissue around her fingers. Reverend Calloway stood waiting at the door in front of her, one hand grasping the doorknob. His cheeks were flushed red as his nose and with lips folded inward, his mouth was drawn into a straight white line.

"Hurry it up, boys. Let's go."

We looked at Mrs. Henderson. Her eyes were tightly closed and she brought the tissue to her lips. She would not look at us and ever so slightly, her body began to shake.

"See ya, Mrs. Henderson."

Reverend Calloway stepped quickly forward and grabbed us by the shoulders with his moist pudgy hands. He guided us to the doorway and just before he ushered us on outside, we both glanced back and caught Mrs. Henderson's eye—and that's all it took.

As the preacher's long automobile swung around under the corner streetlight and carried us toward the Grand River Police Station, we could still hear the echoes—lifting up out of our house, spilling out into the night air—of our kind old neighbor lady's loud exploding laughter.

* * *

By the time Reverend Calloway, Franklin, and I reached the police station, Sergeant Floyd Nichols, the arresting officer, had already gone home. Despite Reverend Calloway's pounding the counter, calling Willie a modern-

98

day Judas, and shouting something about a higher law, the receptionist and finally the police chief himself, persuaded the preacher that Willie was safely locked up for the night and that our pressing charges and identifying him could wait until the next day.

He drove us back home and the only words he muttered, just before letting us out of the car, were to get a good night's sleep because it was very important that we remember everything that had happened that day. Mrs. Henderson still sat in our mom's stuffed rocker, her head back and mouth open. At the sound of the front door closing, she let out a quick snort, raised up, and looked around.

"I swear, this place is like Grand Central Station tonight. You two get on in here and get down there to bed. And don't think, just because I got a little tickled, that what you did at the church was okay. If your daddy was here you'd be tanned but good. By rights, I should've done it myself. Now you two go an' get those filthy clothes off before I change my mind."

We trudged through the living room and kitchen and went downstairs, only to find Mary sitting on Franklin's bed, waiting. She was barefooted and had on her pink bathrobe. A white towel was wrapped around her head and tucked in front. She sat in the middle of the bed, stacking baseball cards neatly in her hand.

Although thirteen months younger than Franklin, Mary had a curious effect on him. She couldn't boss him around even if she tried—which she didn't—but she could still move him to do things he would never do on his own. The year before, Franklin was invited to go to his first junior high dance by a friend of Mary's, Becky Stevens, who lived down the alley and had moved to Grand River from a small town in Florida. Becky Stevens had a crush on Franklin but unfortunately for Franklin, her likeness to Marilyn Monroe began and ended with gender. She wore thick horned-rim glasses and braces and when she talked, all that wire and silver seemed to catch at her words, stretching them as they left her mouth. And there was that same feeling of length when she walked—all neck, elbows, and knees. But Becky Stevens was intelligent. She had Mary ask Franklin to the dance for her. And when Mom brought Franklin home after dropping Becky Stevens off, Franklin glared at Mary, went straight down to his room, and didn't talk to her for an entire week. Mary's influence was as much a mystery to him as it was to anybody else.

"Are you guys okay?"

"Yeah."

Mary rubbed her bare foot over the top of her other one. "Reverend Calloway wants me to ask you something."

"What?"

"He wants to know what you want to do."

"What do you mean?"

"Well, now that Mom and Dad's gone."

Franklin and I glanced at each other as Mary studied her toes. Franklin shrugged.

"Reverend Calloway said we should pray about it and to let him know soon. He said it's important that we ask God to help us. I was thinking maybe if we'd pray together God would listen to us better."

Mary got down on her knees and clasped her hands. I knelt and with head bent forward, peered to the side over at Franklin. He bit at his lower lip and then ran the back of his hand over his mouth. He looked around the bedroom as though memorizing it—the walls with the pictures and posters, the ceiling with his model airplanes hanging from it, the floor strewn with more baseball cards and dirty socks—until his eyes came to rest on Marilyn Monroe's white glossy face. And as Mary began to whisper to God there on the cool hard cement floor—the floor our father had poured with his own two hands—Franklin let out a low sigh before slipping quietly down beside us.

10

Mr. Dugan, a solid barrel-bodied man with blue whiskers the same length and color as the stubble on his head, didn't understand.

When Franklin showed up at the filling station Monday morning for work, he sat in a swivel chair with his boots crossed and one heel reaching out just enough to catch the lip of his metal desk. A wad of Red Man Chewing Tobacco bulged like a goiter from his left cheek. The string of keys he always carried hooked to his belt loop now lay in front of him next to the half-empty bottle of RC Cola with a layer of Planter's Salted Peanuts floating on top. Mr. Dugan rarely spit and must have needed something solid to help wash down his chew. "Nice of you to drop in."

As usual, the top of the red pop machine sitting in the corner was flung open—Mr. Dugan never paid for his own pop but then neither did anyone else—and he nodded at it with his head. Franklin pulled out an orange.

"Thought grape was your drink."

Franklin shrugged.

"You, too, if you want."

I took out an orange and following Franklin, popped the cap using the opener on the front of the machine.

On a shelf behind Mr. Dugan's desk, a rotating fan, which no longer rotated, blew sun-faded pink streamers straight out like tails on the ends of kites. On a calendar next to the fan, a big-chested redheaded woman wearing only a white vest, matching shorts, cowboy boots—one of which she rested on the chrome bumper of a semi-tractor-trailer—and a smile, held a big wrench in front of her: VALLEY MECHANICS—We Have Just The Tool For You. The months rustled and flapped gently in the hot office air.

"Pete, isn't it?"

"Yeah."

Mr. Dugan bent his head down and looked up at the sky out the filling station window. "Gettin' just a hair cooler. Can you feel it? Just a little bit of an edge. 'Bout time to stock up on anti-freeze and go watch that puny football team up at the high school lose another game. Why they keep that dad-gum coach I'll never know."

He swigged his cola, washing down spit and the memory of Grand River High School's twenty-one straight defeats. After the last football game the year before, the principal, Mr. Richman, expelled the school newspaper's sports editor for publishing the headline: *Trojans Spring Another Leak, Father Another Goose Egg*. The ex-editor was Mr. Dugan's nephew, Bernie Dugan, and his article was pressed between the desk and the scratched glass top where Mr. Dugan could sit and read it out loud to customers so he could laugh all over himself again. He was almost as proud of his nephew as he would have been had Bernie been the quarterback on a winning team. Before the article came out, Mr. Dugan had referred to Bernie as "four-eyes."

The double ding of two rolling sets of tires pierced the office. Franklin glanced out at the car and rubbed his hands on the legs of his work pants.

"You like working here, Franklin?"

"Yeah."

Mr. Dugan chomped down on his tobacco cud, his lower jaw moving in two tight circles. "Ain't you even going to tell me where you been for the last week, for cryin' out loud?"

Franklin looked down at the floor.

"You didn't even call."

"Sorry, Mr. Dugan."

He set down his cola and picked up his keys, clipping them back onto his belt loop. He squinted out through the window at the car stopped at the pump and shook his head. "Dad-gum kids today. Can't play ball, can't make it to work, can't do for squat." Wiping his hands on the oily red cloth he took from his back pocket, he nodded at the car. "Well, better get on out there before they drive away. Whole world don't end just because you took a vacation."

"Thanks, Mr. Dugan."

Franklin hurried out the door.

"And don't forget to check the oil!"

Mr. Dugan shook his head and chewed vigorously on his Red Man then looked grumpily over at me as though I were just as guilty for missing work as Franklin.

"And what about you? You going to want to work here when you get older or not?"

I looked down into the round mouth of the pop bottle at my orange soda. "I dunno."

Mr. Dugan quit working the tobacco and the words that came from his mouth were softer as though they had been chomped on for a while, too.

"You're getting pretty big. How old are you now?"

"Almost eleven."

"I ain't seen you around here all summer. What've you been doing with yourself?"

"Nothin'."

"Well, 'bout time you did do something, don't you think? Come see me next summer. If you work half as good as your brother out there, maybe I could use you now and then, too."

"Thanks, Mr. Dugan."

Franklin trotted up to the office door and stuck his head in.

"Thirty-weight, Mr. Dugan."

Leaning back in his chair, Mr. Dugan grabbed a quart of Mobil Oil from the rack over his shoulder and tossed it to Franklin. Franklin hustled back out to the car. Mr. Dugan stood and walked around behind the cash register as another car pulled up to the side pump. And Franklin was there, again, getting instructions, starting the gas flowing, and then hurrying back to the office.

"Five eighty-six on pump one, Mr. Dugan." Franklin handed him a ten and ran back outside.

He rang up $5.86 on the cash register and made change. Then, as was his custom, Mr. Dugan, hitching his pants, walked out to pump number one, gave the lady her change, and thanked her as she drove away.

I drained the rest of my bottle and set it in the wooden crate of empties next to the machine. I went outside and waved good-bye to Mr. Dugan, who was watching Franklin check the tire pressure on a pickup truck.

Mr. Dugan was right. The day did seem just a little bit cooler. And as I walked away from the filling station to find Fudgie, I wondered why today the smell of gasoline didn't seem half bad, either.

* * *

I walked along the Indian Wash watching for the snakes and muskrats Erwin was always talking about. All I could see were cattails and willows growing along its muddy banks and clumps of moss anchored with sludge waving in the current like green hair.

Erwin wasn't allowed to go swimming with us in the canal so he took solace in the shallow waters of the wash, catching water snakes and frogs and chasing the family of muskrats that he said lived there. No one else but Erwin had seen the muskrats so no one else believed him—that is, except his best friend, Timmy McGee, who would have believed old man Hillar was a priest if Erwin had told him so.

The neighborhood gang did believe Erwin about the snakes, though. The evidence was all over the place, having slithered down the back of Patty Higgins' dress, found its way into Timmy McGee's first-grade Sir Walter Raleigh pencil box, and even coiled into one of the pockets of Lee Hooker's black multi-zippered motorcycle jacket. It was the first time Lee Hooker showed us anything resembling fear and if it weren't for Erwin's small size and Franklin's quick tongue—Franklin swore to Lee Hooker that he had seen the snake crawling toward the jacket where Lee Hooker had laid it on the ground while we were playing football—Erwin would most likely have been murdered.

How the snake managed to zip the pocket back up wore heavily on Lee Hooker but he accepted Franklin's explanation. After all, pounding someone half his size and age would have been almost as humiliating as the high-pitched gasp that came out of Lee Hooker's throat when he reached into his pocket for his pack of Lucky Strikes and came out, instead, with a handful of snake. It was one of the few times Franklin got Erwin out of a fight instead of into one.

Because of the flood of 1959, when the Colorado River overflowed its banks and all our neighborhood went crazy with riding bicycles through the ankle-deep water that stood on the streets, the town leaders decided the Indian Wash should be dug, just in case. It cut into the clay and alkali ground below the canal along Willow Avenue before veering south down 28 Road and then spilling into the Colorado River on the other side of town. It was dug deep, its sides as steep as the Grand Canyon. And in Erwin's eyes, even though it usually ran as little more than a drainage ditch, it *was* the Grand Canyon and he, Erwin, its lone explorer.

When it rained, the gutter pipes which stuck out here and there along the top of the trench spouted waterfalls and Erwin would hold a piece of screen he tore from an old porch door under them and pan for rain-shiny nuggets and drowning earthworms. On hot days, he moved through the willow saplings and cattails and tamarisk that sprang along the bank, catching insects and reptiles and stalking the phantom family of muskrats.

Now the pipes were green with algae and leaked sewage and gutter-run like snot from Beanie Livers' nose when she had a cold, which was almost always. I threw clods down at these pipes and started dirt avalanches with the sides of my feet while I walked along toward Hill Avenue. There, the wash tunneled under the street through a big corrugated tin pipe tall enough for even Franklin to stand up in. City workers had already painted the sides of the pipe silver, as they did every year, but new words had already appeared there in dripping black paint, words I recognized as the Ute Indians who used to travel through the valley might have recognized another tribes' smoke signals without fully understanding their meaning.

Fudgie had told me Hill Avenue was the street the Luceros lived on so I walked along checking names on mailboxes. Finally, I crossed the street and came back down the other side before finding the one that read: Helen and Joe Lucero.

The house was small and whitewashed, with a gravel driveway and a tall sycamore tree in back. Red geraniums bloomed along the sidewalk leading to the front door and there was a cluster of shaggy evergreen shrubs hugging the wood siding underneath the front window.

I tapped on the door, but no one answered, and then again before going around to the side of the house. At the corner I pulled back. A girl was unpinning laundry from a wire clothesline in the back yard. Her hands stretched working above her and long black hair fell straight down her back almost to her waist. She wore a long white cotton skirt and when she stooped down to the wicker basket, it flared slightly at her hips.

"You like her, man?"

"Fudgie! Geez, you scared me."

Grinning, he raised his chin toward the girl.

"See?"

"What?"

"My sister. That's Carmalita."

"Oh."

The girl continued to take down the laundry.

"Where you been, man? Yesterday I wait in the tree for a long time."

"Church."

"All day?"

"Yeah."

"Eee, you momma must be like mine, always go to church. You papa go, too?"

I shook my head.

"Hey, jus' like my papa. He no go, neither. Our families the same, huh, man?"

"Yeah, I guess."

Fudgie slapped me on the back. "And we both have pretty sisters, no?"

He yelled at Carmalita but she picked up the wicker basket of clothing and began to carry it up the walk to the house. Fudgie waved, and she looked over and smiled. I felt my face and neck heating up.

"Carmalita, this is my frien', Pete."

She looked at me, still smiling—her eyes large and brown, the color of root beer, with long lashes, and a small upturned nose set between high cheekbones, above slightly white, slightly crooked teeth—and stuck out her hand. Looking past her at something of great interest in the yard, a rose-bush or maybe a rock, I shook her hand imagining that this is how Franklin would probably have handled it had he ever met Marilyn Monroe. Resting the wicker basket on one hip, she turned and walked into the house. I, in turn, let out my breath.

"I think she like you, man. When you let me meet you sister?"

"Anytime."

Fudgie grinned.

"Come on."

I followed him into the house. Carmalita had set the basket on the kitchen counter and I could smell the warmth of the sun on the clothing and the aroma of cooking food. The walls were yellow and in a milk bottle sitting in the middle of the table stood a cluster of daisies, their centers that same color.

A short chubby woman with a round face and wearing a white nurse's uniform stood over the stove, stirring the contents of a black cast-iron pot with a wooden ladle. She had light orange hair, and her skin was red and freckled.

"Pete, this is Mrs. Lucero."

"Hello, Pete. It's nice to meet you."

"Hi."

"Luis tells me you and he are quite the friends."

I looked down at the toe of my tennis shoe I was working into the lino-leum floor. "Yeah."

Mrs. Lucero smiled. "Luis, would you like to invite Pete to have lunch with us?"

"Yeah! Come on, Pete, eat with us."

"It won't be much because I have to get back to the hospital but at least you'll get to meet everyone."

"Fudgie, maybe I better get home. Mrs. Henderson'll be wondering where I'm at."

Fudgie looked at me. "Who is Mrs. Henderson?"

I shrugged and continued gazing at my shoe. Mrs. Henderson had told Franklin and me to get back by noon because Reverend Calloway was coming to pick us up and take us back to the police station. But Franklin had to work and I, well, I had to see my friend.

"Okay."

"You can eat, man?"

"Yeah."

Fudgie slapped me on the back and then suddenly looked past me outside.

"Pete! Look!"

A man with thick wavy black hair and long sideburns stood outside, flattening his nose against the screen door and holding his hands up beside his head like bear claws.

"Grrrrr."

Fudgie started across the kitchen for the other room but the man flung open the door and caught him by the back of his T-shirt.

"No! No, José! Stop!"

Fudgie struggled as the man grabbed him around the neck and began poking him in the ribs.

"Joseph! Quit roughhousing. You're going to wake Manny."

The man paid no attention and began dragging Fudgie across the kitchen, his fingers digging into Fudgie's armpits. Fudgie tried to get away, grabbing at the kitchen chairs, but it was no use. He was laughing hysterically as they finally tumbled through the doorway and outside onto the grass.

Mrs. Lucero stood with her hands on her hips, shaking her head. She was smiling. I smiled, too, and looked out through the screen door, out at the man who continued to growl and maul Fudgie on the lawn.

I can feel the whiskers on my cheek and smell the grass and the aftershave from the bottle with the ship on it mixed with his smell. He pins my wrists to either side and works his jaw, works his stickery cheek against my neck. He growls and tickles and lets me pull his hair and ears and nose. He lifts his head—his hair's all mussed—and laughs and I laugh and then his face comes close again and I can smell him and feel him and I say his name over the breathing and growling and I know it's him and I know no different. And me and him, me and my pa, we laugh.

"Aren't you glad you're staying to eat with this crazy family, Pete?" Mrs. Lucero shook her head, again, and continued stirring. Carmalita walked into the kitchen from the darkened doorway and went over, put her hand on Mrs. Lucero's arm, and nodded. Mrs. Lucero handed Carmalita the ladle and then left the kitchen.

I watched Carmalita work the pot of what I could smell to be beans and wished I could think of something to say, something funny that would make her laugh. Her hair looked even blacker here inside the house and longer and, strangely, even more alive as though it were moving on her head. And then I realized her hair was moving because her back moved, heaving and then relaxing as she smelled the beans.

"They smell pretty good, huh?"

Carmalita said nothing, only continued stirring. I walked over behind her and peeked over her shoulder at the beans. Her eyes were closed and her nostrils flared.

"They look good, too."

Carmalita whirled around with the ladle and it flew out of her hand and dropped to the floor, splattering bean juice. I jumped back, bumping against the kitchen table. We stood gawking at each other.

"I'm sorry. I . . . I didn't mean to scare you."

Carmalita's face turned red. She grabbed a dishcloth, knelt down, and began wiping up the juice.

"Here, I'll help you." I knelt beside her and reached for the ladle when I felt a hand tighten on my shoulder. I half stood and was half lifted to where I was nose-to-nose with a large burly man wearing only a pair of trousers and black rimmed glasses with white tape wrapped around the middle of them.

"What you wan', *gringo*?" He was bent over and leaned heavily on the back of a kitchen chair.

"Manny! You shouldn't be up." Mrs. Lucero came quickly into the kitchen and took his hand from my shoulder and helped him sit down. His black hair was messy and flecked with white, shoulders slumped forward.

"What you wan' with my daughter, *muchacho*?"

"Manny, this is Luis' . . ."

"*Gringo* has a tongue. I heard it, no? *Plática, mulo!*"

"Manny! This is Pete, a friend of your son's. He is a guest in this . . ."

"*Quieta, mujer!*"

Mrs. Lucero turned and went outside. Carmalita stood next to her father and put her arm around his shoulder. Turning his head, he squarely faced her and quietly spoke Spanish. Carmalita stared at his lips, nodded softly, and took the basket of clothing into the other room. Manny gazed after her. His eyes were bloodshot and pouches lay like tiny bird nests beneath them.

But then his eyes snapped alertly back to mine. "Don' touch my *florecita, mulo.* Or I break your *cabeza.* Your head! Crack!" Manny slapped the back of his hand in the palm of his other and I winced.

"Pete is our amigo, *Tío.* Be nice to him." Joe walked into the kitchen with Fudgie, winked at me, and patted Manny on the shoulder.

"Hi, Pete. I'm Joe, Fudgie's cousin . . ." He glanced at Fudgie. ". . . as well as his teacher, master, and juvenile delinquent officer."

Joe smiled and stuck out his hand so I shook it. But Fudgie didn't smile, only looked at his father.

"And this is Fudgie's father, Manuel Manzanares. Say 'hi' to Pete, Manny."

Manny sat and stared into the other room. Joe grabbed him under the arms and began easing him off the chair.

"Put me down, José. You trea' me like a *hito.*"

"You are weak, Manny. You must rest to get well."

"I am tired of res'. I mus' go back to San Felipe."

"You are still too sick. Your sons will take care of everything there, *Tío.* Don't worry."

"I mus' talk to Rosita, José."

"There's no phone in San Felipe, Manny. We've been over this. How are you going to talk to her?"

"Call Ensenada. Tony's boy, Gabriel, live there. Call him. He has a phone."

"Then what?"

"I will sen' him to San Felipe for Rosita so she can call me."

"Manny, this is crazy."

"I mus' talk to her."

Joe looked across the kitchen at Mrs. Lucero. She nodded.

"Okay, Manny, we will try. But first we eat."

"*Sí,* José. *Gracias.*"

The meal tasted good even in the heat. Fudgie and Joe sopped up bean juice with flour tortillas and washed it down with coffee. Mrs. Lucero tended Manny, dabbing bean juice from the corner of his mouth using a towel and giving him water when he coughed, which was often. And Carmalita just watched, her brown eyes unblinking, the largest eyes I had ever seen.

Mrs. Lucero and Carmalita began clearing the table.

"No bread and jam, Helen?"

"The bread is for supper."

Joe lit a cigarette and leaned back in the chair, rubbing his belly through his T-shirt. He had taken his dress shirt off after the wrestling match with

Fudgie and hung it on the back of the chair. He was long and wiry—a little like Willie—but had a slight paunch that, had he been shorter, would have been much more pronounced. His hair was combed straight back from a broad flat forehead.

"*Muy bueno*. Was that good, Manny?"

"I mus' talk to Rosita, José."

"Okay, *Tío*."

Fudgie and I sat at the table as Joe spoke first English and then Spanish into the telephone. Mrs. Lucero sat down as Carmalita began washing the dishes. Manny listened, slumped in the chair with his elbows on the table, cupping his jaw in his hands. Joe motioned for Fudgie and after a few more words, handed him the phone. Fudgie spoke quickly in Spanish and then hung up.

"Was that Gabriel, Luis?"

"*Sí*, Papa. He say Uncle Tony will call soon as he get there."

"How did he get 'hold of him so fas'?"

"He didn', Papa. Uncle Tony go see Gabe, anyway."

"You a good boy, Luis. Come here."

Fudgie went to his father's side, and Manny pulled him down and hugged him. "You Papa is sick but he will be well soon, *hijo*. Don' worry."

"*Sí*, Papa."

Manny squeezed Fudgie's shoulders with his hands before letting him go. "Is this you frien', Luis?"

"*Sí*, Papa. This is Pete."

Manny looked at me, running his hand over his upper arm. "How you know him?"

"We jus' meet, Papa."

Manny nodded. I tried to imagine him as the man Fudgie had told me about—the man who had drunk tequila and carried Fudgie's uncle halfway across town on his back and who had gone off on adventures into California, Arizona, and Texas. The man sitting down was tired and sick and couldn't even get out of his chair. And he scared me. But his arms were big and I could see where Fudgie got his chest and broad shoulders. And then he looked at me, his eyes smiling now, and I knew he was Fudgie's pa.

"Sorry I get angry, *amigo*. I get older and meaner every day, like a tired jackass that spill all his seed and have no more lef' and nowhere to put it, anyways."

Mrs. Lucero came over, looking sternly at Joe who was red with choking back laughter, and gathered up the tablecloth by the corners. Carmalita took it from her and stepped outside where she shook off the tortilla crumbs.

"Why don't you boys go outside for a while and play while we clean up."

"Come on, Pete. Let's throw the ball."

Fudgie grabbed a couple of mitts and a baseball and we went outside to the front yard.

"What's wrong with your pa?"

Fudgie stood across the yard and tossed the ball in the air a couple of times, catching it in his bare hand. "I don' know, man, but he real sick. He never get mad at people." Fudgie rubbed the ball and then flung it to me. It popped as it struck the heel of my glove.

"I shouldn't have scared your sister." My hand tingled so I slipped three fingers into the first finger of the glove before throwing the ball back.

"Good arm, man. You scare Carmalita?"

Fudgie threw it back and I nabbed it in the webbing like I thought Moose Skowron might at first base for the Yankees.

"I just said something and she dropped the spoon and beans went all over the place."

Fudgie grinned as he caught the ball. "What you say didn' scare Carmalita, man."

"It didn't?"

"No."

Fudgie threw me a ground ball and I scooped it up and pretended to step on first base.

"Talk never scare Carmalita."

"What scared her then?"

"I don' know. Carmalita don' hear what we hear, man, but she hear things no one else hear. She is always like that, since she born."

Fudgie put the baseball in his mitt and took it off, folding the leather thumb over the ball. "Carmalita know things, too, man." Fudgie walked across the lawn to me.

"She does?"

"Sí."

"What?"

Fudgie shrugged. "Many things. She jus' know." Fudgie stood in front of me now and he glanced around us before his eyes settled back onto mine. "Pete, tomorrow me and Carmalita will go back to Mexico."

"Tomorrow!?!"

Fudgie held his index finger to his lips. "Shhhh. No one can know. We mus' go tell Mama how sick Papa is. Tomorrow we will go to the orchard. Lot of *Mexicanos* in the orchard now. Maybe we get a ride."

I took off the glove and handed it to Fudgie. "You can't go yet."

"Why, man?"

I rubbed the sweat off my left hand onto my pant legs. "Well, we just met and . . . and you haven't even met my sister."

Fudgie grinned. "Eee, I wan' to meet you sister but we can't wait, man."

Carmalita came running around the corner, waving for Fudgie. He started after her but I grabbed him.

"Fudgie. Um, tomorrow . . . tomorrow I want to go to the orchard with you."

Fudgie smiled and nodded. "Okay, man."

We ran around the house after Carmalita and back into the kitchen where Manny sat yelling into the telephone in Spanish. His free hand covered his other ear and his voice sounded stronger and younger than before. Fudgie and I sat down at the table with Joe and Helen just as Manny abruptly hung up the phone.

"Who was it, *Tío*? Did you talk to Tony?"

"*Sí*, it was Tony."

"What did he say?"

"Rosita is upset. She is in church praying . . . always praying."

Manny's voice trailed off and once again it sounded tired.

"Why is she upset, *Tío*?"

"The *presidente*. He upset her."

"López Mateos?"

"No, no. Cárdenas."

"Cárdenas? Why?"

"Somebody has to. I no there, so somebody has to."

Manny shook his head, looking down at the floor.

"How did he upset her?"

"I don' know." Manny waved his hand over his head. "Cárdenas say the church is rich and won' help Mexico so Rosita, she get angry. She say Kennedy should be our *presidente*. Kennedy."

Manny shrugged.

"She hate America but she love Kennedy. I mus' go back, José. I can' let Rosita do to the *presidente* what she do to me."

Joe and Helen smiled across the table at each other.

"Okay, *Tío*. As soon as you get a little better you can go back."

"No, José! No later. I mus' go back now. Now!"

Manny shouted angrily in Spanish but his words sputtered and he began coughing. Mrs. Lucero rushed to him and gave him a drink of water. Joe helped him up and into the darkened room, a living room, and helped him stretch out onto a bed that was folded out from their couch. Mrs. Lucero poured medicine into a spoon and propping his head up with one hand, slipped it into his mouth. Carmalita went to her father's side and slid his glasses off and set them on a table next to the bed.

"Joe, we've got to get him to the hospital."

Joe shook his head. "We do that, Helen, and he's on the next bus heading south."

"Maybe we can get Rosita back on the line. Maybe she can convince him."

"Helen, we've been over this. He'll never go. I know that."

"But he's getting worse, Joe. This prescription isn't helping. Let me talk to Doctor. . . ."

"Helen. If we check Manny into the hospital against his will, it'll take everything right out of him. It'll kill him."

Helen looked down at Manny and wiped his head with a washcloth. "But lying here all day might do the same, Joe. Can't you see that?"

Fudgie and I watched from the kitchen doorway as Joe took Helen in his arms and hugged her. The small living room smelled of vapor rub and menthol and rubbing alcohol. Manny's eyes were closed and his coughing stopped. Carmalita pulled the sheet up to her father's chin just as the men at the hospital pulled the sheet up over my pa. But the men at the hospital went all the way over Pa's head and I didn't see him anymore after that, except at the funeral. But that really wasn't him. I'm not sure who it was but it wasn't my pa.

And then Mrs. Lucero turned on a lamp next to the fold-out couch and it glowed against the wall and ceiling and there above it in the soft light hung a man from a cross, the same man I saw on the nun's mirror coming back from the hospital.

"Do you love Jesus, son? Well, Jesus loves you and to prove it He's going to be your new daddy."

I heard my name trail after me as I burst through the screen door out into the bright sunshine. I could hardly feel my feet—I could hardly feel anything—as I ran down Hill Avenue and then along the Indian Wash. When I reached Dugan's filling station there was a police car parked alongside the office in the shade. Mr. Dugan stood beside it, talking to the policeman who was sitting in the driver's seat. Two cars were parked at the pumps but I couldn't see Franklin anywhere. As I came running up, Mr. Dugan turned, wide-eyed, and looked at me.

"Pete! Look, here's Pete!"

Mr. Dugan came over to me and hugged my head to the bib of his greasy overalls. "Son, you shoulda told me. You and Franklin shoulda told me. I had no idea, son. I'm sorry. I had no idea."

The policeman got out and opened the back door and there slouched Franklin. Mr. Dugan let go of me and I slid in next to my big brother and the policeman shut the door. He got back in and started the engine, and Mr. Dugan peered in on us and then stepped back and watched as the police car pulled away, out around Mr. Dugan's red gas pumps and down the street toward the Grand River Police Station.

11

When we arrived at the front desk, four officers were huddled around a portable television on the far end of the counter. An upright rocket billowed smoke from its base as a voice vibrated from the set, counting backwards with numbers flashing at the bottom of the screen. ". . . 18, 17, 16 . . ."

Behind the counter, shuffling papers, sat the same tall thin policeman we had seen the night before. Light through a half-pulled Venetian blind fell across his arm, shoulder, and the side of his head and then up the wall behind him, illuminating a clock. The second hand circled as though fanning the motes glinting in the angled slats of light.

". . . 13, 12, 11 . . ."

Franklin fidgeted, crossing and uncrossing his legs and pulling at his work pants, the smell of gasoline still about him. The policeman behind the counter finally stood and glanced toward the television, shaking his head.

". . . 8, 7, 6 . . ."

I could hear the click of a typewriter and cars gasp and accelerate in rushes outside. The policeman who brought us craned his neck, squinting over at the television set.

". . . 3, 2, 1 . . . ignition . . . we have lift off."

"This'll show them commie bastards. Let's see 'em try and copy this one."

The four neatly trimmed heads at the end of the counter tightened their knot as the rocket lifted off in a straight line and then arced, disappearing and reappearing through clouds until only a tiny spark of light was visible in the vast grayness of the small television sky.

"There she goes."

"Is this Franklin and Peter Caviness?"

The policeman brought his gaze back over from the television. "Sure is, Al."

"You were the two in here last night with the preacher, right?"

Franklin nodded.

"Yeah, I remember. I'll take them from here."

The policeman who brought us went over and joined the group tied to the television. Al came around the counter and led us toward a hallway past the others.

"Hey, Al. Come take a look at this."

Al stepped back and looked. "I don't see anything. What are we looking at?"

One of them pointed to a speck of white dancing over the screen like a firefly in a fruit jar. "There. See it? It's the Mariner II on its way to Venus."

Al squinted and shook his head. "That's it?"

"Yep."

Al looked closer. "Says who?"

"Walter Cronkite for one."

"Well, if Walter Cronkite says so I guess that's good enough for me."

Al took us on down the hallway and into a room. There, sitting on one side of a long table, were Reverend Calloway and Mary. Mary started to stand but the reverend stopped her by placing his hand on her shoulder and pushing gently down.

Al pulled a couple of chairs out and we sat opposite our sister and the preacher. Mary's gaze was on her lap and I could imagine her twining fingers underneath the table, as usual when something was bothering her. Franklin and I sat there quietly, stealing glances at her.

This, I recalled, was Mary's second trip to the station, the first one, oddly, being with Lee Hooker. As ornery as Lee Hooker could be, he was always polite to Mary and was even known to have blushed around her although no one dared point that out to him. A few kids on our block even thought Mary was the real reason Lee Hooker always hung around with Franklin although, again, no one would mention it unless certain Lee Hooker was out of town or at the very least, locked up in the local juvenile detention hall. Strangely, Mary liked Lee Hooker. About this, no one had the slightest theory.

It was two summers before that Buddy Phillips showed up in our front yard with something urgent to show Lee Hooker. It was the first year Franklin began helping Mr. Dugan at the station and he hadn't gotten back from his shift yet. Pa wasn't home from work, so Mary sat out on the front step with Lee Hooker and talked. With Mary around, Lee Hooker was indifferent to Buddy Phillips, which made Buddy all the more desperate to take him to whatever it was he wanted to show him. Finally, Lee Hooker agreed to go but only if Mary could go, also. Although Buddy didn't like that idea, he knew it was his only chance.

The three rode their bicycles over to the vacant house across the canal near the brickyard. It was a shell of a house with windows broken and the outside showing wood under cracked peeling paint. There were holes in the roof and floor, and on the inside walls were written words, mostly misspelled four-letter words that told us a lot we didn't know about the world—or at least about the neighborhood.

Buddy took Mary and Lee Hooker through the living room, littered with magazines and beer cans and stuffing from an old gutted davenport, and into the bathroom. There, scribbled on the wall in red crayon above a cracked porcelain toilet, which held everything from cigarette butts to an old Grand River phone directory to a tumbleweed that had somehow found its way in, was what Buddy wanted to show Lee Hooker: Buddy Phillips did it with Della Mae Nagel, August 1962.

What they did together must have been pretty significant to drag Lee Hooker over for the purpose of simply reading about it. But Lee Hooker wasn't too impressed, especially with Mary standing there. Ironically, Mary's being there may have been the only thing that kept Buddy Phillip's face intact.

Seeing Lee Hooker's unexpected reaction, Buddy stammered that he was pretty upset about it, too, that he had no idea who wrote it but that if he ever found out he would make sure the kid was plenty sorry, that's for sure. Then Lee Hooker and Mary left the house to see what treasures might lurk among the sagebrush and old rusted appliances standing around the place and to try and forget what embarrassing thing they had just read.

Buddy came out a short time later. He didn't stay, though, jumping on his bicycle and hightailing it as if the house were on fire.

Lee Hooker and Mary didn't notice anything, with their noses in the weeds as they were, until Lee Hooker suggested they go chase after the sirens that were whining away in the distance. But by the time they decided to leave and do just that, the sirens were on top of them and they didn't have to go anywhere. The sirens found them: one fire engine and two police cars worth.

The fire caused little damage to the old house. It turns out Buddy Phillips had lit what had been deposited in the dried-out toilet all those years and the combination of things had smoked like old tires being burned. But the Grand River Fire Department took up where the fire had left off with old Gordie Scroggins, the fire chief, directing his men to fire axe the doors since there were no more windows to be broken and to hose the whole place down, just in case. All this, long after the smoking toilet had been success-fully doused. Chief Scroggins and his men were bored and the old vacant house became the victim of their boredom, along with Mary and Lee Hooker.

They were whisked away to the police station in the same scream of sirens, questioned like criminals (which, for Lee Hooker, had become com-monplace), and then finally released—Mary to the custody of Pa and Lee Hooker to his probation officer.

Pa's anger about Franklin's association with Lee Hooker was a single cinder in the bonfire of rage he now felt as he picked his little girl up from the police station. And, driving off, Pa had fuel thrown on his rage when Lee Hooker came out of the building, flicked a cigarette butt into the middle of the street, and swaggered away scot-free as though it were all in a day's work.

Mary tried to explain that Lee Hooker had nothing to do with the fire, that Buddy Phillips had started it, but Pa wasn't in the mood for explana-tions. For Pa, Lee Hooker's being with Mary was enough of a crime.

Lee Hooker wasn't allowed to come to our house after that, while Buddy Phillips continued to make tackles in the football games we played on our front lawn. And, as for Mary, she for some reason (maybe in the injustice of his being barred from seeing her) continued to hold a soft spot in her heart for the neighborhood hood.

But now there was no Lee Hooker—only the three of us sitting in that same police station with a church preacher.

"Now don't you boys worry about anything. You're not going to get into any trouble. I should have made that clear to you last night. When the po-licemen come in, just tell them what happened at church with the wine and all and nothing will happen to you. Just relax and stay calm. Ask God for help and He will give you strength."

The preacher smiled his clown smile as he folded his pudgy hands on top the table.

"Hi, fellas. I'm Sergeant Nichols. I'm glad we could finally get together."

A man wearing horn-rimmed glasses with a black elastic band sat down at the head of the table. His huge head was stubbled and sidewalled by a recent haircut, making his ears look large and red.

"When Mr. Truman gets here, I'm going to ask you a few questions and I want you to answer them as truthfully and as accurately as you can. Okay?"

Sergeant Nichols opened a folder and began reading, his mouth mov-ing silently. I could feel Franklin bouncing his leg up and down under the table like the old dog we used to have, Duke, scratching his ribs for mites.

Reverend Calloway unfolded his hands and began drumming his fingers on the table, the four dimples that were his knuckles creased and blinking.

"Excuse me, officer?"

"Yes, Reverend."

"Is Truman to have a trial in the near future."

"Not if we can help it."

"I beg your pardon."

Sergeant Nichols looked up from the folder. "Well, Reverend, like they told you yesterday on the phone, we'd kind of like to get this thing straightened out today if we could."

Reverend Calloway's hands clasped together in front of him. "Straightened out? You mean still not file any charges so Truman can go free?"

"I'm just saying that if we can get to the bottom of it maybe we can save everybody some time and save the taxpayers a few dollars."

"And let that pervert go free? Never."

"Just hold on there, Reverend."

The door opened and Sergeant Nichols held his hand up for Reverend Calloway to be quiet and there stood Willie, wearing light gray coveralls that hung loosely from his lean body. His eyebrows rose when he saw Franklin and me but he didn't say anything as he sat down at the far end of the table opposite Sergeant Nichols.

"Thanks, Miller. Okay, let's get started."

Sergeant Nichols scooted his chair forward and the policeman who brought Willie left the room, closing the door behind him. Reverend Calloway's hands separated and he curled his thumbs inwardly between his fingers and palms.

"Do you two boys know this gentleman?"

Willie gazed at us, his gentle friendly eyes watery and bloodshot. Franklin coughed.

"Yeah."

"What's his name?"

Franklin poked me under the table but I was quiet.

"Willie."

Willie's eyes smiled and he nodded.

"Good. Mr. Truman, how about you? Do you know these two youngsters?"

"Yes, I do."

"And their names?"

"Franklin and Pete."

"Where did you boys meet Willie?"

"Church."

"What church?"

Franklin nodded his head toward Reverend Calloway. "The preacher's."

"Reverend Calloway's?"

"Yeah."

"Is that accurate, Mr. Truman?"

"Yes, it is."

"And you are employed as a janitor at the First Pentecostal Church, right?"

"*Was* employed."

Sergeant Nichols shot a look over at Reverend Calloway. "Is that right, Mr. Truman?"

"Yes, that's right."

As Sergeant Nichols scanned his papers, I could see Reverend Calloway's hands clench.

"How did you two boys meet Mr. Truman?"

Franklin squirmed in his seat and nudged me again with his elbow. I stared straight ahead at Reverend Calloway's hands.

"Well, we was looking for the Sunday school class."

"And?"

"Willie asked us to come into his office."

"Is that right, Mr. Truman?"

"Yes, it is."

"You have an office?"

"I call it my office. Actually, it's a room where I keep my tools."

"Oh, the room we found them in."

"Yes, sir."

"I see. Why were you two in the basement if you were looking for your Sunday school class?"

Franklin shrugged. "Because the preacher didn't tell us where to go."

"I most certainly did!"

"Please, Reverend. You'll get a chance to talk in a moment."

Reverend Calloway took his hands from the table and put them underneath. Mary looked up at him.

"So you didn't know where your Sunday school class was being held?"

"Nope."

"Why didn't someone tell you?"

"Because we were late for church."

"Why were you late?"

"Pete wasn't ready."

"Is that true, Pete?"

I nodded.

"So, you were late and didn't know where to go so you went downstairs and ran into Willie. Right?"

"Yeah."

"And Willie invited you into his office. Then what happened?"

Franklin glanced at me and then down, gnawing on his bottom lip. "Nothin'."

"Nothing? Are you sure, Franklin?"

Franklin raised his head and looked from Sergeant Nichols to Willie and then to me. "Don't he have to say nothin'?"

"Pete will get his chance to talk. Now just answer the question, son."

Franklin stared at the middle of the table and took a deep breath. "We had some juice."

Reverend Calloway's hands came back out and he rubbed the top of one with the other.

"What kind of juice, Franklin?"

"I don't know. Just juice."

"Did Willie give you the juice?"

"Yeah."

"Did you get some juice, too, Pete?"

I nodded.

"And how about Willie, did he have some?"

"Yeah."

"Did Willie tell you what kind of juice you were drinking?"

"I don't remember."

"You don't remember, Franklin, or you don't want to remember?"

Franklin said nothing.

"Do you remember, Pete?"

I shook my head like Franklin had. Reverend Calloway's hands tightened and were turning white.

"How about you, Mr. Truman. Do you remember what you gave the boys to drink?"

"Just a minute here! I object! You expect this, this derelict to tell the truth? These poor innocent boys weren't told what they were drinking then, so what makes you think he's going to tell the truth now?"

"Reverend, please. This isn't a trial. We're just trying to find out what happened. I'm not entirely pleased with your version and the boys don't seem too anxious to supply any information so maybe Mr. Truman can help us out a bit. Go ahead, Mr. Truman."

"Officer, if you don't mind, I would like the boys to tell you. I know what it was I gave them but it won't mean anything unless they say it."

"Seems the boys don't want to remember."

"Do you mind if I talk to them?"

"Wait a minute! He can't do that! He's already perverted their minds and you can't allow him to put words into . . ."

"Reverend, one more word out of you and I'm going to have to ask you to leave. I'm running this show, so be quiet. You told me earlier what you think and now it's their turn to talk."

Reverend Calloway looked just as he did the night before when Mrs. Henderson laughed, lips folded inwardly in disgust. Sergeant Nichols nodded at Willie to continue.

"Franklin, remember when you and Pete first came into my office and sat down on the boxes?"

"Yeah."

"Remember my asking you if you would like something to drink because I was thirsty and was going to get something for myself? Remember that?"

"Yeah."

"Remember what I called it? The stuff I got for you?"

Franklin took another deep breath and licked his lips and rubbed the palms of his hands on his pant legs. "I don't know."

"Remember, it had a name?"

Franklin stared straight down and said nothing.

"Pete, do you remember?"

I looked at Willie. His hair was as white as Mary's Easter dress, white as clouds or feathers or snow when it first falls in late autumn. Reverend Calloway's hands sitting there on the table were a different kind of white. They were white because they weren't anything else. Linthead white.

"Don't be afraid, Pete. It's okay. Sergeant, I don't want to put the boys through any more. Sometimes I can't remember things very well, either."

Willie licked his lips and smiled and winked at me. Sergeant Nichols closed the folder in front of him and picked it up, scratching one of his large red ears.

"Well, I guess since the boys can't seem to remember much, we'll just have to . . ."

"It started with a W."

The sound of my voice drew everyone's eyes to me. I twisted the end of my shirt under the table. Sergeant Nichols put the folder down.

"What's that, Pete?"

Reverend Calloway's hands were even whiter and I wished they weren't there. I wished he wasn't there. But Mary was there and that made me feel better.

"Pete, go ahead. What did you say."

"What Willie give us to drink. The name, it started with a W."

Reverend Calloway sprang to his feet like a jack-in-the-box popped up. His eyes were lit up and his big clown's smile was spread out over his face.

"Wine! I told you Sergeant! Didn't I tell you? It was wine! They didn't get drunk drinking soda pop, for heaven's sake!"

Sergeant Nichols was on his feet now, too, shouting at Reverend Calloway who shouted back. Another policeman came in and Mary stood up and Reverend Calloway was leading her away by the hand. She looked back at us like she had at the preacher's church.

Willie sat still, a slight smile on his lips, shaking his head. Another policeman came for him and Willie got up slowly from his chair and walking over behind us, bent down and whispered: "See, boys? Words—they can mean anything or nothing, but they can never change what already happened. Don't worry, everthing'll be okay."

Willie patted Franklin and me on our shoulders and then he was led away.

Sergeant Nichols returned and his face was as red with anger as Mrs. Henderson's had been with laughter. He picked up his folder and motioned to us, so we followed him out of the room and down the hallway. We walked by the television, which was quiet now, and through the empty lobby around the corner of the counter. The white-faced clock was there on the wall and I could hear the faint whine of the second hand, and through the window where the sun had shone I could see car lights passing in pairs out in the gray twilight.

Sergeant Nichols drove us home and tried to make us feel better by talking about being a policeman. But those things didn't mean anything to us now. We just sat in his car, watching night come.

* * *

Sergeant Nichols dropped us at the curb in front of our house and, waving good-bye, drove away. Right behind him, before we could even open the gate of the picket fence, came Reverend Calloway in his Lincoln Continental. The preacher whistled a song I had heard before—something about a battle and a wall falling down—as he hopped out and around to open the door for Mary.

"Hi, boys. I'm certainly proud of the way you two handled yourselves today. I told you the Lord would give you strength if you just asked Him. 'For the Lord abhors the bloody and deceitful man.'"

With a quick turn of his head, he made a clucking sound as if to say Franklin and I were chips off the old block. He helped Mary out and still whistling, put his arm around her. Mary looked down at the sidewalk as the preacher opened the gate, and I could hear the crash of boxcars coupling down at the railroad yards south of town and wished what I was really hearing were those walls in Reverend Calloway's song come tumbling down onto his bald head.

As we filed through the gate the porch light came on, spotlighting Mrs. Henderson in the doorway. Her feet were spread wide and elbows bent out from her body with the back of her wrists resting waist-high on either side. Her hair, usually wispy and wild, was now tightly wound against her head with a million bobby pins and the smell of peroxide.

"Good evening, Mrs. Henderson."

"Don't you good evenin' me, preacher. Where've you been with those children?"

"Mrs. Henderson, I told you we had to go to the police station to get this matter sorted out."

"You told me nothin' of the kind. You said you'd bring them back home first."

"The police found Franklin and Peter, Mrs. Henderson. They were hiding out in that filthy gas station."

"Wait a minute, you. That gas station is where Franklin works making honest money, which is more than I can say for some people."

"Mrs. Henderson, I didn't come here to quibble with you about a gas station. I don't think you really understand the severity of what has happened. My church, the Lord's temple, has been defiled. The blood of our savior . . ."

"Hold on there, bub. I was goin' to church while you was still crawlin' around messin' in your britches, so don't you tell me what I do and don't understand."

She pulled out a long white envelope from the front of her dress and waved it at Reverend Calloway.

"And here's something else I'll bet you don't think I understand. What an' the devil do you suppose this is?"

Reverend Calloway leaned forward as if he were trying to pick up the scent with his round nose.

"This here come in the mail today. It's addressed to Herbert T. Merriweather and it's from some fancy lawyer named Lister. He ain't your lawyer by any chance, is he, preacher?"

Reverend Calloway grabbed for the letter but Mrs. Henderson yanked it away and stuffed it back into the crease of her sagging bosom.

"Now try an' get it, you mealy-mouthed boob, an' I'll have you throwed in jail for tryin' to ravage a sweet old lady!"

She turned to us. "You kids get on in the house and get ready for bed. You've heard enough for one day."

Mary turned and went straight through the living room and into her room, but Franklin and I doubled back and stood just inside the door at the front window.

"You sure seem all excited about Mr. Merriweather's mail, preacher. Why is that?"

Mrs. Henderson glared down at Reverend Calloway from the porch and looked as if she were going to pounce on him. Reverend Calloway closed his eyes and took a deep breath. When he finally spoke, his words were measured and his voice quivered like a tuning fork that has been sharply pinged.

"Opening someone else's mail, Mrs. Henderson, is a federal offence punishable by several years in . . ."

"Who 'n Sam Hill said anything about openin' mail?"

Reverend Calloway stared at her and then looked away to the side, pulling at his nose.

"If I knowed you two were in cahoots, I would've skinned you alive like a couple of Siamese cats. Now get off this property before I change my mind."

The preacher looked back at Mrs. Henderson. "Please, be reasonable. I don't want any trouble from you. Mr. Merriweather and I are God-fearing men who only want the best . . ."

"For yourselves! Now git!"

Although Reverend Calloway didn't jump as gracefully as a Siamese cat, he did move quickly, hopping into his car and gunning it down the street, the white-wall tires squealing against the pavement. Mrs. Henderson stood shaking her head and watched the taillights disappear around the corner.

"Lord of Mercy, what's happening to our churches in this country today? Come back here, you two."

Franklin and I had tried to make it through the living room and downstairs but dragged ourselves back to Mrs. Henderson as she closed the front door and turned off the porch light.

"What'd you two hear?"

Franklin shrugged his shoulders.

"Well, whatever it was, you never mind it. Ya hear? I'll see about this business if it's the last thing I ever do."

Mrs. Henderson plopped down on the rocker and picked up her wicker basket of yarn and set it on her lap. She took the knitted material and began smoothing it in front of her. "Now tell me what happened today. You first, Pete."

"Nothin'. I just went to the gas station with Franklin and then to Fudgie's."

"Fudgie's? Who's Fudgie?"

"A wetback."

"He's not a wetback, Franklin."

"Is, too. Everybody says so."

"Franklin Caviness, you never mind what everybody says. If you believe everything people say around here, your brain'll turn to oatmeal and start runnin' out your ears. I swear, in this neighborhood I've heard everything from old man Hillar keeps a bastard son chained up in his cellar to Mrs. Livers gives her children dog food and feeds those yappy little overgrown rodents of hers TV dinners."

She chuckled. "Now that I think about it, maybe that last one's true. Now tell me about this Fudgie character, Pete."

"He's my friend."

"Why ain't I never seen him."

"Ya did. In the tree."

"That little Mexican fella?"

"Yeah, I just met him over at the kindergarten. Him and his family's from Mexico and they just come here to work but his dad's sick and their friends, the Luceros, are taking care of him 'cause Fudgie's mom and brothers left so . . ."

"Hold on there, Pete. You're talkin' so fast I can hardly keep up. You say his daddy's sick?"

"Yeah."

"What's wrong with him?"

"I don't know, but he coughs a lot and lays in bed all the time."

"Where is he?"

"At the Lucero's."

"Joe and Helen Lucero?"

126

"Yeah. I ate lunch with them."

"You did? Why, Joe Lucero's daddy used to work with my Milton on the railroad. A fine man. Ain't Joe Lucero a lawyer or somethin'?"

"Yeah, and Fudgie says he's real smart, too."

"Maybe he's somebody we oughta talk to 'bout this mess. You two sit down. I ain't through talkin' to you, yet."

We sat on the couch while Mrs. Henderson began working the yarn with her long blue knitting needles. She wore a multicolored mumu and her nylons were rolled down and sagged around her swollen ankles. When she was deep in thought, Mrs. Henderson's eyebrows and lips would pull together and wrinkle like a couple of raisins.

"Now tell me what happened at the station, Franklin."

"A policeman asked us questions and I had to answer everything 'cause Pete wouldn't talk."

"No, sir. I talked."

"Yeah, you talked, all right. You lied and told them Willie give us the wine."

"No, I didn't!"

"You did, too."

"Did not!"

"You two quit your bickerin'. Now what's this business about lyin'? Did you lie to the police about something?"

"I didn't but Pete did."

I felt a knot rise up from my stomach and settle in my throat. I didn't tell the police Willie gave us wine. I told them it started with a W, that the word of the stuff Willie gave us to drink started with a W and it did. The preacher said it was wine, not me.

"I didn't do it."

Pa looks at the small basement window, the pieces of glass lying in the sill. He has a frown on his face as he turns the torn screen away and carefully lifts the baseball out and holds it in his big hand.

"This yours, Petey?"

Pa hands me the baseball, and I look at it and can see the initials P.C. through the roughed cowhide and grass stains. I give the ball back to him.

"Yeah, Pa, but I didn't throw it."

Pa looks at the ball again and then down at me.

"You sure?"

I nod my head. Pa's looking blurry, now, and I can feel the hot starting to fill up in my eyes.

"Who did throw it then, son?"

I don't know who threw it but I can't tell Pa because my throat's feeling funny now and I can hardly swallow. Pa puts his hand behind my head and leads me into our house, carrying my baseball in his other hand.

"If you say you didn't break it, Petey, I believe you."

Pa's on one knee, now, and his hands are on my shoulders and he looks straight into my eyes. I swallow hard and shake my head.

"I didn't."

Pa squeezes my shoulders and it's no use then and I close my eyes and bite my lip and can feel the button of his shirt hard against my hot cheek.

"Petey, what did you say to the policeman?" Mrs. Henderson reached over and picked up the wicker basket, laid her yarn and needles into it, and placed it on the floor beside her. Then, with a slight smile across her face, she opened her arms to me. She held me and I could smell the sting of peroxide from her curly blue hair and it must have watered my eyes because they were wet against her collarbone.

"Petey, you never mind, honey. You kids have been through more in a couple of days than some people go through in a lifetime. That preacher, or whatever he is, has you so mixed up you probably don't know if you're comin' or goin'. He's got that dear sister of yours studyin' and prayin' 'til she's darn near blue in the face with it. But I figure whatever can help you get through all this is okay, so I'm goin' to leave her to herself for a while. But you mark my words, honey, as soon as I can I'll put that preacher right where he belongs and he won't bother you kids no more."

"Mrs. Henderson?"

"Yes, Petey?"

"Willie said Mom an' Pa are just sleepin' an' Mom won't ever be sick again. Is that true?"

Mrs. Henderson didn't say anything for once, just held me tightly to her breast. The peroxide must have been bothering her, too.

12

Franklin sat at the breakfast table in his orange baseball T-shirt, Crown Appliance stenciled in black lettering across his chest. To see Franklin up so early was a big surprise. Usually, after late summer evenings of work and late nights of play, he wouldn't be up before ten. But there he was reading the sports page of *The Grand River Sentinel*, which wasn't a surprise.

"How'd the Yanks do, Franklin?"

"Three-nothin' over the Orioles."

Mrs. Henderson stood at the stove. Bacon popped and sputtered at her from the skillet and she poked back with a fork.

"Mornin', Petey. How you feelin'?"

"Fine."

"After all the commotion yesterday, I thought you two scamps'd still be out like a couple of light bulbs. And here it is not even eight o'clock."

I stood behind Franklin and squinted over his shoulder at the sports' page. "Where's the standings?"

"Here. The Yanks are still three up on the Angels and Twins and the way Richardson is playing, they got it in the bag."

"I could've told you that. They always got it in the bag. The only question is who they going to beat in the World Series."

"Let's see, the Dodgers are only up two and a half on the Giants and Willie Mays is clobberin' it, again. Cincy's still in it, too."

"Sister Irene says the New York Giants are going to win it all."

"New York *Giants*? Who said that?"

"Sister Irene, that nun."

"Oh, yeah, and Y.A. Tittle is going to hit a homer in the seventh game with two out in the ninth and the score tied. Right?"

"Right."

Franklin had a milk mustache and was dunking cinnamon toast into his glass, leaving a dark ring around the inside. Mrs. Henderson had the bacon draining now and was scrambling eggs and buttering toast.

"You two oughta read something 'cept that sports page and start improvin' your minds. There's a lot to know in this here world."

"We do. We read the comics."

Franklin and I grinned at each other but Mrs. Henderson pretended not to hear.

"Take that there rocket ship they blasted off yesterday. That dang thing's goin' to go clear to Venus or some dang place. You know how far that is?"

"How far, Mrs. Henderson?"

"Don't you get smart, Franklin Caviness. It's a dang sight farther than Willie Mays can hit a baseball."

Franklin rolled his eyes at me and continued studying the pennant races.

"The first thing my Milton would do after supper every night was read *The Grand River Sentinel* from cover to cover. Every word, mind you. He could tell you just about anything you wanted to know about this place or any other, for that matter. Weddings, temperatures, wars, births, accidents, anniversaries, TV schedules. You name it, he could tell you. Shoot, I didn't even have to read it myself. If I needed to know somethin', I could just ask Milton. Course, now that he's passed on I read it, but I just can't remember things as good as I use to when Milton was alive."

Mrs. Henderson carried the black skillet to the table and scraped yellow clumps of egg onto our plates. She set a plate of bacon and toast between us and sat down. "What are you fixing to do so early in the mornin', Pete? You going to go play baseball with Franklin?"

"He can't. I'm substituting on a team and you have to be at least thirteen to play on it."

"Naw, I think I'll just go climb trees or something."

"Well, if you ain't got nothing to do, just tell me 'cause that garden out there needs weedin'."

Franklin smirked at me from behind his glass but I didn't say anything, just concentrated on my bacon and eggs. After finishing, I put on my Yankees baseball cap and hurried outside, imagining I were Roger Maris hitting my sixty-first home run. The sun burned low over Spruce Mesa and beads of dew glinted in the grass, wetting the tops of my sneakers as I ran across lawns toward Hill Avenue.

Helen Lucero answered the door. She was a short plump woman but attractive in a freshly scrubbed sort of way, with orange hair pulled neatly back into a bun and a white nurses uniform pressed to a shine. She always gave the impression that she had just stepped from a long hot shower. She smiled.

"Hi, there, Pete."

"Hi."

"Are you feeling okay today?"

"Yeah, I'm okay."

"I sure hope we didn't scare you off yesterday."

"No, it's okay. Is Fudgie here?"

"No, Fudgie and Carmalita left about a half hour ago. They said they wanted to go over to the orchards and watch the peach harvest. Manny won't let them pick without him so they were just going to take a look. Have you eaten breakfast?"

"Yeah, I just did, thanks. Do you know what orchard they went to?"

"No, they didn't say. But they usually go to the Morrison's. It's just on this side of the canal below the water tank."

"Yeah, I know where it's at."

"Are you sure you don't want anything to eat?"

"No, thanks. I got to go now."

"Take care and come over anytime."

I was already around the house, running toward Morrison Orchards north of town. The clay hills washed white in the morning sunlight and the glare made me squint as I reached the dirt road that ran along the canal bank. The irrigation water was light brown and it moved in a steady flow, eddying back into small whirlpools along the edges near the bank. After a good rain, the water would turn red as an Irish setter because of the runoff from higher up where there was more iron in the soil. Debris often floated by—tree limbs, cardboard boxes, metal containers, and sometimes even the carcass of an animal—and there were undercurrents, too. But despite these it was still a favorite place for cooling off in the hot Grand River summers. No summer day could equal one of floating endlessly down the canal in the middle of a shiny black innertube, arms and legs dangling in the current.

The peach harvest was in full swing in the valley, and I could hear the clatter of tractors pulling flatbeds of bushel baskets and crates across furrowed rows of trees and the distant voices of fruit pickers talking to each other from their ladders or singing while they harvested the crop. Dogs with cockleburrs in their fur and tongues lolling out of their mouths lay under trees, already too hot to bark or sleep or do anything other than pant. Up ahead were cars, mostly old, parked along the dusty road, and down below was a one-story ranch-style house with a lawn and two pruned apricot trees in the yard.

At the end of a gravel driveway, a wooden post was stuck in the ground with a piece of plywood nailed to it. On it, in dripping red paint, was written: PEACHES FOR SALE. A neater, professional-looking sign stood beyond: MORRISON ORCHARDS.

A short stocky man in bib overalls with the pant legs turned up and a toothpick working in his mouth was standing with one foot on a flat-bed trailer. The trailer hitch was nosed into the dirt, rusted orange. The man held a pencil and a clipboard and was writing down the names of a small group of pickers gathered around him. A stack of wooden ladders with numbers spray painted on them were behind him and a pile of canvas picking bags sat on the edge of the lawn nearby. The pickers were quiet as they were issued the tools of their trade, and the man gave them a kind of pep talk after which they would, one by one, walk off into the orchards to begin work.

"You can work five minutes or five days, it don't much matter to me as long as you bring back your ladders and pickin' bags. No hourly wage here. It's how much you pick, just remember that. Get that fruit in and leave here rich, that's what I say. It's up to you. I'll pay twelve cents a bushel. Can't beat that, can ya? No, sir, ten cents is tops around here, but I treat my people right. Give me a day's work an' I'll pay you for it. You can count on that. Yes-sirree, that's money hanging from those trees, people. Think of it that way and you'll do just fine, by golly. I'll guaran-damn-tee it. Just keep after it and we'll all do just fine, believe me."

A woman in a long light-blue skirt smudged with dirt and a sleeveless blouse sat in the crook of one of the apricot trees and cradled an infant in her arms. Her blouse was discreetly unbuttoned and strands of blond lank hair hung loosely around her face as she gazed down at the baby greedily suckling her white breast. Her husband went to her then and still holding the ladder and bag, kissed her on the head before turning and walking into the orchards with the rest. She looked after him for a moment before dropping her eyes down onto the feeding infant.

Finally, the man issued a ladder and bag to the last picker and began to stride across the lawn toward the house.

"Hey, boy, you here to pick or just take in the sights?"

I quickly looked away from the woman and shrugged my shoulders.

"Excuse me, missus. Can I get you some lemonade or something? It's going to be a hot one today."

The woman looked up and smiled at the man. "Thank ya. That would be nice."

"How 'bout you, boy? You want to work or drink lemonade?"

The man winked at the woman.

"No, thanks. I'm just looking for my friend."

"Who's your friend?"

"His name's Fudgie Manzanares. He's about this tall and he's got black hair and brown skin. Have you seen him?"

"Yeah, I've seen him. And about a thousand of his relatives."

The man got a big charge out of himself, laughing heartily as he went on into the house. The woman held her baby over one shoulder now and she lightly bounced it up and down patting it on the back.

"What'd ya say his name was?"

"Fudgie Manzanares."

"How old?"

"Twelve."

"Does he have a sister?"

"Yeah, did you see him?"

"Well, a little while ago somebody like that asked Sonny, my husband, if we could give him and his sister a ride down to the highway but we just spent all night drivin' up here from Cortez."

"That's him. Did you see where he went?"

"I think him and his sister went off in that direction."

"Thanks."

I waded off through the orchard grass to find Fudgie and Carmalita. The peach tree branches grew together overhead, sunlight only breaking through in muted blotches. But the pickers higher up on the ladders bore the full intensity of the heat on their necks and faces even though most of them wore some kind of hat. They wore long-sleeved shirts to protect themselves from mosquitoes and gnats and the clinging itch of peach fuzz which, when mixed with sweat, could rub skin raw. Down below in the shadows, the air was cooler but smothering in the trapped humidity coming off the weeds. The mosquitoes were thicker there and as the workers congregated around big aluminum water jugs to drink and talk and compare the number of bushels they had picked, I could smell snatches of insect repellant about them.

Up and down the rows I went but could find no sign of Fudgie and Carmalita. On the outer edges of the orchard lay a field gone to seed, yellow butterflies flitting over it. At the far end, near the road, stood a fruit stand with peeling white paint. An old green truck with wooden slats on the sides was parked in front so I walked across the field to it. The front of the stand was boarded up and the man in the bib overalls whom I had spoken to earlier was on his knees, taking tools from a toolbox.

"Find your friend?"

"No."

"Well, I don't doubt it. This is a big orchard."

The man picked up a crowbar and a hammer and began to pry boards from the stand. Nails, rusty with age, squeaked as he loosed the lumber from the frame.

"Want a job, son?"

"I don't know."

"How old are you?"

"Ten an' a half goin' on eleven."

"I'll tell you what, I'll give you five bucks to help me tear down this fruit stand. Is it a deal?"

It took Franklin a month of watering and mowing one lawn to make five dollars. Five dollars was the most money I had ever been offered for anything.

"I want to but I kind of need to find my friend."

"Well, if you change your mind, get on back here after lunch. You know where I'll be. But I want to get it done this afternoon."

I turned and started down the trace of road beaten in the weeds toward the house, thinking of what I could buy with five dollars. And then I thought of Fudgie and how, maybe, if he helped me, we could earn enough money to help him and Carmalita get to Mexico. By the time I reached the yard, it was noon and people were sitting in the shade eating sandwiches from paper bags and lunch boxes. A few lay out under the apricot trees on the lawn and napped, hats over their faces and outstretched arms as pillows for their slumbering heads.

I walked up to the canal road where people were milling around watching a man change the oil on his truck. A few others were sitting in cars, the doors flung wide, listening to the radio. In the water, a group of wet glistening heads bobbed down the canal like buoys and then emerged farther down current attached to young brown bodies.

One of these bodies coming back up the canal road belonged to Fudgie Manzanares.

"I've been looking all over for you. Where'd you go? I thought maybe you already left."

He didn't answer and the other boys smiled and nudged each other and lifted their chins in my direction.

"Fudgie, what's wrong?"

"Fudgie, what's wrong?"

All the boys but Fudgie laughed at the boy who mimicked my question. He glanced back at them and they went quiet.

"What you wan', *gringo*?"

He stopped walking and looked at me for the first time.

"Fudgie, I thought we . . . nothin'."

I stepped to the side and looked after them as Fudgie and his friends pushed by me down the road. They laughed, elbowing and poking each other. With hoots and shouts and Fudgie leading the way, they all sprang back into the water.

I walked to the house and back down the road toward the old fruit stand. In the shade of a packing shed set off in a grove of globe willows sat a group of women and children. A hand shot up and I could see it was Carmalita's but I didn't wave back and I didn't stop.

When I arrived at the fruit stand, the man's truck was gone so I lifted myself up onto the dusty counter under the eaves. The sun was straight up and there was little shade. For a time I sat staring at the dirt before I noticed the man had left the crowbar leaning against a short stack of old lumber. I hopped off the counter and picked it up, feeling the weight and heat of the metal in my bare hand. And then, taking the end of the crowbar in both hands, I raised it over my shoulder and with a short quick step and long even swing, smashed the side of the fruit stand—as though I were Willie Mays hitting a baseball all the way to Venus.

* * *

"I guess we have a deal."

I hadn't heard him drive up. He startled me so I stopped swinging and wiped my face with the front of my shirt. My hands and arms tingled from the impact of the crowbar on wood.

"Well, it doesn't look too scientific but I guess it's pretty effective."

The man smiled at the hole in the side of the building.

"I was kind of hoping to save what lumber I could, but maybe this wood is too old and splintery, anyway."

He picked up a piece of board and examined it, turning it over in his hands.

"If you slide the flat of that crowbar under the siding and pry 'er, they'll come off a lot cleaner and you won't kill yourself in the process."

He took the crowbar and jammed it behind a broken board and pried out, pulling the wood and nail from the stud.

"See?"

He handed back the crowbar, smiled, and resumed work on the front. He was right. It was much easier his way. After the siding and roof were stripped away and piled into the back of his truck, only a dusty skeleton of two-by-fours remained upright.

"I think we can keep most of these, Pete. The rest of it I'll just save for smudging in the spring. I'll go unload the truck and you can start taking down those studs. Try not to splinter them and don't forget to take the nails out."

The man drove away as I began knocking the walls down and yanking the nails out with the claw end of the hammer. Dust and cobwebs clung to my hair and skin and covered my T-shirt and jeans, but it somehow felt good doing this in the heat and dust, doing this hard sweaty work.

When the man returned in the truck, Fudgie and Carmalita were sitting next to him.

"Hey, Pete. I found your friends for you."

They got out of the truck but I continued working, bent over pulling the nails out. Fudgie walked over to me while the man began stacking the two-by-fours into his truck bed and I could smell the canal still on him. Carmalita stayed near the truck, watching.

"Here, man, let me give you a hand."

Fudgie reached down to take the hammer from me, but I yanked it away.

"I don't need no help."

Fudgie stood silently by and watched me work and then went over to the man and said something to him. He returned with another hammer and began working beside me, pulling nails from the two-by-fours. Soon, Carmalita joined us, carrying the boards we had taken nails out of and placing them in the truck. We worked late into the afternoon until finally nothing remained but a bleached rectangular outline in the dirt.

"By golly, you boys did one heck of a job. Here's your five bucks I promised, Pete. And here's a couple of bucks for you and your sister. *Gracias.*"

The man got into his truck and drove away with the last load of two-by-fours.

"Here, Pete, you did mos' of the work, man. Take it."

Fudgie held out the two one-dollar bills.

"I got my money. Keep it. You'll need it for your trip."

I brushed off my pants and started across the field up to the canal road.

"Hey, Pete! Wait for us, man. We'll go with you."

Fudgie and Carmalita picked up two gunnysacks stuffed with their belongings and hurried after me.

"Me and Carmalita didn' find a ride, man. No one is leaving 'til all the peaches is picked. Maybe two weeks. I don' know what to do. Maybe we try again tomorrow. Hey, Pete, I'm sorry I call you a *gringo*, man."

"I thought you were my friend."

"I am you frien'."

"Then why didn't you talk to me?"

"The water in the canal is so dirty, man, it messed my eyes up. I didn' see it was you."

We were walking along the canal now and we both looked at the water and didn't say anything. Carmalita walked behind us with her gunnysack slung over her shoulder. It hadn't rained for a couple of days and the low light slanting through the water made the canal look cleaner than usual. I could even see reeds and moss waving green in the current along the edges. Suddenly, in what seemed like one fluid motion, Fudgie dropped his gunnysack, stripped off his clothes, and plunged headlong into the water with a loud yelp. Carmalita's face broke into a smile and her body shook silently with laughter as Fudgie surfaced on his back, spewing water up at us from his mouth. I laughed too and before I knew it we were floating down the canal, splashing each other as we went.

Soon we came to a green pipe that ran above the water from one side of the canal to the other. Floating under it, we each reached up and grabbed the metal flange. As we clung there, the current sweeping us out horizontally, I became suddenly aware of my body for there I was, folds of water gushing over my hips and between my legs.

"Hey, man, I go get our things."

Fudgie was crossing his hands over, pulling himself along the pipe toward the bank.

"Fudgie, wait! I'll go with ya!"

"No, man, stay here with Carmalita. I will be back pronto."

Fudgie pulled himself out of the water and started down the road hunched over and with short quick steps as though he were running on hot coals.

"Fudgie! My money's in my shoe!"

"Okay, Pete!"

Carmalita was stretched out beside me, her head back in the current and water streaming through her long black hair. Her eyes were closed and she was smiling. I looked at her small breasts, erect and round, and down her slender body to the thinly shadowed triangle between her legs. Except for Mary when we used to take baths together and Beanie Livers when I was five, I had never seen a girl before.

I let go of the flange then and swam to the bank where I huddled shivering in the reeds, arms wrapped around my knees, waiting for Fudgie to bring my clothes. Carmalita lifted her head finally and searched the water and bank before spotting me. Dusk was sifting down through the summer sky, but there was still light and I could just see Carmalita's round buttocks under the water as she swam over to me.

"Carmalita, maybe we oughta . . ."

Carmalita placed her fingertips to my lips. I stopped talking and she smiled. She closed her eyes then and moved her touch along my nose to my eyes and forehead and into my hair. She took my hand, brought it to her lips, and brushed my eyes closed with the back of her free hand. It was easier to touch her without looking and I could feel the smooth wet skin of her face against my fingers and feel hair damp against my hand. She stayed halfway in the water and as I squatted in the grass I could hear nothing but breath against my skin. I traced my hand down the length of hair along her ear, down the curve of her neck, down to where it soaked in the canal water. And through it, in what little current flowed through the reeds, I felt her nipple hard against the palm of my hand. I took my hand away and opened my eyes. Carmalita was still smiling, her large eyes looking at me. Then she turned her face upstream as though she had heard something.

"Pete! Where you go, man?"

"Over here, Fudgie!"

He walked down the embankment and handed us our clothes. I slipped into my pants and went with Fudgie back up to the road to wait for Carmalita.

"I thought you said Carmalita can't hear."

"She can't, man. She was born that way."

"But she heard you coming before I did."

Fudgie smiled and nodded.

"I know, man. She always do that. I tol' you before, she don' hear what we hear but she hear something else, something we don' hear."

"But how?"

"I don' know. Maybe she hear with her nose."

I began to laugh but Fudgie didn't smile.

"What do you mean?"

"'Member las' night? I tol' you we have to go to Mexico?"

"Yeah."

"Now Carmalita say no. We no have to go."

"You don't?"

Fudgie shook his head.

"Why?"

138

"I don' know. Her eyes tell me, man. I just look at her eyes."

Carmalita walked up to us, combing her long hair out in front before flipping it to one side. I stared at her eyes. They looked the same, happy. There was nothing but happiness in them.

We left the canal and walked down a ditch bank toward home. There was a faint bluish glow over the desert in the west and stars were just beginning to show in the east over the dark rim of Spruce Mesa. Fudgie and Carmalita walked me to our picket fence.

"See you tomorrow, man?"

I looked at Fudgie and nodded. "Yeah, see you tomorrow."

Fudgie slapped me on the side of my shoulder and he and Carmalita started off down the street. I opened the gate and was walking up the sidewalk when I remembered: my money. I quickly patted the front pocket of my shirt and turned my pants pockets inside out. How could he have? I stuck my hands in my back pockets but there was nothing there.

"Hey, Fudgie! What about my money?"

"What money, Pete?"

"You know, the money from the fruit stand."

"Oh, that. I put it in you pocket, man."

And then he and Carmalita hurried on. I frantically searched my front pants pockets again, watching them move farther away, but again found nothing. I couldn't believe it. First he called me gringo and now this. I had worked hard for that money and no Mexican kid was going to take it from me no matter how tough he was or how beautiful his sister.

I angrily started out the picket fence gate to go after them when I felt something rub against my chest. Reaching into my front shirt pocket, I felt crisp paper and pulled it out. I was relieved. I didn't want to fight Fudgie anyway. He probably would have killed me.

I walked back up the sidewalk to our house, unfolding the five-dollar bill from around two ones.

13

She took the five-dollar bill from my hand and held it to the kitchen light as if expecting to see through it. Abe Lincoln's crinkled face gazed back at her. She shook her head. "Where'd you get this?"

"A man at Morrison's Orchards give it to me 'cause I helped him tear down a shed."

Mrs. Henderson handed it back and looked down her nose at me like she did when threading one of her darning needles.

"Well, I'll be. You're a regular little breadwinner now, ain't ya? What do you think of your big brother here, Winnie?"

Erwin sat between us, holding a pencil and pinning a piece of notebook paper against the kitchen floor with his forearm. His tongue worked as furiously as his pencil as he drew squadrons of airplanes across the blue-ruled sky.

"He ain't my big brother. Franklin is."

"Excuse me, Mr. Big Stuff, but Pete here's your brother, too, you know." Erwin kept drawing.

"Well, I think it's wonderful. What are you going to do with all that money, Pete?"

"I don't know. Maybe save it."

I tucked the bill back into my jeans pocket with the other two dollars.

"Yep, I think you've got some of your pa in you, all right. He'd have done the same thing. He was a dandy, your pa was, and I'm betting you grow up just like him."

I looked down at Erwin's picture as the first leaden stream of fire streaked across the page from the wing of one airplane and exploded into another on the opposite side. The plane burned gray from the end of Erwin's busy pencil and a crashing sound came from between his tongue and the roof of his mouth.

"Who's fightin', Win?"

"The good guys are fightin' the bad guys."

"Who's winning?"

"I dunno. They just started."

Another missile of gray arched across the sheet and exploded. Mrs. Henderson peered down over Erwin's shoulder at the battle.

"Which ones are the good guys, Winnie?"

"I dunno. The ones who wins the other guys."

Mrs. Henderson shook her head and smiled.

"I wish the real world was like that, Winnie, because sometimes the good guys don't always win."

Erwin, frowning, looked up at Mrs. Henderson.

"Roy Rogers always wins and he's good. The Lone Ranger, too."

Erwin turned back to his paper, studying it. Then, holding the pencil as though it were a knife to stab with, he scribbled a tornado of circles over half the page. "See, these guys are the bad ones. They're all killed. And these ones are good guys."

Erwin held the paper up to Mrs. Henderson, pointing at the planes safe from the cloud of gray lead. "See?"

"You've got kind of a one-sided war goin' on there, don't you?"

Erwin put the paper down on the floor and folded it more or less in half. He then got up, stuffing the war picture in his back trousers pocket.

"Where's Mary?"

"That's a good question, Winnie. She hasn't been around all day, has she?"

"Huh-uh."

"That darn preacher has her so wrapped up in religion she barely knows where she is herself lately. Pete, why don't you take your little brother and go see if you can't find her."

"Okay."

"Maybe Franklin's seen her. He's over at the gas station."

We ran out the back into the carport and jumped on our bicycles, the screen door banging behind us.

"Don't stay out too long, though, ya hear? I'll have a treat waiting for you when you get back."

Night was coming sooner to Grand River now. The leaves on the big elm across the street in the vacant lot and on the aspens in old man Hillar's back yard rustled in the cool evening breeze, rustled like a thousand tiny hands applauding the approaching darkness.

By the time Erwin and I skidded into Dugan's gas station on our bicycles, the sign and pump lights were turned off and the car bays stood dark, the only light streaming out through the narrow windows of two big sliding garage doors. Mr. Dugan rolled out from underneath a '59 Oldsmobile just long enough to tell us that he had let Franklin off early. We jumped back on our bikes and headed toward City Park.

I let Erwin ride in front of me, short legs pumping like crazy and his small bullet-shaped head bobbing from side to side. His bike was a hand-me-down from Franklin that had passed through Mary and me before reaching him. It had only one speed and no coaster or brakes, so if you wanted to slow down or stop you had to lift one of your feet off the pedals and drag your toe along the ground or else find something soft, like sand or somebody's wet lawn, to run it through. The toe of Erwin's left shoe was always worn to the nub from this and his elbows and knees wore constant scabs. But like almost everything else in his six-year-old life, pain meant almost nothing to him in the face of fun.

Through pools of shadow we rode, through neighborhoods loud with hide-and-go-seek and tin can and tag, through older grown-up neighborhoods, quiet save a Grand River Eagles' ballgame heard from a radio through an open window, a pair of rockers creaking against wooden porches, the hiss of lawns being watered, and the constant chorus of crickets and through it all, not a sign of our sister.

"Now where?"

Erwin stood straddling his bike at the steps of the public swimming pool. City Park was empty except for a couple standing off to the side in the darkness near the mulberries, which hugged the chain-link pool fence.

"Beats me. We could probably ride around all night like this and not see nothin'."

Erwin laid his bike on its side and sat down on the steps. "I hate school."

"Me, too, Win. Everybody does."

"Why do we hafta go then?"

I swung my leg up over the bicycle seat and kicked the stand down, propping my bike upright. I sat down next to Erwin and watched the couple move deeper into the shadows.

"'Cause summer's almost over, Win."

"I know. But why can't we just play."

I shrugged. "I don't know. We just can't, that's all."

"Mom and Pa won't know."

"Win, don't say that."

"Why?"

"Just don't."

"But they won't."

I thought about this, listening to the chit-chit-chit of sprinkler heads and the chirp of crickets and then the sudden nearby explosion of a motorcycle kicked on and the explosion throttled into a buzz, building and backing off, building and backing off down Garrison Avenue until fading out of earshot.

"It don't matter if they know or not, Win."

"Why?"

"It just don't. School's school and we got to go."

"So? I hate Miss Sterling and I ain't gonna go."

"That was first grade, Win. You won't have to have her this year. You'll probably have Mrs. Kelly. She's nice."

"I still hate her."

Franklin, Mary, Erwin, and I had all had Miss Sterling for first grade and the truth was, we all truly hated her. Not only because she was strict, but because she was mean. And all four of us, even Franklin, had wet our pants in her class. But it was our little brother Erwin who had wet his with the most gusto.

Miss Sterling allowed her students to go to the bathroom only twice a day, before morning recess at ten and before afternoon recess at two. We would line up like soldiers in front of the miniature bathrooms—girls at one door, boys at the other—and squirm and fidget while we waited our turns. Miss Sterling would stand between the rows, carrying a ruler and wearing a scowl. If it took too long, she would rap the door with that ruler and I would flush the toilet whether I did anything or not. It was then, shortly after one of these nervous unfinished staring matches with myself, that I wet my pants. Erwin, though—it was widely known—had wet his not after, but during this process.

When Miss Sterling rapped her ruler for Erwin, he didn't flush the toilet as I had four years before. Instead, he pressed his tongue to the roof of his mouth or maybe tried tickling himself. When she rapped again, he remembered Franklin's trick to get him to wet his bed while sleeping, so he reached over to the sink and turned on the hot-water faucet and stuck his outstretched hand underneath to see if the water's warmth had the same magical impact on him awake as it did when he was asleep. Miss Sterling didn't rap her ruler a third time. She came barging into the bathroom to see what was keeping him just as Erwin was beginning to spout in the general direction of the toilet. At the sound of her coming, Erwin whirled around to turn the sink water off while letting his own run full-force, which was now aiming far from the porcelain target and was, instead, hitting a new one: Miss Sterling. In twenty-one years of teaching first-graders, Miss Sterling had never once come close to screaming and her shrill sound brought the next kid in line, Marvin Weaver, to push open the door and make a solemn pronouncement to his classmates who were pressing and craning in behind him:

"Lookie. E'win pottied on Miss Stewleen."

Franklin would tell this story over and over and every time, at the end, there could be heard a chorus of "Lookie! E'win pottied on Miss Stewleen!" echoing through our neighborhood. And no one who had Miss Sterling for first grade ever grew tired of hearing it. To all those who had suffered the same wet humiliation in Miss Sterling's class, it was a kind of adolescent justice which, until then, we could only dream about. Erwin was a hero and his tough reputation in our neighborhood was forever sealed with his christening of Miss Sterling's legs.

"I shoulda peed on her more."

"Yeah, and Pa would've spanked you harder than he did."

The lovers hugged and their dark outline looked like one, like one fat man with his arms crossed. I nudged Erwin with my elbow.

"Yuck. I hate girls."

The couple parted and there were two heads again—one shorter than the other—and they walked arm-in-arm out of the shadows of the mulberries toward the one lamplight that stood guard in front of the public swimming pool building.

"Let's go, Pete. I wanna go home."

Erwin stood and pulled his bike up off the damp grass. I followed while keeping my eyes on the couple walking across the park toward the street and the lamplight. Erwin pedaled down the sidewalk toward them. Barely aware of being on my bike, I coasted along behind him. The man's arm held tightly around the smaller figure's shoulder, bringing her close into his chest as they walked. We were coming up on them, the lamplight shining like a single flashlight directly off the man's gleaming bald head. Erwin was past them now, turning down 12th Street toward home. My head spun and my stomach drew up into itself and I shivered. The lovers walked right in front of me and I could hear their footsteps fall against the pavement. I edged slowly by, my bike wavering and, holding my breath, glanced back at them: a small red-haired women nestled up underneath a large bearded face.

"S'cuse me."

I pedaled as hard as I could, past Erwin, and didn't stop pedaling until I skidded into our carport, leaving a dark patch of rubber across the driveway. With one hand still holding the handlebars, I leaned against our house—my forehead flat against the crook of my elbow—and, gasping, waited for quiet to return to my pounding chest.

* * *

Mrs. Henderson took the cookie sheet out of the oven. The whoosh of warm air filled the kitchen with the rich aroma of cookie dough and melted chocolate chips.

"Where's Winnie?"

"He's coming."

"Did you see Franklin?"

"No. Mr. Dugan let him off early."

"My, that's different. I thought Dugan had his nose all out of joint."

"Naw, Mr. Dugan's all right."

Erwin soon showed up, his hair standing straight up from the wind. It so often stuck up that one summer we took to calling him Pine, short for porcupine.

"Why didn't ya wait for me?"

I shrugged. "I don't know."

Erwin went straight for the stove, plucked a cookie off the sheet, and quickly dropped it onto the palm of his other hand. He blew the heat from the ends of his fingers. "We didn't see her."

Mrs. Henderson scooped the cookies onto a plate using a spatula. She then placed round gobs of dough laced with chips on the cookie sheet and slid it back into the oven.

"Don't be bashful, Pete."

"No, thanks. I'm not hungry."

Mrs. Henderson gawked at me. "Peter Caviness, I have never knowed you to turn down a cookie. And a chocolate chip one, to boot."

I shrugged and sat down at the table with Erwin, who was already wolfing down his second cookie, his hands covered with chocolate. Mrs. Henderson set a glass of milk in front of him.

"How about some milk, Pete?"

"No, thanks."

Mrs. Henderson put the bottle of milk back into the refrigerator and sat back down with us.

"So where'd you two go?"

"Over to the park."

"See anything?"

"No, not really."

Erwin looked up from his fingers which were fishing in his milk for soggy cookie bits. "We saw two people kissin' in the bushes."

Mrs. Henderson smiled. "You did?"

"Yeah, it was yucky so we left. Huh, Pete?"

"Yeah, Win. It was real yucky."

"Winnie, quit playin' in your milk and drink it. It's gettin' past your bedtime, anyway."

"I wanna wait for Mary."

"Mary's not going to be home 'til late so get on in there and wash that chocolate off your jib and get to bed."

Erwin, his chin crinkling like a used paper sack, got up from the table and stalked down the hallway.

"That little dickens. He never gets upset unless it's about that big sister of his."

Mrs. Henderson rubbed her eyes and let out a sigh. The curls of her permanent were already loose and tangled and when her hands came down, her eyes seemed redder and older than I could ever remember.

"Is Mary going to be late?"

Mrs. Henderson got up and untied her apron string and laid the apron across the back of the chair. She walked over to the stove and peered down through the window of the oven.

"That last batch was a little too chewy. I think I'll leave these in a couple of minutes longer. My Milton hated nothing more than something that wasn't cooked clear through. Ate his eggs hard-boiled, his toast crispier than a saltine, and his bacon so burnt it half fell out of his mouth when he chomped down on it. And anything raw made him green around the gizzard. What a man."

Mrs. Henderson shook her head, staring down at the stove burners.

"Mrs. Henderson?"

"Another thing Milton hated was anything soft or gooey. Could be anything. Jello, syrup, pudding, taffy, even spaghetti if it wasn't cooked just right would send him right into the bathroom. My, my. But give him something he liked and he ate it 'til there was no tomorrow. How that man stayed so slim all those years I'll never know."

She looked over at me.

"Is Mary going to be coming home late, Mrs. Henderson?"

Mrs. Henderson came back over to the kitchen table and sat back down heavily. She folded her hands in her lap and shook her head.

"No, Petey. Mary's not going to be coming home late."

* * *

The house washed cool over my burning skin—the wooden steps, the painted plasterboard walls of the stairwell, the varnished handrail, the cement basement cool against my bare feet, against my tingling fingertips stretched before me. Through the workshop and into my room I walked, around the bed to the built-in drawers. Kneeling down, I felt the smooth curve of the metal handle, slid out the bottom drawer, and crawled into my secret hiding place.

The rectangle of gray where the drawer had been fell dimly across my middle. In the faint shadows I could make out the boards of the wall and across the underbelly of the staircase and along its runners. And as my eyes began to adjust, the faces tacked up around me began to appear like specters instead of sports heroes and just then I wanted to rid myself of them. I reached out and grabbed the handle, dragged the drawer up off my bedroom floor and back into place. I lay down on the mattress, stared into the perfect pitch-black darkness of the house my pa built until finally, I closed my eyes—though my eyes, just then, didn't know the difference.

"Aaahhhh!"

A piercing light struck me in the face and jerked my head up.

"What are you doing in there?"

Franklin clicked off the flashlight. I rubbed my eyes and propped up on my elbows and squinted at him as he pulled off his workshirt and T-shirt. He threw them in at me and they hit me in the face, the gasoline smell burning in my nostrils, mixing with some other smell. I shucked the shirts off me into the corner and crawled out his side of the stairwell.

"What were you doing in there? Spankin' your monkey?"

Franklin sat on his bed, kicking off his pants. He threw them back under the stairs with his shirts and slid his drawer into place.

"Was that a mattress I saw in there?"

I shrugged. Franklin shook his head and flopped onto his bed.

"Pete, you're going wacko. Don't you know there's probably spiders under there?"

Franklin grabbed a deck of baseball cards and began shuffling them on his bare stomach, his head propped on his pillow.

"Why weren't you at work?"

Franklin looked at me. "I had to go do something."

"What?"

"Why should I tell you?"

"Me and Win went looking for you."

"When?"

"Tonight."

"Tonight? What are you, my mother?"

Franklin stopped shuffling the cards. He looked over at me. "Sorry, Pete. I didn't mean . . ."

"I know."

Franklin put down the cards. He brought his hand up and rested his forearm across his forehead, shielding his eyes from the bedroom light. "I went to the church."

"The preacher's?"

"Yeah."

"See anything?"

Franklin nodded. "Yeah. Willie."

"Willie?"

"He was cleanin' out his office."

"How'd he get out of jail, Franklin?"

"Walked, I guess. They just let him go."

"Did Willie talk to you?"

"Yeah, a little. He said he was sorry." Franklin shook his head. "Willie said *he* was sorry."

I looked at the floor.

"Franklin, I didn't tell 'em Willie give us wine. I only said it started with a W, the name of the juice. I only wanted to tell them the truth, that Willie . . ."

"It's okay, Pete. Forget it. It doesn't matter. Willie's out now."

I took a deep breath and looked up at the ceiling. Willie was out. He was out of jail and now maybe he could go back to Wisconsin, back to his home where he grew up before Uncle Sam sent him away, before he came to Colorado and got a job at the church, before he even knew a Reverend Calloway ever existed. Willie could go home now.

"Did you see anybody else, Franklin. Was Mary there?"

"No. I don't know where she's at. Off with that preacher somewhere."

"I thought I saw them tonight."

Franklin sat up. "Where?"

"At City Park, but it wasn't them. Some big guy with a bald head and a beard was kissin' some lady about the size of Mary."

Franklin looked at me. "But it wasn't Mary, right?"

"No, she had red hair."

Franklin lay back down and stared at the ceiling for a long time. I sat on the edge of his bed and looked at the *Life Magazine* picture of Marilyn Monroe.

"Why'd she do it?"

"What?"

I nodded at the picture.

"I don't know. I guess she was sad."

I looked at the white-blond hair, the watery eyes, the puckered lips, the filmy white dress hiked up her leg.

"How could she be sad? She's too pretty. 'Member when she sang Happy Birthday to President Kennedy?"

Franklin got up and walked to the foot of the bed and stood next to me in front of the picture, staring. The smell of gas was about him even without his dirty clothes and that other smell was there, too.

"Yeah, I remember."

"She even talked pretty."

Franklin reached out and took the picture from the wall with a short tug. He gazed down, holding it between his hands.

"Pretty's not nothin', Pete. Just because somebody's pretty, don't mean they're happy."

"Like Mary?"

Franklin looked down at me and nodded.

"Yeah, like Mary."

Marilyn Monroe crinkled in Franklin's hands as he wadded the picture up and threw it across the room, the odor of gas flying with the sudden motion. He stood shaking, his fists and eyes clenched tight, his lower lip quivering. I closed my eyes and didn't move, didn't do anything. But the smell, the smell of my big brother standing next to me I suddenly recognized: cigarettes. Gasoline fumes and cigarette smoke.

"We gotta get Mary."

Franklin had stopped smoking. He hadn't smoked since Pa got mad at him over Della Mae Nagel and her underthings, since before summer when we were still in school and everything was the way it was supposed to be. Franklin unclenched his fists, rubbed his hands on his legs. I opened my eyes and looked up at my big brother. His lips were white and his red eyes stared down at me.

"Pete, we gotta get Mary."

Franklin hadn't smoked cigarettes since Lee Hooker was in town. Lee Hooker was in town. Lee Hooker.

I nodded. We had to get Mary.

* * *

Mrs. Henderson sat sleeping in the rocker, her head tilted way back and a loud snore rattling around somewhere between nose and throat before blowing out her gaping mouth. I tiptoed down the hallway so I wouldn't bother her and into Erwin and Mary's room. Mary's small ballerina night lamp cast a gray light onto the back of Erwin's head. He lay curled on his side. He had kicked his covers down around his feet so I pulled them up around his small shoulders, clicked off the lamp, and turned to leave.

"No."

Erwin rolled over across his back and onto his other side. I turned the light back on.

"You awake, Win?"

Erwin smacked his lips and brought a knuckle to his nose, rubbing it. His eyes were closed.

"Where's Mary?"

"She isn't back yet, Win."

Half of Erwin's face was buried in the pillow, his mouth slack and slightly open.

"Sleep, Winnie."

I pulled the blanket up under his ear.

"Momma?"

"No, Winnie. Go to sleep."

"Where's Momma?"

I patted him on the shoulder and tried to shush him back to sleep the way Mom used to. He rolled to his back, eyes blinking.

"Where's Momma, Pete?"

"Asleep, Win. Asleep with Pa."

"Oh."

He rubbed his eyes with the backs of his small fists.

"You gonna sleep with me?"

His hands came down again and rested on either side of him.

"Yeah, Win, I'll sleep with you."

Erwin's eyes closed and his head turned to the side. His breathing was soon regular and then heavy. I lay down next to him and put my arm across his small expanding chest and closed my eyes. Our house was quiet. Not even the hum of the refrigerator or the tick of the clock on the kitchen wall was there. I held my breath and listened, ears straining to hear something, anything. But there was nothing. Nothing except the rhythmic breathing of my little brother next to me. For that one night, that was all the sound there was—and it was enough.

14

Lee Hooker stood in the sunlight. And there was plenty of it splashing off the hoods and windshields of cars parked along Main Street. The unseasonal cool of the last week had vanished, replaced with feet-blistering sidewalks and glaring glass storefronts downtown. Hot weather had returned to Grand River as though it had never left and Lee Hooker stood in it, smoking a cigarette.

He wore a light green shirt with tails hanging down past the seat of his blue jeans and its top two buttons undone in front. The short sleeves were rolled high on his shoulders and in the sun, the long blue veins in his arms swelled. His was the body of a wrestler, short but lean and sinewy with these swollen veins running every which way, as prominent as the knotty muscles that stretched as tight as catgut over his stocky frame. Lee Hooker's body didn't just look as though it were molded from metal; it was molded from metal, having been beaten and bent since the age of eleven in the sweaty apprenticeship of his father's auto-body shop. After school and on Saturdays, Lee Hooker banged car fenders, puttied dings, and sanded surfaces smooth for the scrutiny of his father's artful eye, for the even sweep of his father's high-powered paint gun.

Mr. Hooker was a perfectionist—it could be seen from the clean lines and mirror finishes of his cars to the razor-white edges of his haircuts, from the spotless cement floor of his small cinder-block shop to the paunchless flat of his stomach—and in matters of work, he expected the same from his son. To Mr. Hooker work was everything, anything else secondary—up to and including education. He hadn't made it past fourth grade and his son's being in seventh was a source of pride. No matter that Lee Hooker had spent a good while there. Anything past elementary school was an added bonus and his father didn't care if Lee Hooker went any further or not. He did, however, care if Lee Hooker landed in the State Reformatory School in Buena Vista. Three months without his son's help hurt and he had to hire another body man to make up for it. The hot-wiring of a '55 Buick didn't make Mr. Hooker happy, either, although he had done the same thing a time or two, repainting the cars and selling them fast and cheap. But Mr. Hooker had never been caught. And the fact that his son had, made all the difference. Lee Hooker had failed and on this, the fourth day of his return, he was beginning to think Buena Vista wasn't such a bad place to be after all.

"Why aren't you workin' today, Lee? Did your pa give you the day off?"

Lee Hooker took a drag off his Lucky Strike and smiled thinly through the smoke curling back up into his nostrils. Franklin and I were standing with him on the street corner in front of F.W. Woolworth's. Earlier we had gone by Hooker's Auto Body where Mr. Hooker not only didn't answer our question about his son's whereabouts but wouldn't even acknowledge we were standing there, filling in each letter of a service order with white-fingered concentration.

"I took the day off."

A red welt sat over Lee Hooker's cheekbone under his left eye, causing the eye to twitch and blink.

"Oh."

Lee Hooker flicked the cigarette butt twirling into the gutter where it hissed in the water left over from the city street sweeper. He looked at me and then back at Franklin.

"So, Frankie, what's up?"

Franklin shrugged. No one dared call Franklin "Frankie" except Lee Hooker and from his lips it sounded okay.

"Not much."

"Not much? What, you go over to my old man's place just for kicks? I guess he's just a fun guy to be around, isn't he?"

Lee Hooker lightly ran the back of his hand over the welt.

"We just wanted to see what you were up to."

Lee Hooker took his pack of cigarettes from his front pocket, flipped it open, and shuffled one out toward Franklin. Franklin glanced over at me and shook his head.

"No, thanks."

Shutting the pack with a flick of his wrist, Lee Hooker slid the cigarettes back into his shirt pocket and stretched his arms above himself, yawning.

"What am I up to? I'm up to no good, least that's what everybody keeps telling me."

"What're you going to do today, Lee?"

"No plans. I was just thinking maybe I'd start the day off with a little silly talkin'. Come on."

Franklin followed Lee Hooker to the front entrance of F.W. Woolworth's. Lee Hooker opened the glass door, letting Franklin go in first, and then looked over at me.

"Well?"

I walked over, too, and Lee Hooker held the door for me as we entered the store together. Once inside, Lee Hooker suddenly stopped.

"Jesus H. Johnson."

Before us scurried kids of all sizes and shapes, most with mothers, some without, but all with hands full of Big Chief notebooks, Elmer's glue, pencils, pens, erasers, crayons, scissors, and every other kind of school supplies.

"Look at these little munchkins, Frankie. Can you believe it?"

"Yeah, school starts next week."

"Don't these ladies have nothin' better to do?"

Franklin laughed but then stopped. Lee Hooker's face went blank.

"They're housewives, Lee. This is their job."

"Oh."

Using both hands, Lee Hooker smoothed the greased wings of his hair into a tighter ducktail in back. The top of his hair was cropped short, as flat as Spruce Mesa. He smiled. "Housewives."

Lee Hooker had never had a mother, at least that he could remember. Actually, she could have been any one of several that moved at irregular intervals in and out of the one-bedroom apartment he shared with his father above the auto-body shop. Or she may not have been any of them at all, which he would have preferred given most of their appearances or personalities or drinking habits or about a hundred other things. A few had claimed to be his mother, though, and more than a few acted as if they were his mother, but none, he thought, actually was his mother and for this, he hated them all.

When his father would show up late from the bowling alley next door with another cheap imitation, Lee Hooker would just grunt and roll over on the fold-out couch, pulling the thin blanket around his ears. Unknown to the women, this was the most conversation they were ever going to have with him no matter how boozy their welcome or sweet their smile. For Lee Hooker, the painted, sequined, perfumed, laughing, loud, drunken companions of his father's and the women now herding children in and out of the aisles of F.W. Woolworth's had about as much in common as a Studebaker and a Corvette.

Franklin and I followed Lee Hooker wading through the crowd down a far aisle to the back, where there was more breathing room and where a box of balloons sat next to a big metal tank.

"Keep an eye out, Frankie."

Glancing around, Lee Hooker took a balloon and slipped the mouth of it over the protruding nipple at the top of the tank. "Clear?"

Franklin craned his neck and looked down the aisle. "Clear."

Lee Hooker slowly turned the handle and there was an abrupt hiss. The balloon squeaked full and shiny under the store's florescent lights. Pinching the mouth off between thumb and index finger, he removed the balloon from the nipple and held it out to Franklin. Franklin brought it to his mouth, inhaling as the helium filled his lungs.

"You dirty rat, I'll do to you what you did to my brother."

Lee Hooker and I snickered as Franklin handed back the half-empty balloon. Lee Hooker started to bring the balloon to his lips but then gave it to me. I breathed in the rest of the helium.

"You dirty rat, I'll do to you what you did to my sister."

Lee Hooker and Franklin covered their mouths, faces red with laughter. Lee Hooker refilled the balloon and then drew on it himself.

"We're off to see the wizard, the wonderful Wizard of Oz, we hear he is a wiz of a wiz if ever a wiz . . ."

Lee Hooker's voice trailed off to its normal speed and pitch so he inhaled the rest and held it. With his thumbs hooked into his front pockets and his elbows and knees bent out, Lee Hooker walked up and followed a kid about the size of Erwin back down the aisle toward Franklin and me.

"We represent the Lollypop Guild, the Lollypop Guild, the Lollypop Guild. We represent the Lollypop . . ."

The boy turned and giggled as the woman in front of him, his mother, wheeled around and grabbed her son by the elbow. Lee Hooker almost bumped into her.

"Hey, you. What are you doing?"

Lee Hooker took his thumbs out of his pockets and straightened up, smiling sheepishly out the side of his mouth. The woman was a good head-and-a-half taller and scowled down at him.

"I was welcoming him to Munchkinland. Ain't you ever seen *The Wizard of Oz?*"

Lee Hooker loved *The Wizard of Oz* almost as much as Franklin loved

Marilyn Monroe. He had seen it dozens of times and knew every song and line by heart, from the Wicked Witch of the West's "I'll get you, my pretty" to the Cowardly Lion's "put 'em up, put 'em up." And every time Lee Hooker recited something from it, everybody laughed when they were supposed to and listened quietly when they were supposed to whether they thought it was funny or well done or not. But at times it was difficult not to laugh even when Lee Hooker didn't want us to. To see the toughest kid in our neighborhood dressed in a black leather jacket and tight T-shirt singing "Some daaaay, ooover the rainnnnbow" was sometimes too much to bear even with the threat of having our noses rearranged. More than once, one of us would go running from the group, face reddened and buried in our hands, faking a nosebleed or an uncontrollable cough.

The woman in front of us, however, didn't understand this rule of etiquette for Lee Hooker and saw nothing funny or redeeming in a slick-haired teenager following her little boy down the aisle of F.W. Woolworth's, singing a song of welcome from Munchkinland.

"You better leave before I call the manager."

Lee Hooker's smile left his face. "Come on, I was just singin'. The kid liked it."

The woman grabbed her son by the shoulders and pulled him closer. The boy wasn't smiling now, either, and his lower lip began to tremble.

"Get away from us, you . . . you . . . you hooligan."

"Lady, come on. Look, you're scaring the kid."

The little boy began to cry.

"Don't cry, kid. Here, have some balloons."

Lee Hooker grabbed a fistful of balloons from the box behind him and stuffed them into the boy's pocket.

"Excuse me! Manager! Manager, could we get some help over here?"

The woman waved her arms at a man in a red smock who was dusting something on the next aisle. The man looked up at us.

"Let's go, Lee."

"Frankie, I didn't do nothin'."

The man stuck his feather duster in his back pocket and started toward us.

"Come on, Lee."

Franklin grabbed Lee Hooker by the arm and tried to pull him away. Lee Hooker jerked his arm free.

"Okay, okay. I'm comin'."

He looked back at the woman.

"Lady, you want to know something?" Lee Hooker stuck his finger in front of her nose. "You ain't a very good housewife."

The manager glared as we threaded our way through the crowd. Reaching the glass doors at the front, Lee Hooker stopped and looked back at the swarm of shoppers. "So this is what normal people do when they ain't workin'." Lee Hooker shook his head. "Jesus."

And then we were outside in the sunshine, running down Main Street.

* * *

"Can you believe that? All I did was sing a song to the little shit and his old lady goes loony tunes."

It was the hottest part of the day and the leaves on the elm trees that lined the streets hung limp, unstirred in the motionless air of what *The Grand River Sentinel* liked to call a scorcher. The paper's favorite illustration of this was an egg, sunny-side up, frying on a sidewalk just like the one we were walking down.

"Lee, uh . . ."

Lee Hooker took the Lucky Strikes from his pocket and tapped one out.

"Yeah, Frankie?"

"Can I ask you a favor?"

"Sure, Frankie. Anything. Shoot."

He stuck the cigarette between his lips and fished in his jeans pockets for his matches.

"Remember you said you'd like to see Mary sometime?"

Lee Hooker quit searching and took the cigarette from his mouth. He nodded.

"Yeah."

"Well, would you?"

We stopped. The downtown lunch hour was over and Lee Hooker looked down the empty street and didn't say anything. We had been walking around in a hurry for over an hour, going no place in particular but anxious to get there. Lee Hooker had been upset about the lady in F.W. Woolworth's but it wasn't the fuming anger that he usually showed when he lost his temper and had to hook somebody a couple of times to get their attention. No, it was more of a rough-edged sadness like he got when he would tell Franklin about his life at the auto-body shop with his father. His words were hard but they would come out soft, as though they didn't know what they were supposed to be. And now, with the mention of Mary, his words decided not to come out at all.

Lee Hooker nodded.

"Well, uh . . ." Franklin looked down at me and rubbed his palms on his pant legs.

I coughed and cleared my throat. "We don't know where she's at."

Lee Hooker stared at me, the faraway look in his eyes coming gradually to focus.

"What?"

"We don't know where she's at. Me an' Erwin went lookin' for her last night and couldn't find her anyplace."

"Yeah, and I haven't seen her, either, Lee."

Lee Hooker looked at Franklin, at me, and then back at Franklin.

"What? Wait a minute."

Lee Hooker shook his hands in front of him as though he had to first wipe the chalkboard of his mind clear.

"First, you ask me if I want to see Mary, like there's some question about that. Now, you're tellin' me you don't know where she's at? What is this, some kind of joke? I've already had enough jokes today, Frankie. What the hell are you tryin' to tell me?"

Franklin took a deep breath.

"Mary's missing. She didn't come home last night."

Grabbing him by the collar with both hands, Lee Hooker pulled Franklin down to eye level. "She's missing? You mean somebody kidnapped her?"

"Yeah, kinda."

"What do you mean kinda?"

Franklin's head jerked with every word out of Lee Hooker's mouth.

"What do you mean, Frankie? Talk to me!"

Lee Hooker stared into Franklin's eyes, his face drained white as the pearl handle of his pocketknife, and then finally let go. Franklin straightened up, pulling uneasily at his collar.

"Sorry, Frankie."

Lee Hooker threw his crumpled cigarette into the gutter and ran his fingers through the wings of his hair.

"I'm sorry. Now tell me what the hell's goin' on."

Franklin had already told Lee Hooker about our parents but he hadn't told him about the preacher or anything else. When Franklin did finish telling him, Lee Hooker pulled another cigarette from his pocket, lit it, and drew heavily.

"The way I see it, Frankie, this is just like *The Wizard of Oz.*"

Lee Hooker held his cigarette cupped in one hand and with the thumb and index finger of his other, picked a piece of tobacco from the end of his tongue.

"The beautiful young girl loses her family, goes off somewhere with a bunch of strangers and is tryin' to find her way back home. And instead of the Wicked Witch of the West, there's this preacher character. Now, the big question."

"What's that?"

Lee Hooker took another puff and blew the smoke to the side.

"Who's the wizard?"

The three of us got up, brushing grass from our pants. We had been sitting and talking in the shade of one of the big elms. Lee Hooker said very little while Franklin talked and now, after over an hour, he had heard enough.

"Where does this preacher guy live?"

"I don't know."

"I thought you said you went there after you got boozed up."

"Yeah, we did, but I was asleep most the time. Do you remember, Pete?"

"No, it was kinda dark. I think it was up by Rimrock Park."

"Boy, aren't you two a couple of Einsteins. Albert and his little brother, Eddie, here."

Lee Hooker shook his head, scratching it.

"Well, let's go by this church, then. Is it the one over on Grant?"

"Yeah, but I told you, I already went by there last night."

"Last night was last night, Frankie. Today is today. I'll meet you there in about twenty."

"Where you going, Lee?"

Lee Hooker took off down the street at a jog.

"Where's he going, Franklin?"

"Beats me."

* * *

When Franklin and I got to the First Pentecostal Church, Reverend Calloway's Lincoln Continental sat in the parking lot by itself. Organ music and singing rang out of the building so we walked around to the back, but the doors were locked and we couldn't see anything through the stained-glass windows. Finally, we returned to the front and sat on the steps, waiting for Lee Hooker. We didn't have to wait long.

"Cargo!"

Lee Hooker was coming down the street toward us a lot faster than he had left us a few minutes earlier.

"Whoa, Cargo! Whoa! Stop, boy! Heel! Heel!"

Cargo, one-hundred-and-thirty pounds of black manginess, forged straight ahead, his mouth stretched smiling and foaming, eyes held wide as he made a beeline for us, pulling Lee Hooker behind him at the end of a chain leash. Earlier, when we had gone to find Lee Hooker at Hooker's Auto Body, we hadn't had a chance to pat Cargo on the head and say hello because he was alseep, sprawled on the cool cement shop floor like an old bear rug. His tongue lolled slobbering to the side, the rhythmic heave of his rib cage and an occasional twitch of one massive paw indicative, no doubt, of the heroic pursuit of some ferocious beast in his dog dreams.

Lee Hooker said Cargo had shown up at the shop as a puppy and the only reason Mr. Hooker had agreed to keep him was because of the size of his paws. He would make a fearsome watchdog. But no one showed him how to be a watchdog, as though size alone were enough of a prerequisite. Mr. Hooker had spent a fortune stringing up a chain-link fence around his business within which Cargo could survey the premises at night and draw a bead on prowlers or aspiring burglars before sinking his long canines into their criminal hides.

At the time, Mr. Hooker didn't realize the only thing the playful pup with the great fondness for sleep was going to sink his teeth into was food. As Cargo grew bigger and bigger, so did his appetite. And to Mr. Hooker's growing concern, Cargo's down time became even more excessive, sleeping ten to twelve hours at a whack. After one-and-a-half years of eat and sleep, when Cargo had grown to almost full height, Mr. Hooker had enough. They had to get rid of the young dog. He was too damn expensive. And that was final.

Lee Hooker and his father loaded Cargo into the back of the tow truck, his tail thumping the side panels as if someone were beating a bongo drum, and drove him across town to the pound. After they returned, Lee Hooker went straight to their apartment while his father went back to another customer's crinkled fender. The rest of that day, to Mr. Hooker's surprise, more than one person asked him about the young black dog and he was finding it increasingly difficult to tell them. Finally, as the day drew long and thin, it dawned on him: the dog was popular. In fact, he may have even been drawing in customers. And Mr. Hooker, in turn, was feeling uneasily unpopular as he more and more quietly had to mumble the word pound to yet another client. So the next day, the big overgrown dog with the droopy eyes and endless appetite was back.

Lee Hooker jerked up to us in front of the church like a cowboy yanked from the stall by a Brahma bull. Cargo immediately lapped our faces before plopping down beside us. He rarely got a chance to go out and about, and in the excitement and heat of romping across town, he was pooped.

"Come on, Cargo. No you don't. Get up, boy. You're not going to crap out on me already." Lee Hooker jerked the chain up a couple of times and Cargo stood, panting and waving his great tail in the hot air.

"Why did you bring Cargo, Lee?"

"Thought he might come in handy. If I do anything stupid I'll be sent back to Buena Vista."

"Oh."

"Come on. Let's check this place out."

"We already did, Lee. It's locked. But that's the preacher's car over there."

"Man, a '62 Lincoln. I bet that baby cost a couple of bills."

We walked over to the car. Lee Hooker bent down cupping his hand over his eyes and peered inside.

"Look at that interior. All leather. So I guess this cat does have a special relationship with the Man, doesn't he?" Lee Hooker pointed skyward.

"Hey! Get away from that car!"

We looked up. Reverend Calloway's gleaming head emerged from a side door and he marched deliberately toward us. Using a handkerchief he snatched from his suit pocket, he rubbed the spot where Lee Hooker had been leaning.

"See, you've smudged this. I just had it waxed." He rubbed more vigorously. "Now move along, boys. We can't have you loitering in our parking lot."

The preacher flicked his pudgy hand to the side as he worked the car's finish. Franklin and I stood behind Lee Hooker, but Lee Hooker wasn't moving. Reverend Calloway stopped rubbing and looked down at us.

"Now, I'm asking you nice . . . Oh, my goodness! Frank Junior, Peter. What a surprise. I didn't realize it was you."

Cargo was sniffing the preacher's white shoes and the preacher glanced nervously down at him.

"My, he's certainly a big beast, isn't he?"

Lee Hooker stared up at the preacher, his muscular arms folded in front of him, one hand holding the end of Cargo's chain leash.

"Huge."

The preacher wiped his moist forehead with his handkerchief before folding it and sliding it back into his pocket.

"Well, I've been trying to get in touch with you boys. We're having a church picnic this Saturday and Mary and I were hoping you two could come join us."

Lee Hooker stood ramrod straight at the mention of Mary's name. Cargo continued to sniff Reverend Calloway's feet and his tail began to tap a steady beat against the side of the car.

"That is, if it's okay with Mrs. Henderson, of course."

"Gee, can I come, too?"

Lee Hooker slid his Lucky Strikes from his shirt pocket, took one, and thumped the end on the back of his other hand.

"Well, I suppose, young man. It's kind of for members only, but if you would like to come and have fellowship with us for a little while that would be just fine, I guess. You can't smoke, though."

"Maybe I could bring my old man, too. He loves a good picnic."

"Well, I don't know, uh . . ."

Cargo's nose had now moved away from the preacher's shoes to one of the back white-wall tires which, to the preacher's horror, was turning into a yellow-wall tire.

"Cargo, that ain't polite. Bad boy. Don't do that to the preacher's car." Lee Hooker tucked the end of Cargo's chain under his arm, lit his cigarette, and then looked up at Reverend Calloway. "Shoot, I'm sorry. Does this mean me and my old man can't come to your picnic?"

"Young man, you'll have to remove that dog from these premises, immediately. We can't have him running around here bespoiling the landscape."

Lee Hooker shook his head from side to side, grimacing. "I'm really sorry. He's such a dirty old mutt. And mean, too. I don't know why me and my old man keep him. If he's not out bespoilin' something, he's rippin' somebody open with those razor-sharp teeth."

Reverend Calloway shuffled back against his shiny red door.

"Now, don't go smudgin' your door there, sir. Wouldn't want to see you scratch the paint or anything. Those little nicks can be some of the toughest ones to get out."

Reverend Calloway, hugging the car with his backside, began edging away toward the church.

"Well, Frank Junior, Peter, you boys think about the picnic and let us know real soon. Okay?"

The church side door suddenly opened and Mary appeared. Lee Hooker started toward her but caught himself. Behind her was the guy at the funeral, the guy who had taken us down to the altar and had asked Willie to dim the lights.

"Mare!" Franklin and I waved. "Mary, over here!"

Mary looked up and waved back. She leaned back into the church and brought Erwin out by the hand and walked toward us.

"What's Win doing in there, Franklin?"

Franklin stared and didn't say anything.

"Hi."

"Hi, Mare."

She hugged me and then Franklin. "What are you guys doing here?"

Franklin looked down at Erwin. "We were going to ask you the same thing."

The preacher reached over to take Mary's arm but Lee Hooker jerked the chain and Cargo padded over and sat between them.

"Mary, you probably need to get back to choir practice, don't you?"

"No, we just finished, Reverend. I'll be in to help put things up in a minute."

Reverend Calloway stood stiffly, his head set straight ahead but his eyes cast downward as Cargo nosed the front of his suit pants. Lee Hooker smiled up at the preacher.

"Looks like he really likes you."

Reverend Calloway backed away along the car, but Cargo's muzzle stayed buried in his middle. Lee Hooker gave Cargo more slack.

"Do you have a dog, sir? I can always tell when Cargo smells another dog."

Reverend Calloway, now on his tiptoes, the heels of his hands braced against the car, inched higher until he was almost on the trunk. Mary turned just as Cargo jumped, his front paws slapping down on the trunk on either side of the preacher.

"Cargo! No!"

Mary shot a look at Lee Hooker so he tightened the leash, but Cargo wasn't budging. Cargo affectionately hugged the preacher, his dewclaws hooking into the preacher's sides. Reverend Calloway's head leaned back, his lips pursed, and his eyes clamped shut as though in the throes of religious fervor. Mary and Lee Hooker grabbed Cargo's collar at the same time and yanked him down.

"Are you okay, Reverend?"

Reverend Calloway didn't answer. He just wheeled around and hurried across the parking lot to the church, his face as red as the smudged finish of the Lincoln Continental.

Mary looked down at Cargo, who had rolled to his back hoping for a scratch.

"Bad boy, Cargo." She knelt and shook her finger in front of Cargo's nose. "That was a bad dog." Mary cupped her hands behind Cargo's ears and jiggled his large head. His tail swished between his legs and he licked Mary's forearm.

"Oh, Cargo, you haven't changed a bit." She ran her fingers through the fur on his chest and Cargo smiled, his tail emerging from between his legs and beating a cloud of dust from the parking lot.

"Except I think you've gotten even bigger."

Mary straightened up and looked at Lee Hooker, shaking her head.

"Hi, Lee."

"Hi."

He threw his cigarette on the pavement and ground it out with the pointed end of his black shoe.

"Nice to see you, again, Lee."

Lee Hooker nodded, staring down as he continued to mash the butt.

"Mary, where'd you go last night?"

Mary turned and looked at Franklin.

"Didn't Mrs. Henderson tell you? We had a youth group meeting at Reverend Calloway's and he was too tired to drive me home so I spent the night."

"Oh."

"Franklin, you didn't miss me, did you?"

Mary smiled and pinched Franklin in the side. Franklin turned away and looked down at Erwin.

"What are you doing here, Win? You going to join the preacher's church, too?"

Franklin lightly shoved Erwin in the chest.

"Don't."

"What's wrong, Winnie? You and the preacher buddies now?"

"Leave him alone, Franklin. What's wrong with you?" Mary walked over to Erwin and put her arm around him.

"What's wrong with me? What's wrong with you?"

"What do you mean?"

"What do I mean? I'll tell you what I mean."

Franklin stepped away and then turned back, facing Mary.

"Come on, Frankie. Take it easy." Lee Hooker put his hand on Franklin's shoulder but Franklin shrugged it off.

"Stay out of this, Lee."

Lee Hooker looked back down at his shoes, shaking his head.

"Ever since Mom and Pa, you've been doing nothin' but hangin' out with that fat preacher and now. . ."

"Don't talk about Reverend Calloway like that, Franklin. It's not respectful."

"I don't care. It's true! And now you bring Win over here and last night you stayed over at the preacher's house and, and . . ." Franklin stuffed his hands into his back jeans pockets. "What're you going to do next, Mary? Move in with him?"

Mary held Erwin in front of her and ran her hand over his hair. Erwin stood still like he used to do when Pa would line us up in the kitchen to give haircuts. But now it was Mary standing behind Erwin and, instead of Pa's comb, it was her fingers. Her eyes moved from the top of Erwin's head to Franklin.

"And what are you going to do, Franklin?"

They stared at each other and then Franklin looked away, wiping his mouth with the back of his hand. He shrugged. "I don't know."

Mary took a step and put her hand on Franklin's arm. "Mom and Dad are gone, Franklin. We've got to start . . ."

Franklin, still looking away, put his hand up to brush her away but let it drop to his side as he took a deep breath.

"Listen, Mary. I've been thinking. Maybe I won't go back to school."

"Franklin, you can't quit school."

"No, wait. Listen to me. I was thinkin' I could talk to Mr. Dugan and get on full-time. You and Win and Pete could keep going and I'd just work. Then in a couple of years, when I'm old enough to get my license, I could buy us a car and it would kind of be like it always was."

Mary looked down at Erwin, shaking her head. "It's a nice idea, Franklin, but it can't work."

"Sure it can."

"No, it can't. We're too young. They're not going to let us stay by ourselves, anyway."

"Who's not?"

"The authorities, Franklin. The people who help with this kind of thing."

"Well, we'll just have Mrs. Henderson stay with us until they will let us. Mrs. Henderson likes staying with us, Mare."

She smiled, shaking her head. "Franklin, Mrs. Henderson is getting too old and it's not fair to her. She's already raised her family and they probably wouldn't want her to."

"Who's this 'they' you keep talking about?"

"The people who run the foster homes and adoption agencies for kids who lose their parents. Kids like us."

Franklin stared silently at Mary and no one made a sound, not even Cargo. Franklin licked his lips.

"So how do you know all this stuff, Mary?"

Mary looked down at Erwin and then brought her eyes up to meet Franklin's.

"Because Reverend Calloway told me. He's already introduced me to them."

* * *

By the time we reached Hooker's Auto Body, it was still over ninety degrees and the sun was still a disk burning white above the horizon.

"Time to face the music. You boys wouldn't want to come in, would you?"

Lee Hooker smirked and took a drag off his last cigarette. For health reasons, he wouldn't allow himself more than a pack a day.

"Lee, why don't you come to the game with us. You're in trouble, anyhow, and it's the last one of the season."

"No. Baseball's not my bag, Frankie. I'll be okay. Maybe my old man's forgot I took the day off and is already slammin' 'em down at the bowling alley. Just so he don't call my probation officer and get me sent back up to Buena Vista and Julian."

"Julian? Who's Julian?"

After Mary had gone back into the church by herself—Franklin had insisted Erwin go with us—Lee Hooker had begun to talk again, partly because no one else would—no one else felt like it—and partly because he had to get something off his chest: the three months in Buena Vista with Julian Crine.

Julian Crine was from Denver. He was fifteen-years old, stood six-feet tall, and weighed well over two-hundred pounds. His head he kept shaved, eyebrows plucked. He didn't talk and he didn't do homework. But he did work. Julian Crine was the best worker in Buena Vista. Julian Crine was also disturbed.

No one knew exactly why Julian was at Buena Vista. He had been there longer than anyone could remember. Not even the reformatory staff could shed any light on it. But there were a lot of rumors and theories. One story had Julian holding his entire school hostage with nothing more than a sharpened butter knife. Another had him torturing his grandmother. Many heard he had killed his junior high school shop teacher for not letting Julian sweep the floor after class. Seeing Julian work on the end of a shovel or unload boxes behind the warehouse made this the most widely believed theory, but no one knew for sure. And no one dared ask him.

The day Lee Hooker showed up in the bus with three other new inmates, the reformatory had just received a shipment of new desks in a semitrailer. The four were sent directly over to help unload. Only Julian and a guard were there, but the guard was only supervising. Lee Hooker and the others started right in, sliding the heavy boxes to the back of the trailer and then hopping down to hoist them out on their shoulders before staggering into the warehouse. After about half done, only Julian and Lee Hooker remained standing. The other three were exhausted and told to go back to the dormitory.

As they worked into the night, the ends of Lee Hooker's fingers were blistered and the blisters were beginning to pop. His shoulder, where he had to rest the box, ached and felt raw. Even the backs of his legs throbbed from pushing and walking the desks into the warehouse. But like Lee Hooker, even Julian grew tired. At first, Julian didn't slide the boxes, Lee Hooker said. Unlike the others, he would just lift the desks up in front of him, walk to the end of the trailer, jump down, and carry them into the warehouse. But soon Julian began sliding desks, too.

Lee Hooker and Julian Crine hadn't said one word to each other up until they each carried a last desk into the warehouse. As the guard pulled the semitrailer doors shut, before escorting them over to their dormitories, Julian Crine, under his breath, had said, "Good work," and Lee Hooker had replied, "You, too."

Those were the only two words Lee Hooker heard from Julian Crine in his three months at Buena Vista. But, unfortunately, it was far from the last he saw of him. The one hour of free time each day found Julian Crine standing beside Lee Hooker no matter where he was or what he was doing. And stand was all that Julian Crine would do.

"At least it kept the other dirt-bags away from me. But it liked to drove me nuts."

"What would you do?"

"What could I do? He could've broke my neck with his pinkie. First I tried talkin' to him and then I just tried to ignore him." Lee Hooker shook his head. "The last thing I saw when I turned around to say good riddance to that place was Julian Crine standing there, starin' at the bus as we drove away."

He reached down, unhooked Cargo's leash, and scratched him behind the ear.

"Cargo doesn't talk much, either, but at least he wags his tail. Don't you, boy?"

Lee Hooker opened the gate of the chain-link fence and Cargo loped across the grounds toward the shop.

"Look at him. It's past his dinner time. My old man probably missed Cargo more than he did me."

Lee Hooker wound the chain leash around his hand.

"Don't worry too much about Mary, Frankie. She'll be okay. We'll make sure of it, one way or the other."

Franklin nodded.

"Catch you cats, later."

He shut the gate and we watched him walk across the dirt, sprinkled white with alkali, to the small cinder-block building. Reaching the front door, Lee Hooker took one last drag off his Lucky, flicked it to the side into the weeds, and disappeared.

15

"Just a minute."

Erwin and I waited in the shadows as Franklin, who was hanging by his fingers from the left-field fence, slowly pulled himself up and peered over into City Park Stadium.

"Ladies and gentleman, please rise for *The National Anthem*."

Franklin let go and dropped to the ground.

"Okay. Soon as the music starts. You first, Win."

"I know."

Franklin bent down and laced his fingers together as Erwin brought his foot up.

"Ohhh-oh . . . say . . . can . . . you . . . seeee . . ."

In one motion, Franklin lifted and Erwin stepped up and was atop the fence. He slid on over and I could hear him hit the ground on the other side and scamper away. Franklin and I looked at each other.

"You're getting pretty heavy. I don't know if I can do it."

I stepped past him and stared up at the dark green fence silhouetted against the stadium lights. Rubbing dirt on my hands and pulling my New York Yankees baseball cap tightly down, I stepped back and then jumped as high as I could but fell back into the shadows.

"Here. Get on my shoulders."

Franklin squatted and I straddled his head and he shakily stood. Grabbing the bottom of my sneakers, Franklin lifted until I could just reach the top. I swung my knee on over as Franklin struggled up and together we dropped to the other side.

"Hurry. Over this way."

We walked quickly along the fence until we were behind the bleachers where Erwin was waiting.

"What took ya?"

Franklin grabbed the bill of Erwin's cap and turned it around on his head as I followed them off into the crowd.

"O'er the laaand of the freee . . . and the hooome . . . of theee . . . braaaave."

We walked between the bleachers—the crowd applauding around us—and along the chain-link backstop. Standing behind home plate, we watched the Grand River Eagles' pitcher warm up his arm and the first baseman throw grounders to the other infielders.

"Good evening, ladies and gentlemen, and welcome to tonight's game between the Grand River Eagles and the Pueblo Merchants."

I peered over my shoulder at the people clapping and settling down into their seats and noticed a woman off to the side near the aisle lean over and whisper to her friend in front of her. They turned, the first lady pointing at us, and they both looked and slowly shook their heads. I nudged Franklin with my elbow, lifting my chin in their direction.

"Did they see us, Franklin? Did they see us sneakin' in?"

Franklin glanced over as the two whispered to their husbands beside them. Turning together, all four of them looked at us. It wasn't as though they were mad or disgusted or anything, just looking like you might look at a colorful rare bird in the zoo or fish in an aquarium. Franklin turned around.

"What are we going to do, Franklin? Are they going to tell the cops?"

Franklin just kept watching the teams warm up.

"That's not why they were looking at us. They don't care if we sneaked in or not."

"They don't? Well, do they know us then?"

Franklin took in a big breath and slowly let it out, not taking his eyes from the field. "No, they don't know us."

"They don't?"

Franklin shook his head.

"Then why're they staring at us, Franklin?"

Franklin lifted his cap and ran his fingers through his hair before fitting the cap tightly back into place, just like a third-base coach would have done giving signals. His eyes drifted from the field then and down at me.

"They don't know us, Pete. They know about us."

Franklin turned back to the Eagles and I, too, looked out through the backstop at the players. "Oh."

The Grand River Eagles wore pin-striped uniforms, like the Yankees', and dark blue caps with GR stitched across the front. Their opponents from

Pueblo had on white pants and jerseys with red lettering and matching caps and stockings. The Merchants milled around the visitors' dugout, stretching and spitting and working over their equipment with rosin, chalk, and saliva.

"Tonight's batting order for the Pueblo Merchants, batting first and playing shortstop . . ."

Beyond the right-field fence the parking lot was full and people continued to file into the bleachers even though it seemed not one more person could fit. Cardboard trays of soft drinks and snow-cones and hotdogs and boxes of popcorn were everywhere in the stands and there were baseball caps of every color. It seemed everybody in Grand River was here to watch this last game of the season.

"What side do you want to try, Win?"

"I dunno."

"Both teams are throwin' righties so maybe the third-base side."

Franklin and Erwin turned and started to walk away.

"Franklin?"

Franklin stopped and turned around. "Yeah?"

I gripped the chain-link backstop and acted as though I were still watching the teams warm up.

"Can't we stay here?"

"What?"

I could hear all the people behind me, talking and yelling and whistling.

"Can't we just stay here and watch the game?"

"Here?"

"Yeah."

"Course not. We've got to go shag fouls. Come on."

I heard Franklin and Erwin move away behind me but I continued to hug the backstop, staring out through the chain link at the diamond. The first batter for the Pueblo Merchants stepped to the plate and pawed a small hole in the batter's box with the toe of his back foot.

"Hey, Petey! Back up a ways, son!"

Pa raises his hand above him and motions me toward the right-field fence as the batter takes a couple of practice swings. I thump my fist into my mitt and then crouch down, placing my mitt and bare hand firmly on my knees.

"Come on, Jake! Hum 'er in there!"

My teammates in the infield begin their chatter. "Hey, batter! Hey, batter! Hey, batter, batter, batter . . ."

Jake, our pitcher, winds up and throws.

"Swing!"

"Thata boy, Jake. Good arm, good arm."

Pa stands in front of our bench clapping his hands. Jake has the ball again and I thump my fist a couple of more times into my mitt.

"Come on, Jake! You can do it!"

Behind the backstop Mom and Mary sit in the bleachers. Mom wears dark sunglasses and I can see the lenses gleam in the low light slanting over the fence behind me. Jake starts his wind-up.

"Hey, batter, batter, batter, batter . . . swing!"

The batter swings and the ball ticks off the bat and over our dugout. The catcher turns to get another baseball from the umpire.

"Way to go, Jake! Just one more, buddy!"

Jake rubs the ball and then gets ready for another wind-up. The team chatters. "Hey, batter, batter, batter, batter . . . swing!"

And the batter swings. There's a loud crack as the ball shoots off the bat. It sails high and I take a couple of shuffling steps forward and then a couple sideways toward the right-field line, watching the ball jiggle against the sky.

"You got it, Petey!"

I prop the mitt Mom and Pa gave me for my birthday out in front, looking over its webbing, the ball growing as it falls toward me.

"It's all yours, Pete!"

The ball gets larger and larger as I stab my hand upward and feel the ball strike the leather webbing at the top of the glove. I turn around, hearing nothing, and see the ball bounce off the fence.

"Go! Go!"

I run back and leap on it, grabbing the ball with my bare hand, and throw it as hard as I can. The runner rounds third as our second baseman catches my throw and whirls around and throws it to the catcher. But it's too late. The umpire spreads his arms.

The other team jumps up and down around home plate as I walk slowly across the field to our bench. Jake sits with his head lowered, looking at the dirt. Our second baseman throws his mitt against the back of the bench and plops down. The people are standing in the bleachers now, but I don't look over there. I don't look anywhere.

"Okay, guys, let's bag up the equipment. We'll get 'em next time."

I'm the last one in and Pa glances up from his clipboard.

"Two hands, Pete. Remember what I told you? You got to get two hands up there."

Pa uses the clipboard as a glove and holds it out in front of him with his other hand. I nod and Pa tries to smile. "We'll get 'em next time."

I tuck my mitt under my arm and walk over to the fence where Mom and Mary wait. Mom hugs me. "Nice try, Petey. You almost had it."

Mary hugs me, too, as I walk by them away from the field, away from my teammates toward the car and home.

"Pete! Hey, Pete! Come on! What're you doin'?"

I turned around, facing the crowd, but I tried not to look at them because I knew they were staring at me and thought if our eyes didn't meet, maybe they'd stop. Franklin waved his hand. "Get over here!"

Looking down, I turned away from the backstop and walked over to where Franklin was standing between the bleachers.

"What the heck are you doin', Pete? The game started and you're standin' over there like the Statue of Liberty. Let's go."

I followed him out behind the bleachers where kids were wrestling and shoving and chasing after each other on the grass. Some of the bigger boys, around Franklin's age or older, stood in groups talking with girls who wore shorts and oversized letter-jackets or sweatshirts.

"See that guy over there, Pete?"

A tall guy about college age wearing a flat-top, T-shirt, and shorts with a canvas apron tied around his waist—like the one Pa sometimes put his nails into—stood in the middle of the grass. The other kids spread out around him.

"That's the Eagles' shagger. It's his job to get all the foul balls back."

From behind the wooden bleachers along the third-base foul line, the game could hardly be seen. But that didn't seem to matter to us because another game, every bit as important, was just getting started back here.

Franklin stood next to the green fence with Erwin crouched about twenty feet in front of him. I joined the rest of the kids in closer near the shagger. Eddie Livers, Rickie Livers' youngest brother, knelt on one grass-stained knee nearby, the bottom of his bare foot black with summer. Buddy Phillips was there, too, standing off to the side talking to two older guys.

"Pete!"

Franklin motioned me away from the shagger, waving me farther down the third-base line toward left field. From here I could see the playing field better. The bullpen was in front of me and I could watch the Eagles' relief pitchers loosen up.

The first foul ball came off the bat with a hollow crack as though the bat had splintered and arced high above the lights, landing just out of the grasp of the catcher into the crowd on the other side of the backstop. I looked back over at Franklin. If we hadn't moved from where we were watching the Eagles warm up, we'd probably already have a ball. But then the thought of the crowd staring at me crept in and I decided it wouldn't have been worth a zillion baseballs.

The batter flipped the bat in his hand and tapped its handle on the plate to see if it was broken. Satisfied it was okay, he dug in with his cleats and on the very next pitch, swung, lifting the ball foul again, this time over the stands and into the middle of Gateway Avenue where it bounded across the street. Every kid in sight moved like a wave toward the fence but it was my little brother Erwin whose head disappeared over it first. Franklin had catapulted him over in the same way he had helped him sneak in.

Franklin sat on the fence, watching, and then like magic, jumped down with the baseball in his hand. He jogged it over to the shagger and flipped it to him. The shagger reached into his apron and handed him a dime. I could see Franklin put it in his pocket as he returned to the fence to help Erwin back over.

The kids returned to the grassy area except for a few who stayed on the fence. Franklin noticed them, too, and boosted Erwin back up.

The Eagles turned the game into a rout in the sixth inning, scoring eight more runs and spraying the ball everywhere their opponents weren't. The team from Pueblo helped them, too, booting the ball every chance they got or throwing it over their teammates' heads. The crowd grew restless and more and more kids trickled out behind the bleachers to go find something more entertaining.

By the seventh the score was 13 to 1, and Franklin and Erwin had teamed up for seven more dimes. The crowd had greatly thinned by then and those who remained sat like stones, bored, or milled around chatting with one another, their children roughhousing on the grass behind the stands.

The Pueblo Merchants were up for the last time and I stayed just outside left field near the foul line, drawing names in the red dirt with the toe of my sneakers. After writing everybody's name I could think of, including my own, I smoothed the dirt over using the edge of my foot and began drawing a tribute to Marilyn Monroe. I had finished toeing in her outline and was making streaks of hair around her head when a line-drive foul ball skipped right in front of me, taking Marilyn's left shoulder with it.

I heard Franklin and Erwin yell my name and, as I turned to run, heard what sounded like the entire crowd thundering down behind me. Leaving Marilyn Monroe there in the dust, I took out after the ball. It rolled all the way to the fence and hopped as it came off the wooden slats. I dived for it. There was a thud and a great weight pressed down on me, a tangle of elbows, hips, and knees. The ball lay underneath, nestled into my belly. I clutched at it with both hands. When the weight lifted I got up, brushing the dirt from my shirt and pants.

In the distance through the cloud of dust, I could see Franklin and Erwin perched on the fence, craning their necks. Many of the guys were already walking away. I held the baseball in my hands, ran my fingers over its stitching and glossy slick leather and over the little scuff mark where the bat had struck. I rubbed it like a real pitcher would and then lifted it up against the stadium lights for Franklin and Erwin to see—and then it disappeared.

"You never learn, Caviness."

I turned around to the grinning face of Rickie Livers. His little brother Eddie stood behind him.

"Hey, that's mine."

"It's yours?"

Rickie Livers glanced around, eyes wide with mock wonder, and looked at Eddie.

"Funny, I thought it was the Eagles'. Didn't you think it was the Eagles' ball, Eddie? Caviness here thinks it's his."

Eddie Livers gummed a grin. I glanced over at the fence for Franklin and Erwin but they were gone.

"Come on, Rickie, I got it first."

"Well, if you want it so bad, why don't you just take it?"

Rickie Livers tossed it in the air between us a couple of times.

"You ain't so tough without that little spic around, are ya, Peter-head?"

"I got it first, Rickie. Now give it back."

"Caviness, you'll just never learn."

Rickie Livers held the ball up to his face as though it were an apple and then pretended to take a big bite, opening and closing his mouth as if chewing. He thrust it out to me.

"Wanna bite, Peter-head?"

I reached for the ball but he quickly flipped it to his little brother and in the same motion, latched onto my fingers with his own, lacing them together and bending mine backward.

"Not quite fast enough, huh, Peter-head. Do you still want it or is Eddie a little too tough for you, too?"

Eddie Livers grinned as his big brother bent my fingers farther back, dropping me to my knees.

"This is what you get, Caviness, for tag-teamin' me with that little spic."

He kept bending my fingers and I could feel sweat popping out over my forehead.

"What's wrong, Peter-head, cat got your tongue?"

"Let's have the ball, pal. Game's almost over."

Rickie Livers turned around and looked up at the Eagles' shagger. He released my fingers.

"Give me the dime, first."

The shagger reached into his apron and handed a dime to Rickie Livers, taking the baseball from Eddie at the same time, and then jogged off toward the Eagles' dugout.

"Look, Eddie. We're rich. Ain't that nice of Peter-head to help us out?"

Rickie and Eddie Livers stared at me as I pressed my fingers against my ribs under my other arm.

"Oh, darn, Eddie. I think Caviness hurt his fingers when he dove for the ball. Maybe Peter-head should run on home and have his mommy kiss it and make it all better."

Eddie Livers laughed as they shoved by me and headed toward the crowd moving through the exits. I got up and brushed my pants off with my good hand. Squeezing my fingers under my other arm, I again looked over at the fence where Franklin and Erwin had been but they had left without me.

The last Pueblo batter struck out and the game was over. The few people who hadn't already left stood up and collected their things. Bat boys for both teams began bagging up equipment and the players tramped out of the dugouts, talking and shaking hands. The American flag, already pulled down in center field, was being folded by a pair of Boy Scouts as the field crew hustled out to collect the bases and to rake and hose down the infield one last time.

The stadium was mostly quiet now. The only sound was the electrical hum high atop the wooden poles, the lights aswarm with moths, millers, and mayflies lit white against the black sky. The announcer and the radio people in the broadcast booth perched above the grandstand were packing up their equipment while the last few fans filed through the turnstiles out into the parking lot below.

Sitting in the first row behind home plate, I watched the last few players disappear into the locker rooms, their metal cleats clicking against the concrete walk. The ground crew finished raking the infield and all that remained were scattered cups and popcorn boxes and blue programs left between the wooden benches. But these disappeared, too, with the blink of stadium lights going off in pairs around the baseball field. The Eagles had won their last game of the season and now it seemed everyone in Grand River had gone home. Everyone except me.

* * *

My fingers throbbed. I opened my eyes. Pinpoints of light volleyed down through the moonless sky, reflecting dimly off the line of cottonwoods over the left-field fence, off the leaves turning and fluttering in the late August air. I sat up in the loose dirt across home plate, pressing my fingers under my arm, and rocked back and forth.

"That was some pretty fancy base running."

I looked around and there stood Willie, leaning against the visitor's dugout. He walked over to me. "Let me help you up there, Pete. What'd you do to your hand? Hurt it sliding in there?"

"Yeah, I guess so."

"Well, that was one Olympian effort, I must say. Were you safe or out? I couldn't tell from where I was sitting."

Willie smiled. I brushed off my pants and shirt.

"I was safe but he called me out."

"Who did?"

"The umpire."

"Oh, of course. The umpire."

Willie shook his head and clucked his tongue. "Umpires and politicians, give them a little sayso and they always say 'no' when they should've said 'yes' and always say 'yes' when they should've said 'no.' Here, let me take a look at that."

Willie took me by the wrist with one of his large hands and bent down, holding my hand in front of his face. He studied my fingers.

"You really sprained these. Must have jammed them in the dirt."

"Yeah."

"These three look a little swollen around the knuckles. Can you move them?"

I wiggled my fingers. Willie released my wrist and straightened back up.

"When you get home, put some ice on them and that'll keep the swelling down."

Willie smiled and then looked around the empty stadium. "Well, another baseball season under the old belt. I guess I better be moseying on home now. It's past my bedtime. Can I give you a lift?"

"Naw, I can walk."

"Are you sure?"

"Yeah."

"Suit yourself."

Willie winked and walked toward the exit gate to the side of the backstop.

"Hey, Willie?"

Willie stopped and turned around. "Yeah, Pete."

I kicked the loose dirt around the batter's box with my sneaker. "Do you think the Yankees are going to win the World Series this year?"

Willie chuckled softly. "Yes, Pete, I believe they are. Don't they always?"

He walked back over to me. "I didn't know you were such a baseball fan, Pete. Seeing your cap there, I guess I should have known."

"Yeah, me and Franklin used to like the Yankees. They always win."

"Yes, they're a dandy, all right. Which team do you like now?"

I shrugged. "I think Franklin still likes the Yankees but I'm gettin' kind of tired of 'em."

"They are a rather predictable lot, aren't they? Seems all they know how to do is win. It's a heck of a note. Me, I'm rather partial to the underdog, the buffoon. This Pueblo team tonight was right up my alley. Offer me a Prince Hal and I'll take a Falstaff every time."

"My pa used to drink those."

Willie smiled. "I've been known to tip a few back, myself, on occasion. Where is Franklin, by the way, Pete? I thought I saw the three of you come in together."

I shrugged. "I guess home. Him and Erwin got eight dimes tonight shaggin' balls."

"Well, that's pretty good. That must be quite an enterprise back there. I've watched those entrepreneurial types hustling after baseballs all summer long but never realized there was real money in it. Shoot, had I known that, I may have been back there myself."

"Franklin and Win are real good at it. This is the first time I've helped 'em, though."

Willie looked down at me, one eyebrow raised. "You do strike me as a more serious student of the game. Am I right?"

"Yeah, I guess."

Willie patted me on the back. "I knew we had a lot in common, Pete. But I'm like you, I get kind of tired of the teams that always win. The Eagles are getting that way, too. Anymore, I just like to come to these games to get the hometown folks riled up a bit. Nothing better than to sit among the fans and root for the other team. Their zeal gets my hemoglobin goin', makes me feel young, again."

Willie smiled. "Sure I can't give you a ride home, Pete. I've got my trusty black steed parked right over there beyond the front gate. It'd be my honor."

I followed Willie through the opening in the backstop and out around the grandstands to the front gate. An old black Chevy pickup sat by itself in the parking lot.

"This is Rocinante. Rocinante, meet Pete." Willie banged on the hood with his hand.

"She ain't pretty, but she's a goer."

He reached through the window on the passenger's side and opened the door for me. I jumped in and Willie went around and got in the driver's side, slamming the door behind him. His back arched and legs straightened as he fished for the keys in his front jeans pocket. Willie wore cowboy boots and a light blue shirt like the ones Pa used to wear—work shirts. His shirt and jeans, faded to the same light-blue color, were pressed clean with sharp creases down the sleeves and pant legs. Willie's hair was parted on one side and the hint of a younger man's hair tonic was about him. Willie wrestled the keys out of his pocket and pumped the gas pedal. He inserted the key into the ignition and turned it. The pickup coughed and sputtered but didn't catch.

"She's a hard one to wake up, Pete, but once she's up and at 'em . . ."

Willie pumped his leg again, the pedal squeaking and thumping down onto the floorboard. Willie revved the engine and let it idle.

"Music for the multitudes. Ah, what a sweet enchanting voice this little hussy has once she's finished clearing her throat."

Willie smacked his lips in the same way he had when drinking wine at the church. His tall lean figure hunkered over the steering wheel, one thick wrist draped over the top of it as we stared out through the cracked windshield across the parking lot toward the public swimming pool, waiting for the engine to warm.

The pickup smelled of pipe tobacco, like Willie's office, and the scent mingled with exhaust the truck belched. The floorboard was covered with magazines, spent wooden matches, rags, and empty beer cans. Strewn across the dusty dashboard were road maps, a pair of sunglasses, and a small notebook with a pencil lying on top. And there, cradled in the ashtray that opened from the dash, sat Willie's pipe.

"Willie?"

"Yeah, Pete."

"Willie, I didn't tell 'em."

"I know, Pete."

"I just said it started with a W, the stuff . . ."

"I know what you meant, Pete. Welches or wine, it doesn't matter. Time is the only thing that separates the two of them, anyway."

"We took it, too."

Willie pressed the clutch in, grabbed the shiny black knob, and eased the truck into gear.

"We took the wine, Willie. Me and Franklin."

Willie looked over at me and nodded. "I know you did, Pete. Franklin told me. It's okay." He turned right and we went around the swimming pool and along the mulberry bushes where Erwin and I had seen the two lovers.

"And you know why it's okay, Pete?"

I shook my head.

"Because you both told me, you spoke the truth and that makes all the difference in the world. Now which way do we go?"

"I guess that way, down 12th is the fastest."

The night air blew in through the door windows, bracing our faces as the old pickup moved down the quiet Grand River streets.

"How'd you get out, Willie?"

"Of the crossbar motel?"

Willie pulled the truck up to a stop sign. He turned to me in the seat, his right arm resting along the back.

"Well, Pete, you know that Sergeant Nichols?"

"Yeah."

"Well, the funniest thing. I told him the truth, and you know what?"

"What?"

"The darn guy believed me." Willie smiled at me, his eyes sparkling from the streetlights shining through the windshield.

"So they let you go?"

"Scot-free. Imagine that."

Willie reached over and ruffled my hair with his large hand. "But freedom's nothing, Pete, if you're not free up here in your old noggin." Willie thumped his middle finger against his temple. "We're supposed to have the freest people in the world here in the good old U.S. of A., but I sure don't see too many of 'em."

"You don't?"

"Nope."

"Where are they, Willie?"

"Well, they're kind of in a jail, too, Pete."

"In jail? Really?"

Willie nodded. "Their bodies aren't but their minds are and some of them will never be free. They're in prison over making money, Pete, and sometimes they don't care how they make that money. That's why it was so good to meet an honest hardworking man like Sergeant Nichols. I've been working for Reverend Calloway for so long that I'd almost forgotten there are still honest people out there."

"You mean the preacher isn't honest, Willie?"

Willie glanced at me as he shifted into gear and we pulled away from the stop sign.

"If honesty, Pete, is believing that everything that comes out of your mouth is the gospel truth then, yes, maybe the preacher is honest. But, Pete, just saying something is so, whether you believe it or not, doesn't make it any more true than if you didn't say anything at all. Things either are or they aren't and all the words in the world can't change the truth. Understand?"

"I think so."

Willie rubbed under his jaw and over his clean-shaven cheek with one hand. "You told Sergeant Nichols that what I gave you to drink started with a W. Right?"

"Yeah."

"Well, Reverend Calloway thought it was wine. In fact, there was nothing in the world we could have said to him that would have changed his mind about that. You know why?"

I shook my head.

"Because he wanted it to be wine."

Willie turned onto our street, the headlights sweeping out across old man Hillar's house on the corner and then lighting up the gutter and our picket fence.

"But it was Welch's, Willie."

"Yes, Pete, it was Welch's. Is this it?"

"Yeah."

He pulled the pickup over to the curb and stopped, then turned and grabbed me by the shoulders, squaring me in front of him. "And one more thing, Pete. Don't worry any more about getting drunk. It was a mistake and you've suffered enough for it. Okay?"

I nodded. Willie squeezed my shoulders and let go.

"And besides, I don't think you and Franklin are the first ones that ever took a little nip at church. In fact, I think you can almost be sure of that."

Willie winked and we smiled at each other.

"Now get on with you, Pete, and be a good lad."

I jumped out of Willie's truck and slammed the door.

"Hey, Willie?"

"Yeah, Pete?"

I looked down at the curb where I was standing next to Willie's truck.

"Do you believe in wizards?"

"Wizards?"

"Yeah. Lee Hooker says there's a wizard, like in *The Wizard of Oz*, but he doesn't know who it is."

Willie scratched his head, his other hand resting on top the steering wheel. "Well, I can't say for sure, Pete, but usually where there's a wizard, there's somebody behind a curtain pulling a bunch of strings."

"Like in the movie?"

"Yeah, Pete, like in the movie."

"Thanks, Willie. I thought maybe you're the wizard."

Willie laughed. "I am, Pete. I'm the wizard of toilet bowls and dirty floors." He shoved his truck into gear. "Take care of yourself, Pete."

"Willie, when can I see you, again?"

"I'm leaving in the morning but I'll be back some day."

Willie revved the engine and he pulled away from the curb and started down the street. "So long, Pete, and tell Franklin good-bye."

"Where you goin', Willie!?!"

He hung his head out the window, his white hair blowing back across his forehead as white as a cloud against blue summer sky. "Wisconsin!"

His arm shot out the window and waved as his old black truck eased down the street and around the corner. Willie was gone. He was going home.

I opened the gate and walked up the sidewalk to the front door. The house was dark, not a single light anywhere. Finding the front door locked, I walked around to the back but it was locked, too. Franklin had forgotten to leave it open for me. And then I saw the white piece of paper stuck in the screen door:

Pete,
My key won't open the door. Me and Win are at Mrs. Henderson's.
                                        Franklin

16

"Look at here."

Mrs. Henderson thrust *Life Magazine* in front of Joe Lucero who sat beside her on the dark green crushed-velour sofa. Pincushion pillows surrounded them and a pink poodle crocheted around a Pepsi Cola bottle stood stiff-legged nearby on the floor.

"I swear they're all the same. Read that. Right there."

The page snapped as Mrs. Henderson thumped it with her short arthritic index finger. She squinted, leaning in toward the printed page and against Joe, who was now as much under her as next to her. Behind them stood a lacquered saguaro lamp Mrs. Henderson had bought in Arizona with her husband during their last vacation together; a panoramic view of the desert at sunset, lit by the light bulb within, stretched around the lamp shade.

"Go ahead, Mr. Lucero. Read it out loud."

"Please, call me Joe."

Mrs. Henderson fumbled with her knitting glasses before perching them on the end of her wrinkled nose.

"See here, calls him a ringmaster. A ringmaster! And that's being polite. Oughta call him a huckster 'cause that's exactly what he is, just like Calloway. Anybody called Oral . . . humph. But the magazine don't want to get sued or nothin', but you know all about that sort of thing, don't ya?"

Mrs. Henderson waved her hand once above her head as though waving away a fly that was keeping her from something important.

"Anyways, let's see here, says he healed a stiff back, deafness, alcoholism, paralyzed face, injured foot, paralysis. What's a paralyzed face, anyway?"

She snatched off her glasses and intently looked up at Joe. He smiled broadly back, a frozen face the perfect answer. They stared motionless at each other and then Mrs. Henderson reared back, her arms flying upward, and then pitched forward, slapping Joe on his thigh, her funny bone shaken loose from deep inside. Joe laughed, too, and patted Mrs. Henderson on the back.

"I'm sorry, Mrs. Henderson. I just can't get serious about a kook like this."

"I swear! My Milton used to tell me how funny your daddy was but I had no idea!"

As she wiped at her eyes with the end of her apron, I decided this was as good a time as any to come in off the porch. The screen door creaked and I stepped inside.

"There's that little dickens."

Mrs. Henderson struggled upright, her face drawn back into a pinched seriousness. She came and pulled me to her, red eyes studying me like they always did. As she sat me in her rocker and plopped back down next to Joe directly across from me, I wondered if her eyes were red from worry or laughter or from the sour vinegar smell of boiled cabbage and corned beef that swelled her house. No matter what meal Mrs. Henderson cooked, whether it was fried chicken with potatoes and gravy or a single fried egg, her house seemed to smell of it. The plastered walls, the wooden floors, even the sofa and twin armchairs and the long dusty gold drapes with the sheer curtains pulled over the windows seemed to soak in whatever flavors were gurgling in the pots and skillets of her big white kitchen.

"You about scared the waddin' out of me, Pete. We was just about ready to go lookin' for you. Didn't you see Franklin's note?"

"Yeah."

Between us on the coffee table over a scattered pile of *True Detective*, Mrs. Henderson's favorite publication, lay the magazine under question, opened to a page with the picture of a man standing on a stage, his arms outstretched like the man's arms I had seen dangling from Sister Irene's mirror and nailed to the Lucero's wall above Manny. A crowd below the man was standing, too, but the people's arms were up in front of them reaching out toward the man. Mrs. Henderson picked up the magazine and closed it on her lap.

"Don't you know Mr. Lucero here?"

"Hi, Pete."

"Hi."

"Mr. Lucero was kind enough to come over and talk to us about this mess and was just about ready to go looking for you himself. We thought maybe that preacher nabbed you, too. Where an' the devil have you been?"

"The ball game."

"Well, you must've seen some extra innings that Franklin and Winnie didn't 'cause they got back over an hour ago."

"Who'd he nab?"

"What?"

"You said, nabbed you, too."

She glanced at Joe and shifted her weight. "I just meant maybe he took you, you know, took you off to church, again, like he seems to be so fond of doin'."

"The preacher nabbed Mary, didn't he?"

Mrs. Henderson stared down at the magazine and riffled its pages with her thumb.

Joe scooted forward, elbows resting on his knees. "Listen, Pete. We don't know what the preacher has or hasn't done. We just know he's trying to get custody of Mary. Do you know what custody means?"

"He's tryin' to be her pa?"

"Well, I guess you could put it that way. He wants to be her guardian. He wants to take care of her."

"Is that why he changed the lock?"

Joe looked over at Mrs. Henderson and then back to me.

"We don't know who changed the locks yet, but we're going to find out as soon as we can. In the meantime, don't you worry. I've talked to Social Services and you and your brothers can stay here with Mrs. Henderson until we get this figured out. Okay?"

I nodded.

"Pete, I'm . . . I'm really sorry about your folks." Joe looked down at the floor between his legs, hands clasped together between his knees, and shook his head. "I want you to know, Pete, that I'll do anything I can to help." He stood and walked to the door. "Thanks for the coffee, Mrs. Henderson. I'll be in touch as soon as I find out something."

"Thank you, Mr. Lucero. Here, let me get that porch light for you so you don't break your fool neck out there."

"Joe?"

Joe stuck his head back through the doorway. "Yeah, Pete?"

"You didn't tell Fudgie, did ya?"

"Tell Fudgie what?"

"About, you know . . . "

Joe stepped back into the house. "Pete, you can trust me. I won't say anything to anybody if you don't want me to. Okay?"

I nodded. "Is Fudgie's pa going to be okay?"

"Yes, I think Manny is going to be just fine, Pete. He's one tough old bird."

Joe smiled and went on outside. Mrs. Henderson followed him out so I picked up the magazine lying on the sofa. The cover had a picture of an astronaut and was dated August 3, 1962. I flipped it open and there were pictures of Marilyn Monroe giving an interview. I couldn't read it all, but it had something to do with her fame and how difficult it was to be beautiful and famous. I remembered what Franklin said about beauty, that being beautiful doesn't mean you're happy. Then I remembered that it was the very next day, August 4th, that Marilyn Monroe had killed herself.

The August 6th edition of *The Grand River Sentinel* carrying the story of Marilyn Monroe's death had turned up missing at our house. Mom had called Warren Hyde, our paper boy, at home but Warren swore he had tossed it right on the driveway like he always did. Pa went out and looked under the car and in the evergreens along the side of our house and finally went next door and borrowed old man Hillar's paper. Pa didn't like to borrow anything from anybody and the missing newspaper ate at him so he finally asked Franklin about it. And Franklin, fidgetting, finally admitted he had burned it. Franklin had even replaced the rubber band before taking it out to the incinerator. Pa could deal with most major growing-up problems like Della Mae Nagel's underthings or Lee Hooker's smoking, but this one he couldn't understand. Franklin burned the newspaper? Pa was so perplexed that Franklin didn't even get swatted or grounded or even chewed out. Franklin, though, acted as if he had gotten all three, staying in the basement most of the time when he wasn't working at Mr. Dugan's or just moping around outside. Franklin was just beginning to act like himself again when Pa and I went fishing, when everything started coming loose around us.

I heard the porch door slam so I put the magazine down. Ms. Henderson came in shaking her head. "Now, there goes one fine feller." She walked over to the television and tilted the large picture of her husband and peered down at his reddened cheeks and lips and blackened-in hair, compliments of Arnie Kirkendahl, the local photographer.

"My Milton used to tell me about Joe Lucero's daddy, about what a good worker he was and what a card he could be, and it sure as shootin' rubbed off on that boy of his."

She sighed, carefully positioning the picture frame back on the television. She began to turn away and then, suddenly, stopped cold. "Pete? What time is it?" She whirled around and stooped down in front of the gold clock standing next to the picture of her husband on the television.

"Oh, for heaven's sake. It's already past ten."

Mrs. Henderson's fingers disappeared into her waveless hair and she shook her head. With hands dropping to her side, she slouched down onto the sofa, legs straight out in front of her. She stared up at the ceiling.

"Mrs. Henderson, what's wrong?"

She looked tiredly over at me and tried to smile. "It's Wednesday night. *Wagon Train's* over."

* * *

The green and white parakeet, Spot, woke up before anybody else. The first peep of sunlight through the kitchen window brought the same from the shrill throat of the bird clinging to the side of his wire cage that stood next to the back door. Spot was named Spot not because of any unusual markings on his wings or tail feathers nor because of what he left splattered all over the newspaper of his cage floor. Rather, he was Spot because every other pet Mrs. Henderson ever had was named Spot, from the high-backed Siamese with eyes so crossed they appeared to be good for nothing but hiding behind its small wet nose to the mongrel, Spot, a mutt so mangy and so friendly that when he saw you his tail thumped and his body twisted so violently that flakes of dry skin and scab fluttered off around him. Mrs. Henderson just plain liked the name Spot and now Spot the parakeet was piping in the new day.

"Spottie! You be quiet in there! Those boys are tryin' to sleep!"

Franklin, lying next to me on the double bed, turned over onto his side pressing a pillow to his head. "Was tryin' to sleep."

Erwin, on the other side of Franklin, didn't stir. Mom used to say Erwin could sleep through a spanking. As though she really knew. Mom could never bring herself to spank any of us.

Franklin lifted the pillow off his head and turned, looking at me. "Where you going?"

I pulled on my pants, buttoned them, and reached for my shoes.

He rubbed sleep from his eyes and yawned. "When'd you get in last night? I didn't even hear you?"

I shrugged. "I saw Willie."

"Where?"

"At the ball park. He gave me a ride home."

"What did he say?"

"Not much. Told me to tell you good-bye."

"Good-bye? Where's he going?"

"Home. Back to Wisconsin."

"Oh."

Franklin propped himself up on one elbow. "Did you tell him about the door locks?"

"No."

"Did you see my note?"

I nodded as I fumbled with the laces on my sneakers.

"What's wrong with your hand?"

"Nothin'."

"Nothin', bull. Your knuckles are all swelled up. What'd you do?"

"I said nothin'."

Franklin swung his feet over and sat on the edge of the bed, rubbing his face. I finished tying my sneakers and started out the door.

"Where you going?"

"I don't know."

"Well, hold your horses a minute and I'll go with you."

Franklin dressed and, leaving Erwin asleep in Mrs. Henderson's guest bedroom, we tiptoed through the kitchen to the back door.

"Shouldn't we tell Mrs. Henderson where we're goin'?"

Franklin stuck his index finger into the bird cage and Spot latched onto it with his beak, twisting his head as zealously as when he attacked the seed sticks Mrs. Henderson fed him.

"Ouch, you little . . ."

Franklin shook his finger and Spot tweeped.

"Tweep, yourself, you scrawny little turd."

"Well, shouldn't we, Franklin?"

"How we going to tell her when we don't know where we're going ourselves?"

But we did know where we were going so we left Spot to his shriekings and quietly went outside. The morning, like almost every morning lately, was cool even though the days had heated up again. The aspen and scrub oak would just be starting to turn higher up on Spruce Mesa and rabbit-brush was already painting the rocky hillsides yellow on the outskirts of Grand River, blooming among the sagebrush and cactus and along the sand-stone ledges. Down in town, the grass shone wet each morning and mist hung low over the river.

Franklin and I stood at the base of the elm tree, our hands jammed stiffly into our pockets, and stared across the street. Old man Hillar's truck idled in his driveway next door, the white exhaust disappearing into the air almost as soon as it seeped out the tail pipe. Old man Hillar left for work at Smitty's Hardware every weekday morning at 7:15 sharp and there he was now, lunch box in hand, standing between the screen and back door, locking his house.

Not everybody in Grand River locked their house when they left home but old man Hillar did. He had been burglarized in broad daylight just three summers before. In fact, after the thieves got away with most of his tools, his 12-gauge shotgun, and a new battery out of the '52 Chevy he was rebuilding, he decided serious measures were in order. First, as a statement of resistance, he strung barbed wire across the top of the fence out back along the alley, not considering that an intruder could easily get around it by simply opening the gate and ducking inside. Then he brought home a faulty alarm system he had salvaged from Smitty's dumpster, rewired it, and hooked it up to both his front and back doors. And last, he secured dead bolts to all doors and windows and also locks that could only be unlocked with a key whether he was inside or out. It took old man Hillar a good while to get used to his new home-protection system. He locked himself in four times that first summer and after the third call, Gordie Scroggins and the boys down at the fire station took to calling him Houdini. And now, looking across the street at our own home, we had a similar problem. But instead of escaping out of our house, we had to escape into it.

Old man Hillar got into his truck, backed out of the driveway, and drove off down the street.

"Come on, Pete."

I followed Franklin across the street and up our driveway. Looking around as though he were breaking into somebody else's house, Franklin reached for the key and brought it out of his pants pocket. Only half of the key went into the lock so he turned it teeth edge down and tried it again.

"See?"

"Yeah."

We ran around to the front door and Franklin tried it there, jabbing at the lock and twisting the key. "Those bastards!" Franklin flung the key across the street into the weeds of the vacant lot. He sat down on the front step and held his head in his hands.

"Franklin, how about the windows?"

"Already tried them last night."

"What about the basement windows?"

"They're too small."

"I bet I could squeeze into them."

Franklin brought his hands down and looked up at me. "No way."

We walked around to the back yard to Franklin's small bedroom window. He got on his knees and peered in.

"Pete, it's not locked. You really think you can do this?"

I shrugged. "Guess I can try."

"First we got to get this screen off."

Franklin took out his pocketknife and unscrewed the four screws from the screen and set it to the side. Next, he jiggled the small rectangular window frame and popped it out.

"Bingo. Now the hard part."

Setting the window next to the screen, he stuck his head into the basement.

"What do you see, Franklin?"

He pulled his head back out.

"My desk is right under the window so you should be okay. My Soap Box Derby trophy is right there so don't kick it over or I'll pound you."

I looked up at my big brother. He grinned. "On second thought, if you can really get through that hole, I'll let you kick a field goal with it."

I pulled off my shirt and cap and handed them to Franklin. I sat down in front of the window, stuck in my legs, and began wiggling into the opening until my legs were completely in. I scooted on my butt, inching my way forward. The window jambs squeezed my hips so I turned sideways and got in a little more but no farther.

"I told you it wouldn't work."

Franklin grabbed under my arms and pulled me out. I got up and Franklin handed me my shirt and cap.

"What about Win?"

"Naw, I don't think Win should get mixed up with this."

"Mixed up with what? It's our house, Franklin."

Franklin scratched his head. "I don't know . . ."

I gave Franklin back my shirt and cap and kicked off my shoes.

"What are you doin'?"

I unbuttoned my pants and bent down, pulling them off. Franklin glanced around us.

"Pete, you're crazy."

I handed him my pants and then my underwear.

"Pete! You . . . "

Getting down on all fours, I stuck my head into the opening and then my arms, wiggling forward. After working myself in up to my hips, I began pushing with my hands against the bedroom walls. I could feel the cold metal edges of the jamb biting into my sides but I kept pushing. Then I felt Franklin's hands against my feet outside and together, straining, we worked me inside. Headfirst, I slid downward—bracing myself against the top of the desk, knocking model dragsters and airplanes to the floor—and then tumbled in, landing against the foot of the bed.

"You all right, Pete?"

"Yeah."

"Good. Go open the door."

Pressing my sore knuckles under my arm, I stood and looked at Franklin's Soap Box Derby trophy standing upright on his desk and then up at the small rectangle of light I had just come through.

"Franklin! Throw down my clothes!"

But Franklin was already gone, running around the corner of the house to the back door. I turned and walked through his bedroom and up the stairs to the back door. I could see Franklin's shadow against the door's window curtain as I reached for the handle of the new door knob and then I heard the jingle of his keys. Why was Franklin still trying to fit that stupid key into the . . .

I sprinted down the stairs and across the cool tile floor through Pa's workshop and into my bedroom. I could hear voices above me as I quickly pulled the bottom drawer out of the wall. I slipped into my secret hiding place and pulled the drawer quickly in after me. I held my breath.

"I'm absolutely certain I heard something."

"I didn't."

"No, it sounded like footsteps and then a drawer opening."

The top drawer slid out and I could see a crack of light and then it slid closed.

"Maybe there are ghosts."

"I don't find that particularly amusing, Mr. Lister."

"Sorry."

"If you'll recall, I lost somebody very dear to me and I certainly don't appreciate any of your . . ."

"I said I'm sorry. Can't we get on with this, please. I've got a court appearance in about forty-five minutes to get these papers signed by the judge. We have to move on this as fast as we can."

"What about the children?"

"We're taking care of it, Mr. Merriweather."

"Now, the deal was that . . ."

"I said, we're taking care of it. How many times do we have to go over this? I'm the guardian *ad litem* and after the judge signs these papers, Calloway becomes legal guardian and you'll be conservator and administrator of the property. It's perfectly legal."

"I understand. It's just that my sister, she . . ."

"Now where were we?"

"Uh, yes, well. As you can see, in here there is a bedroom and one like it on the other side, a workshop in here and there's an extra bathroom . . ."

I lay face-up on the mattress, the voices fading in the cool naked darkness, in the cool wooden box of the house my pa built, until only silence. And then the voices, they fade back in, filling the box until I'm almost drowned in them.

The Lord is my shepherd; I shall not want. Petey, I got a new cap for you today. Just like the kind Maris and Mantle wear. *He maketh me to lie down in green pastures.* Pa fell. Me and Pa was fishin' and he just fell. *He leadeth me beside the still waters.* Sorry about your ma and pa. If there's anything I can do. *He restoreth my soul.* Do you love Jesus, son? *He leadeth me in the paths of righteousness for His name's sake.* Well, Jesus loves you and to prove it he's going to be your new daddy. *Yea, though I walk through the valley of the shadow of death.* Hey, Caviness, even Erwin can pound you, puss. *I will fear no evil.* It started with a W. *For thou art with me.* What Willie give us to drink. The name, it started with a W. *Thy rod and thy staff, they comfort me.* Things either are or they aren't and all the words in the world won't change it. *Thou preparest a table before me in the presence of mine enemies.* Hear your wind chimes, Mom? *Thou anointest my head with oil.* Wine! *My cup runneth over.* Now I lay me down to sleep. *Surely goodness and mercy.* I pray the Lord my soul to keep. *Shall follow me.* And if I die before I wake. *All the days of my life.* I pray the Lord my soul to take. God bless Mommy and Daddy and Franklin and Mary. *And I will dwell in the house of the Lord forever. Amen.* And the house we live in. Amen. Forgive me, Father. Nine, eight, seven, six. N-E-S-T-L-E-S, Nestle's makes the very best. Five, four, three, two, one. Chooooco-laaaate. We have lift off. You got him, Franklin. Is he dead? Forgive me, Father. Is he dead? Yeah, let's eat worms for supper! Is he dead? Amen. It's not just a screen door, it's our house. Amen. Our house.

* * *

"Pete?"

There was a tap on the wall.

"Pete, are you there?"

I pushed the drawer out. "Yeah."

Franklin pulled the drawer the rest of the way out and helped me from under the stairs. Erwin stood next to him, pointing at me. "Lookie. His whanger."

Franklin laughed. "Not much of one. Aren't you freezing?"

I reached into the drawer and pulled out a pair of underwear.

"Here's your shoes and the rest of your stuff." Franklin dropped my clothes on the bed. "Did they see you, Pete?"

"No."

"Boy, that was a close call. They didn't notice the window, either."

"How'd you get back in?"

Franklin nodded toward Erwin. "I had Win come in the same way you did."

Erwin looked up at Franklin and shook his head. "Huh-uh. I got my clothes on."

"I mean through the window, Win." Franklin rolled his eyes.

"Yeah, and I broked Franklin's trophy."

Franklin shrugged. "Did you see Uncle Herbert?"

"No, but I heard him. That other guy said maybe there's ghosts."

"Oh, no. Not ghosts, again."

Franklin shook his head as Erwin looked back up at him.

"Ghosts? There's ghosts, Franklin?"

"Great. Now you've got him wonderin' about it."

"I didn't think Uncle Herbert was coming back, Franklin."

"Me neither. Wait 'til Mrs. Henderson finds out."

"Yeah, she'll have him tarred and feathered and hanging from a tree."

"Yeah, we better hope so."

I slipped on my shoes and followed Franklin into Pa's workshop. A skiff of sawdust clung to everything and when we walked in, seemed to lift like sand brushed by the fin of a fish at the bottom of an aquarium.

"Hey, look at this."

Pa's unfinished coffee table, no longer upside down across the saw-horses, sat upright on the floor. I walked over and ran my fingers over the smooth top and down the finely sanded legs. I looked up at Franklin, who was watching me.

"Look at this, Franklin. Pa's coffee table he was makin' for Mom."

Franklin shrugged. "So?"

"It wasn't sanded like this. It was sittin' up here on the sawhorses. Pa just glued the legs on. I watched him."

Franklin put his arm around Erwin and started back across Pa's work-shop. "Maybe you're right, after all, Pete."

"What do you mean?"

Franklin turned at the doorway. "Maybe there are ghosts."

17

When Rosita Maria Gonzalez de Manzanares arrived in San Felipe, a letter awaited her on the kitchen table. It was from her brother, Carlos, in Mexico City. Weary from the four-day journey with her two sons, she slumped down at the table and opened it, leaving her canvas suitcase at the door. She was alarmed. Carlos had never written her a letter. At different times over the years, she even wondered if he knew how. But as she began to read, her alarm—which she could already feel settling into her shoulders, where she harbored most her troubles—relaxed into relief and then joy. Despite the misspelled words and broken sentences, Carlos could write. In fact, his letter was a treasure she would read many times over the next three weeks. Carlos had seen the Kennedys.

Mexico's relationship with the United States had become strained. With Castro and the communists' overthrow of Batista in Cuba three years before, the recent salinity problem of Mexico's share of the Colorado River, and the ever-increasing flow of itinerant workers over the border, President Kennedy decided it was time to return to Mexico. Though he and his wife had honeymooned there after they were married, he knew, given all these tensions, that this trip would be no second honeymoon. Or so he must have thought.

Carlos had written that on the day of President Kennedy's arrival, he had gone to the streets of Mexico City, like his neighbors, in his finest attire. It seemed everyone was there for never had he seen the normally crowded streets of the city this crowded. Swept up in the festive atmosphere, Carlos had climbed a tree like a kid so he could get a better look: a sea of sombreros reached out in colorful waves on all sides with small Mexican and American flags bobbing like buoys against the tide, a beautiful sight for the visiting president. But as the motorcade slowly moved down the boulevard from the airport to the presidential residence, shouts of "*Bienvenido, Presidente Kennedy*" showering its way, it wasn't President Kennedy who was presented with the most beautiful sight—it was, instead, the Mexican people. For sitting next to the American leader was the most beautiful woman Carlos had ever seen: Jacqueline, the president's wife.

Jacqueline, Carlos wrote (again and again, as though the mere act of writing her name was a way of paying homage, a way of bringing her closer), was a gift from heaven. She was tall, was Jacqueline, with dark hair and milky fair skin. When she moved, it was with an elegance befitting a queen. When she spoke, it was the soft thrush of an angel's wing and when on the following day she stood before the Mexican people and greeted them in their own language, it was as though a spell was cast over the entire nation. Everyone fell in love with her.

After only two days, President Kennedy and Jacqueline once again moved down the boulevard and Carlos returned to the street and to the tree. But this time, Carlos wrote, instead of "*Bienvenido, Presidente Kennedy*" it was "*Hasta luego*" on his countrymen's lips as the American president and his angelic wife waved farewell. And long after President Kennedy and Jacqueline disappeared down the boulevard, Carlos remained in the tree and watched his people standing along the curbs talking and smoking and dabbing their eyes until finally dispersing. Yes, the Kennedys' trip to Mexico was as sweet a honeymoon as anyone could imagine and Rosita's brother, Carlos, had been there.

Although she didn't actually read it in the small painstaking print, Rosita knew from his passion—from the not-so-simple act of this letter to her—that Carlos had wept also. And now, as she sat at her kitchen table, Rosita Maria Gonzalez de Manazanares felt this passion and began to cry. Though she cried for her brother's good fortune, she also cried for her homeland and her people's poverty and the Americans' wealth. She cried for the farmers and fishermen and shopkeepers, for the whores in Tijuana and the bare-footed children who sold tourists trinkets and flowers in the dirty streets there. She cried for the thousands of itinerant workers—wetbacks the Americans called them—who had to cross the border into a foreign land every year to make a living. She cried for her husband and his illness. She cried for her children and their future and for missing them. She cried from weariness and anger and sadness and she cried from this passion. Finally, when she thought she could cry no more, she cried for something she hadn't cried for since she was a little girl. She cried for herself.

Rosita pushed herself up from the table. She took her shawl and tied it around her head. And though weary, she walked out of the house down the dusty streets of San Felipe to the Catholic Church where she knelt at the flesh-worn altar and prayed to the Virgin of Guadalupe to forgive her weaknesses.

The following three weeks were oddly quiet in San Felipe. With no one to cook for, save herself or maybe one of her sons if they stuck around long enough to eat, she had decided to get out of the house and spend some time at the curio shop. Uncle Tony would surely welcome her help.

After Manny had given Uncle Tony dominion over the curio shop by leaving him the key in an envelope with explicit instructions about the shop's management, Uncle Tony had become a changed man. No longer were his afternoons and nights spent in the company of cronies at the local cantina, telling lies about days thankfully gone. Nor were his mornings lost in drunken stupor at the bottom of a tequila bottle, head drumming with another hangover, the only remedy being the same as its source. Uncle Tony was now a businessman.

Mornings he could be seen, black pocketbook in hand, standing in the aisles of the curio shop taking inventory with a thick pencil, marking an X for every item sold. The rest of the morning, if he wasn't mopping the floor or wiping the windows or unpacking new merchandise, he was dusting the shelves. Afternoons found him sitting as squarely and solidly behind the counter as the counter itself. And at nights he was at that same counter adding and subtracting and adding again the day's take. Some evenings one or two of his old amigos would turn up to ask for a short-term loan or see if he wanted to join them on a moonshine stroll along the beach. Or they would just show up to heckle him for no longer being their buddy, for no longer being the same old fun-loving tequila-guzzling Tony.

One such night, not long before Rosita's return, Uncle Tony's best friend, Albino Venegas, appeared at the shop waving a barracuda in his face. Albino would sell him the fish, still so fresh its gills were flexing, for a bottle of mescal. When Uncle Tony said no, Albino fumed so threateningly that Uncle Tony had to wrestle the barracuda from his old friend's hands—before Albino broke something—and thump him alongside the head with it. Albino Venegas was a slight man, though wiry, and the impact of the fish left an impression of the barracuda's jaw along the flat of his temple, which, down at the cantina, served as further evidence that Uncle Tony had gone drunk with making money.

At first, Rosita welcomed the new Uncle Tony. His diligence and enthusiasm were remarkable. This transformation may even have been a minor miracle although Rosita had given up praying for him years before, so disgusted had she been with his drunken influence on her husband. And at first, Uncle Tony had seemed equally happy with Rosita and the new respect she showed him. He had even given her a little copper cross that he had tapped out of an American penny using his anvil and a ball-peen hammer. Though it was primitive, Rosita was delighted and wore it every morning to the shop so Uncle Tony could see for himself how much she liked it. Yes, at first, it seemed a match, if not made in heaven, at least made somewhere between there and purgatory. But that was before Albino Venegas and the boys from the cantina showed up, before all hell broke loose.

On the afternoon of Uncle Tony's transgression, Rosita had appeared at the curio shop just as she had for a solid week. It was a Friday in San Felipe and the wind was whipping off the Sea of Cortez in hot gusts, leaving whitecaps in its wake. Both Rosita and Uncle Tony knew that Fridays, especially in the summer, were often the busiest days with rich Californians and college students beginning their weekends early. Uncle Tony was standing out front, his great belly exposed under his sports shirt as he stretched up to cinch down the canvas canopy that had come loose in the wind. Rosita laid her shawl across the back of a chair and began untangling the legs of rubber scorpions and spiders that Uncle Tony had put in a box on the counter. Though Rosita didn't fully approve of such merchandise or its location near the front, she knew it sold well and decided not to rankle him by moving it elsewhere. Besides, he had made so many concessions in his behavior lately that perhaps it was time she made a few herself. She smiled inwardly and looked out the window for this hulking man, this man turned businessman in a single summer. But Uncle Tony wasn't there.

Rosita got up still holding the scorpions and spiders and walked to the window. There, off to the side at the edge of the street stood Uncle Tony with five men. She recognized them as the good-for-nothings from the cantina. Trinadad Reyes was there and Julio Gallegos, Juan Mendoza, Gilbert Ríos, and that little wire of a man, Albino Venegas, his jaws working like a tight pair of pliers as he looked up at Uncle Tony.

Rosita started out the door, thought better of it, and returned to the counter. Tony had made it this far without her assistance and there was probably no need for it now. Setting the box down, Rosita said a short prayer and began dusting the shelves. Her prayer was quickly answered. Uncle Tony walked in and sat down behind the counter.

The rest of the day was slow. The wind must have driven the tourists away as it did the large seagulls that usually flew along the shoreline, scouring the beaches for food. At first Rosita thought Uncle Tony's silence was due to this lack of customers. But as the day drew out and light dropped behind the great spit of land that is Baja, Uncle Tony's mood darkened. Rosita had made it her habit to stay late to help unpack merchandise and count the money. As she neatly stacked a shipment of towels from Tijuana along the wall, his brooding eyes silently bore into her and she decided to leave early. Maybe he was just tired and would feel better in the morning. Rosita left quickly, murmuring good-bye on the way out without looking at his face.

That evening was disquieting. She couldn't get the image of Uncle Tony out of her mind. She fixed rice and beans for supper but could only manage to rearrange the food on her plate with the turn of her spoon, eating little. She went to bed early only to toss fitfully. Finally, she got up and put on her robe and sandals and boiled some water for tea. As she took the kettle from the fire, she heard something: a high scream or maybe it was just a gull. She poured water into the cup and was about to put in a pinch of tea when she heard it again.

Draping her shawl around her head, she stepped outside onto the patio. Often, late at night, she could hear a ruckus down at the cantina on the far side of town. But tonight the noise was closer and drew Rosita Manzanares down the dark streets of San Felipe to the curio shop.

When Rosita stepped inside it was like a nun entering a whorehouse: everyone stopped and stared. And Rosita stared back. There was a lot to see. In the corner, over one of the towels she had unpacked not five hours before, a game of poker was being played by two men she had never seen before. One of the men smoked a cigar and the other had a woman leaning over his shoulder, studying his hand and holding a glass of smoky brown liquid. The cards each man held were postcards, substitutes for playing cards, but the money lying out on the towel was real.

Behind the players stood a second woman, her waist wrapped in the dark hairy arms of Julio Gallegos. Rosita had known him since he was a small boy and she liked him (although she never let Julio know) and it had saddened her when he had become like Uncle Tony, staggering back and forth from the cantina. Julio had a T-shirt on his head that fell back like a woman's hair and the woman in his arms wore make-up and little else.

Gilbert Ríos, a half-empty bottle in his hand, leaned back against the shelves where the religious merchandise was kept. Gilbert's profession was mud—he had stuccoed half the buildings in San Felipe—and one encrusted boot now rested on the shelf with the clay crosses. But when Rosita looked at him, he brought the boot down and you could hear its muddy heel scuff the floor in the silence.

In front of him over the shelf that stretched down the middle of the shop hunched Trinadad Reyes and Juan Mendoza, their right hands firmly clasped, arm-wrestling. What had been neatly stacked on top of the shelf—shoulder bags, leather sandals, T-shirts, and small plastic bags of incense—was strewn at their feet. They were brothers-in-law, these two, and spent more time together in competition—whether it was a foot race or beer-chugging contest—than they spent collectively with the woman who had made them relations. Although they, too, stared at Rosita, the tension of their arms remained unchanged so great the competitive fire between them.

Standing on a chair which had been dragged out from behind the counter, refereeing the arm-wrestling contest and the entire proceedings, was Albino Venegas. A bottle in one hand, a cigarette in the other, he was the only one still smiling after Rosita appeared at the door and scanned the disaster before her. Albino Venegas knew who Rosita was looking for and with a turn and an outward sweep of his arm, he presented the main attraction.

Rosita hadn't moved from the door, and Albino Venegas and the arm wrestlers were blocking her view. Craning her neck, she took a few steps. There sprawled across the counter—feet dangling, shirt torn wide, eyes closed, and mouth agape—lay the slumbering, miserably drunk Uncle Tony.

She had seen enough and started to turn away. But something caught her eye. Lifting the hem of her robe, Rosita stepped over the upturned post-card rack. What was that fluttering around Uncle Tony's mouth each time his huge hairy chest heaved? Rosita bent down, squinting, and then slowly straightened up, raising her eyes to Albino Venegas who was still standing on the chair grinning fondly down at his best friend, down at the legs of spiders and scorpions dancing rubberly between his friend's lips.

It took very little, really, given Albino's intoxicated state and the fact that he had proudly but unsteadily lifted one boot onto the back of the chair to gaze down on Uncle Tony as he might have posed with a prize fish for the click of a tourist's camera. Yes, it took just a smart kick of the chair. And as Rosita stepped back over the postcard rack and walked to the front door—Albino swimming in the air behind her—she felt a sudden lift of her spirits and then, if not joy, something very akin to it as the crash of Albino Venegas shattered the quiet behind her and she walked outside and away from her family's curio shop.

She loosened the shawl from under her chin and let it fall across her shoulders. The breeze through her hair felt refreshing as she walked back home. It was now midnight and she knew she wouldn't sleep so she pulled her canvas suitcase out from the closet, slung it up on her bed, and began to pack. With a little luck, she could catch a ride on her second cousin's bottled-water truck to Ensenada first thing in the morning. Once there, it would be easy to find a ride to the border. She would only have to figure out a way to cross. But no matter. She would find a way. Rosita Maria Gonzalez de Manzanares had always found a way.

* * *

A pot of steaming coffee sat on a wicker pad in the middle of the table. Six pairs of hands surrounded it: Helen Lucero's, small and pale yet nimble and sure, lifting the lid of an apple-shaped ceramic jar and plucking out two cubes of sugar and dropping them into her cup; Joe Lucero's, long-fingered and square with half-moon cuticles white as milk against his skin; Fudgie's, brown and fidgety, turning his cup this way and that, fingernails rimmed black with grit; Carmalita's, soft but wise, cupping the coffee's warmth between them; Manny Manzanares', broad, high-knuckled and scarred, resting on either side of his mug, one thick finger hooked through the handle; and Rosita Manzanares', clasped loosely to the side near her husband's. Mine I kept under the table as those other hands moved—lifting and sliding and talking—cups clattering into saucers, coffee poured and drunk and repoured, and all the while steam rising between.

"Want some more, *Tía?*"

Rosita shook her head so Joe set the pot on the pad and sat down.

"So, *Tía* Rosita, how did Uncle Tony feel the next day? Did you see him before you left?"

Rosita nodded, patted her stomach, and said something in Spanish. Everyone groaned, sipping their coffee and shaking their heads at the thought of Uncle Tony waking up sick with another hangover and with such a mess to clean up.

"And Albino?"

Rosita shrugged, said something else, and quickly crossed herself. Fudgie leaned over to me. "She say she don' care what happen to Albino Venegas." Fudgie smiled and I looked at his mother.

When I first arrived on Hill Avenue after sneaking out of our house and making sure the door was locked behind me, everyone was hugging and kissing Rosita in the Lucero's front yard. Even Manny was outside in his bathrobe, leaning heavily on his cane with one hand and pressing his wife's head to his chest with the other. I watched from behind a bush across the street and when everyone began to file back into the house, I turned to leave, only to be spotted by Carmalita. She ran to me, eyes dancing with laughter and joy. Taking me by the hand, she spirited me back across the street. Joe and Helen, Fudgie, and even Manny greeted me with hugs and then introduced me to Rosita. And as soon as she held my hand and looked into my eyes, I knew where Carmalita got her beauty. And when everyone settled around the kitchen table and spoke Spanish—talking about San Felipe and Rosita's brother and Uncle Tony and the curio shop—with everyone joining in to interpret, I knew Carmalita's silence was as rich as the language she had never spoken.

"Fudgie, why does Carmalita only talk to your mom?" We stood in the Lucero's spare bedroom, Fudgie holding his mother's canvas suitcase.

"She the only one that understan'. Momma trade for a book with a *touriste* an' they learn signs together."

"Oh."

Fudgie set the suitcase down.

"And why didn't you and Carmalita leave like you said you was?"

Fudgie smiled. "Papa is better. An' now Momma is here."

"But you didn't know she was coming."

"I didn', but . . ."

"Carmalita did."

"Hey, man, you catch on fas'. You no so stupid for a gringo."

Fudgie and I stared at each other and then fell spinning and giggling onto the bed, my arm locked around his head.

"Luis!"

We stopped wrestling and looked up at his mother who stood in the doorway and sharply clapped her hands. She spoke quickly in Spanish as I followed Fudgie up from the bed and out of the bedroom.

"Momma is back."

Fudgie smiled sheepishly, shaking his head as we walked into the kitchen. Carmalita and Joe stood at the sink washing the cups and saucers as Helen sat with Manny at the table. Helen looked up from her cup. "Yes, she is back, Luis Manzanares, and a good thing, too. Now maybe you and that overgrown teenager over there will start acting like human beings, again."

Joe nudged Carmalita with his elbow. "I don't think you're overgrown, Carmy."

"Joe Lucero, you know which overgrown teenager I'm talking about."

"Fudgie, are you just going to stand there and let this mean woman insult me like that?"

"*Sí, José.*"

Joe stared blankly at Fudgie and then scooped up a handful of suds from the sink and tossed it, hitting him across the face. Fudgie, head lowered and arms wide, charged Joe and grabbed him around the legs.

"Joseph!" Helen jumped up from the table and rushed over to grab Fudgie before he could tackle Joe to the kitchen floor. A fluffy glob of soap thwacked against her forehead.

Slowly she wiped the suds with the back of her hands, staring straight at Carmalita whose own wet hands now covered her mouth, eyes wide with something between terror and glee. After Helen removed most of the soap except for a few globs that clung to her hair, she walked over to the sink and stood between Joe and Carmalita. Fudgie sat watching from the floor, his arms still wrapped around one of Joe's legs. Helen, one hand on her hip, looked at Joe and then at Carmalita, scooped up a handful of soapsuds, and plunked it down on Carmalita's head. Carmalita didn't move as Helen turned to Joe.

"Honey, no . . . no. We were just . . ."

Joe jerked his hands to his face a fraction too late. The soap, now more soup than suds, drenched him and the fight was on. Joe clung to the side of the counter as Fudgie pulled on his leg. Helen and Carmalita splashed at the sink, soaking each other as well as Joe, Fudgie, and the kitchen floor. Manny roared from the table, slapping his leg and pounding his cane to the tile as white puffs of suds and streaks of water filled the air and everyone slipped to the floor.

Rosita Manzanares rushed from the spare bedroom to the kitchen, eyes wide and hands covering her mouth. Seeing Manny doubled over at the table, she clutched him by the shoulders and eased him upright and, looking into his face, realized it was only laughter that left her husband limp in his chair.

She raised her head, eyes meeting those staring up at her from the floor, and slumped into a chair next to Manny. Her eyes drooped tiredly and then narrowed—studying the crazy wet family sprawled gasping before her, the family she had traveled over one-thousand miles back to—but finally crinkled as she joined her husband and laughed, laughed thankfully into her hands.

* * *

Joe leaned back in the sun against the fence. His T-shirt hung drying from one of the pickets as he ran a comb through his wet hair. "You like this crazy family?"

I nodded.

"We like you, too, Pete."

Joe slid the comb into his back pocket. "You got wet, too, didn't you?"

I looked down at the wet splotches on my shirt and pants and then grinned. "Yeah."

"Pete, the reason I asked you to come out here is because I wanted to talk to you about what I learned this morning." Joe folded his arms across his chest and looked down. "I talked to Social Services, to a woman named Bonnie Finch who is handling your case. She's a good friend. I went to high school with her. Do you understand what Social Services does?"

I shrugged. "Kinda."

"Well, they do a lot of things but in your particular case, it's their job to find you and your brothers and sister a place to live."

"We have a place."

Joe unfolded his arms and rubbed one forearm with the palm of his other hand.

"You mean Mrs. Henderson's?"

"No. Our house."

Joe sucked air through his nose and blew it out his mouth. "Pete, there seems to be some dispute about that."

"What do you mean?"

"Well, you know those locks that were changed?"

"Yeah."

"I think I know who did it. After I talked to Social Services, I went by the courthouse to check on the deed. A deed is a document or a piece of paper they give you when you receive a piece of property. In this case, your folks' house. Did your folks buy the house, Pete?"

"No, my pa built it. With his own hands."

He nodded. "Well, somehow Herbert Merriweather—your uncle, right?"

"Yeah."

"Somehow he's got the deed transferred to himself and I think he's the one who changed the locks."

"Uncle Herbert?"

Joe nodded. "Anyway, that's my guess. After I go back to the courthouse today and figure out how the deed was transferred, I'll see if I can't find your Uncle Herbert."

"Uncle Herbert said he was goin' back to Wichita."

"I don't know anything about that, Pete."

"Is Uncle Herbert going to be staying with us, Joe?"

He looked down at me and then lifted his head to the sun and clasped the back of his neck. It was another scorcher in Grand River. There wasn't a cloud anywhere. The sky stretched pale in the heat and the sun burned white, fading everything in its reach. Joe dropped his hands to his sides. "That's what I was kind of starting to tell you, Pete. Bonnie Finch and the people at Social Services are, uh . . ." Joe looked down at me and placed his hand on my shoulder. "They're trying to sort all this out for you."

"Uncle Herbert's mad at us, isn't he?"

"I don't know, Pete."

"He is."

"Why do you say that?"

I looked down at the dirt, wiping my sweaty hands against the front of my pant legs, and shrugged.

"Well, you let me worry about your Uncle Herbert. Okay?"

I nodded.

"I guess we better get back in there and help them clean up the mess. Helen'll make my life hell if we don't." Joe smiled and unhooked his shirt from the picket and slung it over his shoulder.

"Joe?"

"Yeah, Pete?"

Joe put his arm around my shoulders as we walked across the yard to the back door.

"When can we start sleeping in our own house again?"

Joe stopped, looked down at me, and opened his mouth to say something but thought better of it.

18

By the time Fudgie and I left the Lucero's house, walked along the bank of the Indian Wash, and got to the gas station it was twilight, the sky a deep blue over the shadowed sandstone walls of Rimrock National Park. Mr. Dugan hadn't turned on his bay lights even though the lamps on the tall lightpoles in the middle of the street were already aglow. Another dad-gum waste of taxpayers' money, Mr. Dugan was fond of saying, whether it was about the city lights or street sweepers or any other lame-brained scheme conjured up by the local self-important mucky-mucks, as he called the city's officials.

What really brought the veins in Mr. Dugan's forehead to surface, though, was the digging of the Indian Wash which, even though it had happened three years before, was his favorite topic. That is, whenever he could get anyone to stick around long enough to hear him out. Not only was the dad-gum thing expensive but it stunk from Grand River all the way to Spruce Mesa and back and you couldn't go near it even if you had half a notion to. And besides that, the dad-gum mosquitoes swarmed together down there in a veritable orgy of insect fornication and bit not only into the ruddy skin of Mr. Dugan's round body but also into his business. Who likes to get their car serviced while being air-bombed by squadrons of those dad-gum blood-crazed mosquitoes?

Mr. Dugan attracted mosquitoes like some shrubs attract dogs. His scent was just too ripe to be ignored. One would have thought with all the gasoline, motor oil, and lubricant that was ground into him, the mosquitoes would have stayed away. They stayed away from Franklin for the most part and he smelled the same. They left Erwin alone, too, and he spent half his time down there among them and didn't smell of gasoline at all. Maybe it had nothing to do with smell because Mr. Dugan had doused himself in everything from Cutter's Insect Repellant to Aqua Velva Shaving Lotion. The only things Mr. Dugan seemed to repel were his customers.

"There's that little sucker. Here, hit him with this."

He leaned across his desk and handed Franklin the fly swatter. Franklin held it above the mosquito, buzzing and tapping against the glass. He flicked his wrist and the swatter smacked against the pane, smearing the mosquito red across it.

"Thata boy."

The window trembled slightly, their reflections quivering as Franklin handed the swatter back to Mr. Dugan.

"Hi, Pete. Come on in and close that screen before another skeeter gets in."

We stepped into the office and closed the screen door.

"Who you got there, Pete?" Mr. Dugan was tipped back in his swivel chair and he held a baloney sandwich in one hand and rested a bottle of RC Cola on his thigh with the other.

"This is my friend."

Mr. Dugan bit off half the sandwich and took a swig of cola. He was so used to cramming his mouth chock-full of Red Man Chewing Tobacco that putting half a baloney sandwich into it was like dropping a jellybean into an empty cookie jar.

"Well, does he have a name?"

"Yeah. Fudgie."

Chewing his sandwich and fishing his fingers into a jar on the desk, Mr. Dugan looked at my friend. "Now there's a interesting name. Fudgie. I like that."

Mr. Dugan shoved the rest of the sandwich into his mouth, following it with a long green pepper he pulled from the jar. He sat up, wiping his fingers across the front of his overalls, and stuck his hand across the desk.

"Clarence Dugan. Nice to meet ya."

"Me, too."

Mr. Dugan picked up the jar and held it out toward Fudgie. "Care for a jelly-peeny?"

Fudgie took one by the stem. "*Gracias.*"

Mr. Dugan looked over at Franklin. "You know Franklin here?"

Fudgie nodded. "I know him. Hey, man."

Franklin raised his chin and stared at the pepper pinched between Fudgie's fingers. A grin began working the corners of his mouth as Fudgie bit off half the pepper.

"Taste jus' like jalapeños." Fudgie stuck the rest into his mouth.

"Nope. Jelly-peenys. You like 'em?"

Fudgie nodded as Mr. Dugan smiled and looked at Franklin, whose mouth now hung wide.

"Well, help yourself to more there. I'll leave the jar here on the desk. And why don't you boys grab yourselves a pop, too, while me and Franklin get this customer. 'Bout time somebody decided to gas up. You'd think we're still in the dad-gum horse-and-buggy age the way things been goin' around here tonight."

Setting his root beer down, Franklin looked up as car lights flashed against the glass and swept across the station before lighting and blinking out on the brick wall of the El Palomino Motel next door. Franklin and Mr. Dugan walked outside.

"How much these cos', man?"

Fudgie and I peered in at the bottle tops of the pop machine.

"Nothin'. They're free."

"Eee, man. This guy mus' be rich."

I pulled out an orange and Fudgie did the same.

"I guess he just likes people to stick around and drink with him. He likes to talk."

We popped the caps off using the opener on the front of the machine. Fudgie tipped his bottle up and gulped the soda as he surveyed the office.

"Hey, man. Look at this." Fudgie wiped his mouth with the back of his hand and stared at the calendar, a red-headed woman holding a wrench. "What's it say, man?"

I walked over and looked up. "Says Valley Mechanics—We Have Just The Tool For You."

"Eeee."

Mr. Dugan came back into the office carrying a ten in his hand and rang up the purchase. The register dinged and the drawer slid out.

"You boys like Miss August?"

"What?"

"The calendar." Mr. Dugan motioned toward the wall as he counted the change. Fudgie and I shrugged.

"Take it if you want. August is almost over, anyways, and I'll just throw her away."

He ripped August from the calendar and handed it to me. Reaching around a corner, he flicked a switch and walked outside with the change. The bay lights flickered on and I could see Franklin kneeling outside, checking the air pressure on the customer's car.

"He like to give everything away, huh, man?"

Fudgie and I looked down at Miss August.

"Here, Fudgie. You take her."

"No, if Momma catch me with that . . ." Fudgie whipped his finger across his throat. I nodded, gazing down at the red hair and lipstick.

"You momma don' care, man?"

I look at the picture and turn the page.

"Petey? What are you reading?"

I slide it under the covers. "Nothin'."

Mom walks over to the bed. "It's late, honey. School's tomorrow. You need to get to sleep."

I nod.

"Give me what you were reading and I'll put it upstairs with the rest of your school books."

I feel the magazine's slick glossy cover under my arm. "That's okay, Mom."

"Don't be silly. You don't want to sleep with your books."

Mom turns back the covers, picks up the magazine, and then pulls the covers up around my chin. She kisses me on the forehead and leaning over to turn off my lamp, flips the magazine over and glances down. She hesitates and then turns off the light. Mom doesn't move, just stands there. "Petey?"

"Yeah?"

"Petey, I . . ." She sits down on the edge of my bed and places the back of her hand against my cheek. "Sleep tight, hon."

She stands quickly and walks to the door and closes it softly. I feel the sheets cling moist to my skin, can hear her footsteps fall creaking up the stairway, and lie rigid-still in the black of my room, wishing I were dead.

"Pete?" Fudgie grabbed my arm.

"Yeah?"

"I ask you why you don' never tell me about you momma an' papa?"

I looked at him and blinked.

"Okay, boys, ready to go to work?"

Mr. Dugan, wiping his hands on the greasy red rag he pulled from his back pocket, walked back into the office with Franklin behind him. "I got league tonight so I thought you two could give Franklin a hand closing things up so I can get out of here a little early."

Mr. Dugan slapped himself on the side of the face. "That is, if you want to."

Fudgie nudged me with his elbow and I looked at Franklin.

"How 'bout it, Pete?"

I quickly folded up the picture and stuffed it into my back pocket. "Okay."

"Good. I'm going to go ahead and count the cash register now. A couple of small bills and some change ought to do it, don't you think?"

Franklin stared at him.

"What do you mean, Mr. Dugan?"

"Well, seeing hows we ain't exactly been a beehive of activity and all."

Franklin continued watching Mr. Dugan, who slapped himself on the back of the neck.

"You mean you're going to leave money in the cash register?"

Mr. Dugan hit the cash register and it dinged open. "Well, unless you think we ought to give out wiper blades and bubblegum, instead."

"No, I just didn't think you'd . . ."

Franklin glanced at Fudgie and me and then looked back at Mr. Dugan. "I already showed you how to run this thing, didn't I?"

"Yeah."

"Well, I figure now's as good a time as any for you to give her a whirl."

Franklin nodded. "Want me to show them what to do now, Mr. Dugan, or should we wait 'til ten?"

"Seeing as I'm still here to watch the front, why don't you go ahead and show 'em now. Have another jelly-peeny, Fudgie. There's only three left."

He slapped himself on the ear with one hand as he held out the jar to Fudgie with the other. Fudgie took a pepper. "Gracias."

"We surely did knock that jar off, didn't we? Have to bring in some more now that I found me another jelly-peeny eater."

Mr. Dugan winked at Fudgie as they ate the peppers.

"Franklin, pour this juice into that empty 7-Up bottle, would ya?"

Franklin took the jar and bottle over to the drinking fountain. Mr. Dugan smiled at Fudgie. "I save it for when I cook beans. Spices 'em up just right."

Fudgie grinned. "My papa like to drink it."

Mr. Dugan whistled through his tobacco-stained teeth. "'Fraid I'd have to draw the line there. Well, guess we better get busy if I'm going to make it over to the alley. Here, why don't you eat this last one?"

"No, gracias, I don' . . ."

"Go ahead. Here, you can take it home with you."

Mr. Dugan dropped the pepper into the empty jar and began counting the money. Franklin set the 7-Up bottle of jalapeño juice down and turned to Fudgie and me. "We'll start with the bathrooms."

He took us into the back room. "Grab those two mops and that bucket and follow me."

We did as we were told and followed Franklin outside.

"Franklin!"

He turned and opened the screen door, sticking his head back inside. "Yeah?"

"You'll need these."

Mr. Dugan unclipped the ring of keys from his belt loop and tossed them.

"Thanks, Mr. Dugan."

"Make sure she's locked up tighter than a skeeter's hiney before you go. And give that little brother of yours and his buddy each a buck. Just keep the rest and I'll take it out of your paycheck. You are coming in tomorrow, ain't ya?"

"Yeah." Franklin looked down at the keys in his hand.

"And Franklin?"

Franklin looked up. "Yeah, Mr. Dugan?"

Mr. Dugan slapped himself on the cheek. "Shut that dad-gum screen door before these little suckers carry me out of here."

Franklin closed the door and we followed him around the building to the restrooms.

"Fudgie, you can do the women's and Pete the men's."

Franklin squirted soap into a bucket and turned on the hose. The water gushed into the bucket, raising the suds to the top. Franklin handed Fudgie the disinfectant and a brush and then led me to the men's. I looked down at the white cake next to the urinal drain. Cigarette butts lay soaked and crumbling around it.

"You got to get these out first."

"How?"

Franklin pushed down the handle and water filled the urinal but didn't drain. "Just scoop them out."

"Scoop 'em out? With what?"

"I don't know. Anything."

"Do I have to?"

Franklin looked at me. "Well, do you want to work here or not?"

I glanced down at the cigarette butts, bobbing on the yellowish water.

"Got 'em lined out, Franklin?" Mr. Dugan opened the restroom door. He had changed into a red short-sleeved shirt that had DUGAN'S MOBIL printed on the back with a flying horse underneath it. Clarence was embroidered in cursive above the shirt's pocket and the pocket, like his cheek, bulged with Red Man Chewing Tobacco.

"Almost."

"Just don't forget to lock her up tight, Franklin."

"I won't, Mr. Dugan. Should I come in early tomorrow since I've got the keys?"

"No, I got an extra set. Just bring 'em in with you at noon. Night, boys."

"Good night, Mr. Dugan. Good luck bowlin'."

Mr. Dugan carried the bowling bag over to his Buick, slid it in the back seat and, swatting the top of his head with the rolled-up *Grand River Sentinel* he took from under his arm, got into the car and drove away.

"I better get up front."

Franklin left, so I looked for a cup or something to scoop out the cigarette butts but couldn't find anything. I walked over to the women's and opened the door. "Geez, you're almost finished."

Fudgie was scrubbing out the toilet. He looked up and grinned. "I work hard. Maybe Mr. Dugan give me a job with Franklin."

"Do you have a cup in here or something?"

We looked around the bathroom.

"That's okay. I'll find one."

"Hey, Pete?"

"Yeah?"

"Thanks, man."

"For what?"

Fudgie looked down into the toilet at the blue water he was swishing. "I don' know. Jus' thanks."

I grinned. "I guess me and you are the wizards of toilet bowls now."

"The what?"

"The wizards of . . . nothin'. Never mind."

I walked back to the office where Franklin was leaning against the cash register, staring outside at the empty bays.

"I need a cup or something."

"Over there." Franklin motioned over his shoulder. "Look. Fudgie's already emptying the trash. Boy, that guy's a worker. And did you see him eat those peppers?"

I nodded and got the cup.

"Pete, after you finish the men's, I want you to take the hose and rinse off the . . . oh, great."

"What?"

"Look who's comin'."

Out past the pumps and the swarm of moths and mosquitoes zigzagging under the bay lights, the front rim of a bicycle flashed over the curb along Gateway Avenue. The rim continued across the pavement and skidded to a stop right outside the office window. Rickie Livers got off his bicycle and walked over to the screen door, letting the bike fall to the pavement. His little brother Eddie came skidding in right behind him.

"Hey, Franklin! Did you see that?"

Rickie and Eddie Livers walked into the office, the screen door banging behind them.

"What?"

"That wheelie. I bet I did a wheelie for about half the block. Huh, Eddie?"

Eddie nodded his head, laughing.

"Hey, Peter-head! Look, Eddie, it's Peter-head. What's he doin' here? Gettin' some gas?"

Rickie Livers bent to the side, lifted one leg, and made a farting sound through his lips. He laughed as I ran my hand over my sore knuckles.

Franklin stepped from around the cash register. "What do you want, Livers?"

"I wanna tell you 'bout what I did today. But first me and Eddie want a couple of those Big Hunks."

Rickie Livers pulled out a dime and, smirking over at me, slapped it down on top of the cash register. Franklin took it and tossed them a couple of candy bars he took from under the glass counter next to the register.

"Anyways, me and Eddie goes down to the canal, you know, and Buddy Phillips is down there with the Carter twins and they got them a big rope comin' down from the tree and they think they're hot stuff swingin' over the water, you know, so me and Eddie hides behind these bushes and we start heavin' dirt clods and I get Buddy Phillips right here under the eye."

Rickie Livers pointed his dirty finger to a spot under his eye and then bit off his candy bar."And you know what? He falls right into the water—kersplash!—cryin' bloody murder and they don't even know who done it."

Rickie and Eddie Livers doubled over in laughter, their mouths full of white nougat and peanuts.

"Should've saw Buddy Phillip's stupid face, Franklin. It was like this." Rickie Livers screwed his freckled face into a mass of wrinkles, eyes crossed and his mouth twisted to the side. Franklin looked over at me.

"Go finish the men's, Pete."

Rickie Livers looked over at me, grinning. "They got you cleanin' the shitter out, huh, Peter-head?"

Rickie Livers bent over and made that farting sound with his lips. He and his little brother laughed but then, suddenly, Rickie Livers stopped laughing. Fudgie walked by the window outside, dragging empty trash cans.

"What's he doin' here?"

"Workin', just like Pete. He cleaned the shitter out, too, Livers. Maybe you'll want to ask him about it."

Franklin grinned as Rickie Livers glanced back at me and licked his lips. "I ain't scared of him."

"Gee, you got a lot tougher than last time you saw him, Livers."

"That's 'cause I didn't see him comin' last time."

"Well, good, because now you can see him comin' 'cause here he is."

Fudgie walked into the office from the garage where he had put the trash cans. "What you wan' now, Franklin?"

Franklin looked down at him from behind the cash register and then over at Rickie Livers. "Well, since you got rid of the trash—at least most of it—I guess you can just have a seat. Thanks, Fudgie."

Fudgie walked deliberately between Rickie and Eddie Livers and sat down on the window sill.

"Fudgie, remember Rickie Livers?"

He looked at Rickie Livers. "*Sí*. I remem'er him."

"Well, Rickie has a question for you. Go ahead, Livers. Ask him what you asked Pete."

Rickie Livers stuck the Big Hunk in his back pocket, jammed his hands into his cutoff jeans, and glanced around the office, his little brother Eddie staring up at him. "I don't have to ask him nothin' if I don't want."

Franklin looked over at Fudgie and then back at Rickie Livers. Franklin was grinning. "If he don't scare you, Livers, I guess you must be pretty tough. At least you've always acted pretty tough around Pete here."

Rickie Livers stared at Franklin.

"Well, let's see how tough you are, Rickie."

Franklin hit the cash register and the drawer dinged open. "Here's two bucks sayin' Fudgie's tougher than you."

Rickie Livers and Fudgie stared at the two one-dollar bills Franklin dangled above the cash register.

"I got money. I don't need to fight no beaner for it."

Fudgie stood, clenching his fists, but Franklin held up his hand.

"Who said anything about fighting, Livers?" Franklin pushed aside the 7-Up bottle of jalapeño juice and picked up the jar. Rickie Livers walked over and looked into it.

"What's that?"

Franklin put the two dollars down, opened the jar, and took out the jalapeño. "This is Mr. Dugan's pepper."

Rickie Livers took it by the stem and held it to his nose. "So?"

Franklin snatched it back.

"So you and Fudgie'll both eat half and the first one to drink something loses."

"And if I don't drink nothin', I get the money?"

"Yep. Two bucks."

"What if neither of us drink nothin'?"

"Well, I guess I'll give you each a buck."

Rickie Livers looked over at his little brother and then slapped his hands and rubbed them together. "Hot dog! It's a deal!"

We gathered around Franklin as he took out his pocketknife, snapped it open, and laid the pepper on Mr. Dugan's desk. Carefully, he ran the blade lengthwise down the pod, splitting it into halves. One he gave to Fudgie, the other to Rickie Livers.

"Okay. You got to chew it all or you're disqualified. I'll count to three and you stick the peppers in your mouths and chew 'em up and swallow 'em. Understand?"

Rickie Livers and Fudgie stood nose-to-nose, the pepper positioned directly in front of their mouths. Rickie Livers licked his red lips and stared down cross-eyed at his half.

"Everybody ready?"

Fudgie and Rickie Livers nodded.

"One . . . two . . . three . . . go!"

They popped the peppers and began to chew. Fudgie ate slowly, as he had with Mr. Dugan earlier. Rickie Livers, on the other hand, chewed rapidly, his jaw working furiously under his freckled skin. Rickie Livers swallowed and Fudgie swallowed. Rickie Livers shrugged and Fudgie shrugged. Rickie Livers' face turned red and Fudgie's smiled.

But Rickie Livers' face had always been red. It was red when he chased me down alleyways, through vacant lots, or around playgrounds. When he stood at the base of trees and yelled at me as I shinnied skyward out of his reach. When he laughed at the mean jokes or the tricks he played on me. And it was red when he collared and punched me, turning my own face bloody red. And now Rickie Livers' face was redder than ever as he and Fudgie stood staring at each other. Rickie Livers' eyes watered and his nose ran. His lips curled back and the tears ran down his cheeks. He made a hissing sound as he sucked air in and out through his teeth. He wiped at his nose with the back of his hand and began to sweat. He fanned his mouth, clutched at his throat, but refused to budge.

Standing in front of Mr. Dugan's desk, taking the 7-Up bottle in my sore-knuckled hand and watching a red Rickie Livers trying to withstand the fire that raged within him, I remembered all the rotten things he had done to me and all the mean things he had said. And when Rickie Livers lunged to grab the 7-Up bottle I thrust out to him, when I saw the hate and fury in his eyes as I wouldn't let go of the bottle and saw him lurch instead, gasping and sputtering across the office to drown himself in the drinking fountain, I knew Rickie Livers would hate me more than he had ever hated me before and I knew, in turn, that I could have made his hate so much worse. But it really didn't matter now. Either way, I was never going to let Rickie Livers or anyone else bully me again.

19

The sky was black, a dark envelope pricked with stars closing down around us as we stood in front of Mrs. Henderson's porch and stared at the light glowing against her living-room curtains.

"Think she's up, Franklin?"

"I don't know. Hope Win is, though."

A breeze washed in through the screen and rustled the leaves of dried-out ferns and geraniums and dusty African violets she had brought back from her last vacation in Arizona. Mrs. Henderson loved house plants. In fact, she loved them to death. Outside, where Mother Nature could help her with watering and sunlight, she did fine. Her iris and gladiolas were the pride of the neighborhood and the rosebush growing up against her back fence was as tall as ours. But once Mrs. Henderson moved inside with her plants, even if it was just inside the porch, her green thumb turned as black as gangrene.

The large waxy spear-like leaves of rubber plants and philodendrons curled up and turned brown as though she had held a torch to them. Healthy full-bodied ferns dried out and shed their leaves like Saint Bernards shed hair in summertime. And every last one of the African violets—which she potted and repotted and set into every empty space on the window sills among all the porcelain Swiss-boy-yodeling knickknacks she collected—died just in time for fresh recruits to be brought in the next year. Mrs. Henderson's house was a house plant's torture chamber and she loved each and every dying one of them.

Franklin opened the screen and we tiptoed past her plants to the front door, the porch swing creaking from its chain. Franklin cracked the door and we slid inside, easing it shut behind us.

"If you two ain't the dangedest pair of night owls, I don't know who is."

Mrs. Henderson sat in her rocker with Spot perched on her shoulder. She wore one of her multi-colored mumus and the saguaro lamp behind her shone off her bare shoulder where the mumu hung to the side. Spot straddled her white brassiere strap, pecking at a saltine Mrs. Henderson held between those short arthritic fingers.

"You two sit yourselves down here while I feed this vulture the rest of his snack."

Spot tweeped as Franklin and I sat on the sofa.

"He is, without a doubt, the racketiest bird I ever knew. If you don't give him his nightly treat, he'll shriek and carry on 'til the sun comes up. And it don't matter what you drape over that cage of his, if he don't get his treat, he's going to throw a ruckus and that's all there is to it."

Spot pecked at the saltine, his little curved beak working furiously and the tiny pearl of a tongue flashing from his mouth. Mrs. Henderson shifted her attention from Spot and looked over at Franklin and me. "Now, where you been off to this time? Keepin' track of you two is like keepin' track of a couple of peas in a tossed green salad."

"I had to work. I told ya."

"Franklin Caviness, you don't tell me nothin' so don't you go an' get your nose all out of joint. And you, Pete, I suppose you were out makin' a fortune again, too. Right?"

"Kinda."

"Well, don't you two move 'cause there's a couple of things I been waitin' all day to tell ya."

Mrs. Henderson struggled up from the rocker and held her index finger in front of the bird so it could have a perch to be put into the cage. Spot knew this routine and beat his wings, fluttering up on Mrs. Henderson's head. He perched in her tangle of hair like a quail hiding in bramble.

"Spotty! Get down off me!"

Mrs. Henderson reached up but Spot had other ideas as he took flight and beat his way across the living room, landing on the drapes where he clung with sharp silver-banded claws.

"Spotty! Come back here!"

Mrs. Henderson started toward him but he inched up the drape, pulling himself along with claws and beak until he was perched atop the curtain rod.

"Get down from there!"

Mrs. Henderson looked helplessly at her fugitive bird.

"If he ain't the dangedest thing. I just got his wings clipped not three weeks ago and look at him up there. Just as proud as if he was one of them there peacocks instead of a little piddley parakeet."

Spot tweeped and began preening his tail feathers. Mrs. Henderson shook her head.

"Oh well, fiddlesticks. Let him stay up then. I swear, between you two and that little feather duster I'm just about plum wore out. Come on in the kitchen and I'll get you a snack."

As we followed Mrs. Henderson down the hallway to her kitchen, Spot flapped by and landed on her shoulder.

"Must've heard me say snack."

She put Spot into his cage and then poured us each a tall glass of milk and set out a platter of Oreos. Sitting down at the table with us, she watched us dunk our cookies into the milk and eat. "Want anything else? There's some cold meat loaf in the fridge."

We shook our heads. Mrs. Henderson took the empty platter and set it on the counter. She then sat back down, clasped her hands on the table, and sighed. "Well, guess who I seen today?"

"Who?"

She rubbed one thumb over her other. "I seen that sister of yours."

Franklin and I sat up. "Where?"

"She come over here to see Winnie."

"She did?"

Mrs. Henderson nodded.

"Did she take him with her?"

"Nope. But she would've liked to. That dang preacher was right outside there in his car waitin' for 'em."

"He was?"

"Yep. And Winnie throwed a fit when I wouldn't let him go."

Mrs. Henderson shook her head, looking down at her lap. "Poor little tyke don't know what to do." Pursing her lips, Mrs. Henderson pressed one of her fists beneath her nose. "Loves his sis but hates that preacher and, all the while, the little guy misses his . . ."

Mrs. Henderson's voice cracked. She took a Kleenex from the pocket of her mumu. "I'm sorry, boys. I just feel so sorry for him . . . for all of you."

Mrs. Henderson dabbed at her eyes and blew her nose into the Kleenex. We fidgetted in our seats and stared down into our now empty glasses. Franklin and I weren't used to seeing Mrs. Henderson cry. When Mom was gone or too sick to take care of us herself, Mrs. Henderson was always the one there to keep us from crying. And now that Mom wasn't there at all, Mrs. Henderson's crying just didn't seem right. But then, little in our world seemed right.

"Mrs. Henderson?"

"Yes, Petey."

"What'd Mary say?"

216

Mrs. Henderson wiped her eyes and nose and stuffed the Kleenex into her pocket. "Said she misses everybody but that she's gotta follow the Lord's will."

Franklin and I looked at each other and shrugged. "What does that mean, Mrs. Henderson?"

Pulling up the brassiere strap that had fallen over her shoulder, she leaned forward in the chair, red eyes narrowing. "Means that preacher's still got her like this." And she brought her old arthritic hand up in front of our faces and clenched it, balling it into a fist until it turned white and shook with emotion—an emotion of a different kind.

* * *

Erwin was awake. The commotion with Spot and Mrs. Henderson had startled him so it was just a matter of getting his clothes on and waiting for the soft sandy shuffle of Mrs. Henderson's slippers against the linoleum floor to cease as she went about her nightly ritual of watering all her house plants—whether they needed it or not. The three of us slipped out the back door without a peep, even from Spot.

"What about them ghosts?"

Franklin let out a sigh and looked down at his youngest brother who, if he were walking any closer, would have been between Franklin's legs. Our street was quiet as usual at this time of night and the tall sycamores along the curb swayed against the sky making it seem even darker.

"There's no ghosts, Win. Don't listen to what Pete says."

"You said there was, too. I heared ya."

"I was kiddin'. There's no such thing. Tell him, Pete."

Actually, we had been telling Erwin ever since he could understand that ghosts and witches and other goblins don't exist. But we could never quite convince him.

As fearless as Erwin was in battle, he was every bit as fearful in sleep. From his and Mary's bed, he could see skeletons and death masks and monsters in every dress and shirt hanging from the closet. Flying rats and monkeys with jagged yellow teeth swooped through his dreams, and late at night he could hear snakes slither across the floor toward him and the heavy footsteps of headless men. And when he was sick with fever, the fiends of his dreams multiplied and Mom would sit up with him all night, stroking his forehead or singing as a way of keeping them at bay.

"How can there be ghosts in our own house, Win? Pa built it. There's no ghosts."

We stood under the elm in the vacant lot, staring across the street at our darkened home. Old man Hillar's house next door was dark, too, as was every other house on the street. But our house seemed the darkest.

Erwin and I followed Franklin across the street, up the driveway, and around to the back. Franklin squatted and lifted out his bedroom window he had left unfastened.

"Okay, Win. Let's go."

Erwin stood next to me and backed away. Franklin looked at him. "Come on. It's easy. Just like you did before."

Erwin shook his head.

"I don't think he wants to, Franklin."

"I can see that, stupid. But he's got to."

Franklin stood and reached for his arm, but Erwin moved behind me. "Get over here, Win. This is the only way. It's too small for us."

Franklin reached around me and grabbed him. Clutching my side, Erwin tried to twist his arm away. I grabbed Franklin's wrist. "I'll do it."

Franklin looked at me. "No, you're not going to take your clothes off again. That's stupid. Win can get in easy. Come on, Erwin."

Franklin began pulling him to the window.

"No!" He struggled to get free.

Jostled between them, I finally shoved against Franklin. He stumbled back and kicked the window leaning up against our house. The glass shattered through the quiet of the neighborhood like a gunshot.

"Oh, great! Look what you did!"

Erwin and I stood looking down at the broken pieces against the cement patio and Franklin squatted to pick them up when the spotlight hit us head-on. We froze like rabbits in a car's headlights.

"Don't budge!"

A second smaller light shone off to the side and grew larger as it moved toward us.

"Much as blink an' I'll blast yas!"

The smaller light jiggled up our sidewalk from the alleyway and then stopped in front of us, shining into our eyes and reflecting off a steel-blue barrel and a pointy metal head bobbing behind it.

"Yous little piss-ants."

The flashlight clicked off and old man Hillar slid the shotgun from under his arm and slumped down onto one of our lawn chairs. He leaned the gun against the house and using both hands, lifted his German pith helmet from his head and set it on the patio. He squinted up at us shaking his head and then looked down running his hands through his hair.

"Yous little piss-ants."

His floodlight from next door continued to bathe us in light as he fumbled with the pocket of the army coat he had thrown on.

"Yous little . . ."

He finally wrestled the cigarettes out and lifted the whole pack to his mouth and bit the butt of one, pulling the pack away from it. He gnawed the end, wadding the rest of the pack in his hands and throwing it to the side.

"Damn it to hell . . ."

Old man Hillar wrung his hands between the skinny bare knees that protruded from his army coat as sharply as table corners from a shrunken tablecloth. Underneath, he wore a pair of boxer shorts and on his feet, a pair of tattered brown slippers. The cigarette turned this way and that in the floodlight as he chewed the end.

"Mr. Hillar?"

Old man Hillar stared down at his hands.

"Mr. Hillar, are you okay?"

Franklin placed his hand on his shoulder but the old man threw it off and staggered upright.

"Yous little sons-a-bitches! Breakin' into your own damn property! Could've filled your butts with buckshot! Spread yous across the yard like fresh horseshit!"

He yanked the chewed-up cigarette from his mouth and pitched it to the concrete, and then picked up the pith helmet and fitted it squarely down over his head.

"March!"

He grabbed the shotgun and we followed him back to his house, through the alley, under the string of barbed wire, and in and around the discarded motors and appliances and rusted-out thingumajigs that seemed to spring from his yard as abundantly as the kochia weed that surrounded them. In all the years we lived next door, he had never invited us to do anything, much less come into his house. And now as we stood just inside the back door, I knew, at least in part, why.

"Come on. I ain't gonna hurt ya—at least yet."

With arms drawn to our sides, we shuffled under a dimly flickering florescent light through the length of what once might have been a kitchen. Lining the counters on both sides, stacked to the ceiling and waffling outward from the sheer weight, sat boxes and fruit crates and metal milk baskets full of everything from old car batteries to the insides of radios, from light fixtures and plumbing elbows to clothes hangers and fruit jars. Greasy newspapers lay across the floor and on the kitchen table, which we had to edge around sideways, sat a lawnmower, belly-up and disemboweled with parts spread around it.

Old man Hillar propped his shotgun in the corner of the living room and sank into the only available chair, an armchair that had just enough spring to keep his bony backside from hitting the floor. The rest of the room resembled the kitchen with the exception of a large cracked aquarium full of cobwebs instead of water, spiders instead of fish, and an orange life jacket smudged brown with dried mud. He tipped his pith helmet back and gawked at us, scratching at his boxers underneath the army coat.

"You gots to get a hold of it."

We stood in front of him, shifting our weight back and forth, arms folded tightly to our bodies.

"When it's slippin' is when you latches onto it and squeezes it." He paused. "Then when you gots it in your hands, you knows it's worth somethin'."

We nodded.

"Otherwize, it just pisses away and there's no gettin' it back."

Old man Hillar lifted his pith helmet, set it on the arm of the chair, and replaced it with the dirty-yellow John Deere cap. He held the point of the helmet and rocked it back and forth and then he did something we had never seen him do before: he smiled—a crusty, grizzled, almost pained smile from under the bill of his cap.

"Life's just that way. You gots to learn it, damn it, or it ain't fish piss."

He pulled himself up then and went crackling off down the hallway over the newspapers to another room, leaving us standing in his living room.

"Let's get out of here, Franklin."

"Look at all this junk. What do you think he does with all this stuff?"

"I don't know, but I want to . . ."

Old man Hillar suddenly came back down the hallway carrying a shoe box. He walked past us into the kitchen.

"Git in here." He set the box on the table next to the mower and rummaged around in it.

"Here." He handed Franklin a doorknob.

"What's this?"

Old man Hillar grabbed it back and held it up to Franklin's face.

"It's a damn doorknob. See? What do you thinks it is?"

Franklin looked at it, again. "Hey, that's ours."

Old man Hillar tossed the knob back into the shoe box and then thrust the box into Franklin's arms.

"Mr. Hillar, how'd you . . ."

Reaching into the pocket of his army jacket, old man Hillar brought out a key. "Here, you needs this." He gave it to Franklin and then herded us back through the kitchen toward the back door. Franklin stopped and turned around.

"Mr. Hillar, how'd you get our doorknobs?"

Old man Hillar pushed us on outside. "I works at a damn hardware store. I put the sons-a-bitches in."

And he slammed the back door. Franklin looked down into the shoe box.

"Put what in, Franklin?"

Franklin shook his head. "I don't know, unless . . ."

The back door jerked open but we couldn't make out old man Hillar standing there for all the shadows and floodlights.

"An' yous damn mower'll be ready tomorrow. Now git!"

The back door slammed again and we could hear him click the locks and thunk the bolts into place. Franklin hurried off toward the alley with Erwin and me trailing after him.

"Was that our mower, Franklin?"

Franklin opened the gate and we ran up the sidewalk to the back door.

"I think that was our mower on the table, Franklin. Why doesn't old man Hillar like us?"

Franklin took the key, held it up to look at its teeth, and then slid it into the lock. Taking a deep breath, he turned the key and the door swung open. Franklin let out his breath and looked down at me. "I think maybe he does."

* * *

"Pete. Come here. I want to show you something."

I got up from lying on my bed and throwing my football in the air and followed Franklin into the workshop.

"Where's Win?"

"I don't know. He was just down here. Look."

Franklin pointed to the middle of the floor where, next to the table saw and sawhorses, stood the coffee table Pa had been working on for Mom's birthday. I walked over to it.

"Don't touch it. It's still wet."

The familiar smell of varnish hung in the room and the coffee table shone.

"Did you do this?"

Franklin stood with his feet wide, hands on his hips. "Do you like it?"

The grain of the table top stood out in deep brown streaks against the lighter brown and glistened under the light. Finely sanded legs were preserved under a sheen of varnish, and I squatted and looked at the underside. It too was brushed smooth. I stood, staring down at the table. Franklin looked at me. "Well?"

"Did you really do this, Franklin?"

He smiled slightly and then his face drew serious as he looked back down at the coffee table. "No, Pete."

I looked up at my big brother, the shine from the table catching in his eyes. "Who did then?"

He continued to stare at the coffee table. "Pa did."

"Pa?"

He nodded slowly, eyes still fixed on the coffee table, unblinking.

"What do you mean, Franklin? How could Pa . . ."

Franklin moved his eyes from the table and looked down at me. "Pa did it, Pete. I just helped him finish." And then he turned away and I followed him out of Pa's workshop and up the stairs to see about our little brother.

* * *

Erwin lay curled up asleep on his and Mary's bed, clutching his teddy bear. The overhead light was on.

"Franklin, where's Mary's lamp?"

He walked over to the nightstand where Mary's ballerina lamp had sat and looked around on the floor. He opened the drawer underneath and then quickly straightened as though he had seen something he didn't like. Turning, he rolled back the closet door. Empty. Franklin strode across the bedroom to the dresser and flung open the drawers. They were empty, too. Wheeling around, he shot out of the bedroom and I could hear him roll back the closet doors in Mom and Pa's room. And at the same moment, I heard the back door.

"Winnie. Winnie, get up."

I pulled Erwin up from the bed. Still clutching the teddy bear, he rubbed his eyes as I turned off the bedroom light and pulled him into the darkened hallway. The back door closed.

"Franklin! Someone's here!"

Franklin appeared and grabbed us by our shirts, yanking us into our parents' bedroom. He quickly bent down to Erwin and held his finger to his lips. Something fell crashing to the floor in the kitchen.

"Quick! In here!"

Franklin turned off the bedroom light and pulled Erwin and me into the closet, clothes hangers tinkling above us. Franklin slid the door in front of us, leaving it slightly cracked.

"Swing loooow . . ."

The bedroom light turned on.

"Sweeeet chaaaa-riii-oot!"

I peeked out through the crack. Uncle Herbert stood in front of Mom and Pa's big dresser mirror.

"Cominnng for . . . to carry meeee . . . hoooome!"

Uncle Herbert threw his head back, tipping a bottle toward the ceiling. He wavered but then caught himself and clunked the bottle down on the dresser. Righting himself, he snapped to attention and saluted sharply into the mirror.

"I look over Jordonnnn . . ."

His saluting hand slid over his brow as knees buckled and he surveyed Jordan around the room in the mirror. His body swayed and his head bobbed to the tune.

"And what do I seeee . . ."

He crouched forward and stared goggle-eyed into the mirror.

"Cominnng for to carry me hoooome!" His arms stretched wide.

"Swing loooow . . . sweet chaaa-ri-ot!"

He rose, his head bent back, arms stretched wider.

"Cominnnng . . . fooor . . . to carrrry . . . meee . . . hoooome!"

Uncle Herbert's arms fell to his sides. His head drooped forward and he stood there, swaying like a willow sapling in the breeze—a tall willow sapling—as we watched him wide-eyed from the bedroom closet. Erwin tugged at Franklin's shirt. "He's sleepin', huh?"

"Shhhh."

Uncle Herbert's head snapped up. He looked around the room. A broad smile broke across his face.

"A baaand of angelllls . . ."

He bent his arms to either side and flapped his hands up and down from his wrists, as Spot had flapped across Mrs. Henderson's living room earlier. He looked at the closet.

"Comin' after meeee . . ."

He was talking more than singing now, as he snatched the bottle and tottered toward the closet.

"Comin' for to carrrry . . . meeee . . ."

He stopped in front of us and reached for the closet door. I scrunched my eyes shut.

"Hooooome . . ."

No one breathed.

"Marge?"

I cracked open one eye. Uncle Herbert still stood in front of us, one arm outstretched, but now his eyes were fixed on something across the bedroom. He wavered.

"Marge?"

His arm dropped to his side. Without taking his eyes from whatever he saw, he threw his head back and guzzled. He wiped his mouth on the sleeve of the same suit coat he wore that first morning he had shown up at our front door and then staggered across the bedroom out of sight.

"Oh, Marge. Marge, Marge, Marge. My little sister Marge. Forgive me, Marge. For I am a simple man with simple needs. I have very little in this old world, Margie. You know that. You know that, Margie, and so does Frank so please forgive me. Why doesn't Frank like me, Marge? Frank never liked me. Why is that? Well, if that's the way you like it, Frankie boy, then that's the way you like it. Don't invite me to eat Christmas with you anymore. I've got plenty of places, plenty of friends I can see. You bet I do. You bet I cockle-doodle-do, Frankie boy. And the duckie went quackety-quackie-quack. And old Frankie went doo-be-ty doop be-do."

The bedroom fell quiet and then we could hear the bed screech against the wood floor as Uncle Herbert bumped into it and reeled across the bedroom toward the mirror. He plopped down in front of it on the edge of the bed. In his hands, he held the framed picture of our mother.

"Margie, Margie, Margie."

He sagged there, looking down at the picture, and then lifted his head to the mirror. "Herbert T. Merriweather. It's my pleasure, madam." Uncle Herbert held his hand out to the mirror and shook hands with the air. "That's T as in Theodore. Old rough and ready Teddy. Yes, he is, as a matter of fact. My first cousin. We grew up together, he and I. Course, he was much older, you see, but we were quite close, nonetheless."

He looked down at the picture. "Isn't that right, Marge? Here, allow me to introduce to you my sister, Margaret."

Uncle Herbert held Mom's picture up to the side of his head, facing the mirror. "No, no relation to Margaret Truman. But they were great friends, weren't you, Marge? Went to college together, those two. Great friends, freat griends."

Mom's picture slowly lowered in tandem with Uncle Herbert's head until finally falling to the floor as his chin drooped to his chest. But with the sound of the frame hitting, his chin bounced up.

"Marge. Marge?"

He glanced around the bedroom and then looked down at the picture. "Oh, Marge. What have I done?"

Bending over, he slid off the bed in slow-motion and pitched forward, pressing his face to the floor. He rolled over and slumped sideways against the dresser, clutching the picture to his chest.

"No, Marge. No, the children are fine. I'm taking care of them, Marge, so don't you worry. They're just fine. They love their Uncle Herbie. And Uncle Herbert loves them. Yes, he does, Marge."

He hugged the picture frame tighter and rocked back and forth. "Oh, Marge. Talk to me. Tell me something, Marge. Please tell me everything's okay. Please, Margie, please . . ."

Uncle Herbert continued to rock, eyes closed, his long body still slumped against the dresser. Slower and slower he rocked and just as the rocking had almost stopped, Erwin turned suddenly to Franklin, tugging at his shirt. Clothes hangers tinkled brightly above us.

"Marge?"

Uncle Herbert struggled to his feet, glancing around the room. "Marge? That's you, isn't it?"

The hangers quieted but it was too late. Uncle Herbert stepped toward the closet, hands out in front as though walking through darkness.

"Marge?"

We stood still, cringing, as he stepped closer.

"It's okay, Marge. Don't cry. It's okay."

Uncle Herbert whispered now, his voice raspy, head down, mouth open, and his nose stuck into the crack.

"Don't cry, Margie. Don't cry."

His fingers appeared in front of us along the inside edge of the closet door and then he rolled the door back. "It's okay . . . Herbert's here."

Franklin and I stared as white as corpses into the bleary drunken eyes straining into the closet. His jaw dropped. He staggered backward against the foot of the bed as Erwin bolted from between us out of the closet.

"Aaaahhhh!" Uncle Herbert stiffened. His eyes and mouth stretched even wider and then fell slack. His head and back bounced against the mattress and his body jiggled and then lay still.

Franklin and I stood gawking from the closet, the clothes hangers tinkling like Mom's wind chime and Erwin screaming from the house like a ghost in someone else's dream—our Uncle Herbert's.

20

Mom's brown couch came out first. It was long and heavy and from where we were sitting in the elm, we could tell the two men were struggling with it.

"A Whitey Ford for a Marv Throneberry? You sure?"

I nodded.

Shaking his head, Franklin took my Whitey Ford and handed me Marv Throneberry of the Mets. We looked up from our baseball cards as the men finally lifted the couch and pushed it into the trailer.

"This makes three Whitey Fords. All I need is a Bill Stafford and I'll have the whole pitchin' staff."

The men went back into the house and another one, a skinny short guy, came out carrying table lamps, one in each hand. He walked up the ramp and disappeared into the trailer.

"Got any more you want to get rid of?"

I shuffled through my cards.

"I don't see how you guys stand it." Lee Hooker perched on the limb above us, holding a pearl-handled pocketknife in his fist—if you could call a four-inch blade a pocketknife—digging it into the elm. A cigarette, the end burnt back with a half inch of ash, hung from his lips and I could see his eyes squint from the smoke curling under his wrap-around sunglasses.

"I mean starin' at those stupid cards all the time, tradin' 'em back and forth."

He shook his head as he leaned into the tree, the elm shavings falling to the plywood floor of our tree house. "Jesus. You know what those guys at Buena Vista would've done to you if they'd caught you with them things?"

Lee Hooker stopped carving for a moment to watch the first two men carry out the Indian hand-woven rug on their shoulders. It was rolled up and tied with twine and the weight of it turned the men's faces red.

"They would've made you eat 'em."

The rug disappeared into the trailer.

"I don't get it, Pete."

"What?"

Franklin scratched his head. "Why you gettin' rid of all your Yankees?"

I shrugged, looking down at my cards, trying to decide the next one to trade. "'Cause they always win."

"So?"

"So, I like the underdogs. They get my hema . . . hela . . . helicopter goin'."

"What?"

The three men were carrying out the kitchen table now. One of its legs caught on the spring of the screen door and the skinny man swore.

"You think they actually pay these guys?" Lee Hooker smirked and then went back to carving.

"Here." I held out Roger Maris to Franklin.

"Roger Maris? You're kiddin'." Franklin stared at me. "What do you want for him?"

"Got any more Mets?"

Franklin flashed through his deck, shaking his head. The kitchen chairs followed the table and then out came Pa's stuffed rocker. One of the men carried it hunched over with short quick steps as he might have carried a keg of beer and then hoisted it into the trailer.

"I can't believe you're gettin' rid of Roger Maris. I thought he was your favorite."

I shrugged.

"What'd you say you wanted for him?"

"I don't care."

Franklin started to say something but then we all turned and watched them bring out the big living-room mirror. It was covered with a sheet and the men carried it carefully down the steps, the skinny guy directing their way, and set it on the grass on its edge.

"Where they taking all this stuff?" Lee Hooker pulled the cigarette from his mouth, blew into the cuts he had carved in the tree, and brushed the shavings from his lap. Some flicked off into my hair. Franklin shrugged, watching the men slide the mirror inside the trailer and tie it against the wall.

"I guess they're takin' everything over to some storage place. Least that's what Mrs. Henderson says. Here, Pete."

I took the stack of Mets from Franklin.

Lee Hooker whistled. "Look."

One of the men was tapping a screwdriver into the hinge of the front door using a hammer. He set the hammer on the floor, grabbed both ends of the door, and worked it away from the jamb.

Lee Hooker snapped his pocketknife shut. "They're taking your whole house apart. How can they do this? Ain't there a law or something?"

Lee Hooker dropped to the tree-house floor. With a kick of each foot, he pulled at his pant legs to keep them from riding up in his crotch.

"Can't we do somethin', Frankie?"

Franklin stared across the street. The men were muscling the box springs of our parents' bed through the front doorway. The man in front backed down the steps and then up the ramp and, together, the two men lugged it into the trailer.

"Here, Franklin."

Franklin turned to me and took the card. "Bill Stafford. Where'd you get this?" Turning the card over, he began reading the back of it. "What do you want for it?"

"Nothin'."

Lee Hooker leaned against the tree and took a last drag off his cigarette, stubbing it out on the callouses of his hand. He blew smoke up through the leaves. "Well, I don't think it's legal. Maybe I'll ask my probation officer about it."

By the time they tied the mattress and box springs alongside the mirror, it was noon. The men stretched out on our lawn in the shade of the trailer with their black lunch boxes. The skinny guy had a thermos and he poured coffee for the others.

Lee Hooker took a couple of cigarettes from the pack jammed into his front pants pocket and flipped one to Franklin. "You know what I like about Grand River?" He snapped his lighter open and lit his cigarette. "Nothin'."

Lee Hooker then tossed the lighter to Franklin. Franklin caught it, as he had the cigarette, and glanced over at me.

"I mean here it is the last week of summer and we got nothin' better to do than watch these goons eat their baloney sandwiches. Shit."

Lee Hooker took another drag and looked up, studying the leaves against the blue sky. "But I guess it beats Buena Vista. Where'd you say Mary's at?"

Franklin lit the cigarette and tossed the lighter back to Lee Hooker. He then took a short puff, staring down at the tree-house floor.

"She's still at the preacher's."

Lee Hooker snorted. "Oh, yeah, the preacher. Old billiard-ball head. Now there's a swell guy for ya. Did you see his face when Cargo jumped him?" Lee Hooker laughed. "He probably thought Cargo was goin' for his throat."

Lee Hooker doubled up and laughed harder. The three men on the lawn glanced across the street at us.

"Oh, man . . . good old Cargo."

Lee Hooker took his sunglasses off and wiped a tear from under one eye with the back of his hand. One corner of the eyeball was shot through with red and his eyelid was a bluish green color.

"What happened to your eye, Lee?"

He quickly slipped his sunglasses back on, shrugged, and smiled out the side of his mouth. "Me and my old man. Guess he didn't like me takin' yesterday off."

Franklin stared up at him. "What about today, then?"

Lee Hooker looked down at Franklin and me and then scanned the sky around through the tree limbs as though he had heard an airplane or the roll of thunder.

"What about today, Frankie? The sun's out. Summer's almost over. We're in a tree like a couple a three monkeys, watching' these goons eat soggy baloney sandwiches while they're takin' a break from takin' your beautiful house apart."

Lee Hooker glared across the street. "That's right! Goons!"

The three men looked up from the lawn.

"And to top it all off, your sister is off with some bald-headed preacher creep while you two Einsteins pass cards back and forth like it's the great-est thing since dual exhausts. So, yeah, what about today, Frankie?"

Lee Hooker suddenly grabbed the baseball cards from Franklin's hand and flung them into the air. They fluttered and turned in the sun like falling leaves, scattering in the weeds and dirt around the elm. Lee Hooker slid down the tree trunk—not even bothering with the splintery footholds nailed into it—and taking a last deep drag off his cigarette, strode across the street and flicked the butt into the middle of our lawn near the men. They fol-lowed him with their eyes as he stomped off down the street, but the men didn't get up and they didn't say anything and they didn't even stop chew-ing their sandwiches.

"What's wrong with him?"

"Shut up, Pete." Franklin stubbed his cigarette out on the tree-house floor; a tree shaving caught fire, glowed red, and then smoldered.

"What'd he write up there?"

"What?"

"See what he carved."

I stood and climbed up to the branch where Lee Hooker had been.

"Well?"

The two marks were etched smoothly. I ran my fingers over them.

"M.C. He carved out M.C."

"That all?"

"Yeah."

Franklin shook his head, biting his lower lip, and stared down at the tiny black cinder on the tree-house floor.

* * *

M.C. Mary Caviness. Mary. Mare. Even her name was pretty. Or maybe it was because she was pretty that made her name seem so. Like Marilyn Monroe. Or Jesus Christ. But they were both dead. Willie had said Jesus Christ was just another name in a history book. Maybe a name is just that, a name. Maybe it doesn't matter what anybody or anything is called. Words are imperfect little creatures, saith Willie. But Mary Caviness was pretty. In name and in person. Inside and out.

Mary never knew she was pretty and there was no explaining why. At school, boys settled into desks around her in almost every class and during the ten-minute break between subjects, sought her out in the hallways as though she were a drinking fountain and they parched P.E. students whose only subject was gym. At lunch in the cafeteria, she would often be the only girl at a table full of boys and after school, the unknowing reason for a shoving match or bloody lip in Crawford Park across the street. Her name and initials could be found doodled across countless desks and notebooks and her picture pressed inside wallets. And if it weren't for her older brother's tough reputation and the fact that he had flunked second grade and was in her same class, the group of boys she attracted may well have been a mob. But Mary didn't seem to notice all this attention. She grew up with boys and treated them mostly the same. Oddly, the exceptions seemed to be the most awkward boys, the ones with thick glasses or two buckteeth.

There was Norman Penderhaughten who lived two blocks away. Norman was the tallest and skinniest kid ever to walk the halls of Grand River Junior

High. From his great height, towering over Mary, he bent forward like the leaning tower of Pisa, shoulders rounded and stooped, head way down as though he were looking out the window of an airplane at the ground far below, the riddled cuticle of one index finger glued to his mouth. Norman Penderhaughten always looked as if he were in the middle of working on an algebra problem and those mornings when he walked Mary to school seemed to be the only time he actually solved one. His doubled-up fist would fall from his mouth to his side and the concentrated network of lines between his eyebrows would smooth out and give way to a slight close-mouthed smile as Mary chatted with him about whatever was on their minds that morning.

And then there was Eugene Kroll, a kid only Mary and his mother could stand. Eugene wore dimples drilled into his cheeks as deep as the puckers in Mrs. Henderson's pincushion pillows. They looked as though they had been sewn from inside his mouth and then tied off to his tongue. His hair was always oiled and combed to a perfect bob in front and didn't move no matter what he did or where he was going. His shirts were always ironed and clean and his shoes shined. Eugene wore horn-rimmed glasses across a straight sharp nose, used words no one else seemed to know, and snorted and whinnied whenever he laughed, which was often. Eugene Kroll had never received a B on any report card in his entire life—but then neither had Franklin although Franklin's grades spanned the other direction—and he told anyone who would listen that his father was a physician, not a doctor, in a place called Madagascar. Franklin swore Madagaskar was a double-A fueler driven by none other than Big Daddy Don Garlitz and did a quarter mile in around eight-and-a-half seconds. Trouble was, no one would listen to Eugene Kroll—no one except Mary. Mary had to tell us everything we knew about Eugene because we would rarely give him the satisfaction of telling us himself.

There had also been boys in grade school: Tony Parks, who had gotten polio and when Mary wasn't around, used more dirty words than Rickie Livers and all his brothers and sisters put together; Marvin Weaver, a chubby flat-topped kid who had a taste for Elmer's Glue and sucking ink from fountain pens; Ethan Drake, whose mother wouldn't allow him to say the Pledge of Allegiance; and Phil Greenwood, a boy so shy that saying hi to him might break him out in a sweat. All these boys Mary had spent time with and had become their friends, which made the more popular and handsome kids try even harder—and end up even further away.

And then there was Lee Hooker. Lee Hooker wasn't exactly handsome although he was good-looking in a kind of greased back sort of way, and he didn't really have many quirks unless you called an occasional swear word or cracked knuckles from auto-body putty a quirk. Sure, he smoked too many cigarettes but he could be discreet about that, and he had those occasional legal problems which no one dared mention. And then there was the mystery of his age. But despite all this, Lee Hooker was just Lee Hooker and for Mary he was in a category all his own.

"Hey, Mare! Up here!"

She turned around and looked up at me in the tree house and then quickly walked over to the vacant lot and began climbing up the foot pegs.

"What are you doing up here, Petey?"

"Nothin'."

She wore a new light blue dress—since the funeral and meeting the preacher, she wore nothing but dresses—and she had to pull it over her knees as she stepped up onto the plywood floor.

"Where's Franklin and Winnie?" Mary leaned against a limb to catch her breath.

"Franklin went to work. I don't know where Win is. Probably over at Mrs. Henderson's."

Mary squeezed my shoulder and smiled at me but I continued to stare at our house. The three men had finished loading the trailer and had driven it away and now there was a white truck backed up into our driveway, Cline's Painting and Remodel stenciled in red across its door.

"Isn't it exciting, Petey?"

My gaze snapped back to Mary. "Exciting? What?"

"This." She motioned with her eyes to our house. I looked back across the street, thinking I missed something. Men in white pants, T-shirts, and caps carried buckets and ladders in through the front doorway.

"What's exciting about it?"

"Our house, Petey. What they're doing."

Mary stared into my eyes. "You don't know, do you? No one told you."

I shrugged. "Told me what?"

Mary smiled and placed her hand on my arm. "Remember how Mom and Dad were always talking about repainting the living room?"

"Yeah."

"Well, that's what those men are going to do."

"They are?"

"They're going to repaint everything and put in new carpet and maybe even remodel a little. Won't Mom and Dad be happy, Petey?"

Mary's eyes danced as she looked across the street. "That's why we had to move out, so they can do all this and we won't be in their way."

I looked back across the street. "Really?"

She nodded, smiling, and then gave me a hug. "I just know everything's going to work out, Petey. I'll bet Mom and Dad are up there right now just smiling down at us."

Through the picture window we could see the men moving around like trout flashing in and out of shadows of the deep fishing holes Pa used to work with his fly rod, drawing the fly along the surface with short tugs of his line, waiting for the strike of fish against hook. But these weren't fish. They were men and they carried paint brushes and rollers and buckets of paint.

"Mare, you mean we can move back in after they're done doin' everything?"

"Well, probably not right away."

"When, then?"

Mary looked at me and shook her head. "I don't know exactly, Petey. Probably when we get to be old enough."

She looked down at her dress and brushed at its front with the back of her hand. "Where'd all these pieces of wood come from?" Mary slid the edge of her hand along the tree-house floor, sweeping wood shavings into a small pile.

I glanced up at the limb where Lee Hooker had carved her initials. "I don't know, Mare. Where do you want 'em to come from?"

But Mary didn't answer—as though she didn't hear me or didn't want to hear me—and just continued to make little piles on the tree-house floor.

* * *

Erwin was in the Indian Wash. Mary and I had tired of watching all those strangers traipse in and out of our house so we went to Mrs. Henderson's, but no one was there. We were walking down Hill Avenue to go see Franklin at the filling station when we spotted him. From the street over the wash we could see his small head parting the cattails below us.

"Winnie!"

Mary waved. Erwin looked up at us and then kept wading. We ran around the railing and scrambled down the steep embankment, knocking dirt clods splashing into the water.

"Winnie, wait."

Erwin stopped but continued scouring the water rushing by him.

"What're you doin', Win?"

"Yer scarin' 'em."

"What?"

"Muskrats."

Erwin wore his pajama top with the Lone Ranger's rearing horse, Silver, printed all over it. One side of the collar scrunched up under his chin from being unevenly buttoned and half the shirttail hung out his pants. The legs were rolled to his knees, and his bare feet and ankles wore stockings of deep gray mud with green moss clinging around them. In one arm he hugged a Mason jar.

"Where?"

Erwin pointed downstream at the other side of the wash.

"I don't see nothin'."

"They was there but ya scared 'em."

I looked at Mary and rolled my eyes.

"What do you have in your jar there, Winnie?"

Erwin lifted it to show Mary: two white feet and a sad half-moon mouth stuck splayed against the glass as though glued to it.

"That's a big one, Winnie. Are you going to let him go?"

Erwin looked at Mary for the first time and then shrugged. "Don't matter. I'll just catch 'im, again."

Squatting down, Erwin shoved the jar under the water as if dunking someone in a swimming pool. The air blub-blubbed to the top and the frog stretched out green in the current and disappeared into the moss.

"He's happier now, Winnie."

"So?" He straightened up, staring into the moss where the frog swam.

"Winnie, why don't you wash your feet off and come with us."

But he just continued staring and then shook his head.

"Come on, Win. I'll buy ya a Big Hunk."

"I don't wanna. I'm gonna catch a muskrat."

Erwin turned and parted the cattail using his free hand and took a few steps downstream. Mud sucked air where his feet were and then filled with water.

"Win, there's no muskrats in there."

"Is, too." Erwin glared up at me through the cattails. "I seen 'em."

Mary placed her hand on my shoulder and shook her head for me not to argue.

"Come on, Winnie. We know there are muskrats. We just want you to come with us to see Franklin."

"I always see him."

"Well, I don't."

"You don't see nobody but that fat guy."

Now it was Mary whom Erwin glared at.

"That's not true, Winnie."

"Is, too. You don't care 'bout nobody."

"Erwin . . ." Mary reached through the cattails to touch him but he jerked away and fell forward onto his hands, dropping the fruit jar and soaking the front of his pajama top.

"Winnie. I'm sorry . . ." She stepped down into the mud to help him up but Erwin was already standing, hands and forearms sleeved with muck.

"I hate you!" Erwin flung his hands out and splattered the new light-blue dress.

Mary stopped cold—as though struck with something more painful than mud—and with her mouth open and hands out to her sides, looked down at her dress like the bad guys in The Lone Ranger look down at the bullet hole in their bellies before they keel over face-first into the dust. But Mary didn't keel over. She only stared at her dress and then up at Erwin before turning and walking slowly up the steep embankment.

21

It was the last weekend of summer. At least the summer we knew, the one that had nothing to do with the position of earth and sun or the length of day and night. With Saturday came cooler temperatures to Grand River as though even the weather acknowledged what we already knew—that what turns the leaves colors, dries them out, and makes them fall from their branches has nothing to do with season and everything to do with the end of summer vacation.

It was the weekend grownups called Labor Day weekend but to us had always been a long three days of dread, knowing what was to come after it was over. School. But for Franklin, Mary, Erwin, and me, this weekend of 1962 was to be unlike any other we had ever had, the heat of one summer collecting as it did on that final Sunday afternoon.

It was also the weekend the Yankees moved three and then four games up on the Minnesota Twins in the American League, the Dodgers a game and a half over the Giants in the National—although the Dodgers' lead wouldn't last and just as Franklin had predicted, it wouldn't matter who the Yankees played in the World Series anyway—and the rest of the world was rife with tension and talk of war. Castro denied Cuba had fired on a U.S. Navy airplane. Algeria was on the brink of civil war—when I asked him, Franklin said Algeria was somewhere down between Alabama and Georgia. And the Reds failed in their attempt to launch a spacecraft to Venus just two days before the launch of Mariner II and pieces of their failure were circling the earth. I couldn't understand why the Reds would want to do anything other than play baseball and when I questioned Mrs. Henderson about it, she laughed so hard I felt stupid for asking.

The paper ran two photographs on the front page of the Saturday morning edition: President Kennedy, his wife Jacqueline, and daughter Caroline returning from a three-week vacation in Italy and a twenty-two-year-old peach picker shouldering a bulging canvas bag, the caption reading Peach Pickin' Whiz for the two-hundred-and-fifty-one bushels he picked in ten hours of work.

In the valley, fruit farmers were getting in their last loads of peaches, packing them into wooden crates to be loaded into boxcars and shipped east to Denver or west to Salt Lake City and beyond. Pickers and packing-shed workers began talk of where they were going next, California or Arizona or back to Mexico. High school boys talked about football and two-a-day practices, and high school girls talked about high school boys and what they would wear on the first day of classes. Mr. Dugan had already purchased his ticket for the Grand River Trojans' first football game as if the bleachers of City Park Stadium would be full instead of half-empty as they usually were for the first slaughter of the season. Old man Hillar had delivered our mower as promised and to prove it worked better than ever, mowed our grass and half the dried-out dahlias Mom had planted near the sidewalk by the alley. Mrs. Henderson continued to bake cookies, drown her house plants, and chase Spot around the living room. And Fudgie and his family, well, I didn't know what they were doing until Fudgie showed up that Saturday morning on Mrs. Henderson's porch.

"Hey, Pete."

"Fudgie. How'd you know where I . . ."

"Here." Fudgie held out an envelope.

I stepped out onto the porch, pulling the door shut behind me.

"What's this?"

Pete was written in cursive on the front.

"For you an' you brothers an' sister. A party."

"A party? For what?"

Fudgie shrugged. "End of picking season, man. Helen and José every year has a party."

Curling one bare foot over the other, I tore the end of the envelope open and took out a single piece of paper, an ink drawing of a peach blossom decorating its corner:

Dear Pete,
You and your family are invited to a party tonight at 7:00 o'clock to celebrate the end of the peach harvest. We all hope you can come and are anxious to see you and meet your brothers and sister.

Love, Helen and Joe Lucero

"I mus' go, Pete. José say if I no help today, I mus' tonight give Mama an' all the ladies tea." He glanced at me, smiling sheepishly, and turned to leave.

"Fudgie."

He hesitated but didn't turn around.

"Yeah, man?"

"How's your pa?"

"My papa, he is *muy bien. Gracias*, Pete. I mus' go now."

Fudgie walked quickly across Mrs. Henderson's porch to the screen door.

"Fudgie, how'd you know I was here?"

He stopped, taking in a deep breath, and stared out through the screen toward the street. "Las' night I help Franklin close *Señor* Dugan's gas station. I go with him to you house to change he's clothings. He tol' me, man. Franklin."

He turned and looked at me. "You house, it is beauty-ful, Pete."

And then he was out the door, running down the street, almost out of sight before the porch screen slammed behind him.

Shivering, I rubbed my arms as I stepped back into Mrs. Henderson's living room. Erwin was up now and he lay on the floor in his pajamas with a pillow, watching *The Magic Land of Allekazam*. Magic hypnotized Erwin. Every Saturday morning he sat wide-eyed in front of the television as if it hung from a golden chain and swung back and forth in front of him. A few other programs—*Mighty Mouse, The Lone Ranger, My Favorite Martian*—completely engrossed him but only *The Magic Land of Allekazam* could send him into a trance.

"Win, is Franklin up?"

He shook his head without taking his eyes from the set.

"What're you watchin'?"

"Magic."

A man wearing a sparkling sequined jumpsuit was sawing a lady in a wooden box in two. When he finished, the lady's top and bottom halves were wheeled out and away from each other. She smiled happily from one end of the stage while kicking her feet up and down from the other to the applause of the audience.

"That's pretty good."

"That's what I'm gonna do to Uncle Herbert."

"You are?"

"Then I'm gonna make him disappear. Allekazam! Poof!"

"Well, just make sure you get both halves gone. Wouldn't want his head layin' around so he can still eat."

"Yeah, I'll keep his head an' we can feed him worms!"

I left Erwin to his magic and walked through the living room down the hallway to the kitchen.

"Mrs. Henderson?"

Spot's cover was off so I looked outside. Mrs. Henderson stood out among the gladiola and iris holding the garden hose and wearing a knit sweater and her straw sun hat, the brim half unraveled with fringe. I turned and got a spoon and a bowl from the cupboard and went over to take out the milk when I saw them, taped together among Mrs. Henderson's recipes on the refrigerator door:

Margaret Caviness

Margaret Louise Caviness, 40, died at 3:00 p.m. Monday in St. Matthew's Hospital following a lengthy illness. She was the widow of Franklin Raymond Caviness, who preceded her in death by one day. Mrs. Caviness was born Margaret Louise Merriweather on September 11, 1922, at Hays, Kansas . . .

I closed my eyes and could see different colored spots shifting before me like light reflected off suspended crystal, slowly turning in the air. I opened my eyes, grabbing hold of the refrigerator door:

Franklin Caviness

Franklin Raymond Caviness, 52, a teamster employed with UGF Trucking, died Sunday on Spruce Mesa while fishing with his son . . .

"Peter Caviness, pick that bowl and spoon off the floor. What's wrong with you, boy? I swear, sometimes you kids act like you don't got a brain one in those heads of yours."

The back screen door banged, and I could hear her pull out a drawer and wrestle with a skillet as I squatted down and retrieved the bowl and spoon. Mrs. Henderson slid the skillet onto the stove and lit the burner.

"Did you see that package for you in there?"

I shook my head.

"Well, get that older brother of yours up and you can open it. It's for all four of you."

I walked down the hallway to the spare bedroom. Franklin lay sprawled out on his stomach, a pillow sandwiched around his head.

"Franklin. Franklin, get up."

I shook his shoulder. Franklin's head shot up like a lizard that has seen something move.

"Come on, Franklin. Mrs. Henderson wants us up."

Franklin's head dropped down face-first into the mattress and then he rolled over, working the roof of his mouth with his tongue. He rubbed the side of his head. "She always wants us up. Just because she can't sleep."

"She says there's a package for us."

"A package? From who?"

"I don't know. I didn't see it yet."

Franklin sat up, yawning, and pulled on his pants, the legs of which had been crumpled over his shoes like an accordian, as if the body inside had suddenly evaporated.

"Look." Franklin pointed to the corner of the room where a pile of grocery sacks stuffed with clothes sat around a table—Pa's coffee table. I walked over to it.

"Thought I better get it out before those goons carted it off, too. We're lucky they left it. You should see the house, Pete. They cleaned us out."

"Is it dry?"

"Of course."

I ran my hand over the top and down one leg. "It's beautiful. What's all this?" I pointed to the sacks.

"Our clothes. I'm surprised they didn't decide to wear 'em."

"Franklin, did you see what's on Mrs. Henderson's refrigerator?"

"Yeah, I saw."

"It's Mom and Pa's . . ."

Franklin held up his hand. "I said I saw."

"Well, why didn't I?"

"I don't know. It was in the paper."

"When?"

"Beats me. Before the funeral."

"Nobody showed me."

"So, what good would it done?"

I shrugged and looked down at my hand, studying my knuckles as Franklin pulled on his T-shirt. "Why'd ya tell Fudgie, Franklin?"

"What?"

"Fudgie said you took him over there last night."

"Yeah, he tagged along. I needed somebody to help me carry the table and all these sacks. So what?"

"So now he knows, Franklin."

"Knows what? About our house?"

"No, about . . ."

I looked up at Franklin, standing there with his hair poking up every which way above half-grumpy half-open eyes.

"You mean about Mom an' Pa? You mean you never told him?"

I shrugged.

"Why didn't you tell him, Pete? Isn't he your friend?"

I looked away, my chest heaving and holding tight with air.

"Didn't want to scare him with his own pa sick. Thought if I told him, he'd think his pa was gonna . . ."

I turned and started to walk away but Franklin caught me by the arm and turned me around. I quickly looked down.

"Fudgie is your friend, isn't he, Pete?"

I nodded and as Franklin put his arm around me, I held my breath, held it tight until my big brother squeezed it—and everything else—all the way out of me.

* * *

Franklin slumped at the kitchen table rubbing his face.

"What an' the devil time did you get in last night, Frank Junior?"

Franklin shrugged.

"I was up past *Hawaiian Eye* and you still wasn't home. When does Dugan close that place, anyways?"

"Depends."

Mrs. Henderson shook her head and looked over at me. "Pete, that package is in there on the coffee table. Why don't you go get it."

I picked up a small rectangular package and brought it back into the kitchen. On the front across brown wrapping paper was neatly printed MARY, FRANKLIN, PETER, AND ERWIN. It was bound with twine.

"Who's it from?"

Mrs. Henderson stood at the stove with a fork in her hand, poking sausage sizzling in the skillet.

"No idea. It was stuffed in my mailbox yesterday. No stamp, no return address, no nothin'."

Franklin took it and held it close to his ear. "Maybe it's a bomb. Tick, tick, tick . . ."

Erwin shuffled in, dragging a pillow behind him.

"Or somebody's eyeballs."

"Winnie, you are the gruesomest child I ever did see."

"What's goo . . . goosemest mean?"

"Means you watch too much of that dang idiot box."

"You watch it, too. Every night. I seen ya."

Mrs. Henderson narrowed her eyes at Erwin and pointed her fork at him. "You be careful, bub."

She turned back to the sausage browning in the skillet and I could see her bite off a smile as she took an egg from the carton, cracked it on the lip of the skillet, and sent it sliding and sputtering through the sausage grease, leaving white lace bubbling after it. As Franklin and Erwin studied the package, I reached over, peeled the two newspaper clippings from the refrigerator, and slipped them into my back pocket.

"Well, are you boys going to open it or am I going to have to do it for you?"

Franklin cut the twine using his pocketknife and began to tear the paper, but then suddenly stopped.

"What's wrong, Frank Junior?"

Holding up the package to Mrs. Henderson, Franklin pointed. "Mary's name's first. Maybe she oughta be here."

Erwin snatched the package and ripped the rest of the paper off. Franklin grabbed the box back. "Erwin, you little . . ."

Erwin lunged at it but Franklin held the box above his head, leaning back in the chair fending him off with one arm.

"Give it, Franklin!"

"Now, you two stop it."

Mrs. Henderson slapped the fork against the table edge. "I swear! You boys been actin' like a couple three hooligans, lately. Now, knock it off an' give me that box."

She took it from Franklin. "Maybe you're right, Frank Junior. Maybe Mary should be here. Here, Pete. You keep it 'til then."

Erwin glared as I took the small parcel.

"Winnie, Pete, sit down there with your brother. There's something I need to tell ya."

We sat, looking up at Mrs. Henderson. She set the fork down and leaned

242

forward, her tan liver-spotted hands flattened out against the kitchen table.

"I talked to Joe Lucero yesterday."

"Who's that?"

"A lawyer, Winnie. He's a friend of Pete's and ours. Anyways, I talked to him about this here mess we got goin'."

"What mess?"

"The mess with the house, Winnie."

Erwin looked around at Mrs. Henderson's kitchen. "Why don't you just clean it? That's what Mama does."

Mrs. Henderson jutted out her bottom jaw and took a deep breath, staring at Erwin.

"Anyways, as I was sayin', Joe Lucero come by yesterday and told me the latest. Seems your Uncle Herbert's tryin' to get his grubby mitts on your house. Fact, he's got the deed and already has half the town over there workin' it over like it's his own place."

"I seen him. Uncle Herbert, I . . . . Ow!"

"Okay, Winnie, what's goin' on? Where'd you boys see him?"

Erwin, rubbing his shin under the table, glared at Franklin. Franklin and I stared down as Mrs. Henderson let out a sigh. "Well, I guess it don't matter. Just as well we all know he's back, anyhow . . . if he ever left in the first place, the no-good-for-nothin' . . ."

"Is that why they're movin' everything out, Mrs. Henderson?"

"Well, Petey, kind of. But as Joe Lucero says, maybe movin' everything outa there ain't such a bad idea so's that scalawag can't lay claim to nothin' else. We got a storage space rented out for all your stuff while Mr. Lucero tries to figure this nonsense out."

"Does Mary know about all this?"

"Franklin, I don't know what Mary knows. I ain't seen hide nor hair of her. But don't you kids worry. We'll git this thing straightened out if it's the last thing we ever do. Now, git on in there and wash your hands for breakfast."

We filed into the bathroom and stood pinched together at the sink, holding our hands under the faucet while staring at the box I had set on the counter.

"Mary don't care."

"What, Win?"

"Mary don't care 'bout nothin'. I told her, too. Huh, Pete?"

Erwin swiped his hands across his pajama tops and then reached for the box.

"Don't, Win. You heard Mrs. Henderson."

"But maybe it's alive and gots to breathe."

Franklin laughed. "What do you think it is? A snake?"

Franklin took the box from Erwin and handed it to me. "Go hide this somewhere until we can get Mary over here. Whenever that'll be."

I carried the box into the bedroom and looked around for a good place to hide it. It was small, about the size of one of the bricks up at the brick-yard, but not as heavy. I walked over to the grocery sacks full of clothing and found one with my things in it and stuffed the box down toward the bottom. Starting for the door, I decided the sack wasn't such a good place after all. I pulled it out and looked at the top: two pieces of tape on either side kept the lid on. I pressed down and the tape buckled and when I let go, the lid sprang up and one of the pieces of tape popped loose.

"Pete, come on. It's ready."

I looked up at Franklin who was leaning into the doorway.

"Put it anywhere, Pete. I just don't want Win to get to it before Mary can be here."

"Look, Franklin."

He walked over and looked down at the box. I squeezed the lid down again and it popped back up, loosing the other piece of tape.

"What do you think's in there, Franklin?"

"Beats me. But we might as well look now that the lid's about to fall off."

Franklin reached over and pulled at the top. A thin piece of white tissue came off with the lid and floated to the floor with pieces of green-colored paper. We stared down at the paper in the box and without saying a word, looked down at the other pieces of paper scattered around the floor, green rectangular paper with the same grandfatherly face staring up at us and the same number printed in each corner: 100.

* * *

"Eighty-seven, eighty-eight, eighty-nine, ninety."

Franklin picked up the pile of bills from the bed as he might have picked up his baseball cards and tapped them together on his thigh.

"How much is that, Franklin?"

"Let's see, ninety times . . ."

Franklin carried the bills over to the chest of drawers, rummaged in the top one, took out a pencil and an envelope, and began to figure. Mrs. Henderson had gone back outside after serving us breakfast and Erwin was back in front of the television. *The Baseball Game of the Week* between the Yankees and the Cleveland Indians had started and I could hear Pee Wee Reese and Dizzy Dean discussing the game's lineup. Dizzy Dean broke into his rendition of The Wabash Cannonball just as Franklin finally put down his pencil.

"How much?"

Holding the envelope in front of his face, Franklin double checked his math. As poor as Franklin was in science and geography, it had been mathematics that always had a way of twisting and turning his brain into one big tangled knot. Just as he was finally getting a handle on long division and fractions, they had sprung algebra on him. Algebra made about as much sense to Franklin as spring cleaning did to old man Hillar; there was just no fathoming it.

"Well?"

Franklin put down the pencil and envelope and looked at me, mouth open. "Nine-thousand dollars."

I leaped from the bed, hands in the air. "We're millionaires!"

"Shhhh. Win's goin' to hear."

I flopped back onto the bed and stared at the ceiling. It was the most money I had ever heard anybody ever having at one time in my whole life. Almost every weekday after lunch Mom would watch *The Millionaire* give away his money to some unsuspecting person. But that was only on television. This was real. "Who do you think it is, Franklin?"

Franklin shook his head and stuffed the box far back into the top drawer. "Beats me. It just don't figure. Unless somebody maybe feels sorry for us."

"Feels sorry for us? What do you mean?"

"Well, after Mom an' Pa and everything."

I looked down at my sneakers.

"Gee, I feel sorry for you girls."

Franklin and I whirled around. Standing in the doorway dressed in a white shirt and black pants was none other than Lee Hooker—at least, I thought it was Lee Hooker.

"Well?"

His flattop and fenders hairdo was now just flattop and didn't have any of the butch wax he usually smeared through it. His shirt and pants were not only clean but pressed, and all but the top button of his shirt was buttoned.

"What's all this crap about feelin' sorry for you? I feel sorry for ya, feel sorry that you're both so damn ugly."

Lee Hooker smirked and leaned against the doorway.

"Lee, how'd you get in here?"

"I tunneled in. I'm here to break the two of ya out of this joint."

Franklin stared. "Lee, what happened to your . . ."

Franklin didn't say hair. Lee Hooker had a way of cutting off other people's sentences with his eyes, as though he had sliced the words off in midair using the four-inch blade of his pocketknife.

"Well, why ain't you two sorry-lookin' girls ready?"

Franklin and I looked at each other and then back at Lee Hooker. "Ready? For what?"

Lee Hooker crossed his arms and shook his head, smiling. "The picnic, Frankie. The church picnic."

"Lee, I don't really think we oughta . . ."

And there was the flash of Lee Hooker's eyes again and Franklin's words fell away. We were going to City Park for the First Pentecostal Church picnic.

* * *

City Park was a park not only for picnics but for about any other thing one could imagine. Formerly the Fair Grounds, it was purchased by the city for $20,500 in 1917 after a vote by Grand River citizenry okaying a two-percent bond for that purpose. What the city received, besides a lot of real estate, was an exhibition hall, race track, grandstand, stables, and enough horse manure to keep every flowerbed in the county fertilized for at least one year. But horse manure was just so deep—the city council had bigger plans. Soon, the track was turned into a football field with an adjoining baseball diamond. A great barn-shaped auditorium was built. Forty acres to the east were planted for a golf course. Two tennis courts were poured. And a swimming pool was dug with the stipulation that every Wednesday and Saturday be designated free day for every kid under 16 years of age.

In 1933, with the advent of President Roosevelt's New Deal, the Civilian Conservation Corp was allowed to build structures at the park, but city council members voted to have the buildings removed ten years later when first there was talk of a German prison camp and then a request by Holly Sugar Company to house Mexican aliens there. In that same year, the council did agree to another prison of sorts: the City Park Zoo.

The zoo not only incarcerated the usual array of overexposed underfed wildlife—coyotes, bears, mountain lions, bobcats, and rhesus monkeys—but also one of the most famous, if not noisiest, inhabitants of Grand River:

Leon the lion. Leon was an African lion whose yellowish gray mane was only surpassed by his great roar which could be heard day or night from any front porch in the entire city. During the summer months, Leon's roar rose above the yelps and shouts of children at play in the public swimming pool and by association, made for many nervous parents. In 1950, when Leon was beginning to get on in years and his teeth yellowed and his eyes began to dim and droop, one brave soul aimed a BB gun through the zoo's bars and shot him. Leon wasn't seriously injured but his vocal irritation at being locked up seemed to increase as he padded back and forth, head swaying and panting behind those bars. Then, in 1953, another sporting citizen of Grand River shot him again—this time with a rifle—and Leon the lion was finally free.

After Leon's death, the Humane Society petitioned the city council to have the zoo closed down and the council responded the following year as it usually did when faced with a crisis; it purchased another lion and two cubs from a zoo in Salt Lake City. That same year, the State Game and Fish Department placed elk and deer at the zoo, and there was an offer of four alligators which was refused when one of the city council members painted a graphic picture of what might happen if the alligators escaped and found their way over to the public pool nearby. By the summer of 1962 and with the addition of a second more modern swimming pool, the council's rough times seemed to be over even though there could still be heard the lonely roar of lions from City Park Zoo.

"What do ya suppose he's thinkin', Frankie?"

Lee Hooker leaned against the railing and stared at the panting lion sprawled across the concrete in the corner of his cage.

"I don't know. Probably wishin' he was somewhere else."

Lee Hooker nodded. "Yeah. Being locked up ain't no fun. Is it, fella?"

The lion yawned and rolled over on his side, rib cage heaving in the sun. Lee Hooker sighed. "Come on. Let's go find this picnic."

We walked through the sour urine stench past the swing sets and merry-go-round and then around the pool where it was the last free day of summer and every kid in Grand River was jockeying for position, trying to get in one last swim.

"That's stupid. How ya supposed to swim with all those other bird-brains crammed in there?"

Lee Hooker shook his head in disgust and patted his front shirt pocket for his cigarettes. He pulled in his chin, peering down into his pocket, and then smirked. "Jesus, I forgot."

"Your cigarettes?"

"No. That I didn't bring 'em."

We walked away from the pool past the cotton candy machine toward a far corner of the park bordered by Garrison Avenue and 12th. Cars lined the curb, and we could see people taking blankets and containers out of trunks and from back seats and spreading them on the picnic tables. Others sat talking on the green wooden park benches while children played nearby, hiding behind trees and chasing after each other.

"You sure about this, Lee?"

Lee Hooker began to run his hand through his hair but feeling just stubble, jerked it to his side. "Yeah. Why not? He invited us, didn't he?"

"Yeah, but we don't know nobody."

"That don't matter. We know Mary, don't we?"

Franklin and I glanced at each other and then looked across the grass. People were dressed in bright clothes, men in pressed slacks with short-sleeved shirts and women with colorful summer dresses, and it made us feel awkward in the white dress shirts and black pants Lee Hooker thought we should wear.

"Look. There's old chrome-dome."

"Where?"

"Over there."

Lee Hooker lifted his chin. We followed his gaze across the grass to Garrison Avenue where a red Lincoln Continental swung up to the curb. Reverend Calloway got out, smiling at the people waving at him from the picnic tables.

"I don't see Mary."

The preacher hitched up his pants and placed his hands on the heads of two small girls who ran up to greet him. He shook hands with others as he strolled over to the crowd which gathered around him until we could only see his sun-splashed head poking through.

"How can they stand that guy? I shoulda brought Cargo. He would've greeted him. One dog to another."

We stopped and sat down as cars pulled up and more people piled out. A wind kicked up, flattening the grass. The poplars and sycamores heaved, and clouds cast shadows across the park.

"What do they do at these things, anyhow, Frankie?"

Lee Hooker lay on his side on one elbow, chewing a blade of grass.

"Beats me. Eat and play games, I guess."

"That all?"

Franklin shrugged, leaning back with his hands propped behind him, legs crossed. "I don't know. I never been to a church picnic before."

"Well, I'm two up on you, Frankie, 'cause I've never been to church or a picnic."

Cars passed by on Garrison and 12th, honking and stopping before surging on. I could hear the shrill whistle of the lifeguard slice the din of voices coming from the swimming pool behind us and the flag in front of the guardhouse snapping in the wind.

"We just goin' to sit here and watch?"

Lee Hooker and Franklin looked over at me.

"Well, I'm hungry. That's all."

Lee Hooker pulled another blade of grass from the ground and handed it to me as he and Franklin continued to study the crowd.

"There she is." Franklin sat up, pointing to a sycamore off to the side of the picnic tables. Mary was leaning back against her hands, which were pressed flat against the tree trunk behind her. She stood by herself, the skirt of another dress I had never seen whipped smooth against the back of her legs and her blond hair blown forward around her face. She surveyed the people congregating in front of her.

"I'm going to go talk to her."

Lee Hooker began to get up but Franklin grabbed him by the arm. "Wait. Look."

Reverend Calloway's bald head moved back through the crowd. He stopped about ten feet from her and rocked forward on one foot, saying something, and then rocked back on his heels, waiting. Mary's head bent down as she traced a strand of hair around her ear. He stood in front of her for a moment—her head remained bowed and she was still against the tree— and then he took her by the arm and led her toward the group of people. Just before they reached them, I noticed the preacher's hand drop and clasp Mary's.

"Come on."

"Lee . . ."

Lee Hooker got up and strode across the grass. We scrambled to our feet.

"Lee, wait!"

We caught up just as he reached the outer edges of the crowd but the people closed in between us. Franklin and I edged through, trying to keep up with him but Lee Hooker was gone. I could see the back of his head bob and weave toward the picnic tables where Mary and Reverend Calloway now stood by themselves. Just as Lee Hooker reached the point where the crowd thinned, right in front of Mary and the preacher, a silence fell over the congregation and with it, chins dropped to chests and the first voice was Reverend Calloway's. "Dear friends, let us pray. Mary."

Reverend Calloway and Mary bowed their heads as Mary brought her hands up and clasped them. "Dear God . . ." Her fingers wiggled underneath her chin, hands tightening together.

I could see the preacher glance to his side at Mary and someone in the crowd coughed and then another and I could hear one of the lions in the zoo roar as the preacher nudged her with his elbow.

"Dear God, thank you for this beautiful day—for the flowers and trees and grass and for all these people here in the park."

The wind kicked up, creaking the tree limbs and I could imagine the preacher's black robe billowing out around Mary's blond head.

"And Lord, thank you for this food You have given us and for this fellowship with our Christian brothers and sisters. And God, most of all, thank you for the giving . . ."

I could feel the shadow from another cloud move over us and there was the lion's roar again, swallowing the shouts and voices from City Park swimming pool.

". . . for the giving of Your only son, God, for having him nailed up on that cross so that we might . . ."

But the preacher's robe didn't engulf Mary. It fell away and Mary's voice rang clear over the bowed heads, over the roar from City Park Zoo.

". . . we might eat this food and . . . and drink this wine . . ."

And the lion roared as a murmur broke through the crowd and I could see the preacher's eyes open and his bald head turn toward Mary.

". . . and buy bigger cars and more expensive dresses . . ."

And there was the preacher grabbing Mary's arm and heads popping up and the freshly barbered head of Lee Hooker bobbing forward.

"Amen! Thank you, Mary."

". . . all in the name of Jesus Christ, Your son . . ."

"Hallelujah! Thank you, Mary! Thank you!"

And the preacher yanking Mary off to the side. "Brother Jones, if you would continue with a prayer of thanksgiving, please."

And Mary still talking and everybody's head up. ". . . and thank you, God, in the name of Reverend Calloway and the almighty dollar . . ."

And everyone watching the preacher jerk Mary to the side and nobody speaking or praying or saying anything. And then the lion roaring and someone streaking forward like a thunderbolt and striking the preacher across the cheek, toppling him across the picnic table onto a pot of baked beans and a bowl of potato salad and, without missing a step, spiriting Mary away through the poplars and sycamores, away from City Park and the lion's loud roar.

* * *

The baked beans had cushioned Reverend Calloway's head like a pillow although he complained bitterly about their temperature as members of his flock helped him from the picnic table and toweled him off as best they could. The potato salad had splatted across his lapel and cheek, launching a single celery seed into his left eye. A member of the church seated him on a park bench and tipped his bean-caked head back in pursuit of this seed, its irritating quality soaking the preacher's bruised face with tears as thoroughly as he soaked new church members' heads with holy water every Sunday morning.

Pickle relish, sliced tomato, mustard, ketchup, bean juice, and the barbeque sauce from a freshly grilled burger turned the back of his white summer sport's jacket into a canvas of greens, reds, yellows, browns, and burnt oranges. He wadded the jacket up and pitched it into a nearby garbage can with the vigor of a frustrated artist discarding a failed painting. His pants and shoes were also splattered, and only the light blue shirt protected by his jacket remained unsoiled although a darker blue had begun to creep from under those flabby white arms. And it was then Franklin and I crept from the preacher's picnic as silently as the two stains and ran from City Park, giddy with the justice of what Lee Hooker had done and Mary had said.

Our sister Mary. She had always known just what to say and once again had said it.

22

Willie had told me freedom is nothing until you're free in your own head. He said some people's minds are in prison forever. The lions in City Park weren't free but maybe when they were stalking back and forth in their cages, they were in their minds running across the open spaces of wherever it was they came from.

Mary hadn't been free until Lee Hooker pushed the preacher into the potato salad. But I thought maybe Mary was free in the way Willie meant—like the lions—and that Lee Hooker just made what Mary was already feeling come true. As for Lee Hooker, I didn't think even Willie could have known what was going on in his head. But by the end of that Saturday night, I was pretty sure that whatever Lee Hooker was feeling, it wasn't freedom.

When Franklin and I got back to Mrs. Henderson's after the picnic, Erwin was sitting on the front porch step with his elbows on his knees and his chin cradled in his palms, lost in the untied shoelaces of his high-top sneakers. *The Baseball Game of the Week* had ended and even though the Yankees had won, he wasn't happy; Mrs. Henderson wouldn't let him go muskrat hunting. But after we told him what had happened with Mary, Lee Hooker, and the preacher and asked him if he wanted to go to a party, he began acting like himself—for the first time in three weeks.

First, he went inside and let the bird out of its cage so Spot could stretch his wings, too. Mrs. Henderson was also going to the party—at Joe's invitation—and she was already dressed and wearing a tan felt hat with a bent-stemmed yellow daffodil growing out of some white mesh when Erwin unleashed her pet. She was torn between scolding Erwin and snagging Spot who kept dive-bombing her from the curtain rod and then the saguaro lamp. Her fake daffodil must have looked like some exotic plant from the jungles of his past in the days before he had ended up in that pet shop where a chubby little woman plucked him from among his brothers and sisters to claim as her own.

By the time Mrs. Henderson lured Spot into the cage using a seed stick, she had forgotten why she felt angry. But it didn't take long to remember because, even before she latched the door to the cage, Erwin was already giving her new cause to be sore. He was playing army with her Swiss-boy-yodeling knickknacks in the clay pot of the drowning philodendron by the front door. One of the knickknacks was aiming a violin at his yodeling round-mouthed counterpart who was perched, hiding, high in the leaves of the philodendron. Just as Mrs. Henderson ordered Erwin to put those precious knickknacks down, the round-mouthed prey fell victim to a bullet from the violin and plummeted from the plant to his ceramic-breaking death on the living-room floor.

That did it. Mrs. Henderson grabbed Erwin by the elbow, yanked him up off the floor, reached back with a grease-laden spatula—which she had carried in from the kitchen—and cocked it back to smack him. But she didn't. She burst out laughing instead. We thought we had finally driven Mrs. Henderson over the cliff. She dropped the spatula, fell back onto her couch, struggled back up, still laughing, and then shuffled into the kitchen and, finally, went outside and stood in her garden among her iris, laughing harder. That was when we decided we'd better go into the bedroom and get ready for the party as soon as we could, before Mrs. Henderson came back in and discovered what we decided to leave her for all her trouble.

* * *

"Pete! Come in."

"Hi, Mrs. Lucero."

Helen Lucero opened her front door.

"Oh, I'm so glad you could come. These must be your brothers."

"Yeah, this is Franklin and Win."

"Erwin."

"I mean Erwin."

"Well, hi, Erwin and Franklin. It's nice to meet you."

Helen shook their hands and closed the door behind us. She wore a red dress and lipstick which seemed to fan the flame of beautiful red curls piled atop her head.

"Where's your sister, Pete?"

"We're not sure."

"Oh, that's too bad. I wanted to meet her. And I know Fudgie did, too. Joe! Come in here. There's a couple of gentlemen I want you to meet."

Joe walked into the living room wearing a black silk shirt and white slacks, carrying a can of beer. "Hey, Pete! ¿Qué pasa? How you doing, muchacho?"

"Fine."

Joe hugged me to his waist.

"Joe, these are Pete's brothers. Erwin and Franklin."

"Erwin and Franklin, nice to meet you. Are you guys as tough and as smart as Pete here?"

Erwin looked up at Joe. "Tougher."

"Tougher? Really?"

Erwin looked down at his own arm and made a muscle, lips pursed and small fist shaking with tension. Joe squeezed it. "Wow. You are tough, aren't you?"

"Yeah, an' you know what?"

"What?"

"I kicked the preacher in the knee."

"You did? Boy, you must be one mean hombre. I better watch out for you, huh?"

"Come on, Win." Franklin put his arm around his little brother's neck and reeled him in.

"How old are you, Franklin?"

"Fourteen."

"Fourteen. Fudgie tells me you work over at Clarence Dugan's gas station."

"Yeah."

"Do you like it?"

"It's okay."

"Fudgie also tells me he and Pete have been giving you a hand."

"Yeah, Fudgie's a hard worker."

"Is that right? Well, shoot, we should've had you over here sooner so you could've helped us get some mileage out of him, too."

"Now, Joseph." Helen shook her head. "He's just kidding, boys. Fudgie does fine. Now excuse me while I get some more cups. Make yourselves at home. Joe, show them where the pop is."

Helen placed her hand on Erwin's head and then walked out of the room.

"You guys don't like pop, do ya?"

Erwin walked beside Joe into the kitchen, looking up at him. I glanced over at the living-room wall above the fold-out couch where Manny had lain. Jesus Christ on the cross was no longer there and I wondered if he ever had been.

"I do."

"Really?"

"Yeah, but Mrs. Henderson only gives us milk."

"Doggone it. Well, maybe I can have a talk with her about that."

"She bakes cookies, though."

"I know. She was supposed to bring some to the party. She is coming, isn't she?"

Erwin shrugged and looked at Franklin. Franklin nodded. "Yeah, she had to feed her bird, first."

"Oh, good. She's a neat old lady." Joe opened the refrigerator. "What would you guys like? How about a Grapette?"

Franklin and I looked at each other. "Do you have Pepsi?"

"No, just Grape."

Joe Lucero chuckled, shaking his head, and took out three bottles of Pepsi and popped the tops. "Mrs. Henderson told me all about your grape-juice-drinking episode. Here, try these on for size. Hopefully, they won't bring up the same memories."

Joe smiled and handed us the Pepsi. "Fudgie and everybody's outside, Pete. Why don't you guys go on out and I'll be there in a minute. I've got to find more paper plates. Didn't know the whole county was going to show up here tonight."

Franklin and I took a swig and followed Erwin out to the Lucero's back yard. People were everywhere, standing on the lawn, leaning against the picket fence, and spilling out over the curb into the car-lined street. They sat on fold-out chairs and on the grass by the sidewalk, on hoods of cars and along the tailgates of pickup trucks. They squatted in the street and smoked cigarettes, ate food from long tables set up around the yard against the house and fence, and drank from bottles and cans and paper cups.

"Where's Fudgie?"

"Beats me. I don't see anybody I know. Look at all this."

Green, white, and red crepe-paper streamers were fastened to the roof gutter and strung twisting overhead across the lawn and into the branches of sycamore. Red and yellow lanterns hung along the wire of the clothesline, and ribbon and bunting of all different colors decorated the front of a plywood platform and the pickets of the white fence. Even the sky was splashed with orange, as though Helen and Joe Lucero had decided it, too, needed some color.

"Pete. Take a look over there."

On a platform along the far fence facing back across the yard toward the street stood four men wearing black sombreros, setting up a drum set and tuning their guitars.

"Look, Franklin. They even got dancers."

Three girls around Franklin's age or older huddled to the side of the platform, talking. Their black hair was bound in tight braided buns pinned with turquoise bows. Their faces were heavily made up and each wore a black satin blouse, a red cotton skirt, and black shoes with straps and clog heels. Three teenage boys in black cowboy boots with sharp silver toes sticking out from under stiff new blue jeans walked over and joined them. Silver buttons with short red tassles ran the length of their pant seams up to turquoise sashes tied at their waists. Their black satin jackets were cut short and broad across the shoulders with fancy red stitching and the same silver buttons across their chests. Underneath, they sported white shirts with short red ties and in their hands, rotated black and turquoise sombreros.

"Hey, Pedro."

Standing on the top step, I scanned the party for Fudgie and Carmalita.

"Pedro!"

I felt something hit my shin and turned around. Manny Manzanares sat in a chair up against the house next to the back door looking up at me. The stiff collar of a wrinkled white dress shirt was buttoned together underneath his stubbled chin, and his white-flecked hair had been slicked over to one side and was now drying and making a curly retreat to its original unruly position atop his head. He brought the cane back to rest between his legs and folded his hands over it.

"You like?" He lifted his chin toward the crowd of people.

"I guess. I just got here."

He nodded. "Who you *amigos*, Pedro?" He looked over my shoulder at Franklin and Erwin.

"Oh, these are my brothers, Franklin and Erwin. Mr. Manzanares, my name isn't Pedro, it's . . ."

Manny coughed and spat to the side, bending over and lifting one hip to pull out his handkerchief. He wiped his mouth and stuffed the handkerchief back into his hip pocket. "You brothers, huh?"

"Yeah."

"Let me meet them, Pedro."

I glanced over my shoulder at Franklin. Franklin furrowed his brow, shaking his head.

"Come here, *amigos.*"

Franklin and Erwin shuffled closer but stayed on the step.

"Come here. Don' worry, I no bite. I bark, but I no bite."

They eased down in front of him. Manny looked them over and then past them at the crowd. "See all these peoples?"

He swept his cane out, and Franklin and Erwin looked over their shoulders and nodded. "They are here to do many thing tonight. Eat, drink, dance, make love—do many thing."

Manny leaned the cane against the inside of one thigh and rubbed his hands along the top of his legs, looking out over the people as though they were his subjects. "Many come from Mexico, many come from America, many I don' know where from they come. Maybe the moon, I don' know."

Franklin and Erwin grinned.

"But, you know, they all come because the peach is picked an' now it is the time to res' an' to have the fun." Manny lifted his hands and placed them on their shoulders. "So here are they—many peoples. An' here are you—two, three peoples."

Manny smiled.

"It is easier to be the many than the few, *amigos.* It is easier." Manny gently shook them for emphasis. "*Comprende?*"

Franklin and Erwin nodded.

"Ah, you are the smar' boys, my smar' *muchachos.*" Manny squeezed their shoulders and let them go. "So no stan' aroun' with you finger up you *culo, amigos.* Go with Pedro an' have the fun. Go be with the peoples."

Franklin and Erwin backed away as Manny turned to me. "Pedro."

I stepped over, and he looked up at me and smiled. "Pedro." Cupping a large hand around the back of my neck, he pulled me down so my ear was next to his mouth. "You a good boy, Pedro, like my Luis. A good boy." He squeezed my neck. "Life, it is like the onion, Pedro. You bite it an' it make you cry but still you bite it because the onion it tas' good."

I nodded and felt the scratch of Manny's whiskers against my cheek.

"An' the ring of the onion—take one an' there is one, take one an' there is one. Yes, the life it is like the onion. I am happy for you an' you brother an' you sister, Pedro. *Muy contento.* It is time for another ring of the onion. I am *muy* happy."

He let me up then and not knowing what to say, I stumbled off into the crowd after Franklin and Erwin as the band broke into its first song of the night and the people began clapping and clasping hands and whirling and dancing around us, sweeping us up into the party so I barely had time to wonder what it was he meant, to wonder why Manny Manzanares was so darn happy about onions.

* * *

Franklin was dancing with a girl almost as tall as he, with short curly hair and eyes the shape and color of almonds. I had never seen Franklin dance before except with Mary once when she was trying to teach him the twist in the living room after Mom and Pa had gone square dancing. Franklin's twist looked more like the tangle and Mary, who was a natural dancer, couldn't understand how Franklin could turn such an easy dance into something so difficult. Even Erwin and I mastered it right away which made Franklin finally say he hated dancing and didn't care if he ever danced another step in his whole life. But here he was now, dancing with the confidence of a Fred Astaire with a pretty girl whose lithe movements were only surpassed by an ability to bring a smile to Franklin's lips—something that had been impossible to do since the death of Marilyn Monroe.

After eating a couple of things wrapped in cornhusks, drinking three bottles of pop, and seeing Mrs. Henderson's daffodil appear above the sea of dancers like the dorsal fin of a killer shark, Erwin decided to perform one of his magic tricks and disappear. He wasn't interested in seeing if Mrs. Henderson's age-worn memory applied to the shattering of her favorite knickknack. I kept my distance, also, and stood at a table at the back of the yard, sipping my Pepsi and holding a paper plate of mostly things I had never tasted before. But I didn't worry too much about Mrs. Henderson after I saw her plant the bulb of her daffodil off to the side of the yard, where she sat yakking with Joe and Helen Lucero.

"*Señoras* and *Caballeros*, may I have your attention."

One of the guitarists stood at the front of the bandstand with his hand raised above his head for quiet. "It is my pleasure to introduce to you tonight's entertainment . . . all the way from Alamosa, Colorado . . . *La Luna y Las Estrellas!*"

The crowd clapped and whistled as six dancers filed onto the platform, the band members moving back out of their way. A man holding a silver horn stepped up onto the platform and after licking his lips, began to play with the band joining in. The three teenage boys stomped their cowboy boots and the three girls moved forward whipping full skirts to either side.

The boys danced around them, dipping their shoulders, hands pressed to the small of their backs. They circled each other, looking over one shoulder and then the other, turning and prancing with the click of heels and the swish of skirts until finally the three sombreros dropped onto the floor and they danced around them. The audience clapped time with the music, and heels clicked and stomped against the wooden platform, dresses rustled and whirled until the sombreros were retrieved as the clapping broke into applause and the music came to an abrupt halt.

"No so bad, huh, gringo?"

I turned around to the grinning face of Fudgie Manzanares. "Hey, Pete."

"Fudgie, where you been?"

He jerked his thumb back at the Lucero's garage next to the alley. "Watching the crap game."

"Crap game?"

"Yeah, you know, craps. *Dados.*"

Fudgie cupped his hand, blew into it, and shook it in front of him. "I watch them throw for money."

"Where's Carmalita?"

"I think she is in the house with *madre*. My momma no like parties, man."

"How come?"

Fudgie shrugged. "I don' know. She like church." He grabbed a couple of things off my plate. "You no like?"

"I don't know. It's a little hot."

"Try this, man." He handed me a fried tortilla filled with beans and cheese as the music started up and the dancers began another number.

"Is Carmalita goin' to stay in the house all night?"

Fudgie glanced at me, grinning, and turned his attention to the dancers. "You miss her, man?"

"No, I just . . ."

"It's okay, Pete. When I no see her, I miss her, too. Carmalita will come out. You will see."

We finished my plate as the dancers finally hopped off the platform and joined everyone else dancing to the music. Overhead, the orange sky had deepened to blue and a sprinkling of stars salted the cool darkness above Spruce Mesa. But in the west, Rimrock National Park was still outlined in red as though the sandstone cliffs were bleeding like watercolors into the streaks of cloud beyond.

"Come on, man."

I followed Fudgie over the picket fence and around to the alley where some men were huddled in a semi-circle up against the back of the garage, squatting and squinting in the growing darkness. A cigarette lighter flickered near the ground, silhouetting the men's legs and illuminating their intent faces and the wooden slats of the Lucero's garage.

"How much do they bet?"

Fudgie shrugged, standing on his tiptoes, craning to see around the men's heads. "I don' know, man. I think how many peaches they pick is how much they bet."

The rapid roll and skid of dice drummed across a piece of plywood and there was the metallic click of the lighter shutting off and the men murmuring in the blackness against the rustle of bills changing hands.

"Is this against the law?"

Fudgie shrugged. "I don' know, Pete. Everybody do it."

"Do you?"

"Me? No way, man. Momma would kill me." Fudgie grinned and then suddenly held his hand up to his chest. "Listen."

The music had stopped and the guitarist was speaking, but this time in Spanish.

"Let's go, Pete."

I followed Fudgie around the garage and over the picket fence. Everyone was facing the platform now, even those in the street who were pressing in along the curb, along the outside of the fence. We threaded our way under the streamers and across the yard to where Manny Manzanares was standing, leaning with both hands gripping his cane. But Manny Manzanares didn't even glance at us. His attention was drawn elsewhere.

The band members moved back and I could see Rosita Manzanares, dressed in a black long-sleeved dress, standing to the side, reaching her arms out as though she had just let go of something. But the outstretched fingers closed then and her hands pulled slowly back to her breast and clasped under her chin as I followed her gaze.

Carmalita Manzanares stepped up to the platform. Her head was bent and her hands were folded in front of her. She walked briskly and deliberately to the center of the platform as people clapped silently before her. Though her cheeks blushed red, she wore none of the makeup, none of the fancy clothing. Her long black hair was pulled loosely back behind her head and clipped with a simple silver barrette. She wore a freshly pressed white blouse, a solid black skirt, and matching black slippers, both clasped to the side with a strap and a silver button.

After a moment, when the movement of hands before her, like the wings of butterflies, fell away and there were only those pairs of staring eyes and a sky full of stars, she smiled inwardly. Silently and slowly her arms raised, her toes flexed, and the long languid curve of back and neck arched in counterpoint to beautifully fluent hands, and Carmalita Manzanares began to dance, speaking a language more beautiful than the music she would never hear. She spoke of her family and her life in San Felipe, of the barren granite mountains and the foamy white waves pulsing against the beaches. She spoke of the collared lizard and the rattlesnake, of the gila monster and sage hen and the graceful leap of the antelope. She spoke of the red blossom of the barrel cactus, the scent of sagebrush after rain, the tall spiny branches of the boojum tree twisting like roots high into the desert sky. She spoke of the wind and the clouds and of sand as fine as wheat flour. She spoke of the earth and sky and of the sun and moon, of light and of darkness. And she spoke of God. And when Carmalita Manzanares spoke no more, when her body was still, eyes were closed, and hands at her sides, there was again the great silence and then a sudden lift of butterfly wings applauding the night air around her.

* * *

"Where's Erwin?"

Franklin turned around from his position at one of the food tables, which were now more tables of ruin, white tablecloths stained with everything from cheese sauce to green chile, from Pepsi Cola to encrusted remains of Helen Lucero's guacamole dip.

"Hey, Pedro!" Franklin grinned, cheeks flushed and bulging with food.

"Real funny, Franklin. Do you know where Win's at?"

"Nope." Franklin wiped his mouth with the back of his forearm. "Mrs. Henderson was lookin' for him, too."

I glanced around the yard. People were pairing up for a slow dance and the light from the street lamp projected their shadows across the yard, up the fence, and into the yard next door. The Lucero's grass had a milky sheen as though the green had been danced right out of it.

"Don't worry. Win's okay."

Franklin wiped his hands on the legs of his jeans and looked across the yard at the girl with the almond eyes. She smiled.

"See you around, Pedro." Franklin slapped me on the shoulder and started across the yard.

"Hey, Franklin."

Franklin stopped and turned around. "Yeah?"

"I thought you hated dancing."

Franklin glanced at the girl and looked back at me, grinning. "I do."

I smiled, too, as I watched Franklin turn and walk over to the girl. There were fewer people dancing now, partly because it was a slow dance and partly because it was getting late. The yard was littered with paper plates and paper cups, empty wine bottles and beer cans, and the slumbering body of a man who had decided to make the shadows of the platform his bedroom and a red bow from one of the pickets his nightcap. Two of the lanterns on the clothesline were burned out and one of the crepe-paper streamers hung limply from the roof gutter and draped over the Lucero's spirea bush. Fudgie and Carmalita Manzanares sat next to the bush on the back step, watching the people dance.

"Hey, Pete."

"Hi."

"You haf' a good time, man?"

"Yeah."

Carmalita smiled up at me and scooted over making room. I sat down and she took my hand. I had never held hands with a girl before except with Mary when we were much younger. Carmalita's hand felt cool and slender and smooth, making mine feel short and sticky as though I were still a little kid with melted popsicle between my fingers.

"Franklin has a good time, too. Huh, man?" Fudgie lifted his chin toward Franklin.

I nodded. "Hey, Fudgie, did you see my little brother?"

Fudgie grinned. "*Sí*, man. He climb the tree." Fudgie pointed to the top of the sycamore. "He go way up. He is a tough li'l *hito*."

"Is he still up there?"

"No, man. He come down an' I no see him, again."

"When was that?"

"Oh, a long time, man. When you firs' come."

I looked up at the sycamore tree and then down at the band and the people dancing in the yard. Joe and Helen Lucero were dancing now, nose to nose, talking and laughing.

"You no fin' him, huh, man?"

"No, I don't know where he went. Maybe I should go back to Mrs. Henderson's. I don't know where she's at, either."

"The ol' lady with the . . ." Fudgie drew a curved line in the air out from the top of his head.

"Yeah. Did you see her?"

"She is in the house with my momma, man."

"I thought your mom couldn't talk English."

"She no like *Inglés*, but she understan' some an' she talk if she wan' to."

"What're they talkin' about?"

Fudgie shrugged and quickly looked down at the sidewalk. Carmalita squeezed my hand at the same time, looking at me with big brown knowing eyes. I gazed back out at the people dancing slowly around the yard, moving as if underwater, streamers above them undulating in the cool night breeze like moss waving in the current of Indian Wash.

"I didn't want to tell ya. Thought if you knew, you'd worry 'bout your own mom and pa. Thought it might scare ya . . ."

The music swam around me faster now and the dancers pivot and swing their bodies and the women's skirts swish as the men twirl the women under their arms and then catch them around their waists and they pivot around the other way.

"They sure do know how to dance, don't they?"

I turn around and there's Trunk Willis, his big friendly nose pointing down at me with a bottle of beer pressed underneath it. I nod and we both look out at the dancing. The music speeds up more and the man's voice at the microphone speeds up with it. They're hand in hand now, skipping around in a circle and then they stop and face each other and bow before they go off in different directions, Mom one way and Pa the other, clasping hands with the other dancers and threading their way around the circle. The curls of Mom's hair bounce as she and Pa skip in the circle and they're both smiling and Pa has a trickle of sweat on his forehead.

"Your ma and pa sure have a good time."

I look up at Trunk Willis as he clucks his tongue and turns his head to the side and takes another swig. I look back at Mom and Pa and they're laughing as they move in and out of the other dancers. The man at the microphone stops talking and the music ends and everybody stands around clapping. Trunk Willis claps, too, and Mom and Pa look over at us and Mom holds her skirt out and does a little curtsy.

"You sure have some fine folks there, Petey."

Mom and Pa walk over to us, hand in hand, laughing. "Well, what'd you think? Pretty good, huh?"

I nodded and swallowed hard. "Yeah."

"Yeah? Is that all you can say: Yeah?" Joe Lucero looked down at me, smiling, and wiped sweat from his forehead. "And what'd the expert think?"

I turned to Trunk Willis but Trunk Willis wasn't there, only Fudgie and Carmalita Manzanares.

"She think so-so."

"So-so? What do you mean, so-so?"

"She think you no so bad for a *loco* lawyer. But Helen, she is *muy fina*."

Helen Lucero smiled, shaking her head of curls as Joe grabbed Fudgie and began jabbing him in the ribs.

"When are you two ever going to quit . . ." Helen turned and looked across the yard toward the street. "Joe?"

Joe let go of Fudgie and straightened up, staring in the same direction.

"Well, I guess I'm surprised they didn't show up sooner."

Two police cars pulled up to the curb, red lights flashing off the row of houses across the street. Three car doors slammed and there were shouts and two policemen sprinted down the street after a short man in a white shirt.

"What the . . ."

Joe Lucero strode across the yard through the people with Helen Lucero behind him. Sergeant Nichols stood between the door of the first police car and the white picket fence, aiming a flashlight at a pad he held in his hand.

"Hey, what the hell is going on here?"

Sergeant Nichols looked up from his pad. "Easy, Joe. It's not what you . . ."

"What're you doing, Floyd? You know we have this party every year. Picking season's over, for crying out loud."

"Joe, it's not what you think, so just simmer down." Sergeant Nichols placed his hand on Joe's chest. "We could've been over here at six-thirty with all the complaints we've got tonight, so just take it easy."

Joe Lucero stood in front of the sergeant, his hands on his hips. "It's not what I think, huh? So what's that all about, then? Tag?"

Joe pointed down the street where the two policemen had tackled the man and were holding him face-down on somebody's lawn.

"Joe, we got a complaint earlier . . ."

"Yeah, that's what you already said. You got a whole slew of them, right? What, did the entire neighborhood call in about all the hardened peach-picking wetback criminals the Lucero's are harboring in their back yard?"

"Damn it, Joe, would you quit being so mule-headed and listen to me a minute?"

The two policemen were walking back down the street on either side of the short man. The man's hands were handcuffed behind him and I could hear a woman's cry in the crowd.

"Bring him on over here, boys."

Sergeant Nichols waved his hand and I could hear the woman's crying get louder and it sounded somehow like our mom's so I turned around and there stood Erwin off to the side near the curb by himself, cradling a shoe box in his arms. He stared down at the box with the same solemn look on his face that he would get when Mom was sick and couldn't take care of us.

"That's him! That's him!" Out the passenger's side of the second police car emerged a bald head, shiny and perspiring.

"Get back in the car, Reverend. I warned you."

Sergeant Nichols pointed down at Reverend Calloway's round nose but the preacher just stood between the door and the car, glaring at the prisoner being escorted through the quietly watchful crowd. Erwin shuffled over from the curb and stood next to me behind Joe Lucero. He tugged on my shirt. "Look, Pete."

Erwin cracked open the top of the shoe box and I looked down into the pink glint of two beady eyes behind a small bewhiskered nose pressing out into the cool night air. "He catched the muskrat."

"Who?"

The crying was softer now, and I looked back along the curb where Erwin had stood, behind the second police car and the preacher, and there stood Helen Lucero. She was comforting the crying woman, stroking her hair and holding her, and then the two of them turned and looked toward the prisoner.

"Him." Erwin pointed up at Lee Hooker who was now standing between the police car and Sergeant Nichols. I looked back at Helen Lucero holding our sister.

"That's him, Sergeant. That's the punk that assaulted me and disrupted our . . ."

"Get back, Calloway, and shut up. Go ahead and take him in, boys."

One of the policemen opened the back door, placing his hand on Lee Hooker's head.

"Lee!"

The two policemen, Sergeant Nichols, and Joe Lucero stopped and turned around, looking at Franklin who came running up behind me. Lee Hooker wore a white sneer on his face and his eyes glanced quickly around the crowd before finding Franklin's. Franklin licked his lips and his eyes flitted nervously around at the policemen.

"Lee . . . Lee, what're you doin'?"

Lee Hooker stared at Franklin. "Guess my vacation's over, Frankie. Guess I get to go back and see Julian."

Lee Hooker looked over his shoulder at Mary, now being approached by the preacher. But Helen Lucero stood between them with one arm around Mary, nudging the preacher away with her other.

Lee Hooker's jaw tightened and he hissed through clenched teeth. "That's right. Keep that bastard away from her."

The policeman tightened his grip on Lee Hooker's elbow and pushed him into the back seat. Lee Hooker twisted his head back, flat steel eyes riveted out the back window at Mary and Helen Lucero and at the preacher who Sergeant Nichols was now ushering back into the other police car.

"It's you, Lee Hooker."

The police car started and Lee Hooker's eyes flicked to mine as the car began to ease away from the curb.

"Lee Hooker, it's you!"

And as the police car pulled away from the curb and took him down the street and out of our lives, Lee Hooker's sneer remained forever in my mind—as did his eyes, those hard-edged eyes that cut into mine as suddenly and as sharp as his four-inch pocketknife.

"It's you, Lee Hooker . . . the wizard."

Those eyes that could suddenly soften. Those eyes that our sister had seen all along.

23

"Luis. Come."

Fudgie Manzanares looked over his shoulder at his mother standing in front of the door of the Greyhound Bus. She wore her usual black dress and scarf and even though it was Sunday, the scarf was off her head and lay loosely about her shoulders. In one hand she held the crucifix that had kept vigil over her ailing husband and in the other, which was wrapped in a rosary, a framed picture of President Kennedy clipped from the cover of *Life Magazine*.

"Momma is happy."

Rosita Manzanares was smiling, her dusty canvas suitcase standing next to her in the morning light. She held the picture out and looked proudly down as though it were one of her babies cradled in her arms. Bringing it up, she crossed herself and pressed the rosary to her lips. She looked up at her new friend Hazel Henderson and hugged her over the suitcase. And then Rosita Manzanares turned to help her husband into the bus.

"Luis! *Ven acá! Rápido!*"

The bus vibrated and whined, spewing a cloud of black smoke into the air.

"I mus' go, man."

Franklin tapped Fudgie on the arm. "Guess we'll see ya next year, huh, Fudgie?"

He nodded.

"We got something for ya."

Franklin elbowed me and I reached down into the pocket of my jean cut-offs and pulled out the tightly folded square and held it out on the palm of my hand.

"Wha's this, man?"

Franklin took it and held it in front of Fudgie's face. "It's the three bucks we owed ya for workin' at Mr. Dugan's and eatin' that pepper."

"*Señor* Dugan already pay me, man. Three dollar, it is too much."

"Naw, a bet's a bet. It was worth it just to see Rickie Liver's face turn red. Huh, Pete?"

I nodded.

"Besides, ya earned it. Here." Franklin held out the square.

"Is this a new kin' of money, man?"

Fudgie started to pull out one of the folded corners but Franklin grabbed his wrist. "Wait."

Fudgie looked up at Franklin.

"Why don't you wait 'til you get on the bus?"

"Why, man?"

Franklin shrugged and looked at me.

"Luis!"

Fudgie glanced back at his mother. Joe Lucero was lifting her suitcase up to the bus driver.

"Okay, man. I wait. *Gracias. Mucho gracias.*"

Franklin and Fudgie shook hands and I could feel Fudgie hesitate, his eyes on me as I stared down at the tire-smoothed pavement between us. The three of us walked over to the bus, and I could see the passengers' heads against the windows and the dark sunglasses of the driver behind the steering wheel. The engine had smoothed, the bus trembling expectantly like a bird dog awaiting its master's command.

"Shoot, Fudgie, I thought maybe you'd decided to stay on here with Pete."

Joe Lucero smiled and slapped Fudgie on the shoulder. Helen Lucero bent down and kissed him on the cheek.

"Be a good boy, Fudgie Manzanares. And mind your momma."

"*Sí*, Helen. I will. *Adiós*, José."

"*Adiós, muchacho.*"

Joe hugged Fudgie. "Take care of your family. You're getting to be old enough, now."

"*Sí*, José."

Carmalita slid by her mother and came down out of the bus. She stepped over to Fudgie and they looked at each other and then at me. Carmalita had on the same slippers she had danced in, black with the silver buttons on the side.

"Luis! *Vente! Ven acá! Ándale!*"

I looked up at the window where Manny Manzanares sat banging on the glass. *"Don' touch my florecita, mulo. Or I break your cabeza. Your head! Crack!"* The edge of his fist pressed white against the glass and then he opened his hand and waved. And I waved back.

"Pete. Carmalita say no worry about you sister."

I looked at Carmalita, at her brown bottomless eyes, as she touched my cheek and ran her fingertips down to my chin and smiled.

"She say Helen and José will take care of her. An' you an' you brothers, too, man."

Carmalita turned and ran up the steps. The door closed behind her and I could hear the brakes hiss free and smell diesel in the air.

Joe walked over and put his arms around Fudgie and me. "You better get going. It's going to leave without you."

I looked at Fudgie, half his face buried and pressed into Joe's shirt with my own.

"Pete, I mus' go."

Joe gave him a little push.

"Adiós, Pete. Adiós, amigo."

The engine revved and a billow of black smoke rose up around us as the bus inched away from the station. Fudgie took after it.

"Adiós, Franklin! Tell Señor Dugan I work nex' year, man! Take care of Pete, José!"

"We will, Fudgie. Don't worry."

Fudgie waved, the door opened, and he jumped on.

I raised my hand as the door folded closed. *"Adiós, Fudgie! Adiós, amigo!"*

The bus eased across the pavement, rolled to a moaning stop for a car to pass on Fifth Street and with a burst of engine and cloud of diesel exhaust, lumbered down the quiet Sunday morning streets of Grand River away from us.

* * *

"Now, you three git back in there and change them clothes. I ain't going to have ya movin' over to the Lucero's lookin' like a band of hobos."

We stood in Mrs. Henderson's kitchen doorway, staring at our T-shirts, cut-offs, and bare feet.

"Bad enough you looked that way to say good-bye to them nice relatives of theirs. The whole bunch of 'em probably already think I'm runnin' a flophouse for a gang of midget winos."

"But we already got everything packed."

"Well, unpack it. You ain't goin' over there dressed like that and that's all there is to it."

Franklin's shoulders slumped forward and his head rolled back as he turned slowly away from Mrs. Henderson's kitchen.

"And that's all there is to it."

"What's that, Franklin Caviness?"

"I said we'll get right to it."

Franklin shook his head, and Erwin and I followed him down the hallway. Franklin fell over backwards onto the bed.

"Geez, am I glad to be gettin' out of here."

"Is Mary waitin' for us?"

Franklin tilted his head up and looked at his youngest brother. "Waitin' for us?"

"Yeah, at them people's house."

"We don't know where Mary's at, Win."

"I do."

Franklin sat up. "You do?"

"Yeah, she's at the party. She's at them nice people's house."

"Well, she was, Win. But she was gone this morning when they got up."

Erwin looked down, studying his small brown hands.

"Did them police git her, too?"

Franklin reached over and took Erwin by the elbow and pulled him to the bed. "No, the police didn't get her, Winnie. They're lookin' for her, though."

"Why'd she leave? Don't she like us, anymore?"

Franklin looked at Erwin and then over at Mom's coffee table against the wall. I sat down next to them.

"Course she still likes us, Win."

"Then why don't she stay with us?"

We sat on the edge of the bed, staring at the varnished sheen of the table top.

"I don't know, Win. That's a good question. Maybe she's at the preacher's, again, now that Lee Hooker's gone."

Franklin stood and walked over to the table, pulling off his T-shirt.

"No, she isn't, Franklin."

He turned and looked at me. "How do you know?"

"I just do, that's all."

"What, did some little bird tell ya?" He bent down and began wiping the table off using his T-shirt.

"No, Carmalita did."

"Carmalita? She can't talk."

"Yes, she can. She talks with her hands and she knows things other people don't. Fudgie told me."

"Well, where is she then?"

"I don't know, but Carmalita said for us not to worry."

Franklin rolled his eyes and ran his hand over the table. "Great. I feel better already. Come on. We gotta get goin'."

Franklin stuffed his T-shirt into one of the grocery sacks as we rummaged around for a change of clothing. I pulled on some long pants, slipped into my sneakers, and took the obituary from my cut-offs and slid it into my back pocket. Franklin reached into the top dresser drawer and pulled out the envelope of one-hundred-dollar bills.

"Where we goin' to put 'em, Franklin?"

Franklin shrugged and riffled the bills with his thumb.

"Whatcha' got?"

Erwin stood on his tiptoes and craned his neck, peering into the envelope.

"Money, Win."

"How much?"

"Well, quite a bit, I guess."

"Did your boss pay ya?"

Franklin and I looked at each other and laughed. "We don't know who paid us, Win, but somebody sure did."

Franklin stuck the envelope into the front of his pants and we headed for the living room where Mrs. Henderson sat in her rocker, a photo album open across her lap. The album was big with black pages and a black shoelace running through it and tied into a bow to keep the pages in order. The photographs were in black and white and they had white borders cut around them in the shape of waves rolling against a black ocean. Small corner pieces kept the pictures in place and under some of the photographs was glued a strip of notebook paper with a date and a notation.

"Why, here we are in Arizona." Mrs. Henderson held out the album and we looked over her shoulder at the pictures. "My, my, look at that cactus Milton's standin' next to! And Milton wasn't no shorty, neither. You'd think not a plant one'd grow in that dirt down there. And hot—my lord, it was hot."

Leaning forward, Mrs. Henderson peered through her knitting glasses.

"Milton with saguaro cactus west of Phoenix, Arizona. October 25, 1953." She clucked her tongue and scanned the next page before turning it. "Why, look it here, boys. Disneyland."

Erwin grabbed a corner of the album and turned it toward himself. "Mighty Mouse!"

Franklin bent down. "That's not Mighty Mouse, Win. It's Mickey Mouse."

"Where's Mighty Mouse?"

Mrs. Henderson chuckled. "I think you got your mouses mixed up there, Winnie."

Mickey Mouse stood in front of a tall castle with pennants blowing along the top behind him. He was waving and smiling.

"Well, my word. Look at there." Mrs. Henderson pointed. Franklin, Erwin, and I crowded around, our heads together.

"Don't you know what that is?"

Franklin drew back and shrugged. "A house?"

Mrs. Henderson smiled and nodded. She leaned over and studied the photograph. "Yep, that's a house all right."

"It's our house. And that's Pa."

Franklin and Erwin looked at me.

"That's right, Petey. How'd you know that? You wasn't even born yet."

We bent closer. Pa kneels down to one side of a concrete foundation and on the other side stands a skeleton of walls, bone-white under the bright sunshine.

"Your daddy was the best danged carpenter around."

Pa holds a tape measure to the edge of the foundation. His big flat carpenter's pencil is slid up at an angle into the crook between his head and ear.

"If you could name it, Frank could build it. He could make just about anything."

Pa slips the pencil out from behind his ear and marks the plywood flooring. He taps a six-penny nail on the mark and pulls his chalk box from his leather pouch, tapping it against the palm of his other hand. He hooks the line over the nail head and reels it out along the foundation, blue chalk dust powdering out from the end. Holding the line taut, Pa kneels down and snaps the line with his thumb and index finger.

"I remember my Milton sayin' there was nobody could build a house as fast and as good as your daddy."

Pa lays out the two sixteen-footers end-to-end, making sure they're flush. He takes out his tape measure and pencil and marks sixteen-inch centers for the wall studs. Kneeling down, he squeezes the boards together, slaps the framing square over them, and draws lines on either side. Pa walks over to the stack of two-by-four fir studs, bends down, and picks up an arm load. He carries them over to the foundation, drops them, and goes back for more.

"And work—my goodness, that man could work."

After he has enough studs, Pa spreads them out between the sixteen-foot plates. He slides out his hammer from the holster of his carpenter's belt and reaching into the pouch with his other hand, pulls out a handful of sixteen-penny nails. Pa bends at the waist, his face reddening, and taps the side of the first stud to bring it flush with the end of the top plate. Holding the two boards in place with one foot, Pa starts a nail and then finishes it off with one-two-three strikes of his hammer. The first two give off the ringing metallic quiver of a driven nail and the third one finds home, loudly indenting the head into wood. Without hesitating or straightening up, he—tap-one-two-three—sinks another nail into the lumber.

"They was so proud of that place."

Pa turns and nails the other end to the bottom plate, his hammer flashing in the sun and the dint of his work echoing off the carport of the house across the street. He steps sideways, lines up the next stud with the marks, and begins nailing. And then another and another until all the studs are nailed in place and the wall is framed.

"And that Marge. She had such an eye for puttin' things right where they belong."

Pa walks over to the top plate, sliding his hammer back into its holster, bends down and lifts the wall upright. The veins in his arms and up his neck swell blue against his sweaty tan. He toenails a brace to the flooring, slaps a level against the outside stud, eyes the bubble, and nails the brace to the wall. He nails along the bottom plate as the sun slants through the skeleton of what will be our house and casts shadows across the plywood flooring. And then our Pa stands upright, his shadow lengthening and becoming one with our house, his day finally done.

"Yes-sirree, your momma and daddy was something else." Mrs. Henderson sighed, closing the photo album and setting it on the hassock. "You boys finally ready?"

"Yeah."

"I suppose you better git on over there, then. Where's that beautiful table of yours and the rest of your stuff?"

"In there."

"Well, you better take everything with you. Don't want Joe and Helen thinkin' all you got to wear is those rags you keep puttin' on. You know, school starts in a couple of days so you best get use to dressin' like young men 'stead of three ragamuffins."

"I'm not goin' to school."

"Franklin Caviness, you certainly are goin' to school."

"No, Mr. Dugan said . . ."

"I don't care what Clarence Dugan says. I talked to Joe Lucero and that's that."

"But . . ."

"No ifs, ands, or buts about it. Maybe you can work after school or on weekends or something, but you ain't goin' to quit school and that's final."

Franklin's face reddened as Erwin and I followed him back into the bedroom.

"Why do you still want to work, Franklin? We got money."

Bending down, Franklin began gathering up the grocery sacks full of clothing. Erwin knelt to help him.

"Shoot, we could probably live forever and never work, huh, Franklin? We could probably just be on summer vacation all year long, huh? Swimmin' and playin' baseball and climbin' trees and . . ."

"Shut up, Pete."

Franklin straightened up. His face was still red but I couldn't tell if it was from what Mrs. Henderson had said or from squatting down to pick up the clothes.

"You think that's what Pa would've done, Pete?"

"I don't know, I just . . ."

"Just quit because somebody give him some money?"

"No, I guess . . ."

"Of course not. He would've kept workin' and that's what I'm going to do, even if I do have to go back to school. I'll work nights and weekends and mornings if I have to."

Franklin's eyes bugged out and he glared at me but I couldn't help it. It started around the edges of my mouth and began working its way up to my eyes, crinkling the corners.

"What's so funny?"

Franklin dropped the sacks onto the bed, grabbed me by the collar, and yanked me up to his face as mine creased into a grin.

"You think it's funny, Pete?"

"I don't . . ."

"Huh!?!"

"No."

"Then why you smilin'?"

I shrugged. Franklin held my collar for a second and then let go with a little shove, sending me bouncing onto the bed. He bent down to collect the bags, but from the look on his face—a look not so much angry as determined—I could tell he really did know why I was smiling. He had finally accepted what Mrs. Henderson had told him. Not that he had to go back to school—an idea he still hated—but that he was now, without question, exactly what Mrs. Henderson had said: the man of our family. An idea he was starting to like.

* * *

We were out the porch and halfway down the driveway when Mrs. Henderson yelled out at us. She wasn't much for sentimentality—although we had seen her cry more than once those last weeks of summer, something we had never seen her do before—shooshing us out her front door as though we were stray cats she had fed for a while but had grown tired of, knowing we would be back now and then, anyway.

"Franklin! Petey! Hold on there a minute!" She disappeared into her house, the porch screen slamming behind her.

"Oh, great."

"You think she found 'em, Franklin?"

"I don't know."

"Where'd you put 'em?"

"In her cupboard under a couple of plates."

She reappeared on the porch, stooped and walking funny as though she were weighted down with more than just years.

"Oh, no. She's goin' to scratch it."

Franklin dropped the sacks on the driveway and ran up to the porch door where Mrs. Henderson was struggling with Mom's coffee table. Franklin nudged the screen door open using the side of his foot and grabbed the end of the table. But instead of helping Mrs. Henderson, Franklin just stood there. They were both shaking their heads. Thinking they were having another one of their arguments, I walked up the driveway just as they were setting the table down inside the porch.

"Franklin Caviness, I swear, if you don't . . ." Mrs. Henderson stared right at him, her hands on her hips, shaking her head. Franklin gazed down at the coffee table and instead of shaking his head, he was nodding.

"If you don't beat all, I don't know who does."

"What's wrong?"

Franklin glanced up at me. Then, without saying another word, he took me by the arm and walked me away, back out to Erwin and the sacks of clothing.

"What happened, Franklin?"

We followed him down the driveway. I looked back at Mrs. Henderson.

"Franklin, what happened?"

Through the screen of her dusty plant-laden porch, I could see the pink of Mrs. Henderson's tissue paper pressed to her nose.

"What's wrong with Mrs. Henderson? Did she find the money?"

Franklin stopped, his head straight ahead. He lifted one leg, hiking one sack farther up into his arms with his thigh.

"Mom and Pa's coffee table."

"What? What about it?"

Franklin turned around and looked me square in the eyes. "We just don't have no room for it, ourselves. That's all." And then he turned and we headed on down the street toward the Lucero's. I looked back one final time at Mrs. Henderson, the pink tissue now waving above her head.

24

It started with words. There had been Uncle Herbert's, stilted, showy, and pretentious, like funeral-home flowers placed on the ground for temporary adornment, unneeded and soon abandoned, left wilting in the sun. Then the preacher's, loud and strange, coming at us like a storm, whirling and enveloping us and even sweeping one of us away. And Willie's, soothing and wise and self-mocking, comforting us from that storm and making sense out of all the nonsense while poking gentle fun at that which seemed anything but.

There had been the Manzanares' words, jumbled and excited and foreign, as though thrown into a bushel basket and then pitched to the sky, raining down around us, weird and wonderful. Carmalita's, which weren't really words at all but which in their movement, beauty, and silence made the most sense. And there had been Mrs. Henderson's, a constant and in their very constancy, a comfort; Rickie Livers's, crude and cutting and hurtful; old man Hillar's, gruff and harsh, but like the summer thunderheads that rolled over the valley, with an occasional silver lining running through them; Mr. Dugan's, gritty and raw like his hands and expansive like his heart; and Lee Hooker's, smart-alecky and slick, yet saavy and vulnerable.

And through all those words in the last weeks of summer 1962, none had the impact that Joe and Helen Lucero's would have, none would change history—as Willie had put it—as completely as theirs.

"Shhhh."

Franklin held his index finger to his lips as we stood at the Lucero's back door, holding our sacks of clothing.

"But why can't somebody do something?"

"Because it's all legal, Helen."

"It's legal? It's legal to con four kids out of their house? They already lost their parents, Joe."

"Look, Helen, I don't like it any better than you do. But like I told you, they have a will, it's been notarized, and this Herbert Merriweather character can do anything he wants with it and there's not a damn thing I or anybody else can do about it."

"So that's how it works, huh?"

"Yes, that's how it works."

"Well, if that's how it works, Joe Lucero, and there's nothing you can do about it, then maybe you should be thinking about a different line of work."

"Oh, Helen."

A door slammed.

"Helen, come on. I didn't write the law. Open the door, Helen. They're going to be over here in a few minutes. Helen?"

Franklin knelt on one knee and let the sacks slip to the ground. He stayed there for a moment, fist pressed to his mouth, and then took the sacks from Erwin and me and set them down, too. Finally straightening up, Franklin motioned us to follow.

Though the sun washed high above Spruce Mesa our street was quiet, curtains pulled and Sunday papers still lying on some of the driveways. Churchgoers hadn't returned from services yet and families out of town for the long Labor Day weekend wouldn't be back until late the next day. Even old man Hillar's house was still, his pickup truck parked in the driveway with another broken-down appliance sitting in its bed.

"You got the key?"

Franklin nodded and reached into his pocket as we hurried up the driveway. He slid the key into the lock and opened the door, paint fumes hitting us in the face. Locking the door behind us, we stepped into the kitchen and stopped. Mom's cupboards and walls which she had painted a light yellow were now so bare and white as to be no color at all. The kitchen table and chairs were gone and the linoleum on the floor was in the process of being ripped up. A crowbar, hammer, and a few other tools lay on the otherwise bare counter, and on the small corner shelf where the telephone had always been lay a heating-vent cover with four screws lying inside it.

Franklin walked across the kitchen and stepped over a roll of old linoleum into the living room, Erwin and I following closely behind as if our house were pitch black and we were afraid of it. But instead of black, the living room was just as invisibly white as the kitchen and we felt just as blinded.

"Where'd these come from, Franklin?"

Four gray metal desks stood on the bare floor, one against each wall with four identical gray chairs rolled up underneath them. Over one of the desks hung three frames as though suspended in midair against the void that was the wall.

Franklin walked over, squinting. "Cer . . . certif . . . certificate of real estate. Gus Calloway. Who's Gus Calloway?"

I looked up at my big brother as he rubbed his head. "It's the preacher."

Franklin jerked around. "The preacher?"

"Yeah. Reverend Calloway."

He turned around and bent back over the desk. "Broker's li . . . license. Gus Calloway. Broker's license. What's that?"

"Maybe so he can break things."

Franklin's eyes moved to the third frame which was above the other two. "Blessed are the meek; for they shall in . . . in . . . in-something-or-other the earth."

He rolled out the chair and tried the desk drawer but it was locked. Slumping down into the chair, he leaned his head back and stared at the ceiling. "The preacher."

Franklin put his foot up on the edge of the desk.

"How come the preacher's got his stuff here, Franklin?"

He slowly shook his head and then drew his knee back and stomped his foot against the desk, sending himself and the chair rolling backwards across the varnished hardwood floor like a bowling ball toward pins. He bumped to a stop against the desk on the opposite wall.

Erwin walked over to another chair and pulled it out. He shoved it across the floor, its metal wheels echoing through the emptiness off the wooden floor before Franklin could reach out and hook it with his foot.

"Don't, Win."

"How come? You did."

Erwin dived onto the seat of the chair on his stomach and elbows, and the chair rolled the rest of the way across the living room dragging the toes of his tennis shoes with it and thudded against the white wall.

Franklin got up and walked over to Erwin. "I said don't." He rolled the chair back and ran his fingertips over the wall, studying it. "You marked it." He looked down at his little brother. "You know, you don't have to do everything I do, Winnie."

Erwin laced his fingers together and wiggled them like the wings of a bat and went skipping out of the living room into the hallway, hands flying above him. Franklin sighed, shaking his head.

"Franklin, is the preacher going to live here now?"

"I don't know. I don't know nothin', anymore."

"Well, what about Uncle Herbert?"

Franklin shrugged.

"What about him? I don't care what Uncle Herbert's . . ."

Franklin stopped as Erwin suddenly reappeared, chin all crinkled up.

"Win. What's wrong?"

Erwin held his breath, his chest puffed out and eyes wide, and pointed down the hallway. We walked over to him. "What, Win?"

He jabbed his finger so we headed down the hallway, peered into the bathroom and then across the hall into Mom and Pa's bedroom. We looked back at Erwin who was now sucking his thumb. "What'd you see, Win?"

Erwin shuffled down the hallway toward us, thumb still in his mouth, and followed us into his bedroom, which seemed as empty and white as the rest of the house—except in the corner.

"Mary!"

She was curled up on her side in a white terry-cloth robe, legs drawn to her stomach, her arms crossed over her chest. Her head lay propped against one wall, eyes staring off somewhere.

"Oh, Mare . . ."

Her blond hair was matted wet to her forehead and fell down one cheek to her neck.

"Come on, Mary. Get up."

Her face was blotchy and, at her temple, red from leaning against the wall.

"Come on, Mare. You'll be okay."

Her eyes were red and swollen, not blinking, her lips chapped white and cracking.

"Let's get her up. Get her outside."

Her feet shuffled across the floor down the hallway and clunked over the roll of linoleum into the kitchen.

"Pete, go get Joe. Go get Joe and Helen. Win, quit cryin' and help me!"

Mary slumped against the kitchen wall, against the white invisible wall.

"Tell them to come quick. Hurry!"

A car door slammed. And then another.

"It's the preacher, Franklin!"

"Oh, no . . ."

We rushed her across the kitchen and down the stairs and then Mary began. Not loud but it was there, over the rubbing against the wall and the tangled fall of our footsteps.

"In here, Franklin!"

Across the cool cement floor of Pa's workshop and into my bedroom, the steady sound was there and with the sliding out of the drawer and all the clatter and with the sliding back in of the drawer. We could hear it above the creaking of the floor and the fall of other footsteps. And even when Franklin clamped his hand over Mary's mouth, it was there. Mary was humming.

"Down here, as you can see, Dave, we've got all kinds of space. We could tear this wall out and make it a storage room. Or leave it, for that matter, and add some more office space."

"Yes, Reverend, we could make it a mailing room or something."

"An excellent idea, Dave. We can send real estate brochures and church material from down here. A wonderful idea. Glory be to God."

"Amen."

"And did I tell you what a steal this was? We got it for a song."

"How much, Reverend?"

"Nine thousand."

"Nine-thousand dollars?"

"Paid in cash. Once all the paperwork and all the legal rigamarole were finished with, it was the sweetest deal I ever made. The guy couldn't wait to get rid of it."

"Praise God."

"He does work in mysterious ways, Dave. Come on up and I'll show you the . . ."

"What's wrong, Reverend?"

"Did you hear that?"

"What?"

"Shhhh . . . listen."

In the cramped darkness under the stairwell of the house our pa built, I could feel Franklin's arm tighten.

"I don't hear anything."

"Hmmm."

"What was it, Reverend?"

"Thought I heard music."

"Music?"

"Yes, humming, like dee-dee-dee-dadee-dadeeee-dee. Dee-dee-dee-dadee-dadeeee."

"Jesus Loves the Little Children."

"Well, so it is, Dave. How about that. Come on, I'll show you the rest of the house."

Huddled together on my old mattress in the black gasoline air, we scooted closer together, our hair brushing against each other's and Mary still humming.

"Franklin, what're we . . ."

"Shhhh—whisper."

"What're we going to do?"

"I don't know. Wait 'til that preacher leaves, I guess. You got a flashlight in here?"

"Yeah, but it don't work."

"Great. How 'bout a candle?"

"I think so."

"Where is it?"

I leaned over to where the stairs went up and groping around among my magazines and boxes of old baseball cards and marbles and kite string, found the smooth length of a candle.

"Here's one."

"Give it here."

I felt around and found Franklin's hand reaching out toward me and passed it to him. I could hear Mary humming and Franklin fumbling in the darkness and then the scratch of a match against cement and there was Franklin's face, orange and flickery.

"Shouldn't smoke, Franklin. It's bad."

"Franklin! Mary talked!"

"Shhhh."

Franklin held the candle out, shadows jumping around us against the walls.

"Just because Lee does, doesn't mean you have to."

"Mary, are you okay? What happened?"

"Lee doesn't want to smoke, Franklin, but he can't seem to help it."

The candle flickered from our breath as we squinted at Mary. Her eyes were closed, a slight smile on her face.

"Jesus'll help Lee, though, because Jesus loves him, Franklin. Jesus loves all the little children . . . all the children of the world."

"Shhhh. It's okay, Mare."

Franklin put his arm around her shoulders.

"Red and yellow, black and white, they are perfect in His sight. Jesus loves the little children of the world."

"Shhhh."

"What's wrong with her, Franklin?"

Franklin looked at me, the candle flame dancing double in his eyes and his shadow big against my sports heroes pinned up behind him.

"It's going to be okay, Mare. Pete, we're going to be okay. Come here, Winnie."

Erwin crowded in as Franklin handed me the candle and put his arm around him.

"Soon as we hear that preacher leave, we'll go get Joe and Helen. They'll know what to do."

"Joseph and Mary, Franklin. Not Helen. Mary had Jesus, but God helped her—Mary."

"Okay, Mare. It's okay."

Franklin hugged her tighter. Erwin whimpered so I put my arm around him, my hand on top of Franklin's arm.

"It'll be all right, Mare. You don't have to go to no more church."

Franklin stroked Mary's head as we huddled together under the house our pa built, staring at the small bluish yellow flame. We could still hear the preacher's weight creak against the floor upstairs but his words we would hear no more.

"Franklin?"

"Yeah."

I studied the cinder of ash in the melted wax before looking up at him.

"Carmalita said not to worry, huh?"

Franklin stared at the candle and slowly nodded. "Yeah."

I looked down into the flame and then up at my sister. Her eyes were closed, her face and throat as smooth and white as the candle.

"Did the preacher buy our house, Franklin?"

"Yeah, I guess so."

"For nine-thousand dollars?"

Franklin nodded.

"Is that why he give us the money?"

"No."

"Why did he then?"

"He didn't give us the money, Pete."

"Who did, then?"

"Uncle Herbert."

"Uncle Herbert?"

"Yeah, Uncle Herbert. The preacher bought it from him."

A tear of wax ran down the candle onto my hand, burned, and then dried against my skin.

"Why don't you put it down, Pete?"

I placed the end of the candle on the cement, tilting it against the edge of the small mattress so the wax could drip and puddle around it.

"Will we have to give it back, Franklin?"

"No."

"Will Fudgie and Mrs. Henderson?"

"Fudgie's gone and Mrs. Henderson don't even know she's got it, yet."

"How much did we give her?"

"Same as Fudgie."

"Three hundred?"

"Yeah."

The wax had built up some around the base so I took my hand away.

"Uncle Herbert wasn't such a bad guy, was he, Franklin?"

"I don't know."

"Maybe if we didn't give him them worms, everything'd be different, huh?"

"Maybe."

"Maybe he wouldn't have got mad at us and sold the house, huh?"

Franklin said nothing as we stared into the candle's flame.

"Franklin, why was Mary singin' that song?"

He slowly shook his head.

"Willie said Jesus is just a name in a history book. Huh, Franklin? And he's not our pa at all."

"That was the preacher's idea."

I reached back and pulled the folded paper from my back pocket.

"What's that?"

I unfolded it and held it near the candle. "Franklin Caviness."

I looked into Franklin's eyes, our heads almost touching, and he nodded slightly.

"Franklin Caviness. Franklin Raymond Caviness, 52, a tea . . . team . . ."

"Teamster."

". . . a teamster em . . . emplooo . . ."

Franklin took the piece of paper.

". . . a teamster employed with UGF Trucking, died Sunday on Spruce Mesa while fishing with his son. Mr. Caviness was a life-long resident of Grand River, having been born here on February 18, 1910. He graduated from Grand River High School in 1928 and enlisted in the Army in 1930. In 1946 he married Margaret Louise Merriweather, whom he preceded in death by one day. Mr. Caviness enjoyed fishing, carpentry, and square dancing. Surviving are a daughter, Mary Lynnette Caviness; and three sons, Franklin Raymond Caviness Jr., Peter Henry Caviness, and Erwin Nathaniel Caviness. Funeral and burial services will be held Thursday at 1 p.m. at Shade's Funeral Home and Cemetary. The Reverend Gus Calloway of the First Pentecostal Church will officiate."

"That's good, Franklin."

"I got it memorized. Margaret Caviness. Margaret Louise Caviness, 40, died at 3:00 p.m. Monday in St. Matthew's Hospital following a long illness. She was the widow of Franklin Raymond Caviness, who preceded her in death by one day. Mrs. Caviness was born Margaret Louise Merriweather on September 11, 1922, at Hays, Kansas, where she lived until moving to Grand River in 1945. She married Mr. Caviness in 1946. Mrs. Caviness enjoyed sewing, gardening, and square dancing. Surviving are one brother, Herbert Theodore Merriweather of Wichita, Kansas; a daughter, Mary Lynnette Caviness; and three sons, Franklin Raymond Caviness Jr., Peter Henry Caviness, and Erwin Nathaniel Caviness. Funeral and burial services will be held . . ."

"How come I'm always last?"

"It's okay, Win. It's 'cause you're the youngest."

"So?"

"So, it don't matter. This is just so people can read about it in the paper."

"I don't wanna be last."

I patted Erwin on the back. "Don't worry, Win. Willie said words don't mean nothin', anyways. Huh, Franklin?"

"Shhhh." Franklin held his hand flat above the candle.

"What is it?"

"The preacher."

The house was quiet above us and we could hear a car start and back out of the driveway.

"They're leavin'."

"Come on, Franklin."

I began to push the drawer out.

"Wait."

Franklin held the newspaper clipping above the candle and a black spot suddenly grew in the middle of it. I grabbed Franklin's wrist, yanking the clipping from the flame.

"Franklin, what're you . . ."

We looked at each other, nose-to-nose, and then my eyes dropped to the clipping.

"You said it yourself, Pete. Words don't mean nothin'. Like Willie said."

I took the candle from against the mattress and brought it up between us. "Things either are or they aren't and no words can ever change 'em."

I steadied the flame and Franklin held the clipping to it, the words burning black into each other and then the paper catching.

"Don't smoke, Petey."

We looked at Mary, the flame growing in Franklin's hand.

"Let's go."

I pushed the drawer open and helped Mary and Erwin out.

"Over here, Pete."

I turned around, holding the candle, and watched Franklin toss the burning paper into the corner where the stairs came down to meet the concrete floor. Franklin reached over to take the candle but I wouldn't let loose. He looked at me, eyes calm and jaw set just like Pa's use to get. And then, together, without saying a word, we tossed the candle into the corner under the stairs, the flame illuminating Franklin's dirty work clothes.

Out of the wall we climbed and joining hands with Mary and Erwin, walked up the stairs out the back door and across the street to the elm. The sun burned high above Grand River and as the four of us climbed the rickety footholds and huddled together on the tree-house floor, a single wisp of smoke curled up through our house, rose from the gabled roof, and emptied above us into the Sunday sky.

* * *

The fire has burned out, the coals black and smoldering. I take water from the coffeepot and pour over them. They hiss and ashes flutter up where the water runs through. It's dawn on Spruce Mesa, a smudge of orange ripening against the sky beyond the treetops on the other side of the lake. I sit up in my bag and stretch. The air is crisp and sucks the warmth from my arms and back. Taking one of the branches left from the pile I had collected the night before, I stir the ashes and empty the rest of the water from the coffeepot. I put on my boots, stand up, and kick dirt over the coals. Then I take the stick and using it as a shovel, bury what is left of the fire.

Marilyn Monroe has been dead now for over thirty years. Some say the Yankees have been dead, too, ever since Maris and Mantle quit roaming their outfield. The whole world is a different place and we're not sure who to root for anymore. Enemies and friends seem to change with every edition of the newspaper. Even beyond the world it isn't the same. President Kennedy's vision of the Last Frontier has dimmed to a glimmer, the race through outer space replaced with one more earthly and less imaginative and decidedly more destructive. They tell us the division between rich and poor has widened and city streets are full of the homeless. Yet immigrants keep pouring in.

Willie, we never saw again but would never forget. Ironically, his words stayed with us, the very things he found such fault with. We never saw Lee Hooker, either, although we heard that he didn't stay long in Buena Vista that last time. Years later Erwin told me he drove by an auto-body shop in west Denver named Hooker's Auto Repair. But it wasn't in the telephone book and I spent one entire Saturday afternoon driving around trying to find it but never could.

Mrs. Henderson helped us through a few more rough stretches in the weeks before we left Grand River with Joe and Helen. We received Christ-mas cards from her for a long time and she even mentioned old man Hillar occasionally. She said he became even more eccentric with each passing year which, to use her own words, seemed to be the pot calling old man Hillar black. Mr. Dugan wrote Franklin that first Christmas after we left Grand River. I didn't read it but Franklin said it didn't say much, just about how business was going and how badly the Grand River Trojans football team had played again that year. But I guessed it must have said more than that from the way Franklin would take the letter out sometimes and reread it. Franklin's eyes always said more than his words ever did anyway.

Fudgie and his family we still see every few years. They quit the migrant worker life that season after Manny became sick. Mrs. Manzanares finally won out and after getting to know her over the years, I'm only surprised she didn't prevail sooner. Manny died a couple of years back and we all went down to San Felipe for the funeral. Baja was almost as beautiful as Carmalita's dancing said it was. We buried him overlooking the ocean with the squack of seagulls above us. The curio shop was much bigger than I expected. Fudgie and his brothers had expanded it and opened a second one in Ensenada which Uncle Tony still tends. When he's sober enough, that is. Carmalita has remained as beautiful as I first remembered her. She's married to a nice guy named Geraldo Lopas and has six children by him. This being my only regret: by him instead of me. Fudgie is married, too, and he and Theresa have two children, a boy and a girl, both of whom call me Uncle Pedro.

Helen is still a nurse at work and at home, and she's still very good at both places. Joe still practices law but instead of private practice, he works for the Public Defenders' Office. He receives a good salary so he doesn't have to bill people, which he wasn't very good at anyway and which was making us poor, to boot. After the fire, though, he proved to Helen that he's in the right business after all by proving in court that Uncle Herbert's will was bogus and the house was ours to do with what we wished. Of course, what we did had nothing to do with what we wished.

Uncle Herbert we never heard from again. Too many ghosts in his closet, I guess. But he did make off with Mom and Pa's Pontiac although no one even noticed for a while with everything else that was going on then. Rever-end Calloway proved as slippery as he had always seemed and didn't get charged for anything—except the money he had paid Uncle Herbert for the house. Joe said Uncle Herbert was one of the worst businessmen he had ever seen, selling low and buying high as he did. He said our house was worth twice the nine-thousand dollars and that model of Pontiac wasn't worth a fraction of it. This last thing Joe said with a wink and he never mentioned the money after that.

As for us kids, well, Helen and Joe Lucero gave us a good childhood, almost as good as the one we had before. Erwin still lives near them in Fort Collins where he works part-time as a youth counselor and goes to Colorado State University for classes in veterinary medicine. Mary is on her second marriage and will be moving with her new husband from Chicago to London soon. She came out of those few weeks in August better than we expected once we got her away from Grand River. Through the rest of the sixties she did a lot of searching and experimenting like a lot of people her age but needless to say, she never did go back to church again. Franklin married young and stayed married. After finishing high school, he and his wife, Vickie, had three babies in three years, and he went back to pumping gas. Now he owns three stations—one for each kid, he says—and a small auto parts shop. But he still can't stand the smell of gasoline.

And me? Well, I've tried a lot of things but nothing notable. I've never married but have seen a bit of the world, I guess. I've gone to college, dropped out, and gone again, but still without a piece of paper in my hand. I guess all those things Willie had said so many years ago somehow stuck and even made some sense. Words against paper sometimes just don't change a thing. Except when you're looking for a job.

The four of us still make it a point to get together every year. Mary flies over to Denver for the weekend and we usually meet at Franklin's house around the time the pennant races are heating up and the air is a little cooler. We have a barbeque in the back yard where Mary and I end up laughing at the silly arguments Erwin and Franklin get into. Franklin is still a Yankees fan, no matter who their owner is, and Erwin loves the Oakland A's for some reason. On Sunday, before Mary catches her flight back to Chicago, we try to make it a point to get up into the mountains for a while even though it's hard to get away from all the people on the eastern slope of the state. We just hike mostly and don't say much to each other. I could never understand this silence between us and it always kind of bothered me. Until now, that is. Now I realize, after coming back to Grand River, that that's just the way Sundays are—quiet, I mean—especially Sundays in August.

The sun is up. The day looks clear, not a cloud anywhere. But the weather can change quickly up here on Spruce Mesa. I pick up my pole and walk off toward the lake.

End